THE TOWER BROKEN

Cover design by Jess Chaplin
Typeset by Jess Chaplin

First published April 2025

Paperback ISBN 978-1-7637553-6-9
Hardcover ISBN 978-1-7637553-7-6
eBook ISBN 978-1-7637553-8-3

A catalogue record for this work is available from the National Library of Australia

I acknowledge the traditional owners of the land and pay my respects to elders past and present.

THE TOWER BROKEN

MARK KRAMARZEWSKI

Also by the Author

The Tower Between Trilogy
The Tower Between
The Tower Besieged

Follow the Author at:

For Lisa
Thank you for supporting me pursue this dream,
And for everything else,
I love you

ACKNOWLEDGEMENTS

The third and final instalment of the Tower Between trilogy is complete and it's been quite the rollercoaster to get to this stage.

Thank you again to my readers. Sharing your time, your kind words, your thoughts, your interest and, sometimes, your reviews, is a real gift. I hope you enjoy how we close the story on these Aussie teens.

I'd also like to thank my wonderful editor, Samantha Elley and my amazing cover artist Jess Chaplin for bringing my lump of words into its final shape.

Thanks to what simply is the greatest of writing communities, I will forever be in debt to the Wabbers. Special thanks to the query support group, Kim, Haley, Sean, Janna, Raechel, Shelby, Lydia and Cayce. And thanks too, to the beta read group, Perla, Deeanna, Chrissie, Sharon, Allison and Karlynn who provide enthusiasm for drafts in their infancy along with their valuable feedback.

And extra thanks to my generous critique readers Becky and Devis, I am so grateful for the much rougher versions that you worked your way through, helping my repair or remove parts that simply weren't hitting right.

Special callout to Taryn, who has continued to be patient and generous in answering questions from outside my lived experience, and to Sam and Danni who were constantly captured by my late night ramblings about whatever I've been drafting or editing that day.

Thanks to Jamie, Luke, Adam, Siân, Brad, Damien, Matt, Maddie and Deanna, who played in the campaign that inspired this story. A few key scenes survived even into the final instalment, even when the rest may look unrecognisable.

And thanks to my childhood friends. Brad, Michael, Luke, Mark and Nick put up with the kid who always wanted to live in a fantasy world, and were willing to visit him there as long as there were slurpees and doritos at the table next to the dice and the character sheets.

And, as before, the deepest of thanks are reserved for my family.

Thank you to my grandparents, who were all storytellers.

Thank you to my parents, Maureen and Andy, who have been constant in their love and support. And to Emma, who offers me valuable insights into the workings of the Australian children-literary world.

And most of all, to Ava and Nicholas, who are far more interesting, and strange, characters than I ever could have written. And to my gorgeous wife Lisa, without your support, I never would have delivered this book. I love you.

CHAPTER 1

Zack sat on the top of the high brick wall separating the suburban shops' rear parking area from the strip of nature reserve behind him. Enjoying the illusion of being tall for once, he closed his eyes and let the hot February sun fall on his skin, while he soaked in the sense of Life that surrounded him. Through the brick, concrete and metal, his magic allowed him to sense the Life of the people in the shops and even a cluster of eight lives moving past, that must have been a bus driver with their passengers.

But it was nothing like the Life at his back. Despite being encroached upon over the last two centuries, the trees had remained and so had the lives that clung to them.

"You know, if you fall off there and crack your head, I can't do anything about it."

Zack opened his eyes and saw the tall mop of blond hair that was his best friend, Art. He dropped down, sliding his sneakers against the wall to slow his fall before landing lightly on his feet.

"Always the healer, never the healed," Zack responded with mock despair.

"Think about it from my perspective," Art said, "you put yourself into a coma and, as the only psychomancer you know, I'll be the sucker obliged to sit by your bedside, chatting with you every day. It would be a real inconvenience."

"You're right," Zack said, straight-faced, "I'm being really inconsiderate with my impending self-inflicted coma."

"Well, recognising it is the first step to self-improvement. Anyway, mission accomplished." Art slapped the top of the three metallic kegs he had dragged around on a hand trolley. "Heavy, though. We should get Bast to pull it. If he's going to have all those muscles, he might as well put them to use."

An athletic, dark-haired teen appeared from around the corner with a broad smile.

"It's nice to hear you've noticed, mate." Bast flexed his biceps, his singlet top allowing the other two boys an unimpeded view.

"You're going to be cold in that," Zack said.

Bast scowled and patted at the flannel jacket tied around his waist.

"My brother looked at me like I was crazy leaving the house with a jacket in this heat. I swear the weather change is the worst part of this gig. So, where are we doing this?"

"Around the corner in the reserve," Art said, offering Bast the handles of the trolley. "There's enough tree cover that we won't be seen and nobody will wander by."

Bast held his hands up.

"Oh, no. I'm the pilot on this little adventure. Ground crew manages the freight."

Zack stepped up to the trolley and picked up the top keg.

"We can't wheel this thing down there, anyway. One each."

The other two shrugged and followed suit behind him. Zack was relieved to be out front so Art and Bast couldn't see the strain on his face from carrying the heavy metal container. He made a mental note to put less work into cardio and more into strength training.

A low wooden barrier separated the car park from the nature reserve and Zack had to be careful with placing his feet as he stepped over it and into the dry foliage reserve. After a few minutes, he judged they were concealed enough and, while he could still easily hear the bustle of suburbia around him, the trees and scrub blocked them from view.

They placed the kegs on the dusty soil in a gap between the trees.

"Is this enough space for you?" Zack asked.

Bast paced around it, stretching his arms over and behind his head as he inspected the area.

"Yeah, should be fine. The normies can't see the orange light when I'm opening the gate and the grey of the gate itself, won't be bright enough to see through the trees. Yeah, this spot is good."

"Maybe, don't open it too close to the cabin," Zack said.

"I don't have that kind of aim, man. I've only been there once," Bast replied.

Zack thought for a moment. "Yeah, okay."

Bast's eyes narrowed. "Why? What's wrong with being too close to the cabin?"

"Nothing," Art answered before Zack could. "It's fine."

Bast ignored him. "Zack?"

"Well, I'm just nervous about the idea of him seeing a gate open up right next to his home and thinking he's under attack."

"'Him' being Odin," Bast said, his voice flat.

"It's fine," Art said and gestured at the kegs, "we're bringing gifts."

"Yeah," Zack nodded, "it's probably fine."

Bast looked unimpressed. "We should have brought the girls."

"They're busy looking at rentals," Zack said.

"And you didn't half pick this time because they were busy?" Bast sounded exasperated.

"Yeah, because we didn't want a thousand questions," Art said.

"Questions like, 'Why are you guys doing something against what the Tower has taught us?'" Bast asked.

"Look," Art replied, "I don't know what Tower lessons to listen to. Not since the end of last year."

Zack was inclined to agree with him. A little over a month earlier, he and his friends had faced down a band of renegade mages, who were ripping holes in the fabric of the world in an attempt to access more powerful magic. Towards the end of the battle, their leader, Armand, had opened a gate into another realm and called on nightmare creatures, made of tooth and bone, to aid him. The only thing was, Armand had been a Mind mage.

"You and I both know that dude was using Mind and Movement magic." Art ran his fingers through his hair. "Something that the Tower told us wasn't possible. And then out pops that other guy…"

"The Traveller," Zack said.

"The Traveller," Art continued, "who tells us that the Tower is lying to us."

"Yeah," Bast replied, "popped out and then popped away, and we haven't seen him since. We all agreed to stick with the Tower."

"And we are," Art said, "but Odin had our back. I'm not talking about risking the Silence or the Watch, I'm just trying to say thank you. So can you open the gate now, please?"

Bast shook his head in disgust. "You two whitefullas get me killed by the whitest of whitefulla gods and I'm not going to be happy about it."

He turned around and incanted; his flickering fingers leaving symbols of orange light floating in the air. A familiar grey ovoid disc appeared in front of him. At first, it was no larger than an apple seed, but as Bast continued his ritual, the disc grew until it reached the size of a door.

"Love your work, mate," Art said as he reclaimed his keg and stepped through the gate.

Zack grabbed his own keg and scrambled to follow Art, not quite as confident of what they were doing as Art was. He moved through the grey. He emerged into another place and a bitter wind assaulted him, making it clear the thin hoodie he had chosen was woefully insufficient.

"Oh, bloody hell." Bast stepped past him and dropped his own keg onto the icy ground. He was shivering as he ripped the jacket from around his waist and stuffed his arms into the sleeves. "This is worse than I remember."

"Worse than when we escaped from mad wizards into a blizzard and nearly froze to death?" Art asked.

Bast reclaimed his keg with shaking hands. "Maybe I've chosen to forget for a reason."

Art pointed away from the gate. "Pretty sure the cabin's up there. Let's get moving."

The three teens worked their way up the slope of the mountain and once they had crested a sharp incline, the cabin came into view. Whatever Bast was claiming to forget, the sight of it triggered sharp memories in Zack's mind. He and his friends had been beaten, threatened and interrogated before becoming lost in these mountains, only to wake up safe and warm in this cabin. Tabitha and Kimmy had told them that a one-eyed man was watching over them and left shortly after they awoke. Art, already referring to this icy realm as Jotunheim, was convinced that man was Odin, All-Father of the Norse gods.

"We'll just leave this stuff at the door," Zack said as they trudged along their approach.

Art frowned but nodded. "Yeah, that's probably the right idea."

Bast's brow furrowed in confusion. "What's the point of this then? I thought we were thanking him."

"We are," Art replied, "in a way. But it's also about trying to balance the scales. We were offered aid and hospitality and so, we're returning with gifts for our host."

Bast shook his head. "My mob doesn't have this kind of thing. We focus more on respecting nature and the existing balance. I suppose it kind of fits that you lot focus more on fixing the balance after you've upset it."

Zack considered this. "Yeah, that seems fair."

They reached the cabin and stopped a few metres away from the door. It was silent and no light from a hearth fire showed around the door or window slits.

"Doesn't seem like anybody is home," Bast said.

"Let's leave it next to the door, then." Zack moved forward.

Art lumbered along beside him, disappointment written clearly on his face. They stacked the kegs against the cabin wall and Bast ran his finger along the plastic tap of his.

"These kegs are a bit modern, reckon he'll be able to work them out?"

"I think it's safe to assume the king of the Viking gods can work out how to get to beer. But I also bought a few other things." Art slipped his backpack off his shoulder and unpacked the contents onto the kegs. "Expensive bottle of mead. Artisanal German sausages. Assorted small goods."

Zack picked up one of the last items. "Pringles?"

"Who doesn't love Pringles?" Art replied.

"How is he supposed to know we're the ones who left all this?" Bast asked.

Zack was worried about that too and was about to share his thoughts when a loud caw sounded from the cabin's thatched roof. The boys flinched at the sudden sound and Zack jumped backwards at the sight of the too-large black bird staring down at them.

"When did that crow get here?" Bast asked, his eyes locked on the animal.

"Raven." Zack and Art corrected in unison.

"So, I'm guessing this means something, then?" Bast said. "Are we okay?"

"Yep." Art's disappointment dissolved into excitement and he stepped forward to face the bird.

"Greetings, noble raven of the All-Father. The mighty Odin recently rescued us from peril and we have come bearing these gifts in recognition of a fraction of the gratitude we feel for his generous aid and hospitality. Please pass our thanks to him."

The raven watched in silence, but when Art took an awkward step backwards, it cawed a second time and dropped down to perch on the kegs.

Art slung his backpack over his shoulder. "I think that's it. Zack?"

Zack nodded, his eyes wide and fixed on the raven that seemed to be more than half his height.

"Alright, home time," Art said, leading them back towards the gate.

"So, Odin has a pet raven?" Bast asked.

"Two," Art replied. "Not sure which one that is, which is just as well because I have no idea how to pronounce either of their names. In some stories, he can see through their eyes, so hopefully he knows about the gifts. Or will."

Bast slapped Zack on the shoulder. "You alright, mate?"

Zack took a deep breath, his heart rate returning to normal. "Yeah, that was just one big bird."

Art laughed. "Oh yeah, Zack's terrified of birds."

"Really?" Bast asked. "After everything we've been through?"

"He got chased by a magpie a couple of times when we were little," Art explained.

"A couple of times?" Zack's voice was loud over the icy winds. "I was terrorised by a feathered demon at the end of my street for years. On the way home from school, every spring, I had to run a claw-and-beak-filled gauntlet of horror to get to my front door."

"He used to hide a bucket in the bushes next to the bus stop to wear as a helmet," Art chuckled.

Bast laughed, throwing his arm around Zack as they made their way down the mountain and through the gate.

"At least now, you're friends with an Animal mage. Get Charlie to put a good word in for you with any scary birds you're worried about."

While Bast closed the gate behind them, Zack pointed a threatening finger at Art. "You want me to bring up your feelings about mimes?"

Art threw up his hands. "I'm not embarrassed about that. Mimes are legitimately and objectively horrific."

Bast wrapped an arm around each of them. "I'm so excited that you've waited until now to reveal what weird roommates I'm about to have. Speaking of which, moving day is in two days. Let me know when the coast is clear and I'll pop over to help."

"I can't wait. And I've organised a full entertainment system to arrive next week. Got a good discount on it, of course," Art said with a wink and a waggle of his fingers.

"Nice," Bast said. "There's a test match that weekend. I'll be able to watch the cricket on a big screen."

Art pulled a face like he'd smelt something rotten. "At somebody else's house, you can. This setup is for movies and gaming. I wasn't even going to bother hooking it up to the aerial."

Zack trailed behind the two as they began what was sure to be a long-fought war over the remote and he was more than happy to stay out of it for now. He simply needed to get home and finish packing.

Zack's mother held her palm to her chest. "Our last dinner as a family all under one roof."

Zack finished scooping mince into his taco shell and rolled his eyes, confident that his mother's distress was mostly exaggerated.

"I'll be back for dinner at least once a week, I promise."

"And you'll still come to Sunday lunch at Deda's?" she asked.

Zack nodded.

"It's important. We need to be there more for him since… now that he's alone in the house."

"I will, I promise," Zack said. "See, you'll see me all the time."

"And there's an even chance he'll be crawling back here before his birthday," his sister, Ellen, said in a dismissive tone.

"Ellie, that's a bit rough," his father responded. "I'm sure he'll last at least a month."

"Jonathan!" His mother slapped his father's shoulder with the back of her fingers.

His father laughed. "I'm mostly joking, Zack, you know that. But you also know my concerns, that you're underestimating how expensive it is. It's not just rent and food, it's utilities, insurance—"

"I know," Zack interrupted the familiar list of worries.

And he felt the even more familiar pang of guilt. All they knew was that he was a seventeen-year-old high school graduate on a gap year. They didn't know he was financially backed by a secret mystic organisation and getting ridiculous discounts through the magical mind control of his best friend. Of course they were worried.

"But we're splitting it all three ways, and we'll be careful with our money."

"I'm sure you'll be sensible, dear," his mother said across the table, "and hopefully, you can stop Art from subletting the front room to some gambling den or whatever other money-making scheme he's likely cooking up."

The four of them laughed. Art had been pitching his million-dollar plans to them for the better part of a decade and most of them weren't brimming with ethical principles.

"But no matter what, you have a place here," his mother said.

"Thanks, Mum. And if you're really missing me, I can always bring over a sack of dirty clothes now and then."

"Of course, dear," she said and, without missing a beat, added, "and no need to bring your own washing powder. You can use mine when you run the machine."

"Are you sure you don't need any help with the move tomorrow?" his father asked. "I could take a longer lunch break and come home."

"Thanks, but I'm all good. I actually don't have that much to take. Mostly clothes, books and electronics. Just a couple of pieces of furniture, but I'm leaving the bed, so everything else is easy."

"Okay, but watch the walls on the way down the stairs," his father said.

"I'll be careful," Zack replied, confident that the gate Bast was going to open between his two bedrooms would ensure the safety of the paintwork.

His father nodded, but Ellen's ears had perked up at the mention of books.

"You aren't packing any of my books that you forgot to return, right?"

"No, I've given them all back."

"Are you sure?"

"Feel free to go through the boxes and look for yourself."

Ellen narrowed her eyes at him. "I think I'll have to."

His mother sniffed, and a genuine tear rolled down her cheek.

"I'm going to miss this."

<hr>

Zack bowed to the animated Samurai statue, ending their sparring session and doing his best to ignore the painful welt on his leg. He drew Life magic into himself as he made his way to the side of the room. By the time he reached Bast and Charlie, his hobble had faded into an easy stride.

Zack's chest tightened, as it always did, when he saw Charlie. The feelings he once held for her had evolved since their drunken kiss and subsequent argument the year before. The torch of idolisation Zack carried, for who he had wanted her to be, had gone and the beginnings of a friendship were seeded in its place, but he still felt awkward around her. He was embarrassed by the memory of how he had treated her and wasn't sure how to get past it. He wasn't sure if she wanted him to.

"How are you guys settling in?" Bast asked Charlie as Zack reclined against the wall.

Charlie, her honey-coloured curls pulled back and up in a messy ponytail for training, idly scratching her wolf-like dog, Max, behind the ears. Her eyes were fixed on where Kimmy and Art were sparring across the room. Kimmy's light axe was only a fraction slower than Art's broadsword and the two danced back and forth, looking for the right opportunity for a quick slash or thrust. Even in singlet tops, they were both gleaming with sweat, emphasising Kimmy's flame tattoo that ran up her neck from her shoulder blade to the edge of her pixie cut.

"Great," Charlie answered. "Kimmy has tried to convince us she should be able to smoke inside since Tabitha can 'snap her fingers and get rid of the smell.' But apart from that, really good. Oh, and Jackie visited yesterday after school. She saw the room we've set up for her. Man, my heart is still aching from how happy she was."

Zack smiled at the thought, momentarily forgetting his awkwardness.

"Yeah, Art mentioned it. And their mum seems pretty cool with the idea of her staying over now and then."

"Tabitha and I have been putting the work in there too, going over to pick Jackie up during the holidays. At first, Sandra was a little confused about why we wanted to hang out with her fourteen-year-old daughter, but she mostly seems good that Jackie's good. And it's not like we need to fake how much we adore her. Speaking of which..." Charlie pointed to the far corner of the room.

Spear in hand, Jackie stepped into a sparring pattern, waiting for one of the Tower's animated statues to join her. Zack gasped when, instead of a regular statue, the Commander's stony form claimed the position opposite. The regular statues, whether a terracotta soldier, a bronze samurai or a Greek sculpture, were tall enough to make Jackie look tiny - and himself, if he was being honest - but most weren't much taller than the average man. The Commander, unlike them, was enormous. At least eight feet tall, its chest, arms and legs were massive, even in comparison to its own height. Jackie was a mouse squaring up to a lion.

"Are you certain?" the Commander's deep Spanish tenor rumbled through the room. "I would not practice with an unhammered sword and I am similarly hesitant to practice with an unfinished person."

Once, not too long ago, those words may have cut Jackie, but the short, blonde girl merely adjusted her grip on her spear and stared back at it.

"Oh, I'm certain."

"So be it, then." The Commander bowed before lunging toward Jackie with a thrust of its stony fist.

Despite looking like the rough half of a mountain, the Commander moved with grace and speed. At the last moment, Jackie slid sideways away from its fist, but the Commander responded, swinging its extended arm around at her, like a hammer. Jackie conjured up a shield of silvery light that blocked the attack, but the strength of it forced her and the shield backwards and she staggered off balance. The Commander spun to face her and spread its arms, ready to slam her between its massive palms.

A flicker of movement to the side caught Zack's eye as Art stepped towards his sister. Zack readied himself as well; the Commander wouldn't kill Jackie, but she'd need healing if any of those blows landed.

The stone hands met in a deafening clap, but Jackie wasn't there. The instant before impact, she had sprinted forward, spear first. She stabbed the point of her weapon into the Commander's thigh and ran past it. The attack had done no real damage to the rocks that formed its body, but the Commander played by the rules and shifted its weight to the other leg as if injured.

Jackie had the momentum now. Without a steady stance, the Commander's fists struck with less force, more than enough to still shatter a bone, but now Jackie's shields were up to the task. The stone punches came in fast, and Jackie deflected them again and again. But she hadn't had a chance to make another attack of her own and her shields were starting to falter.

Rope-a-dope, Zack thought, wondering if he could sneak a thread of Life into her before the Commander took the advantage back.

But it was too late. The Commander feinted with its left and when Jackie turned to block it, the Commander's right fist came down like a hammer and slammed into her skull.

Art screamed and Zack was already running towards her when he registered what happened next. The Commander's fist clattered off Jackie's head against her shoulder and onto the training room's floor tiles. Unfazed by what should have been, at least a concussing hit, Jackie leapt up onto the Commander's wrist. Off balance from its 'bad leg' and from throwing what should have been a finishing blow, the Tower's weapons master lifted its arm up, but this only made it easier for Jackie to run along it.

The Commander threw a tight hook at Jackie with its left hand. Jackie knocked the incoming punch aside with a shield that had none of the shakiness of her last three and, as she approached the massive, stony shoulder, thrust her spear into the Commander's face. The point clattered off its rocky exterior, but the Commander ceased its movement.

"I yield," it said, plucking her between two fingers and setting her down beside it.

Jackie looked up at it, a tight smile on her lips and pride blazing in her eyes.

"Well done. I expected you to be unready and to falter, so you fed that to me and I choked on it. When your construction has finished, I look forward to training you properly." And with that, the Commander strode away across the training floor.

Zack and the others gathered around her.

"It could have given you a little more in the way of props," Bast said.

"Probably embarrassed that it underestimated you," Kimmy added.

Jackie shook her head, her smile widening across her face.

"Are you kidding me? That's the nicest thing the Commander's ever said to me."

"Well, you deserve it, Jackie." Charlie threw her arm around the shorter girl. "You kicked its butt."

Zack looked over at Art. Where he had expected to see lingering worry, there was only pride.

Art beamed.

"My sister, the spearmaiden. Slayer of rock monsters, eater of the last chicken nuggets in the freezer."

Jackie shrugged.

"Clearly, I'm putting the protein to good use."

The group shared a laugh, and Tabitha entered the Training Room, her brown hair tied back in a braid.

"I've clearly missed something good," Tabitha said.

"Only my sister getting ready to be the Tower's next Commander," Art said.

"Tell me all about it on the way," Tabitha replied. "We've got a job."

CHAPTER 2

"Just once, I'd like the Tower to send us into an air-conditioned building to hunt monsters." Art slashed at a slick, leafy branch.

Bast glanced back at him from where he was taking point.

"There was that imp in the game shop."

"Doesn't count," Art replied, "was guard duty. We just ended up at the store. I thought it was only Junie that had it in for us, but all the liaisons must be sadists."

Art had been groaning about the heat and the humidity since they arrived in the Amazon, but it was all background noise to Zack. His head was overflowing from the Life around him. He'd given up trying to find human Life amongst it all; there was no filtering out the Amazon.

Charlie sidled up beside him. Awkward nervousness wrenched through his chest and the calming vibrancy of the Life around him fled. It should be easier now, without his childish infatuation clouding the space between them. Charlie was great; the real Charlie, rather than the imagined one he'd built up in his mind and he desperately wanted to be her friend. But he didn't know what to say and he didn't trust himself with what he might say, so he'd avoided talking to her much at all. But he had to bite the bullet and say something. He was the one who had made it difficult it between them and it was up to him to fix it.

"It's a bit overwhelming, right?" Charlie said, beside him.

"What?" Zack's voice came out in a splutter.

"Life. Or at least, I assume it is." Charlie smiled at him. "Your face was all twisted in thought. I assume you're feeling as much Life as I'm feeling Animal. Or probably more. I can't get over how much is around us, let alone above us."

Zack's chest relaxed in relief. "Yeah. Lots of birds, I imagine."

"Yeah." Charlie nodded before adding with a wink. "And monkeys."

Zack's eyes lit up. "Monkeys? Can you—?"

"I think I've found it," Bast called out from the front of the line.

"Maybe later," Charlie said to Zack before they hurried forward to catch up with the others.

Bast was standing next to the trunk of a massive tree, its branches stretching up and out to meld with the canopy.

"And?" Kimmy asked, gesturing towards it, "it's a tree."

"Very good, Sis," Bast replied with a tone usually reserved for complimenting toddlers, "but look closer."

Zack followed the line of sight from Bast's pointed finger. The familiar grey light of a gate was hidden within the wrinkles of the wood.

"This is the breach?" Tabitha asked.

"The remains of it, yeah," Bast answered. "It's slowly shrinking on its own, which means whatever came through hasn't been using it. I can help it along and sew it up properly."

Tabitha nodded and Bast traced symbols in the air an inch away from the trunk.

"Sweet," Art said, "does that mean we can go home now?"

"No," Tabitha replied, "we need to find whatever came through."

"How?" Kimmy asked. "There's some joke here about tracking a needle through a haystack forest."

"We ask those who live in the haystack, that's how." Charlie turned back to Zack with a half-smile. "I'm about to make your day."

Charlie incanted and the reddish-brown light of Animal gathered around her fingertips. She gestured up toward the canopy and ceased chanting.

Nothing happened.

"Um, Charlie?" Art asked, looking around.

"Wait for it," Charlie responded, still facing upward.

The lower branches of the canopy quivered and a brown-furred creature came scurrying down the trunk of the nearest tree.

"Is that a —?" Zack asked, awe in his voice.

"Monkey?" Bast finished.

"Spider monkey," Charlie specified.

Zack's joy bubbled up in a squeal through his closed lips. The monkey stopped a few metres above them and surveyed the group, its dark eyes filled with suspicion.

"It's okay, my friend." Charlie took half a step towards it. "Nobody here will harm you. I just want to ask you something."

The monkey focused on her and scratched its chin.

"Of course I do," Charlie replied to a question the others couldn't hear. She reached into her backpack and withdrew a muesli bar. After unwrapping it, she broke off a piece and offered it with an outstretched arm.

In a single smooth action, the monkey slid down the remaining length of the trunk, snatched the offering and leapt back onto a nearby branch, where it tested the muesli. After a gentle nibble, it jammed the rest into its mouth and held out its palm.

"Not until you answer my questions," Charlie said, "then all of it is yours."

The monkey sat down on the branch.

"Thank you." Charlie stepped close to the monkey, so they were standing eye to eye. "Have you seen anything strange today? Something that doesn't belong?"

The monkey pointed at the rest of the group.

"Very funny. Something before us, maybe something very strange?"

The monkey stopped pointing and looked at her. Its eyes seemed to lose some of its mischief.

"Will you show me where you heard it?"

The monkey looked down, avoiding her eyes.

"We promise to keep you safe."

It scratched its cheek for a moment and shuffled closer.

"Would you like to sit on his shoulder?" Charlie gestured to Zack. "He's a very good friend and he'll look after you."

Zack's eyes widened and the monkey hopped across from the branch onto his shoulder. It shifted from side to side, finding its balance, before pointing deeper into the rainforest.

"I guess we have a guide," Tabitha said.

Zack stifled a second squeal.

Charlie and Max accompanied Zack and their local travel advisor in the lead, with the rest of the group behind. The monkey chittered constantly and from Charlie's answers, it seemed that most of the conversation was about the ingredients of the muesli bar. Zack's cheeks ached at the strain of containing his smile and he caught Charlie staring at him. He mouthed a 'thank you' to her and she smiled back. Maybe he didn't need the exact right words after all.

They had been moving through the rainforest for over an hour, when Max let out a low, rumbling growl.

"She's found something," Charlie said and the monkey screeched, "Okay, okay, we'll take it from here. You've been very helpful and you've earned every bite of this."

The monkey snatched the muesli bar in one of its hands and scampered into the safety of the canopy. Zack reached out with his mind in the direction of Max's growling. The torrent of Amazonian Life rushed toward him, but he stilled his mind and sifted it as it flowed.

"I don't think the creature is there."

"Let's go see what is." Tabitha waved them forward.

Zack pushed through the foliage, following Max's growls. The leaves peeled back to reveal a clearing that had become a butcher's yard. Human bodies lay torn apart and scattered to such a degree that it was unclear how many lives had been lost here. Charlie ran forward to pull Max back, struggling with the dog while trying to keep her own eyes off the corpses. Jackie gasped, holding her hand to her face.

Art didn't show the same hesitation as his sister and wandered to the nearest cluster of body parts.

"What in the other-worlds could have done this?"

"Something strong," Kimmy replied, circling around the clearing.

Bast stepped carefully in between the corpses.

"Probably big, too, to take out this many. I reckon there's at least eight people here."

"Who were they?" Charlie asked, "and why were they out here?"

"I don't think they were locals," Bast replied, "unless there's a tribe of whitefullas out here."

"I think they might have been a doco-crew." Tabitha held up a broken video camera. "Or maybe researchers. There's some other electronics here, too."

"Any chance they got some footage of whatever did this?" Art asked.

"The thing's a paperweight now," Tabitha said, "but I'll take the memory card to destroy later, to keep the Silence."

While Tabitha got to work prying open the camera, Zack inspected the bodies. Not all breaches could be closed before magical creatures could enter and do harm. Zack and his friends had been lucky in their first encounter, escaping with some bruises and scrapes from the tendrils that had attacked them almost two years before. But his mentor, Sara, had been the only survivor of her first encounter with magical creatures, a few thousand kilometres northwest of here. Still, this was worse than anything Zack had seen himself. And something else didn't add up.

"Whatever did this didn't do it for food."

"What do you mean?" Kimmy asked, moving up beside him.

Zack pointed at the wounds.

"Look, there are no bite marks, no missing mouthfuls."

"Zack!" Jackie looked pale.

"Sorry. I just mean, if something did this to eat them, you'd expect to see more signs of... well... the eating. These people were simply killed."

"And look there." Kimmy pointed at where a pool of blood congealed between two torsos. "There's a trail of blood heading off in that direction."

"Did anything good ever come from following a trail of blood through a forest?" Art asked.

Kimmy hefted her axe. "Nothing good for whatever's leaving the trail, that's for sure."

"Okay, Max, you're up." Charlie walked the dog around the bodies towards the thin line of blood.

Max sniffed at her in defiance.

"Don't be like that. I needed her help to find this place, but now that we have a trail, all I need is the best and smartest tracker in the world."

Max yapped and dropped her nose to the forest floor, sniffing.

"What do you reckon we're after?" Art asked, falling in beside Zack as they followed Max's lead.

"Could be a lot of things. Ogre?" Zack replied.

"Minotaur?"

Zack nodded. "A minotaur would be cool. Bigfoot?"

Art smiled. "A bit tropical for a bigfoot, but who knows?"

"We'll find out soon enough," Tabitha said from behind them, "so maybe you two should calm the geeking out and focus on being ready."

"Just trying to keep my mind off the heat, Tabs," Art replied with a huff, "but fine."

Charlie called back down the line. "Max smells water up ahead, maybe a river."

Art's eyebrows rose.

"We didn't consider aquatic monsters. Could be a creature from the black lagoon situation."

"Or a kappa," Zack replied.

"Are they big enough to do that?" Art asked.

"I don't know," Zack said, "we've never actually seen any of these things, remember?"

Art laughed. "I forget sometimes. When so much of the stuff we read about as kids has turned real, I lose track of what hasn't."

"Yeah. Last week, when we ran into that pair of gargoyles, I couldn't get their dungeons and dragons stats out of my head. Hit points, armour class, the whole stat block."

Kimmy turned around and shook her head at them, her face filled with disgust.

"I don't know how two people who I've seen do so much cool stuff can still manage to be such big losers."

Art elbowed Zack in the ribs. "Hear that? She said we do cool stuff."

Zack laughed and Tabitha and Jackie joined in behind him, taking a slice out of the tension they were all feeling from finding the bodies.

Kimmy was about to say something else when Max started barking. Charlie sprinted ahead.

"She's found something by the river."

When they caught up to Max, another horrific scene was waiting for them. This time, the victims appeared to be a group of local men who, based on the two boats pulled up onto the riverbank, had taken a break from fishing. Their remains were dressed in a combination of soccer jerseys and simpler cloth that Zack assumed was more traditional clothing. He was about to move closer to inspect the wounds when Bast shouted.

"There's something here."

Zack brought his quarterstaff up and looked in Bast's direction but couldn't see anything. Tabitha was standing closer to Bast.

"Well, that can't be what we're looking for, it's tiny. Hey, you two experts, I think we've got an elf or a gnome."

Zack still couldn't see what they were talking about and moved to the side. Once his line of sight was free from Bast and Tabitha, he saw what appeared to be a two-foot tall man, bald, but with a full white beard.

"Yeah," Art said, "that looks like a gnome to me."

"Reckon he hitched a ride here with whatever did this?" Charlie asked.

"Let's ask him," Kimmy said, stepping towards the gnome. "Hey little Santa man, did you see the big scary thing that did all this?"

The gentle jingle of a warning bell rang in the back of Zack's head.

"Why did you call him Santa?"

"Oh, I don't know, Zack. Because he's chubby, with pink cheeks and a big bushy beard?" She moved a little closer. "And see, he's even got a little red hat on the ground next to him."

The warning bell grew into a chorus of sirens.

"Oh hell, Kimmy. Watch—"

The gnome that was not a gnome leapt into the air towards Kimmy with impossible speed. In his left hand was a rusted cleaver almost half his height and in his eyes was euphoric madness. Kimmy turned away from the attack, protecting her face and chest, but leaving her side vulnerable.

The creature cackled as it swung forward with its knife, before crashing against the steel light of Jackie's shield. It tumbled back and landed in a crouch on a dismembered torso. Tabitha whirled her flail low at her hip and moved to stand near Kimmy.

"So, we got some kind of evil gnome?"

"Kind of," Zack said, "I think it's a redcap."

Kimmy brought her axe up, keeping her eyes on her attacker.

"You and Art are really scraping the bottom of the name barrel these days."

"Not our name," Art said, "and if Zack's right, it's the one that did all this. Don't write it off because it's small."

The redcap scampered past Kimmy and launched itself at Bast's legs, only to collide with another shimmer of steel light.

"Shouldn't write anything off just because it's small," Jackie said with a half smirk.

Bast incanted and the redcap screeched before lashing out again with its cleaver. Jackie responded with another shield but this time, with its feet planted, the redcap's swing broke through cutting into Bast's ribs. The redcap screamed in triumph and wrenched the blade out. Blood sprayed from the wound.

Zack ran to where Bast had collapsed to his knees, while Tabitha, Kimmy and Art pushed forward towards the creature. Outnumbered and outsized, the redcap should have fled, but it stood its ground and swung again at Bast, this time at his neck. Bast fell back, clutching at his wound, and Art leapt in between them, his broadsword held forward in both hands. The cleaver clanged against the longer blade and the force of it knocked Art off his feet. He thudded into the ground a metre and a half from where he'd been standing and the redcap pursued him with fevered delight.

An arrow streaked through the air and found its home in the redcap's thigh. The creature grunted and stopped in its pursuit of Art, turning to face Charlie, who hurried to set a second arrow to her bow. Reaching down, the redcap wrenched the arrow from its leg and stalked towards her. Max growled.

"Stay back, girl," Charlie said, "this thing is too dangerous."

Tabitha and Kimmy moved around the bodies to flank the redcap. It slashed from one to the other, but they stayed light on their feet and when one was forced to retreat a step, the other struck with an attack, forcing the redcap's attention onto themselves.

Hopeful that the threat was occupied for the moment, Zack focused on Bast's wound. The cut had been brutal and deep and the way the cleave had been wrenched free did him no favours.

Zack poured Life into the wound, directing it in a complex weave toward bone, muscle, veins and arteries. Each needed to be treated with individual care and Zack accepted his familiar struggle with focus, welcoming the distracting thoughts into the process rather than pushing them away. The wound closed.

"I've done what I can, but you've lost a lot of blood and I can't do anything about that just yet."

Bast nodded and stayed on his knees.

"I'm alright," he said in a soft voice, "go help the others."

Zack moved in between Kimmy and Tabitha, holding his quarterstaff in a defensive grip. Art had found his feet and moved to stand opposite Zack. They had the redcap surrounded. Not that it seemed to care. What it lacked in reach, it made up for in speed and fervour. It lashed out again, knocking Kimmy's axe aside and causing her to stumble back a step.

Only Zack's thrust towards its legs kept it from following her.

Kimmy swore in frustration.

"Why is this garden gnome so bloody tough?"

"It's a magical murder gnome." Art swung his sword only to have it battered away by the redcap's cleaver.

The attacks continued and while the teens tired, the redcap only seemed to be warming up. If not for Jackie's shields slowing some of the attacks, the cleaver would have found its mark. Zack was sure that it soon would.

"Get it towards the river," Charlie shouted.

Her voice sounded strained but Zack couldn't risk taking his eyes off his foe.

Tabitha swung her flail at the redcap, forcing it to take a step towards the water but it turned on its heel and lunged right back at her. They attacked and feinted, but nothing seemed to work. Art looked over the redcap to Zack.

"You better have enough juice left to patch me up."

Zack nodded and swung his quarterstaff towards the redcap's head, grabbing its momentary attention. Art charged forward and rammed the creature with the bulk of his body. The redcap reacted with a flurry of cleaver strikes and, while Art caught the first two on his blade, others cut deeply into his lower arms and thighs.

Art collapsed to the ground, clutching at his wounds as blood leaked through his hands, but the redcap was at the end of the riverbank, teetering off balance. It cackled and spun on one leg before planting the other firmly. The redcap pointed its bloody cleaver at Kimmy and took a step towards her. But as it moved, orange light flickered on the muddy ground beneath its foot and it slipped, tumbling into the water.

Zack glanced over to see Bast grimacing as he worked the incantation. But then a loud splashing sound ripped his attention back to the river. A massive reptilian jaw burst from the water and snapped close around the redcap before dragging it back under. The water rippled and then stilled.

"The redcap's dead," Charlie said.

The surface of the river darkened with blood. Blood! Zack snapped out of his daze and ran to Art's side. His friend was pale and drenched with sweat where he wasn't with blood.

"I got you, mate."

Art nodded weakly, his eyes unfocused. Zack channelled Life towards his wounds, staunching the bleeding, but he didn't stop there. He reached the Life down into Art's bone marrow and spurred it into action, stimulating the creation of more blood cells. It was exhausting work and Zack became lightheaded. He broke off the connection, before his wavering attention could do any damage, and collapsed back on the ground.

Art sat up, still covered in far too much of his own blood.

"Um, should we also get away from the river?"

"It's safe, for us," Charlie said, her voice still strained.

Zack looked over and saw the russet glow in her eyes.

"Great work on the croc," Tabitha said, helping Bast up.

"Caiman." Charlie spoke like she was recalling study notes from a flash card. "Closer to an alligator than a crocodile. Different teeth."

"It's a better name than 'redcap'." Bast sat leaning back on his hands. "Who names a psychotic muppet after its fashion accessory?"

"It's named that because it soaks the hat in the blood of its victims," Zack said.

"I really could have made it through my entire life without knowing that little fact," Bast replied.

"Want to take us home, then?" Tabitha asked.

Charlie's eyes had returned to their normal colour and she looked around at the bodies of the locals.

"Should we do anything about this before we go? Like bury them or find their families?"

Bast clambered to his feet. "I know my mob would want to find them as soon as possible and make sure our business was done right. Art, is there a way you can find out if their people are nearby and maybe coax them over?"

Tabitha shook her head. "Our job here was to protect the Silence. Killing the redcap will prevent more people from discovering magic and if we do anything extra, we might undo all that."

"I think I can do something subtle." Art closed his eyes and reached out his hand. "There's a significant group of people not too far away. Kids too. Probably a village." Purple light collected around his hand. "There's a candidate."

The light faded and Art opened his eyes. "I found someone who was about to head out looking for this group. He won't know why, but he'll come this way first. They'll be found soon."

Bast clapped him on the shoulder. "Thanks, mate."

"Good work," Tabitha said, "but if they're on their way, we'd better get moving. Are you up to it, Bast?"

"Yeah, a gate home is easy. We might not get our security deposit back if the property manager looks under the rug and finds my markings, but they sure make the trip home a breeze."

Art smiled. "Well, we didn't actually pay our security deposit, but I'll make sure we get it back anyway."

"I still feel bad for them," Charlie said. Max rubbed her head against Charlie's hip in comfort.

"We may not have been able to save them," Art said, "but that village really isn't far away and we stopped that evil gremlin from going there next. We have to take the win on this one."

Bast gestured to the completed gate.

"Either way, we've done what we could. Their people will know how to look after them from here."

Zack took a last look at the gruesome scene and stepped through the grey.

CHAPTER 3

The cemetery was peaceful in the late morning sun. No funerals were taking place in this precinct and the only traffic was from a pair of groundskeepers tending to a garden and half a dozen visitors paying their respects to those they had lost.

Zack included himself in the half dozen, although he sat on a nearby bench rather than standing at his grandmother's headstone. He told himself it was because he didn't truly think of this as her resting place. The contents of the coffin buried beneath the stone weren't her anymore. In fact, for a long time before she'd died, they'd been her prison more than they'd been her. His grandmother was her voice, her thoughts, her fierce looks and her laughter. She was the impact she had on the world and the people around her and she was the love he'd felt when she held him. And none of that was buried in the wooden box.

That was the reason he didn't bother to walk all the way up to her plot. The only reason. It certainly had nothing to do with the guilt he still held that she had a plot in the first place. She had made the choice herself in the end and he should be able to respect that. He did respect that. But it could have been different.

"Are you okay, young man?"

Zack startled at the voice that came from a man he hadn't noticed sitting down beside him.

"Yes," Zack answered, "okay enough, anyway. Thank you."

"I can only imagine how much it hurts to lose somebody you care about when you have your particular abilities."

Zack spun his head to the right and immediately recognised the speaker, despite only having met him once. It was the man who, in the aftermath of their fight with a group of renegade mages performing a dangerous ritual, had told his friends not to trust the Tower.

"You're the Traveller."

Zack tensed his legs, ready to run. The man had never threatened him, but he was against the Tower. And Zack was a Tower mage. The man tapped his empty hands gently against his knees.

"I mean you no harm, Zack. I've just come here to talk. I'm not going to hurt you or threaten your precious Silence."

Zack turned his body on the bench to better face the man. He was tall and wiry, dressed in an oversized coat that emphasised his slightness and his hair and beard were a messy nest of salt and pepper knots.

"How do you know my name?"

"I do my research these days. Thoroughly. I've been burned before by the mistakes made from insufficient careful consideration. You met them."

"Armand," Zack said.

"Indeed." The Traveller nodded, plunging a hand deep into his matted curls and giving his scalp a good scratch. "Among others. I taught them too much before I learned who they were. They became blinded by ambition and the hunger for power. I lost them."

"What do you want from us? To replace them?" Zack asked.

"No. Yes?" The Traveller looked away for a moment as if lost in thought. "All I want right now is to meet with you all and have you hear what I have to say."

"Tabitha's the one you should be speaking to, then."

The Traveller screwed up his face.

"No, no, no. She's too close to the Tower, that one. I need you to convince her not to run straight to your mentors."

"Why me?" The gears of Zack's mind were whirling at top speed.

"They listen to you. You convince them the Tower's lying to you all and they'll agree to meet me."

"How do you know they'll listen to me?"

"I told you; I've done my research."

It sounded like he'd been spying on them, which begged a dozen more questions, but Zack put that to the side for a moment.

"Okay then, but what makes you think I'll believe you about the Tower?"

The Traveller straightened up on the bench.

"Two things. One, you saw Armand cast multiple Schools of magic. According to the Tower, that is not possible."

Zack remembered the night when Armand, the Mind mage, had used Movement magic to open a gate.

"Okay. What else?"

"Please consider accepting that as proof enough." The Traveller looked Zack in the eyes.

"It's not enough to convince them." It might be. It was certainly enough that Zack knew something was wrong within the Tower. But if the Traveller had more information to share, he wanted it. "You said you had two examples."

"Okay, but I take no pleasure in what this information might do to you." The Traveller slumped to lean over his knees before taking a deep breath. "Tell me, what has the Tower taught you about magical creatures?"

Zack's eyes narrowed as he thought, not only about the answer, but also where the Traveller might be headed with the question.

"That they are magic itself, given form."

The strange man did not seem satisfied.

"And the nature of that form, of that existence?"

Zack thought back to something Junie had once said. "They are magical energy that mimics life."

The Traveller closed his eyes and exhaled.

"That night on the mountain, when you fought Armand and the others during their ritual. At some point, one of them opened a gate to a terrible place. I saw the remnants of the creatures they called forth. Tell me, did you use your magic to sense them?"

Zack shuddered at the memory of the creatures made solely of sharp bone.

"Yes, it was awful. And wrong."

"And have you ever used it on the training statues or even the Commander?"

Zack nodded. "They aren't alive, though, just magically animated."

The Traveller stared at the grass, clearly avoiding eye contact.

"Now, think about that. Life told you that those things Armand unleashed were of something that was not Life. And Life told you it was not present in the statues."

Zack knew the next question before the Traveller asked it.

"What does Life tell you about the other magical creatures you have encountered?"

"No, Life is just detecting the mimicry," Zack explained, "they aren't actually alive."

The Traveller sat in silence, a look of patience on his face and a shimmer of sadness in his eyes.

Zack continued, "And the Life feels different in magical creatures. Because it's not really Life."

The Traveller's quiet was broken only by the soft brush of the wind through the trees.

"And you can't trust magic, anyway." Zack tried again in vain to convince the Traveller.

But more importantly, he hadn't come close to convincing himself. None of his responses were genuine thoughts. Even as he voiced them, he recognised them as merely desperate attempts to not face the truth. Every creature they had encountered, fought and defeated had been alive. As alive as he was. It was as if the truth shattered the ground beneath him and he was dangling in the air, ready to drop.

"No, son. You can trust magic. It will show you the truth if you are willing to see it." The Traveller patted him on the shoulder. "It's the

Tower you can't trust. They've been lying to you since the beginning."

Zack pushed away his spiralling thoughts with a shake of his head.

"How do you know so much about the Tower?"

"Not now. You convince your friends to meet with me, then I'll share more." The man stood up and pulled a business card from one of his many pockets. The corners were split, and there was a stain at one end. "When you're ready, call that number and say, 'I'd like to see a man about a seahorse.' The woman who answers doesn't know anything about me, but she knows what to do if somebody says that. What will follow is a tiresome game of telephone that is, unfortunately, necessary for my protection. But you don't need to worry about that. You call that number, say the phrase, and somebody will find you."

Zack took the card, his mind distant as he repeated, "I'd like to see a man about a seahorse."

The Traveller nodded. "I'll leave you here with your thoughts now, young man. Don't try to follow me. I hope to see you again soon."

Zack nodded, clutching the business card in his hand. The Traveller turned and stalked away through the cemetery, his coat and hair fluttering in the breeze, bouncing with each step until he disappeared behind a chapel.

Twice now, Zack had met this man. The first time was for a few seconds and this second time was not much longer. With simple conversations he had let loose a cyclone into Zack's life. When he first appeared to the group and told them that the Tower was lying, Zack had believed him. But he had thought they would be lies about who could do what kinds of magic. Lies that, perhaps, revealed the masters of the Tower were keeping more powerful magic for themselves.

But this revelation, that Zack had been too blind to see on his own, shook the foundation of what the Tower was. No, not merely the Tower, about the world and its relationship with the other realms. He hadn't even begun to sort through all the thoughts that were spider-webbing out in his head, but this wasn't for him to work through alone.

Zack took a deep breath and pulled his phone from his pocket.

He opened up the group thread.

Emergency meeting. Boys' house. One hour.

"I was pretty sure we agreed to call this place 'Casa del Macho'," Art said as Zack walked in and plonked down onto a chair. "Not 'boys house'."

"That's pretty much what it translates to," Bast said from the kitchen, his head in the fridge, "or at least 'male house'."

"It doesn't mean 'the castle of manly men' or something like that?" Art asked with surprise in his voice.

"Nope, but if you want to go to a place with a name like that, I know of three or four clubs over in Darlinghurst that would fit the bill." Bast appeared from the kitchen with a beer in his hand.

"You know what? I think I'm good, but thanks anyway." Art turned and looked at Zack, who hadn't cracked a smile. "That bad, is it?"

Zack blinked a few times, drawing his gaze and thoughts back into the room.

"I don't know. I think so, but maybe I'm just overreacting."

"Want to talk about it a bit before the girls arrive?" Art asked.

Bast shook his head. "Nope. Dude called for a group meeting. We talk about it together."

"Maybe I could have a teensy little peek inside." Art wiggled his finger in Zack's direction.

Zack crooked an eyebrow in a silent response.

"Fine." Art crossed his arms. "But you know they're going to take ages. Kimmy is probably—"

The doorbell rang. Bast smirked in Art's direction before heading to the front door. He returned with Tabitha, Kimmy and Jackie.

"Charlie?" Zack asked.

Bast picked up his phone from the coffee table. "Should be any minute now."

The other girls claimed spots on one of the couches before Bast's phone dinged.

"Excellent," he said, walking to a corner of the room where a square rug lay on the floor. "One Charlie coming up."

Bast placed the phone on the rug beside him and incanted. The orange of his magic gave way to the rippling grey light of a gate and Charlie and Max stepped through. Charlie had a backpack over one shoulder and an impressive-looking camera around her neck.

"Thank you, Bast. First class travel at its finest."

"Any time, Sis." Bast smiled. "Don't suppose you've got any souvenirs?"

Charlie patted her bag.

Art pointed at Max. "She's toilet-trained, right?"

The dog stared at him with an expression that could only be described as unimpressed before tilting her head to look at Charlie.

Charlie shrugged. "I don't know. Maxie, are you?"

Max padded across the room to Art, where she promptly lifted her back leg against his shins.

"Okay! I'm sorry. Of course, you are. You are a lovely, brilliant dog."

Max sniffed and settled in at Jackie's feet. Charlie dropped her bag and camera on the table and claimed a seat beside Zack.

"Okay. We're all here," Tabitha said. "What's up, Zack?"

He took a deep breath, mentally flicking through the different versions of this conversation he'd been having in his head for the last hour. "I met with the Traveller today."

His friends gasped and swore in response.

"What do you mean 'met', Zack?" Tabitha asked.

"He found me. I was out in public and he sat down and started talking."

"Are you okay?" Jackie asked.

Zack nodded. "He didn't do anything. Just talked. He wants to meet with all of us to tell us what he says is the truth about the Tower. But only if we're willing to talk."

The others all started speaking at once. Art said something about pulling the information right out of his head, while Tabitha spoke about letting Junie know what had happened. Bast mentioned that the Traveller clearly knew Movement magic, Jackie mumbled a question about how he had found Zack and Kimmy described what would have happened if the Traveller had gifted her with the surprise visit instead.

Charlie's voice, calm and steady, broke through.

"Why did he approach you, Zack?"

Kimmy answered before Zack could open his mouth.

"Well, he's the least threatening out of all of us, isn't he?"

The words slammed like a fist into Zack's stomach. He hadn't considered that, but it made sense. All the others could have attacked the Traveller with their magic, but not Zack. He decided to put that thought aside to revisit when he was alone in the dark, where it could join in the group discussion with all his other worries and doubts.

"That's possible. But I think it also had to do with convincing us that the Tower can't be trusted," he said.

They all looked at him in confusion.

Zack took a slow, steadying breath.

"He said it was because of my Life magic. He pointed something out to me that I should have realised from the beginning and, now that he's shown me, I can't deny it. The Tower has been lying to us. The creatures we've been fighting are not just magical energy. They are as alive as we are."

Silence descended on the room, all eyes staring at him. Zack could tell they were digesting this information, but their expressions gave no clue what they were thinking.

"I don't know," Charlie said, breaking the silence, "this guy comes out of nowhere, tells you the opposite of what the Tower has told us. Why should we believe him? Seems like a pretty obvious move to set us against them."

Zack shook his head.

"He didn't tell me. He just asked the question and I realised the truth. Life has always told me these things are alive. Since I first sensed that imp in the game store, part of me has known they have Life."

"No, I think he's playing with you," Tabitha said. "Your magic is picking up the way they are mimicking Life, that's all."

"I said almost the exact same thing at first," Zack replied.

"See?" Tabitha looked around to the others for support.

"But it's not that. Life tells me what is alive, not what pretends to be." He gestured towards Kimmy. "Mr Shanks doesn't have Life. I can tell the difference."

"Maybe you can't," Tabitha said, "come on, think about the source here. This guy is definitely bad news."

Zack had been thinking about it since he stood up from the bench and made his way back here. And he'd been imagining the different ways this conversation could have gone.

"You can sense Air, right?" Tabitha's eyes narrowed warily as she nodded. "And when we're in other realms, you can still sense the Air there."

"Yeah, but it often feels different."

Zack nodded. "Exactly, even though it's different, Air knows Air. But what if Bast used his magic to sway a tree's branches or rustle the leaves. Would Air tell you that it was a magical kind of wind?"

"No. I'd know it wasn't Air that moved the trees."

"And you trust that. Your ability to understand what is and isn't Air. Because something either is Air or is not, regardless of what it does?"

"Yeah?" Tabitha seemed unsure of the conclusion.

"Then you need to trust me when I tell you that Life knows Life," Zack said.

"And Mind knows minds." Art had a look of realisation on his face. "Some of these creatures have had real thoughts, emotions… memories! They're real. I think I just sort of decided I was picking up some kind of virtual mind. Like the magic had worked out how to pass a mystical Turing test or something. How didn't I see this before?"

"Because we were lied to," Charlie replied.

"We don't know that they are lying," Tabitha said.

Art threw his hands out in frustration. "Oh, come on, Tabs."

"Does it matter?" Kimmy asked. "I mean, yeah, they probably lied to us. But does it make a difference about what we do?"

Bast leapt to his feet and stormed away to the kitchen, where he leant heavily with his elbows on the counter. He locked eyes with Kimmy across the room.

"Are you kidding me? Bunch of people in power decide that some lives aren't really lives? That they don't count? And therefore, we can do whatever we want to them? And you want us to be okay with that? You want me to be okay with that?"

"So, we're not supposed to defend our world against monsters like that creature that hunted me?" Tabitha asked. "Or fairies that steal children?"

Bast stood up from the counter.

"I'm not talking about that. Defending ourselves is one thing. I'm talking about all those times we've been sent out into other realms to do whatever the Tower wants, take whatever they want, fight whatever they want, because nothing there counts as real. Feels a whole bunch like Terra Nullius to me. And we've done it by stepping through my gates. The Tower has turned me into a bloody coloniser!" He paced back and forth. "I think I'm going to throw up and punch a hole in the wall at the same time."

Zack didn't know what to say and nobody else seemed to either. He sat there in the silence and with no small amount of shame that he hadn't considered this from Bast's perspective.

When the silence was broken again, it was Jackie.

"You said he wants to meet with us?"

Zack nodded and pulled the business card from his pocket, holding it out between two fingers. Tabitha took one more glance towards Bast before facing Zack.

"We can hear him out. Make the call."

CHAPTER 4

They arrived in Melbourne two days later and found their way to the steps of the Flinders Street railway station.

"What are we supposed to do now?" Bast asked.

The others all looked to Zack.

"I don't know," he replied, "I told you what the message was. Someone will meet us here and we do what they say."

"I don't like this," Tabitha said, rubbing her arm through her sleeve, "we're handing ourselves over on a platter. We don't even have our weapons."

"We're not completely unarmed," Kimmy smirked and patted her jacket. "If this turns out to be a trap, they'll pay for it."

Zack wanted to object to the notion that this could be a trap, but he wasn't convinced either. And, despite this being a group decision, he was pretty sure he would wear the blame if it turned out to be one.

An overweight man in a chauffeur's uniform approached them, holding a handwritten sign against his chest. *Zack and guests.*

Great. If this went south, he was definitely getting the blame. Zack waved an awkward hand at the man. "That's us."

"Follow me, please."

"Oh no," Kimmy replied, "tell us where you're taking us first."

"Follow me, please."

Kimmy's lips tightened. "Don't ignore me!"

"He's under a spell," Art said, stepping closer to the man.

"And these are the good guys, are they?" Tabitha said. "Mind controlling innocent people?"

"He'll be okay," Art replied, even though Tabitha had clearly been directing her comments at Zack, "he's just locked down a bit until he does this job."

"If we want answers, we do what we're told," Charlie said, "lead on, we'll follow."

The man turned and led the group to a taxi bay. He walked up to a black van and opened the sliding door. There were no seats inside.

"Get inside, please," he said, gesturing to the floor.

"This definitely feels like another line in the 'this is a kidnapping' column," Bast said.

Tabitha shook her head before climbing into the van.

"If we're doing this, we're doing this."

The others followed her in and sat on the hard floor of the van. The man slid the door closed before climbing into the driver's seat.

"Is it safe for him to drive if he's being mind-controlled?" Jackie asked.

"I don't know what they've done to him, but he's probably fine." Art squinted at the driver. "Maybe be ready with your shields, just in case."

"That's my secret, Art. I'm always ready," Jackie replied with a wink.

The van started up and Zack placed his hands against the floor to brace himself from the movement. They had only been travelling a minute or so when the van stopped at an intersection.

Bast tilted his head as if he heard or smelt something. "I think I sense a—"

Zack and the others fell through the floor of the van and crashed onto what appeared to be an old mattress that only somewhat broke their fall. The impact pushed the air from his lungs. They seemed to be in a bedroom of an old apartment, lit only by a lamp in the corner.

A bald, middle-aged man sat facing them on a chair beside an unmade bed. He pointed at them, one by one, as if counting them off.

"What the hell?" Art said, wincing from the impact of the fall.

"Sorry," the man said, "but if you didn't enjoy that, you'll hate this."

He clicked his fingers and Zack felt himself plummeting again. This time, the descent persisted. He caught brief glimpses of other rooms, some dark, some bright and even an image of somewhere with sunlight and trees, before he landed with a slap on some crash mats. The cushioning, no doubt, saved him from some broken bones or worse, but the impact still left him stunned and he'd thumped against the others on the way down.

He and his friends lay disoriented as three women and a man approached them. All four appeared to be in their twenties and were wearing warm, casual clothes. This time, they seemed to be in a shed or barn of some kind.

"No glamours or masks," one of the women said.

"No mind weaves either," added the man.

"And I'm not seeing any evidence of shifts," the second woman said.

"What is going on?" Tabitha said, pushing herself up off the mat.

"Stay seated, please," the third woman said, "we're just making sure you are who you're supposed to be before we send you on your way."

"On our way?" Bast replied. "You sent us through, what, eight gates?"

"Eleven. Our way of making it hard for your masters to follow." The third woman's voice was thick with disdain. "Each of you state the name your family gave you."

"I thought you knew who we were supposed to be," Kimmy said with a sneer.

"The dude's a psychomancer," Art said as purple light collected around the man's eyes, "it's why he's worded it so specifically and giving us no way to skirt around the answer. My name is Arthur Stevenson."

The rest of them stated their names.

The man nodded.

"All true. Can't make any promises on the beanpole. If the Tower has taught him how to mask a lie, I might not have seen it, but I think we're good."

"So, are you going to drop us through the floor again?" Charlie asked.

"I could if you like," the third woman replied. She turned and traced circular patterns in the air beside her, leaving behind orange light and opening a gate. "Or you could step through."

They pushed themselves off the crash mat and Charlie lingered to help Max onto the floor. Max looked unsteady from the multiple falls and her hackles were up as she approached the strangers.

Tabitha hesitated in front of the gate.

"What's to stop this from being a trap?"

"Nothing," the woman replied, "although we could have had you fall through a hundred different portals before dropping you down a volcano, but sure, maybe there's an angry bear on the other side of this one."

Kimmy rolled her eyes and stepped through the gate, muttering, "After all this, I could go a round or two with a bear."

The others followed and found themselves in a dimly but warmly lit room. A tall man sat in a high-backed leather chair. With his wild, unkempt hair, Zack recognised him as the Traveller. He gestured to two mismatched couches facing his chair.

"Thank you for agreeing to meet with me and I'm sorry for the runaround to get you here. Please, take a seat."

Tabitha crossed her arms against her chest.

"What is to stop us from capturing you and handing you over to the Tower right now?"

"Nothing is stopping you from trying. And you very well could succeed." The Traveller opened his arms and smiled. "But what have I done to warrant that? I have not broken their Silence or attacked them."

"You said you were responsible for Armand and the others," Zack replied.

"I did. But by the end, they were against me as much as they were against the Tower. Please, sit. I will tell you what I know and answer any questions I can. After that, you can decide what you do."

Tabitha looked unsure, but Bast shrugged and whispered, "We came all this way. And I can get us out of here any time we want."

"Okay," Tabitha said and walked across the room to take a seat.

Zack claimed a spot next to Kimmy on the other couch. It was a nice piece of furniture but had seen better days. The stitching of a patch on the inside of the armrest rubbed against his arm. The room contained one door on the opposite wall and no windows. Something suggested they were underground, like in a basement or storage area, but he couldn't articulate it. Tabitha's voice brought his thoughts back.

"We're listening. What do you want from us?"

"Thank you," the Traveller replied, "as I told Zack, all I want is a chance to tell you what I know about the Tower. About their deceits and their true motives. Then, you can decide what you do with that information."

"Go on, then." Tabitha leant forward to rest her elbows on her thighs. "Start with how Armand was able to use magic from two different Schools."

"Not just Armand." The Traveller held out his hands to his sides, palms up. A tiny flame danced in his left while, in the other, a two-inch whirlwind moved up and down his fingertips.

"How is that possible?" Charlie asked.

The Traveller closed his hands and returned them to his lap, ending the display.

"Because the thirteen Schools are a fabrication. There is no Fire magic and Air magic; there is only magic."

"That makes no sense," Kimmy said, "why would the Tower want us to be weaker?"

"Because it makes the Tower stronger," Art said, his eyes wide with realisation. "If none of us can do everything alone, then we need to rely on the Tower to get the job done."

"So, like, divide and conquer?" Bast asked.

"I think more like divide and unify," Zack said.

"Or, because it allows for specialisation," Tabitha said, "it's why we have different faculties at university, so we get engineers and doctors and lawyers."

"But those are choices, Tabs," Charlie replied, "a law student could still pick up a few IT subjects if they really wanted to."

"You are not wrong, Tabitha," the Traveller said, "the specialisation is valuable. I imagine your focus within each of your so-called schools helps you excel at what you do. But I believe the others are right. It is about control."

"Then how come I can sense Fire?" Kimmy asked. "If it's not real."

"I didn't say the Fire isn't real," the Traveller replied, "just that it isn't separated from anything else by an impenetrable wall. You see Fire because you are looking for Fire. You can't see anything else because you're looking too closely at Fire."

"So, the Tower lies to us to control us. That doesn't exactly make them unique in this world." Art lounged back on the couch. "I reckon they'd say it's necessary to protect the world from being invaded by magic."

The Traveller's mouth twitched.

"That is their greatest lie. They aren't keeping the magic from invading. They are keeping it from returning. Our world is no different from any other, except that over a thousand years ago, the Tower arose and locked out all the magic other than what they keep for themselves. And the scraps and crumbs that the rest of us pick up."

"So?" Tabitha said. "The world is safer without magic swarming in."

"Says somebody who gets a little for herself, regardless?" the Traveller asked with a smirk.

Tabitha leapt from her seat.

"Says somebody who was nearly killed by a magical invader two years ago!"

The Traveller held up his hands in partial surrender.

"Perhaps you would have been more prepared for that attack outside the shroud of the Tower's Silence. They keep the world vulnerable and then justify all their actions against their role as its sole protectors."

Tabitha sat back down and a stillness settled over the room.

"So, what's your pitch?" Charlie asked. "Do you want us to quit the Tower?"

"And let me guess," Kimmy added, "swear allegiance to you instead?"

"No. I don't ask for, or accept, any oaths." He looked to Charlie.

"Yes, I think you should quit the Tower. But before you do, we have an opportunity."

Art nodded along. "You want somebody on the inside."

"He already has somebody on the inside," Zack interrupted.

The Traveller quirked an eyebrow while the others stared at him with their mouths open in surprise.

"He does?" Bast asked.

"I think so. He knows too much about the Tower. Stuff about the oaths, the Schools, the Commander, even about us." Zack thought of the Traveller's comment that Tabitha was too close to the Tower.

"You're right, Zack. Over the years, I have helped some others see through the Tower's lies and a few of them have been willing to stay to help me investigate." The Traveller levered himself out of his armchair and walked to the wall before turning to face them again. "But the seven of you are an unprecedented opportunity."

When he was answered with confused faces, he continued, "Do you know how many other teams within the Tower are composed exclusively of people who knew each other before their 'Awakening,' as the Tower calls it?"

"Yeah," Tabitha replied, "we've heard it's rare."

"No, not rare. Unique." The Traveller spoke rapidly now, his eyes alight with excitement. "Groups of four or more people who become Awakened to magic are rare, although not unheard of. But often the Tower does not give a group that size the choice to take the oaths. They just send in the memory wipers. And in the even rarer cases, when they do let them take the oaths, they split them up amongst other groups.

"But not you. I don't know why. Perhaps they thought you were too young to split amongst older members. Or the fact you all lived so close to a Tower entrance made you easier to manage. Whatever the reason, you are the only group in the Tower that is in a position to trust each other before anybody else."

Kimmy's eyes flicked to Art, but she looked away when Zack noticed.

"You know," Charlie said, "Junie said almost the same thing last year.

When she sent us hunting for potential traitors in the Tower."

"Turns out she was right to be suspicious." Tabitha stared at the Traveller.

"And perhaps that is the reason you were kept together," he replied, "regardless, you are an opportunity that is unlikely to come by again."

"You've said that twice now." Jackie leant forward, looking tiny in between Art and Bast on the other couch. "An opportunity for what? We won't attack other members of the Tower who have just been lied to like we were."

"And what? They are innocent then?" The Traveller scoffed. "The seven of you were given a couple of breadcrumbs and, within the day, you were demanding to know the truth. Some of them have been there for decades."

He strode back to his armchair and sat down again.

"But no, I'm not asking or suggesting you attack anybody. I want you to help me gather more information. I already know a great deal about the Tower, but I have a blind spot when it comes to the Thirteen."

"The Tower's leaders?" Tabitha asked. "None of your sources know who they are?"

"No, they don't," the Traveller answered, "nobody seems to. But more than that, I'm beginning to suspect they are not simply the ones in charge. I believe they're magically linked to the structure of the Tower itself. I also think the regular rituals they perform, when you do your guard duties, are part of it. And that's your opening."

"But we don't even know where the rituals are performed," Art said.

"You won't need to." The Traveller drew something from a satchel bag next to his chair and placed it on the table between them.

It was a white opal, maybe five inches across and even in the dim light, it sparkled with a rainbow reflection. Next to it, he placed a folded piece of paper and tapped it.

"This is a ritual using what you call 'Movement' magic. The next time you are called for guard duty, Bast follows these instructions and creates a tiny portal connecting this opal to the magic churning around the Tower.

The enchantment within the opal will capture a record of what is happening and, with a little luck, we'll finally learn something about the Thirteen."

"And how do we know you're telling the truth?" Tabitha asked. "And that we aren't bringing in a magical bomb or something?"

"Bast will be able to tell you when he's read the ritual and examined it. I don't expect you to trust me, just to give what I say a fair hearing."

"You seem to trust us," Art replied, "what if we go straight to the Tower and tell them about this? Or what if we just sell that thing? It's got to be worth thousands."

"It is. And that's the question you must ask yourself. Do you want to stay where you are, despite the lies you have been told, and live a life of privilege and luxury built on your role within those lies? Or, do you want to take the opportunity that so few get and help shine a light on those who control our world from the shadows? How you answer this, with your actions, will tell me if I can indeed trust you."

The Traveller sat back in his armchair, leaving the opal and the ritual unguarded on the table.

"It's time for you to decide what you stand for."

CHAPTER 5

The new shirt Art had forced Zack to wear, chafed around the collar and he rubbed his neck as he climbed the stairs to the bar. A security guard eyed him, perhaps mistaking his fidgeting for a guilty conscience, and waited for Zack to reach the top. Zack's cheeks flushed as he presented his driver's licence. He had never done this without Art, but as of today, he didn't need to. The man reviewed the licence and flashed a bright smile.

"Thank you, Sir. And Happy Birthday."

Zack offered an awkward nod and shuffled inside. It was easily the most expensive bar he'd ever been to. The place was a mixture of marble and wood that somehow still looked modern, with wide floor-to-ceiling windows. He caught glimpses of the dark, splashing waves of the harbour through gaps in the crowd of well-dressed patrons.

"There he is!" Art's voice rang out over the clamour of the bar. "Hit it, maestro!"

The song that had been playing was abruptly cut and replaced by the voice of 50 Cent. Zack's heart dropped through his knees as Art danced his way through the crowd, singing loudly and drawing every pair of eyes in the room to Zack.

"... gonna party like it's ya birthday!" Art hugged him.

Zack did not return the hug and, after a moment, Art untangled himself and dragged Zack deeper into the room.

"So, you coming early to get Charlie in was just cover for setting this up?" Zack asked.

Art looked back over his shoulder. "It can be two things. See?"

They reached the end of their shuffle through the room and Art pointed to where Charlie was sitting between Bast and Tabitha. As of that morning, Charlie was the only seventeen-year-old in their exclusive group, but there was a cocktail in her hand, regardless.

Tabitha placed her glass down and leapt into his arms.

"Happy Birthday, Zacky! I'm so sorry about Art. I tried to talk him out of it."

"You don't need to apologise for him, Tabs," Zack said, "I'm the one who stays friends with him after twelve-something years. I should be more surprised he hadn't organised a literal spotlight."

Art beamed with undisguised pride.

"You know, I asked. But they didn't have one set up that could reach the door. I had to make do. So come on, Shorty, it's ya birthday. Let me buy you your first legal beer."

"Second," Zack said, "had one with my dad this afternoon."

"It'll have to be your third, then," Kimmy said, appearing from the crowd with a margarita in one hand and a schooner in the other. She handed the latter to Zack and kissed him on the cheek. "Happy birthday, handsome."

"What? I'm the best friend." Art stared at the beer. "How very dare you?"

"Well, while you were dancing like a twit, I very dared to make sure your best friend wasn't thirsty."

The two squared up and Zack gingerly sipped from his glass. Bast slid along the seat and patted the gap he'd left between himself and Charlie. The two of them clinked their glasses against Zack's and Charlie followed up with a peck on Zack's cheek.

"Happy birthday, brother," Bast said, clapping his arm around Zack's shoulder. "Welcome to the club."

Charlie stuck her tongue out at him.

"Thanks for rubbing it in, I'm still months away."

"You're hardly missing out. It's just now Art's got one less person to keep track of when security or bar staff start asking for IDs." Bast gestured to where he and Kimmy remained in their standoff.

The two were trading barbs that had long since diverted from the beer in Zack's hand and into well-travelled ground. Tabitha reached out and pinched Art by the ear.

"Come on, boy. Let's go dance and find a girl to make jealous."

Art's attention snapped away from Kimmy. "Yes, ma'am."

The two disappeared into a throng of dancing patrons and Kimmy collapsed into the lounge opposite Zack and the others.

"I don't know why she humours him so much." Kimmy sipped her drink and reclined out, her knee-high boots resting on the table between them.

"He's harmless," Charlie said.

"But he's not, is he?" Kimmy replied, "not with his kind of magic. He can make anybody - any of us - think, feel and remember anything he wants."

"Not this again." Bast took a swig from his glass.

"Yes, this again." Kimmy waved her arms, nearly spilling her drink. "I don't know how you can all be so relaxed about it."

"We agreed to trust him," Charlie said.

"Well, actually," Bast said through a second mouthful, "we agreed to trust Zack. And trust Zack's trust in Art."

"I've been thinking about it." Zack put his beer down on the table. "The reason you don't trust Art, Kimmy, is because he has Mind magic and you can't trust that he hasn't changed your thoughts and memories."

Kimmy scrunched up her face.

"Duh, Zack. I literally just said that."

"Yeah, but the problem is, the logic doesn't let you stop there."

"What do you mean?" Bast asked.

"If you don't trust Art because he's a Mind mage, you're accepting that Mind magic exists. But if you accept that Mind magic exists, you have to accept the possibility that anybody, including any of us, could be Mind mages."

"Yeah, we could be, but we aren't," Kimmy replied.

"How do you know that?" Zack asked, his eyes alight with his argument. "Do your thoughts tell you that? Your memories? How do you know Bast isn't the Mind mage instead of Art, and every so often he tweaks our memories so that we think he's the Movement mage, when it's actually Art making gates? My point is, if you are going to play with scepticism, you have to play the whole… however many yards there are in football. Whatever it is that means you can't trust Art to have not played with your memories, also means you can't trust the rest of the world. And since one option means you can't interact with anything, I choose to trust Art."

The other three sat there in bewildered silence, their minds processing behind their eyes. Zack reclaimed his glass and took a deep draught.

"I call bullshit," Charlie said, eyeing him with suspicion.

"I don't know, Charlie," Bast said, "it makes sense to me."

"Oh, I don't disagree with that," Charlie said, leaning into Zack, "but that's not why you trust him. That's an argument you've made after the fact to convince us."

Zack's face went slack with surprise and he hid it behind another sip. That didn't fool Charlie either.

"Aha! I knew it. Spill. Why do you trust him so easily?"

"Because I've known him since kindergarten."

"So? Those memories could be fake." Kimmy sipped from her glass pointedly.

"Not this one." Zack tapped his temple with a smirk. "I remember a five-year-old Art dropping his shorts all the way to his ankles to use the urinal. When he pulled them back up, they were soaking wet and he burst into tears."

Kimmy spat her drink out in a coughing laugh and Bast and Charlie joined her.

Zack shook his head. "No master of psychomancy is putting that memory into my head. Or leaving it there for that matter."

"Having a good time?" Art leant on the bar as he waited for their drinks to be ready.

Zack nodded. "It's a nice place."

He scanned the room. It was crowded and the music was loud. And most of the other people there were better dressed and seemed to have far more confidence than Zack could imagine pretending to have, but it certainly was fancy.

"Yeah, I know it's not really your scene." Art handed over payment to the bartender. "But my best mate is only going to turn eighteen once, so he's going to do it in style."

"No, I like it." Zack followed behind him, balancing three of the drinks between his hands.

They reached their seats and found Tabitha and Bast in conversation.

"I don't care what they've given us," Bast said, "that doesn't mean we don't get to ask a few questions when things don't add up."

"This isn't asking questions, though, is it?" Tabitha replied. "It's messing around with the Tower's ritual. And we have no idea if it's even got anything to do with the Thirteen."

"Hey, no shop talk tonight," Art said, handing over the drinks.

Zack put Charlie's and Kimmy's down on the table for the girls to get when they returned and sat down next to Art.

"Nah, it's all good. It's playing over in the back of my head, too. And Tabs has a point. What if we're being set up to be a Trojan horse or something?"

Bast shook his head.

"No, I don't think so. I still need to study it some more, but the ritual the Traveller gave me shouldn't be able to do anything destructive. It's basically like a phone tap."

"We don't need to settle this tonight," Art said. He gestured around. "Tonight is for celebrating. There's plenty of time before the next Tower ritual for us to argue about it."

"When is the next one, anyway?" Tabitha asked.

"I can't keep track of them," Zack answered, "there's basically one a month."

"Nope." Bast drained his drink before replacing it with the one Art had just brought over. "It's a little more than that. I noticed it last footy season. I had to miss every fourth game to do guard duty."

Zack's eyes narrowed and he pushed past the gentle buzz of intoxication to take a firmer hold of his thoughts.

"So, you're saying they are every four weeks."

"Yeah." Bast nodded. "Why?"

"I just never noticed before, but I think that might be significant."

"Why is that?" Art said, surrendering to the conversation.

"Because of how many rituals that would add up to each year," Zack replied.

Tabitha's eyes widened. "Thirteen. Yeah, okay."

"What are you four losers doing up here when the party is down there?" Kimmy, with Charlie a few steps behind her, approached their seats.

From the sheen of sweat on their arms and faces, they'd clearly been dancing and Zack passed them their drinks. Kimmy took a long draught from hers.

"But seriously, you're not talking about the job, are you?"

"That's what I said." Art waved his glass at the others.

"C'mon, birthday boy," Kimmy continued, without any indication she'd heard Art speak, "let's get out there and find you a lady."

All thoughts of the Tower evaporated from Zack's mind, replaced by terror.

"I'm good. With everything that's going on, I'm not looking for a girlfriend right now, anyway."

Kimmy stared at him like he'd spoken another language.

"Who said anything about a girlfriend? I'm talking about a birthday hook-up. Let's find you a lovely lady and put those superb kissing skills to work. And this time, remember to take the opportunity to feel her up a bit." Kimmy winked at him.

Charlie and Art looked at Kimmy and then at Zack, their mouths slack.

"Superb kissing skills?" Charlie asked.

"What do you mean 'this time'?" Art stammered.

Zack tipped the rest of his beer down his throat and escaped with Kimmy onto the dance floor.

The light and warmth from the sunshine through his bedroom window roused Zack from his sleep. His throat was dry and it tasted like something old and furry had died on the back of his tongue. He rolled over to reach for a bottle of water his drunken self had not remembered to place on his bedside table and he groaned at the pain in his head.

Zack lay there for another five minutes, cursing every drop of alcohol he'd had before he remembered what he was capable of doing. Two minutes later, with a stream of Life dissipating behind him, he exited his bedroom, hangover-free. The smell of eggs and bacon wafted in from the kitchen where Art was cooking.

He grinned at Zack. "Good morning, old man. Hungry?"

"I could eat." Zack claimed a stool at the counter and Art slid a plate over to him. Dipping his bacon in some gooey yolk, Zack asked, "How did we get home last night?"

"I sobered up enough to bundle us all out the door, reluctantly pulling you away from that brunette amazon Kimmy hooked you up with and found us a maxi-taxi," Art answered through a mouthful. "We dropped the girls off and then I rolled you and Bast into bed. And don't think we're not circling back around to discuss you and Kimmy, but I'm worried the nausea from my hangover will return if we talk about it now."

Bast staggered in from the hallway, looking pale.

"I need one of you two to either kill me or cure me."

"I'll do it," Zack said, pulling a thread of Life toward him, "I can actually get rid of the hangover. Art will only make you think you are fine."

"Outrageous." Art slapped his sandwich down onto his plate. "Our entire existence is experienced through our perceptions. What makes what you do any different to me?"

"I reduce the chance of liver damage, for one." Zack directed the Life into Bast.

Art shook his head, reclaimed his sandwich, and mumbled, "Basically, no difference at all."

"Life saver. Thanks, Zack." Bast clapped him on the back, looking himself again. "Art, can you throw a bit more bacon on? Zack's magic can't do anything about this smell, so I'm going to grab a quick shower."

"I already cooked you some." Art pointed to the frypan.

"I noticed, which is why I said more," Bast said over his shoulder, "thanks, though."

Art grumbled and pulled more bacon from the fridge to cook. He turned back to Zack.

"It's not like we're made of money. Well, we are, but if we do cut ties with the Tower, it'll get a bit tighter."

Zack finished chewing.

"I've been thinking about that. I suppose it would mean giving up this place."

"Not necessarily," Art said, "it just means I need to focus a bit more on my side hustles."

"You're not going to rob a bank or anything, are you?"

"Oh, I wish. No. The problem with robbing a bank is, you either get caught on camera or you screw over the poor bank worker who's just doing their job. Same for armoured cars. I think the easiest way to make money is to find a private, high-roller poker game. As long as I can make sure there are no cameras, I can take them for everything they have, wipe myself from their memories and get out of there."

"How are you going to find those poker games?" Zack asked.

"I need to hit up some public games. The casino, tournaments, that kind of thing. Get people talking and go from there."

"Feels like a longshot," Zack said.

"I got this. Nah, it's not the money that's my biggest worry. It's the magic."

Zack's brow scrunched in confusion.

"They can't take our magic away."

"Technically, they can, with the right use of Mind." Art finished his sandwich. "But that's not what I mean. I'm talking about the lessons. I'm so close to implanting memories and, after that, ideas. No chance I can do that without Timur teaching me."

"You having second thoughts?"

"I'm still on my first thoughts. Maybe there's a middle ground. We do the Traveller's mystic wiretap, so we learn a bit more, but instead of just quitting the Tower, we pick and choose what we do. Defence and clean up only."

"I don't know, man. That feels like turning a blind eye."

"I'm just saying, the Tower does good work along with the dodgy stuff. If we stick to the good parts, rise up the ranks, maybe we can help steer it in a better direction."

Zack wasn't sure there was a viable compromise position.

"We might not get a choice either way, if we get caught using that crystal."

"Mr Extra-Bacon will have to get practising, then." Art dropped his plate in the sink. "I looked up the calendar and, if he's right about the four weeks between each ritual, we're due for one next Saturday."

CHAPTER 6

Bast was right.

A week later, armed with their preferred assortment of weaponry, they were assigned to stand guard in a library storeroom. Rows upon rows of books were boxed onto shelves, archived through a complex system of notations beyond Zack's understanding.

Kimmy paced between the shelving.

"Not a huge fan of this room. Barely space to swing my axe."

"I'm more worried about how much of the room is basically kindling," Art said, eyeing the boxes.

"Duh." Kimmy rolled her eyes. "Which is why I'm worried about my axe. It's too cramped."

"You say cramped." Bast knelt behind a row of shelves, to be hidden from the door. "I say excellent cover for my special project."

He placed the opal on the stone flooring and traced some shapes around it with his fingers.

"Are you sure about this, Bast?" Tabitha asked. "The only reason I'm going along with it is you've promised me it collects information. If it looks like it's going to harm the Tower, you stop immediately."

"Yeah, for sure," he answered, "but, if I stop, then it ends and the crystal will have caught whatever it's caught."

"We've got you covered," Charlie said, "whether the interruptions come from the door or the other way."

Bast nodded.

"No time like now then, I guess." He sat back on his heels and began his incantation.

It was slow at first and the orange light of Movement took a few minutes to collect on Bast's fingertips. The tiniest of gates, less than a coin in size, opened in the air next to the opal, but rather than grow, it stayed that size while another opened beside it. More and more opened until at least a dozen miniature grey gates hovered beside Bast.

The opal responded, blooming into white light. Wisps of the light reached out to the gates like fairy floss in the wind. When the white strands connected with the gates, they pulsed gently and, perhaps in response, strands of multicoloured light flowed out of the tiny gates. These strands crept up the white radiance, following it back along its path to the opal.

Zack tried to count the colours. There was the orange of Movement, the deep blue of Water and the purple of Mind. Others were there too, but very quickly, they were overwhelmed by a deep green light. He thought through what he knew about the other schools of magic, but Tabitha beat him to it.

"That's Plant magic, right?" she asked, staring at the streams.

"Yeah, I think so," Charlie said, "and a lot of it. What do you think it means?"

Zack pushed his mind into the much thinner stream of turquoise magic.

"It feels like the Life is… I don't know, 'encouraging' the Plant?"

"I think you're right," Art said, staring deep into the fragmented streams, "the Mind in there feels a bit the same way, maybe more like it's—"

"Um, everybody!" Jackie shouted over the top of Art and Bast's chanting. "We've got a breach opening."

"Are you kidding me?" Art picked up his sword, repositioning himself beside his sister. "The last three guard duties, nothing. But when we've got something else going on…"

"Just keep whatever comes through clear of Bast," Tabitha said.

"Max and I have him covered," Charlie said, knocking an arrow and readying to draw.

Zack and Kimmy moved forward, creating a wall between Bast and where Jackie was pointing with her spear. A spot of grey light appeared between the stone bricks but, unlike a gate, it grew out unevenly, flowing across the wall like an ink stain on tissue paper. Zack's fingers tightened with anticipation around his staff when Jackie tilted her head as if she was listening to something.

"Another one. There." Jackie pointed with her spear to the wall on her right.

"Two breaches?" Kimmy raised an eyebrow. "We've never had two at once before."

"Might just be probability," Art said, "most rooms get one or none, while some get two?"

"Or three?" Jackie sounded alarmed as she pointed to the wall to her left.

"No chance that's a coincidence," Zack said, "it's got to be Bast's ritual."

"Do we stop him?" Charlie asked.

Bast didn't seem to be hearing them. His eyes were locked on the network of coloured streams flowing from his gates and into the opal.

"No," Tabitha said, "you guys talked me into this. Now that it's started, we've got to see it out."

A guttural growl sounded as a creature emerged from the centre gate. It appeared to be feline, around the size of a panther, with sharp, oversized teeth spaced unevenly around its maw. Devoid of any fur, its body was covered in a shiny hide that ranged from fleshy pink through purple to a blue that reminded Zack of veins. Its claws clacked against the Tower's stone floor as it stepped fully into the room. Another sauntered through the gate behind it.

"Charlie?" Tabitha called, not taking her eyes from the creature.

Charlie's face scrunched in effort.

"No dice. Whatever that thing looks like, it's not Animal enough for me to do anything about it."

"Well, let's see if it's flammable enough for me to do something about it," Kimmy said.

As if understanding, or at least sensing, Kimmy's threat, the first creature snarled and bounded towards her. Art lunged out as it passed, slashing with his sword. The tip of the blade cut into its side, but only an inch or so, before the creature's movement knocked the sword away.

"Look out," Art said, "these fleshions have a crazy thick hide."

"Fleshions?" Tabitha replied. "Really?"

"Flesh lions. Fleshions." Art shrugged as he rebalanced his sword in his hand. "It's a work in progress. Watch out!"

The second creature pounced towards Tabitha and she dodged backwards while it crashed against one of Jackie's shields. Two more emerged from the central breach, but Zack's eyes were on the right-hand breach, which had grown to over a metre wide. He braced himself, ready to attack the first fleshion that emerged and try to force it back through the gate.

Instead, what emerged from the grey light was smaller and airborne. A snake, around a metre in length, hovered above the ground on colourful feathery wings. Its yellow eyes fixed upon Zack and, with a hiss, it darted towards him. Half a dozen more entered from the breach.

"Flying snakes!" Zack swung the length of his quarterstaff at the charging serpent, landing the hardened end against the creature's head. It flopped lifelessly to the ground but the others echoed its earlier hiss and flew towards Zack.

Zack shifted his hands into a more defensive grip, his eyes flitting between the serpents' bared fangs. They surged forward in a V formation and Zack did not like his chances of remaining unbitten, but then an arrow flew over his shoulder, piercing the middle snake through its abdomen. It fell, flailing with its wings and crashing into the two on its right.

Those were better odds. Zack spun his staff towards the other two, shifting his position and catching a glimpse of how his friends were faring against the fleshions.

Tabitha traced precise shapes, her fingers glowing with blue light and a narrow, but focused, jet of air slammed into one of the fleshions and threw it backwards. It crashed into the two behind it, knocking both of them to the ground and leaving only the first fleshion standing.

Art and Jackie took the opportunity to charge it, trapping it between themselves and Kimmy. Art gripped his sword in both hands and swung it down on the fleshion's flank. Again, while the blade cut into the creature, its thick hide prevented the edge from cutting deeper.

Art's blade may not have drawn blood, but it did draw the fleshion's attention and it rounded on him, raking out with its talon-like claws. Art parried the attack with the middle of his sword, but the strength of the blow knocked his weapon aside and left him off balance.

Kimmy swung her axe wide, missing a bookcase by half an inch and struck the fleshion in the head. Its hide was thick there too, but while it could stop the axe's blade from penetrating, the force of the blow knocked the creature back into a stumble.

Jackie slid in behind the fleshion, an expression of concentration fixed on her face, and thrust her spear into the space above the fleshion's hind leg. She grunted as she forced it forward and the head of the spear slid deep into the creature. It roared in pain.

"I think the hide is thinner around its joints." Jackie wrenched her spear out.

"Good to know," Kimmy said, readying her axe for another swing.

Zack's attention was drawn back to his serpentine attackers and he fended them off with the ends of his staff. Another arrow zipped past him and clipped the wing of one of the other snakes. A fourth snake darted towards Charlie, who was hurrying to knock another arrow, but Zack spun away from the two facing him and swung with the full length of his quarterstaff. The hardened wood met the snake's body with a loud crack, sending its limp form back through the portal.

"Nice aim!" Charlie said, pointing an arrow at the snakes behind him.

"Total accident," Zack said, spinning back around.

A chilling howl filled the room and Zack's eyes were drawn to where the third breach had finished expanding. A bestial figure had emerged. On two legs, it towered well over two metres and it was covered in brown-grey fur. Its hands and feet ended in sharp claws and its head resembled a wolf's.

"Is that a freakin' werewolf?" Art shouted.

The beast's face turned with a snap, its muzzle pointing at Art. A deep, rumbling growl vibrated up from its chest and out between its bared teeth as it bounded towards him, propelling itself forward with its arms and legs.

"Aw, hell." Art brought his sword up as the beast crashed into him, carrying him forward and down onto the stone floor.

Taking advantage of the confusion, the flanked fleshion pounced at Jackie, who brought a hasty shield up to protect herself, while the other three fleshions untangled themselves and spread out, skulking towards Tabitha.

Zack looked over his shoulder at Charlie.

"Help them, I've got these things covered."

"You sure?" she asked. When he nodded, she dropped her bow and quiver to the floor. "I'll never get a clean shot in all of that. Come on, Maxie, let's get in there."

Russet light collected around her and Zack turned to face the flying snakes. Charlie-wolf and Max bounded out from the cloud of light and into the fray; two more of the snakes entered through the breach. Zack hoped he had them covered.

He whirled his staff around his body, both to keep it ready and leave the snakes unsure of where the next attack would start. And it was working. Their black diamond-shaped pupils snapped left to right, back and forth, as they tracked both ends of Zack's weapon.

Content, for the moment, with the hesitation he was provoking, he realised, too late, that the pause had allowed other snakes to form up. He now faced five of them, including one with an arrow-torn wing that skip-bounced along the floor at him. Not wasting any more time, he attacked, snapping the staff out mid-spin and striking one of the snakes on the front of its skull. The speed of the blow crumpled its head and sent it straight into the floor.

The remaining four snakes darted at him, jaws open wide. Zack fended two away as he brought his staff back and kicked out at the wounded snake, but the last closed in and bit deep into his shoulder. Zack yelped from the pain and spun around, attempting to shake it free, but its fangs were long and it was firmly latched on. He waved his staff around with a one-handed grip, frantically trying to keep the others at bay, while he used his free hand to pry his unwelcome passenger from his body. Zack gritted his teeth from the renewed pain as the fangs sliced through more of his shoulder on the way out, but he held on tight and, when it was free, he slammed the snake against the end of a bookcase, snapping its spine.

His sense of Life warned him that something was wrong and he sent a thread of it in to probe his shoulder. The wound was painful but more of an infection risk than an immediate problem. Deeper in, Life revealed the true threat. Venom. Zack grasped more strands of Life and guided them towards his lymph nodes.

Back in the room, away from his internal struggle, the snakes pressed forward. Pain seared down Zack's arm and into his chest, but he ignored it and pushed forward with his quarterstaff. He danced around the grounded snake and fended a second off before swinging hard at the third. At the last moment, the flying snake strafed sideways and the quarterstaff landed a glancing blow to the base of its wing, knocking the creature away but doing little damage.

Trusting the instincts born from his intense weapons training, Zack turned his attention back to the toxins writhing their way through his body. The venom wasn't alive, so Life couldn't read it, but Life could read the cells around it and see what it was doing. The answer did not fill Zack with relief. His blood was under attack. The venom was tearing through his red blood cells and reducing their ability to clot. The minor wound was no longer insignificant; if Zack didn't do something soon, he was going to bleed out.

Zack reached for Life and poured it into his arm, closing the wound but also reaching out to his immune system to fight the venom and to his bone marrow to replace the blood he was losing. The relief was immediate but was followed by an equally immediate wave of fatigue. Healing usually drew Life from both the mage and the patient and double dipping was costing him dearly.

The snakes lashed out again and Zack caught their snapping bites on his quarterstaff. His body ached. He wouldn't last much longer. Speed over finesse, then. Zack pushed against the two flying snakes with his staff, forcing them backwards and causing them to flutter as they struggled to maintain their flight. Taking advantage of their confusion, Zack turned and bounded towards the grounded snake. It exposed its fangs, but Zack stepped to the right and approached from its side, kicking it in the head with all his weight. The snake skidded across the floor and lay still against the wall.

Zack spun around to find the remaining two snakes darting towards him. He lifted his staff and brought it down in a two-handed swing. The strike was strong and on target, shattering one snake's bones and sending it straight to the floor, but it had left Zack completely exposed to the last snake. It sunk its fangs into his upper arm, not far from the wound he had closed seconds before. A fresh wave of venom flooded into his limb and overwhelmed his already struggling lymphatic system. He bit his lip to distract from the pain and charged the nearest wall. The snake struggled to loosen its bite, renewing the pain with each thrash, but its long fangs worked against it, holding it in place as Zack collided, arm and snake first, with the Tower's stone bricks. Bright red light and pain exploded in his head and he slid to the floor.

Zack took a deep breath and sealed away the pain and fatigue, directing Life back into his body. While Life weaved its way through Zack's injured cells, he looked to see how his friends were faring. Two of the fleshions were down and Charlie had the last flanked between herself and Max.

The beastman situation was dramatically less under control. It crouched over where Art remained prone on the floor, raking down at him with its massive, clawed hands. Art was doing his best to fend it off, or at least roll aside to avoid being torn apart, but the creature was incredibly fast. Only the distraction caused by Tabitha and Kimmy's attacks and Jackie's shields were keeping Art alive. And those shields were beginning to fail.

Tabitha's flail and Kimmy's axe did not seem to be causing the beastman any particular harm. Was Art right? If this was a werewolf, did they need silver to kill it? It lashed out at Kimmy, who leapt backwards, the claws missing her face by less than an inch. Zack forced himself to his unsteady feet and wobbled towards them.

As he approached, he realised that what he had thought was a shadow cast by the beastman crouching above Art was, instead, blood pooling on the stone floor. Art's blood. Zack shuffled faster and the movement caught the creature's attention. It lifted its head toward Zack and sneered, saliva dripping from its sharp teeth, as it raised its arm high, ready for a devastating blow down onto Art's trapped body.

"Hey, Scooby." Kimmy's voice drew the beastman's eyes and Zack's, towards her. Her axe's head glowed with orange-red heat. "Let's see who's under that mask."

The beastman moved to protect itself, but its raised arm was on the wrong side and it was off balance. Kimmy swung the axe with the full weight of her body and the superheated metal sliced through the creature's neck. The head bounced away but the bulk of its body collapsed down onto Art. Jackie and Tabitha ran forward, tipping it off him before it settled. Behind them, Charlie and Max brought the last fleshion down and finished it off.

"Right." Bast's voice sounded casual and distracted. "That's finally done, what do we— What the hell happened here?"

Zack knelt beside Art, fumbling for some strands of Life to stop the bleeding. Art was a mess, with deep gashes on his chest, arms and legs.

"Hurry, Bast," Tabitha said, standing over Art, "close the breaches before more things come through."

Art tried to speak but it came out in a spluttering cough.

"It's okay, mate." Zack poured a thin stream of Life to close the worst of the wounds. "Just lay still, we've got this."

Art shook his head and held up a single finger as he tried again.

"Too many… different. Leave one."

"What does he mean, Zack?" Tabitha asked.

"No idea," Zack replied, "he's lost a lot of blood. It's probably nonsense."

Kimmy gave a sigh that turned into a grunt.

"It's not nonsense, it's actually smart. He's saying that there's too many different creatures here and it looks suspicious. We need to leave one breach open long enough to hide the bodies."

Art smiled and closed his eyes.

Kimmy looked at him in disgust.

"Fine. Let's leave Scooby and throw the rest through. He's too big, anyway."

Tabitha nodded but fixed Kimmy with a confused look.

"You've never really watched that cartoon, have you?"

"No, I prefer anime." Kimmy picked up a pair of snakes by the tail. "Why?"

"It's not important," Tabitha replied, collecting a pair of her own.

Zack had managed to stop the bleeding and was trying to coax Art's body into replacing the loss. Around him, the others pushed the bodies of the fleshions and flying snakes through the breaches while Bast worked to close them.

Art's voice, faint and slurred, whispered up to him, "Does this mean I'm going to become a werewolf too?"

Zack dropped to sit with his back against a bookcase.

"I don't think that was a werewolf, dude. At least I couldn't find any diseases or toxins."

"Oh, okay. I probably wouldn't have looked good in a beard, anyway."

Zack laughed, but it made his head spin. He tried to lift his arms to steady it, but they had become so heavy.

"Zack?" Jackie's voice seemed to be coming from another room. Had she left?

Tabitha ran to his side. "What's wrong with him?"

"Oh, no!" Charlie appeared next to her. "I think he must have been poisoned by those snakes."

"Why was he left alone to fight them?" Now Tabitha's voice seemed far away. Was she still there? With his eyes closed, he couldn't tell. When had he closed his eyes?

"He said he could handle them," Charlie replied.

"Next time, ignore him." Tabitha's arm wrapped around him, forcing him to his feet. "Somebody help me get him to another Lifer."

Another arm gripped Zack from the other side. It's good to have friends, he thought as his mind slipped away.

CHAPTER 7

Sara was by Zack's bedside when he awoke, suggesting his friends had taken him to the infirmary. Her eyes met his as he opened them, meaning she was likely using Life to actively monitor him. A tiny, wrinkled woman, his mentor had the presence of an ancient tree - immovable and constant, as if deep roots anchored her to her place in the world.

Her face was fixed with an expression of patience.

"How are you feeling, Zachary?"

Zack didn't answer right away. Sara could sense any obvious harms; she was asking him to assess himself more deeply. He turned his own sense of Life inward. His lymph nodes and immune system needed a little more time to recover, but there was no sign of the toxins and the bite wounds were completely healed. The bite wounds! He remembered his friends hastily throwing the snakes and fleshions through the breaches to hide any evidence of their covert ritual. And now he was in a position to blow it. He had to walk a careful line with what he said here.

"I'm okay." Zack pushed himself back and sat up. "My lymphatic system is showing some distress, but nothing more sleep won't fix."

Sara nodded. "Yes, I sensed you had taxed it. What were you countering?"

"I'm not sure." Time to be vague, he thought. "Poison? Disease?

Bacteria? I was too distracted by the fight to analyse it, but I could see that it was attacking my blood, so I split my response between closing the wounds, replacing my blood and fighting the toxin."

Sara sat in silence, idly scratching at her lip, her eyes distant.

"Do you have any advice on what I should have done?" Zack asked.

"No," she replied, "there is no trace of any toxin left in your body, so your course of action was effective. You burnt yourself a little low, which worried your friends enough to bring you up here, but you would have recovered on your own."

"Oh, good." Zack swung his legs off the side of the bed.

"If I knew more about the nature of the toxin, I might be able to provide more specific guidance. I sent someone down to examine the creature, but they could find no trace of any poison or bacteria on it. How did it injure you?"

"It bit me on the shoulder." Zack indicated the vague region of his upper left arm. "Why would there be no trace of it?"

"I don't know, but I have some idle theories." Sara's eyes were fixed on his shoulder before she clapped her hands against her thighs. "But the important thing is that you are well. I imagine you want to catch up with your friends, so I won't keep you any longer."

Zack stood up. "Thank you, Sara."

"If you are free for a lesson next week, I thought I could teach you some responses to circulatory issues." Sara walked with him to the door.

"Yes, please. That would be great."

"Excellent. Let's say Tuesday. Come find me at the usual time."

"I will, thank you."

Zack left the infirmary and made his way out of the Life quarters and down the stairs. Discussing time remained a challenging concept in a Tower that had entrances across the globe. The 'usual time' Sara had referenced was around four in the afternoon Sydney time for Zack, but he was pretty sure Sara ran on Paris time, which made it early morning for her.

His friends were waiting in the Entrance Chamber and Art gave a short cheer when Zack reached the bottom of the stairs. The others turned and he was met with smiles and looks of relief, although Bast was missing.

"You didn't have to wait for me," he said as he approached.

"Of course we did," Charlie said, "Bast would have too, but he had a family errand to run."

Zack took that to mean he had taken the opal out of the Tower at the first opportunity.

"Are you okay?" Jackie asked.

"Yep. I just emptied the tank lower than I realised, that's all."

"Good to hear," Tabitha said, "but no more Lifers on the front line, okay?"

"There was more than one front line on this occasion," Zack replied with a lowered voice.

Tabitha scrunched up her face, and Kimmy groaned.

"What?" Zack asked.

Charlie laughed.

"That's like word for word what Art said when Tabitha brought it up while we were waiting."

"Great minds," Art said, slapping his arm around Zack's shoulder, "you're good though, yeah?"

"Yep. But I could use a hot meal and a good night's sleep."

"Let's grab some takeaway on the way home." Art patted his right pocket. "I picked up our pay, so let's splurge a little."

"Burgers?" Zack suggested.

"That's splurging?" Art replied as they stepped through the Tower entrance and arrived back in Sydney.

"Fancy burgers?"

"Fine, but only because you both saved my life and nearly died today." Art shook his head in disappointment and then looked back at Jackie. "Do you want to grab some food with us or get dropped off at home first?"

"Neither." Jackie wore a massive grin. "Mum said I could crash at Les

Chateau Des Femmes tonight."

"Nice," Art replied, "although, you know that just means 'the girl house', right?"

"It really doesn't." Tabitha put her arm around Jackie. "The four of us will come over to yours tomorrow and we'll check out how Bast's project went before we decide whether to hand it in."

Zack nodded. "We'll see you then. Have fun, Jackie."

"We're getting Vietnamese for dinner!" she said by way of farewell and followed the others to Kimmy's car.

Art shook his head, a smile on his face, watching her leave.

"Alright then, fancy burger time."

⸭⸻⸻⸻⸻⸻⸺❊❊

Zack lounged along the two-seater sofa, scrolling through his phone while Bast reviewed last night's sporting highlights on the television.

"What a ridiculous catch!" Bast shouted.

"Terrible," Zack replied, without looking up from his phone.

"What?" Bast asked in confusion. "That was amazing, I don't know how he got his hand on it."

"Oh, yeah." He tried his best to respond appropriately to Bast's commentary but often got it wrong.

Art crashed down between them, munching on some toast.

"You guys don't think Tabitha is really going to push back on us returning the opal, do you?"

"I don't know, mate," Bast replied, one eye still on his program, "she's pretty tight with Junie. Look, I love the girl, but the fact is, she's always been comfortable with the people in charge. Like at school. She would have been the teachers' pick for school captain as well as the students' if Tower stuff hadn't overtaken things."

"But if the Tower is dodgy, she won't want to be a part of it," Zack said, "that's not like her."

"Nah, you're right about that." The highlight segment ended and Bast switched off the television. "But we've got to let her be thorough. We all, more or less, talked her into leading our team. That doesn't mean we don't get a say, but we've got to listen to and respect hers."

"Yeah, fair call," Art said, "so, when are they coming over?"

Bast's phone rang and he picked it up, looking at the caller's name.

"Speak of the devil."

"We were talking about Tabitha, not Kimmy," Art said, melodramatically deadpan.

Bast shook his head.

"You two just need to go find a room and get it out of your system."

"I don't think a duel will solve anything," Art said, "and I'm pretty sure she'd incinerate me."

"Not at all what I meant." Bast turned away and answered his phone. "Hello, this is your Uber driver. Pick up for five? Of course, I'd never leave her out. She's a valued frequent passenger. Step away from the carpet and I'll open it."

He put down the phone and began tracing patterns in the air before him. The gate sprang into being quickly, thanks to the markings Bast had made on the floorboard, as well as his familiarity with both ends of the gate. He reclaimed his phone.

"Okay, come on through."

Jackie emerged first, bringing her overnight bag with her. Max padded through next, followed by Charlie, Kimmy and, lastly, Tabitha. Zack sat up, taking his feet off the sofa, making room for Jackie and Charlie.

Bast set the opal on the coffee table. The white stone glimmered in rainbow diffraction but otherwise seemed entirely unmagical. The three-seater sofa had been claimed in his absence, so he sat on the kitchen counter.

"Okay, Tabitha, start us off."

Tabitha clasped her hands together.

"Right. I get that I'm probably alone in my reluctance about all of this, but I just want us to be sure."

"You're not alone," Jackie said, "it's a big call."

Kimmy nodded along.

"So, the Tower's lies mean nothing?" Charlie asked.

"Of course not," Tabitha replied, "but it's not exactly like the Traveller has been honest with us. He didn't tell us about the risks in that ritual and we could easily have died."

"And I could have become a werewolf," Art added.

Zack rolled his eyes.

"It was not a werewolf."

"Maybe he didn't know," Bast said, "but even if he did, there's a difference between a person holding back some details and an institution built on lies."

"Why are you so quick to trust him?" Tabitha asked.

"I'm not." Bast hopped down from the counter. "But I'm willing to deal with him to find out the truth. And that's why I think we should give him the opal."

"How do we even know what that thing has in it?" Kimmy asked. "And what we'd be giving to him?"

Tabitha rubbed her chin.

"Is there any chance you can look inside it, Bast? If it was designed to respond to Movement magic?"

Bast knelt beside the coffee table and rested his fingers against the opal.

"I think so, but I don't love the idea of triggering breaches."

"And I don't love the idea of triggering evictions and loss of rental bonds," Art said.

Zack scratched the back of his head.

"Wouldn't the breaches have just been because of the bigger ritual in the Tower?"

"Maybe," Bast replied, "but whatever I did, still attracted them."

"Do we do it somewhere else then?" Charlie asked.

Jackie shook her head.

"There's still a risk that the Tower would sense the breach and send a response team. Especially if it's multiple breaches."

The group sat there for a few minutes, each lost in their own silent thoughts.

"Jackie, can you put up a shield or something that stops breaches from forming?" Tabitha asked, clearly thinking out loud. "Like you've done to protect us from the weather or that time in Hades."

"I'm not sure." Jackie's gaze drifted as she thought it through. "No, I don't think so. I could make the barrier, but, unlike toxic air or cold wind, if I wait until I can feel or see the breach, it'll be too late. And breaches aren't inherently dangerous, so Protection can't feel them coming ahead of time."

"Oh, fair enough." Tabitha frowned. "What about you, Bast?"

"Kind of the opposite problem, sorry." Bast stood up and stretched. "I can feel the breaches before they arrive, but I can't stop them. Movement doesn't work that way. I can only reverse them after they've formed."

The room lapsed into silence again and Zack plunged back into his scattered thoughts. His eyes bounced around to each of his friends and when they landed on Art, they widened in excitement. Art noticed the look and raised his eyebrow in question.

"What about an Art original?" Zack asked.

"What do you…?" Art's voice trailed off as he looked between Jackie and Bast. "Oh! Yeah, that could work."

"Is this game just for you two boys, or can everybody play?" Kimmy asked.

Zack turned to face the others.

"Last year, Art linked Charlie and I together so we could see each other's magic. Basically, it allowed Charlie to use Animal while being guided by what Life could detect."

Jackie nodded. "I remember. Yeah, I think that could work."

Tabitha's eyes narrowed in suspicion as she looked between Zack and Art.

"Why did you call it an 'Art original'?"

Zack swallowed awkwardly.

"Well… because it's not something the Tower teaches. Art invented it himself."

"Deadly!" Bast looked impressed.

Tabitha didn't.

"Absolutely not. It's bad enough that we're considering going behind the Tower and dealing with this renegade, but playing with untrained magic is out of the question."

"It was good enough to save my life," Charlie said, and she looked at Art, "but I didn't know you had invented it. Thank you."

"There's a difference, Tabitha, between untrained and untaught," Zack said, "Art knows what he's doing with this. It's just something that the Tower doesn't teach."

"Maybe that's for a reason," Tabitha said.

"Yeah, I think it is for a reason," Art replied, "and it fits with what we've learnt so far. The Tower wants to keep us cleanly divided."

"We keep assuming the worst of intentions for them. These rules might just as much be there for our safety." Tabitha looked around the room for support, but none was on offer.

"Kimmy?"

"Sorry, girl. While there's no way in hell I'm letting him inside me and my magic, just because Art's magic isn't 'Tower approved' doesn't make it wrong."

Tabitha held up her hands.

"Fine. I said my piece and I'm clearly outvoted on this. So, what's next?"

Art stood up, rubbing his hands together.

"Okay, I'll need a bit of quiet. Jackie, you stand up here next to Bast. And maybe you too, Zack."

"Really?" Zack joined the others. "Why?"

"If I link you up with them, you can help channel energy around to wherever it needs to be," Art replied. "Okay, now, everybody needs to stay still and quiet. No reactions to whatever happens next."

"That's not exactly filling me with confidence," Bast said, wincing in anticipation.

"No, it's nothing like that. Just a side effect from it being a spell I invented."

"See, this is what I was saying." Tabitha pointed at Art. "It's too dangerous."

Zack realised then, what Art meant and laughed.

"No, Tabs. It's okay. It's my favourite bit of this whole thing. Try to stay silent."

Art glared at him through a side-eye. "Screw you. Okay, let's do this." Art traced some patterns in the air, and purple light gathered at his fingertips. He chanted, soft murmurs at first, but they grew in volume and the lyrics became clearer.

"What?" Tabitha's mouth swung open.

Kimmy looked on either side of her. "Is he singing Lady Ga—"

"Shhh!" Charlie shot her a glare before turning back to watch Art.

"I was distracted the first time. I'm not missing a second of this."

Art continued with his unusual incantation. Blush formed on his cheeks before dark purple clouds rolled in around them. Unlike in the alley, the clouds weren't as dense and the room was still visible behind them.

Yeah, I've made some adjustments. Art's voice sounded in his head.

Including telepathy? Zack asked.

Art nodded. *It's faster than speaking and it means I can keep chanting. Now get on with it. I can't hold this all day.*

Me next, then. Zack opened a channel connecting Jackie, Bast and himself. The other two looked down at the streams of turquoise Life that flowed between them.

Jackie's eyes lit up. *This is beautiful.*

Zack smiled. *It's over to you two now.*

Jackie worked her own incantation. So often her magic was fast and reactive and it had been some time since Zack had seen her do something complex. She drew circles on the ground with her fingers and, as the circles grew, steely grey light collected around her. Inch by inch, the light pushed out, forming a dome that crept out across the room, made from a lattice of light beams so thin they looked like wires.

Okay, Bast. Jackie's thoughts sounded. *I'm making this bit up as I go. I've made the beginnings of a barrier, but I haven't told Protection what it's keeping out. I think that's where you come in.*

Bast pulled his attention away from the barrier. *This is amazing, little Sis. It's so detailed and so stable. Movement is always swishing around. But yeah, I think I can help you out.*

Unlike Jackie, Bast didn't really incant. Instead, he flicked his hand upwards towards the barrier and a dozen thin streams of orange Movement flew out. No, not streams. Streamers, about a foot in length. The orange lights certainly were not stable. They darted away in every direction and wove themselves through the grey lattice, sparking when they met and leaving behind an orange glow in the lattice.

Jackie's smile broadened. *Wow. Yeah, okay. This is so weird.*

Is it working, though? Zack asked, feeling the gentle tug of Life as his energy was called on to support their work.

Oh definitely. I still can't grasp the concept of a breach enough to block it myself, but the barrier can. I just need a little longer to lock it in place. Jackie's gestures increased in size and speed, and the barrier expanded past the walls of the room while the orange streamers chased it and continued their dance between the wires.

Jackie stopped. *Done. You can bring us out, Art.*

Nice work, Jacks. Art replied and the purple cloud retreated.

CHAPTER 8

"Did it work?" Tabitha asked.

"Yep. This room and most of this house, is sealed off from breaches. For a little bit anyway." Jackie tapped her head. "It's not too hard to hold a barrier like this in place, but eventually, I'll get a headache."

"That was an awesome piece of magic, Art," Bast said, "I can't believe you made that up yourself."

"The 'incantation' could use some work." Kimmy's voice was dry as she made air quotes with her fingers. "You kept repeating the chorus towards the end."

Art's blush was in full bloom now. Tabitha gave a sharp giggle but reined herself in.

"Leave him alone. Now that we're protected, Bast, can you show us what the opal captured?"

"Pretty sure I can." Bast knelt beside the coffee table and held his hand over the opal. He whispered to himself and traced shapes in the air above it. His fingers glowed orange and the opal responded with white light. A kaleidoscope of colour flowed out of the stone in a wide arc before looping around back into it.

"That's not what it did yesterday," Charlie said, leaning closer.

"No," Bast replied, "yesterday, it was capturing the streams of magic. Today, I'm getting it to show what it captured. I think."

Zack knelt down next to Bast to get a better look.

"I think I can count all thirteen colours in there. Anybody else?"

"Yep," Tabitha replied, "but more green than any of the others."

"More than anything else put together," Kimmy added.

She was right. The stream of lights had a thick core of Plant's deep green glow in a spiral with much thinner strands of the other twelve Schools' colours.

"What does it mean, though?" Tabitha asked.

"Yesterday, Zack said Life felt like it was encouraging the Plant," Art said, "I think I kind of feel the same thing, like Mind persuading it."

Charlie nodded.

"I was going to say that it feels like Animal is herding something, but of course, Animal would feel like that, so I'm probably picking up the same thing as you two."

The others voiced their agreement.

"So, what?" Art said, "Every month, the Tower does a ritual to use twelve schools of magic to capture a massive amount of Plant magic? Why?"

"We don't have enough information to answer that," Kimmy replied.

"That wasn't even really the question we were trying to answer, though," Zack said, "we wanted to know if it was safe to hand this information back to the Traveller."

"Looks safe enough to me," Bast said.

"How?" Tabitha leant back against the sofa. "We don't know for sure what information we're giving him."

"Come on, Tabs," Art said, "be honest for a moment. Can you imagine any answer we got from this that would have changed your mind?"

Tabitha bit her lip. "No."

"Then it's not really a fair argument," Art continued, "you're just looking for more hurdles before we contact him. At the very least, we've found nothing in here that appears dangerous for him to have."

She crossed her arms. "Fine. You're right. Let's do it then."

Zack ran a finger over the hardened end of his quarterstaff while Bast prepared to open a gate in their living room. This time, the phone call to enquire about buying a seahorse had been met with the reply that a package was on its way. Two days later, some ink had arrived with the note, *See you there.*

"I'm still not sure about going armed," Art said, his broadsword resting across his knees as Bast worked.

"We've been through this." Tabitha held up her fingers as she counted off. "One, the note said nothing about being unarmed. Two, Bast said this ink will take us off-world, to who knows where."

Art remained underwhelmed by the idea that Bast was opening a gate to a mystery realm in their home.

"I just think it doesn't really communicate trust."

"Good." Tabitha held up a third finger. "Three, the Traveller realises he's got a long way to go before we trust him."

"Damn right." Kimmy patted her axe for emphasis.

Bast exhaled sharply. "This is weird."

"Is something wrong?" Charlie asked.

"Not wrong, exactly," Bast replied, his hands still moving in controlled patterns, "considering the source, I figured this ink would work a lot like the inks Armand and his merry psychos were using. And it does… except it's like something is pushing back against the gate opening."

"We should call them back and refuse to jump through these hoops," Tabitha said.

"Nah, it's okay, I'm getting there." Bast tilted his head to where Jackie was standing nearby. "Plus, we've got a drawbridge ready to pull shut if we need it."

Tabitha didn't look happy, but Jackie stood a little taller from Bast's confidence.

Slowly, the orange swirls of Bast's incantations widened into the grey light of a gate. Weapons low but ready, they stepped through.

They emerged into an idyllic forested landscape. Zack instinctively raised a hand to shelter his eyes but dropped it again when he noticed the light was gentle and warm.

At first glance, this could have been Earth, but a closer look revealed the colours were wrong. An orange sun sat behind pale blue clouds within a sky so deeply blue it approached purple. On the ground, the grass was too dark, the soil too yellow and the odd colours continued in the trees in the distance. It was as if somebody had been painting this world but had made do with an incomplete paint set.

Zack reached out to test the local Life. It was there in abundance and, while it was different to home, nothing particularly strange stood out to him. Around him, the others opened their eyes from what he assumed was their own check-in with the native magic. Nobody raised any concerns until Bast stumbled forward, clutching the side of his head.

"What's wrong?" Tabitha said, reaching for him.

He steadied himself and took three deep breaths before answering.

"Movement here is way out of whack. I think that's probably why it was so hard to open the gate to get here. Speaking of which…" Bast turned back to the gate and incanted. It was the slowest Zack had seen him close a gate in a long time, but the grey light steadily shrank until it disappeared.

"Um, was that a good idea, Bast?" Jackie asked. "If Movement isn't being friendly to you, shouldn't we have left it open?"

Bast shook his head.

"Nope. I don't want my Movement playing with this Movement any more than is necessary."

Zack crouched down in the dirt beside where the gate had been.

"There are some stones here with markings on them."

Bast joined him and ran his fingers over the engravings.

"These aren't symbols I've seen the Tower use or the ones in the 'gates for dummies guides' Armand's crew were peddling."

"What does that mean?" Art asked.

"I don't know." Bast stood back up. "Just that whoever did this probably learned their magic from someone else, I guess."

"So, where to now?" Kimmy asked.

"Towards the woods," Jackie replied.

"I think getting to the top of that hill would be a better idea." Art pointed to a rise away from the forest. "We can get a better look around."

"But I can see the Traveller from here," Jackie said with a grin, "and he's walking towards us from the woods."

Art spun around and shot his sister a look.

"Fair enough then, let's go that way."

They moved along a rough dirt path towards the forest and when the Traveller saw they were headed in his direction, he slowed down, meeting them not too far from the tree line.

"How are you all?" the Traveller asked with a brisk wave of greeting.

"Fine, no thanks to you," Kimmy replied.

Zack looked at her in surprise as did the Traveller.

"I'm sorry?"

"You should be." Kimmy pointed a finger at him, her other hand on her hip. "You didn't warn us that your little magic stone is like a magnet for breaches. You could have got us killed."

"Kimmy, I'm not sure it was quite that bad," Zack said in an effort to lower the tension.

"Not that bad?" Kimmy threw her arms up. "You nearly died!"

Zack felt his cheeks burning.

"Not really," he muttered, mostly to himself.

The Traveller held his hands open in front of him.

"I am very sorry about that. I promise, it was entirely unforeseen. Perhaps a complication from the Tower itself. Was it worth it, though? Were you successful?"

Bast pulled the opal from his pocket. "We were."

The Traveller clapped.

"Fantastic. Now come, we'll examine the findings together." He turned and strode back towards the forest.

The others hurried to keep up and Tabitha darted to his side.

"Why did you bring us here?"

"A few reasons," the Traveller replied, "first, as your young man there has likely mentioned already, this realm is challenging to reach without aid and that keeps us just a little safer from the Tower. And second, there are some people here I'd like you to meet."

"People? You didn't say anything about other people," Charlie said.

"I also didn't say anything about bringing weapons," the Traveller said with a pointed look at her bow. "Please don't threaten anybody. They are a kind bunch and this is their home."

"You said a few reasons," Zack said.

The Traveller looked over his shoulder at Zack with a grin.

"I'll get to the third if it comes up. We've got a bit of a walk ahead of us and I recommend you look around. It really is a beautiful place."

He wasn't wrong. The path took them deeper into the forest, winding its way over gentle rises around trees. Light filtered through the canopy in rays, casting scattered shadows around them. Zack passed by a massive tree, its trunk at least three metres wide. Its branches hung over the path, purple streaks clear within the green of the tree's leaves. Zack shuffled beside Charlie.

"Any animal life around?"

Charlie nodded, her eyes lingering on the treetops.

"Yeah, plenty. Birds, rodents, insects, or at least animals close enough to fill those niches. Nothing bigger nearby, though. I'm getting vibes that this area doesn't belong to them."

"Belong to them?" Jackie asked from behind. "What does it belong to then?"

"People."

"And it's time to meet them," the Traveller said.

The path hooked around a wide, rock-strewn hill and brought them to a clearing. The irregular nature of the forest gave way to ordered rows of shrubs, fruit trees and other plants and the path between their feet gained paving stones. But most dramatically, in the centre of the clearing, was a house.

The group halted. Zack's eyes flicked across it, bouncing from feature to feature. On one hand, it was an odd mish-mash of different styles.

The front wall had the appearance of a mediaeval stone cottage, but the bay window sticking out of it was modern and the veranda that wrapped around it looked almost organic - grown rather than built. Dark iron piping ran down one side and gas lamplights were perched on each corner. Zack lost count of the different styles and eras dotting the house.

On the other hand, it worked. At least to Zack's limited sensibilities. Something about the building suggested care, comfort and a personal touch. It radiated 'home'.

The Traveller turned to face them.

"I am about to introduce you to the Nistroms. They will speak for themselves, but I must be clear that I am a guest here as well. I have vouched for you only so far as to make this introduction, which is still quite a statement of trust. The Nistroms are protective of their privacy and I ask you to be considerate of that. They won't take lightly to any threat to it."

"Are they… dangerous?" Art asked.

"Everybody is dangerous," the Traveller replied, "just be respectful."

They followed him along the path, through the garden and up towards the house. Insects that could have been bees or butterflies zipped and hovered between the leaves and flowers, but the plants themselves resembled those from home. Zack recognised pumpkins, tomatoes and what may have been a strawberry bush.

The front door of the house opened and a short, matronly woman appeared, wearing a loose shirt and jeans. She stepped down from the veranda and, when the sunlight shone on her, it revealed a greyish tone in her skin. And her orange-red hair, held up in a messy bun, was a deeper colour than any natural hair he had seen. The woman stopped at the bottom of the steps and looked each of them up and down as they approached.

"Welcome to our home." Her face held the faint offer of a smile, but no more. "My name is Mishalia Nistrom, but you can call me Misha."

Tabitha took a half step forward and introduced the group,

including Max, who panted happily with her tongue out in response. Misha nodded in acceptance.

"I will be honest. My family is not friendly with the Tower and I was hesitant to agree to you coming here. But I have been told that you are beginning to see the truth behind their lies and Trav says you can be trusted. Whatever else happens and whatever choices you make, please remember that I have invited you into my home, one that would be destroyed if you shared your knowledge of this place with the wrong person."

Tabitha looked back and the others and Zack nodded in silent agreement.

"Nobody will hear about this place from us," she replied to Misha.

"Thank you." Misha turned and beckoned them to follow. "Come inside. Leave your shoes outside, if you don't mind. And those weapons, too."

Zack stepped onto the veranda and slipped out of his sneakers, placing them and his staff against the outside wall before he entered the house. The inside matched the outside with a jumble of old and modern in each direction. Most of the furniture, including the grand dining table, might have been hundreds of years old, but the sound system on the bookcase behind them certainly wasn't. Misha and the Traveller sat at the table and Zack claimed a seat between Kimmy and Jackie.

"Let's get straight to business, then," the Traveller said, "may I have the opal?"

Bast leant across the table and placed the stone in front of the Traveller.

"With your permission, Misha?" The Traveller looked to their host, who nodded.

He whispered a string of syllables and the opal sprang to life, showing the same arc of light as it had two days before.

"What do you see?" he asked Zack and his friends.

"Plant," Zack replied, "being tethered by the other Schools of magic."

"Yes." The Traveller's excited eyes reflected the opal's light. "To what purpose, do you think?"

"We don't know," Charlie answered, "do you?"

"I might." He sat back in his chair, allowing the arc of spiralling lights to continue. "I said to you before that I think the rituals have something to do with the Thirteen and this may be the confirmation I was looking for. When I said that nobody seems to have seen the Thirteen, I meant it. Not that their identities are a well-kept secret, but that nobody knows who they are."

"That doesn't make sense," Tabitha said, "how can they be in charge if nobody knows who they are?"

"An excellent point." The Traveller clapped the tips of his fingers together. "And that is where the Tower itself comes into play. The Tower is something of an interdimensional construct and it acts as an intermediary, passing instructions to those in higher positions who, in turn, pass them down."

"If this is true, why haven't we heard about it?" Kimmy asked.

"Because the Tower defaults to secrets and covets them as a means of reward," the Traveller replied.

"So, what you're saying," Tabitha said, pointing at the opal, "is that every month the Thirteen use Plant magic to bind themselves to the Tower?"

"No," Zack answered before the Traveller could speak. Different pieces of the puzzle were clicking in his mind as he spoke. "It's every four weeks, not every month. Thirteen times a year. They only bound one person to the Tower, the Plant member."

The Traveller nodded.

"The Master of Plant, I believe they are titled, but yes, that is my theory, too."

"And next month, it will be some other school," Charlie added.

"Knowledge," the Traveller replied, "again, if my theory is correct."

"Why Knowledge?" Bast asked.

"The Tower does not simply categorise magic," the Traveller said, "it orders it. Life is first, then Creation, Animal, Plant, followed by Knowledge, Movement, Protection, then through to Mind, Body and the elementals, Fire, Earth, Air and, lastly, Water."

"These are interesting theories," Tabitha said, "but I don't see how it's evidence that the Tower is in the wrong."

"Perhaps it isn't," the Traveller replied, "although, the fact that it is layered in secrets is not the best sign. But any information is useful."

"So, you can use it against them." Tabitha did little to mask her accusatory tone.

"If necessary, yes. But also, to help inform others about the Tower, so they can make their own choices."

Any further reply from Tabitha was interrupted by a woman entering the room from the back of the house. Zack estimated she might be only a year or two older than him and she looked enough like Misha that she was probably her daughter. She was short, around Zack's height, and had the same greyish tone to her skin as the older woman. Her hair was a deep yellow colour, not blonde. The young woman was carrying a wooden box filled with firewood and placed it beside the hearth on the other side of the living space. She turned and stopped when she noticed the group of people sitting around the table. She pulled ear pods out and approached.

"Sorry, I forgot we had company."

"Yes," Misha said with dryness in her voice, "because having guests is such a common occurrence. This is my daughter, Nell." She introduced Zack and his friends.

"Nice to meet you all," Nell replied with a smile before turning to address the Traveller. "Trav."

"Nell," he replied, "perfect timing, actually. I was hoping you could do me a favour. I'd like to equip these young people for what lies before them and I could really use some bronze-stone."

Nell's lips tightened.

"We don't keep it sitting around, I'll have to go get some. And the tunnels will have shifted again."

"I'm sure they'd be happy to help you with it," the Traveller replied, indicating Zack and the others, "I promise it's for a good cause."

Zack's eyes flicked to Tabitha, expecting her to object to them being volunteered. Instead, she stood up.

"Yes, we can help. It would be nice to see more of this place."

Nell smiled and looked at her mother, an unsaid question in her eyes. Misha eyed Zack and his friends in open assessment.

"I'm trusting you, Trav, that these young people are on the level." She turned back to Nell. "Fine. But be careful and come back empty-handed if it's too dangerous."

"Alright, you lot." Nell stepped toward the front door. "Come with me. I hope you're comfortable in dark and narrow places."

CHAPTER 9

Nell led them back out to the veranda, where Max had been waiting with a modicum of patience. The yellow-haired young woman squealed with excitement.

"Who is this?"

"This is Max," Charlie said, slipping her shoes back on, "Max, this is Nell, a friend."

Max brushed happily against Nell, who returned the greeting with a vigorous head scratch.

"Oh, I wish I could get a dog, but they don't like the native wildlife or some of the plants."

Charlie looked at Max.

"Did you hear that? You stay close to me, okay?"

Max whined.

"I don't care. We'll go somewhere fun when we get back."

Max sniffed in a way Zack interpreted as vague acceptance and padded off the veranda to wait. Shoes and weapons reclaimed, they followed Nell around the house and deeper into the forest.

"It's a long walk to where we're headed and I'll explain what we're up for when we get there," Nell said as she walked, "but I want to know a bit more about you all, first. I'm told you're Tower folk? But maybe not for long?"

"Yeah, that's probably a fair description," Art replied.

"We're not sure," Tabitha said, "we've done some good things with the Tower, protected people."

Nell looked back, her eyes scanning Tabitha up and down.

"Fair enough. I get it, you know. If you're the kind of people who try to do the right thing and the Tower is helping you do it, then, of course, the Tower seems good. And then along come strangers and tell you the Tower's crooked. You've gotta weigh it all up."

They came to a fork in the path and Nell led them to the left where, up ahead, the trees started to thin out and softer ground gave way to stones.

"It was simpler for me," Nell continued, "the Tower has been hunting my family for almost two centuries. Great-great-great-grandma wasn't exactly human, you see, and that bothers them. Makes it much easier for me to pick a side. Anyway, what part of Australia are you from?"

"Oh… um, Sydney," Tabitha answered.

"Never been." Nell maintained her casual, matter-of-fact tone. "Been to Perth. I studied engineering there for a semester."

"My mother teaches metallurgical engineering," Tabitha said.

"Really?" Surprised excitement filled Nell's voice.

The two of them chatted with each other and Zack turned his attention back to the surroundings. He extended his senses out. Unlike Charlie, he could not discern the difference between the various kinds of animals beyond a vague notion of their size. Still, Life found them amongst the grass, leaves and branches.

Almost two hours later, the forest changed. Away from either side of the path, the foliage was darker and overgrown. Larger Life signatures approached, not within eyesight, but close enough that Zack felt he'd entered their turf and that he wasn't particularly welcome. He was tracking a nearby lurking aura of Life when the path opened into a clearing. Unlike the one that held Nell's homestead, this one had not been opened up by felling trees. Instead, it was a natural break in the forest's expanse, where the soil had given way to stone and held back the roots. The stone rose several metres above the surface in the centre of the clearing and the dirt trail led to where a wide opening had been carved into the side.

"Um, Nell," Art said, interrupting Tabitha mid-sentence.

"Yes?"

"Can you fill us in on what we're doing?" he asked. "I mean, I get that we're picking up some stone—"

"Bronze-stone," she said.

"Thank you, bronze-stone," Art continued, "and you mentioned tunnels before. So, what does this involve?"

"There's nothing much to it. We go down there." Nell pointed towards the opening. "We go in, prod around for some bronze-stone — which looks pretty much like it sounds — gather it up and leave."

"Gather it?" Bast asked.

"Well, mine it," Nell said with a shrug.

"Are there tools for that inside?" Charlie asked.

"Nope." Nell stretched out her arm in front of her and drew a long, deep breath. Yellow light collected around her fingertips and rippled outward, past her right hand, coalescing into a pickaxe. "I'll mine it. You can help me lug it out."

"Awesome," Art grinned.

"Thank you." Nell gave a joking bow.

The tunnel led down at a steep angle and they were plunged into darkness in less than a dozen steps.

"Hold up a second," Nell said, "I got something for this."

But before Nell could act, a red glow flashed and five flames, like candle lights without the candles, illuminated Kimmy and drifted out to float amongst them.

"Sweet," Nell said, "conjuring lights is something I've always struggled with."

"But you can snap your fingers and make a pickaxe appear," Tabitha replied.

"Well, yeah." Nell held her hands out. "Light isn't made of anything. I'm better with things I can hold in my hands or that I can feel with my fingertips."

"Oh, okay."

The firelight made it hard to tell, but it looked like Tabitha was blushing.

"How far down do these tunnels go?" Charlie asked.

Nell spun around and seemed almost surprised to see her.

"Deep. Potentially for miles. But don't worry, we won't need to go far at all. Miss Sunshine's flames should be perfect for finding bronze-stone. They'll be reflected. So just look around for the flickering." She took the lead again, descending deeper into the tunnel.

"Miss Sunshine?" Kimmy breathed through clenched teeth to Bast. "I could show her a sun, up close if she asks for it."

"Play nice, Sis," Bast replied. "We're guests."

At first, the stone beneath Zack's feet felt like rough steps, but by the time they came to the first junction, it had changed and the tunnel floor became more curved; it was deepest in the centre.

"Which way do we go?" Art peered down the three choices.

"For first-timers, it's best if we just keep taking lefts." Nell turned the corner without checking to see that they followed. "That way, if you need to get out without me, keep taking rights."

"You don't have a map?" Bast asked.

Nell laughed with a soft chuckle.

"A map won't do you much good down here."

"Why not?" Kimmy asked.

"Because the tunnels shift," Zack answered, remembering Nell's comment back at the house. Nell pointed to Zack with a wink.

"Exactly."

"What?" Kimmy pushed forward. "The tunnels move around and you're only bringing that up now?"

"I was getting to it," Nell said, seemingly unfazed, "it's rare I get to talk to somebody new. I was enjoying the chat first. Yes, the tunnels move, but we'll have plenty of warning before they do and we'll get out of here. Now, let's focus on the job at hand."

They turned left twice more, winding ever downwards before they found the first piece of bronze-stone. As Nell had suggested, Kimmy's flamelight reflected off a fist-sized piece a third of the way up the tunnel wall. With easy confidence, Nell swung her pick and chipped away at the rockface around the bronze-stone. When it was fully exposed, she landed a blow precisely at its base and broke it free.

She picked it up and, with a wave of her hand and a shimmer of yellow light, a heavy sack appeared. Dropping the bronze-stone inside, she passed the sack to Art.

"Here, Longlegs, you can play mule."

Art accepted the sack, pinching the edges and sniffed it. Zack caught a glimpse of the expression on his face as a light floated by and guessed what he was about to say.

"Nell, I don't suppose the magic that made this can make gold or jewellery?"

Kimmy groaned.

"You are always looking for something to scam."

"Oh, I'm sorry." Art's voice was drenched with sarcasm. "I didn't realise you were happy to give up the Tower income without a replacement."

"I'm sure the moment you see a new belt you like," Kimmy said with a sneer, "you'll just mind-jack a bank teller and clean out the till."

"The hell I would," Art replied, "the teller would get fired and probably charged if I did that. It's immoral."

"Like you could even find morality in a dictionary."

"Are they okay?" Nell whispered to Tabitha.

Tabitha sighed.

"Probably not, but it's nothing new. Please lead on."

With Nell at the front, they continued down the tunnel, while Art and Kimmy's argument echoed off the stone.

"I can make gold," Nell said, "but like everything else I make, it dissipates soon enough and then you'd have one angry buyer on your hands. I prefer to use my magic to make more permanent value. Like that." She pointed at another lump of bronze-stone glimmering in the dim light. As Nell worked to pry it free, Bast, Zack and Charlie wandered a little further down the tunnel.

"Don't wander off too far," Tabitha called out after them, but when Zack turned to reply, she was busy watching Nell and her pick.

One of Kimmy's roaming candle lights followed them and they hadn't walked more than a dozen metres when several more reflections revealed a cluster of bronze-stone.

"Hey, Nell," Bast said in between clangs, "when you're done with that one, we've got a bunch more."

"Sensational," Nell replied before swinging her pick again, "we'll have Longlegs' sack filled in no time."

Kimmy snorted with laughter, distracting her from her latest retort. She walked to stand between Jackie and Tabitha while Art ignored her and collected the second piece of dark orange stone.

Five minutes later, another two pieces had joined it and Nell was working on a fifth when Jackie shouted in alarm.

"We've got trouble!"

"What is it?" Tabitha asked as the tunnel shook.

"Back to the surface, now!" Nell ordered, stopping mid-swing to run back the way they'd come.

"Is this the tunnels changing?" Art asked as he matched her strides.

"Not exactly," she replied.

On a whim, Zack reached out with his mind while he ran with the others. He didn't have to reach far.

"Nell, why are there five living things coming towards us through the stone?"

"Five giant bugs," Charlie added.

"Five?" Nell sounded concerned rather than alarmed. "That's not good. Might want to move a bit faster then."

"What?" Kimmy screamed. "Being attacked by giant bugs has been on the cards and you've been keeping it to yourself?"

The rumbling increased, dislodging pebbles and dust from the tunnel's ceiling.

"'Giant bugs' is a bit of an overstatement." Nell's voice sounded through the grey cloud. "They're more like people-sized worms. And it's really unlikely that we're actually going to be attacked."

A loud crack sounded as the rockface to their left broke away. Through the puff of dust, a chittering, beak-like maw snapped at Zack. As a reflex, he thrust his quarterstaff forwards to fend it off, but the maw closed down on the staff and wrenched it from his grip. The dust settled, revealing the rest of the creature. The worm, as Nell had described it, seemed to have no face beyond the maw, and the rest of its body was made of rings of translucent flesh. It moved faster than Zack had expected and he dived to his side as it lunged toward him. He landed on his knees and the hard stone tore through his jeans and gashed open his skin.

From behind the worm, Art charged forward and hacked at its body with his blade. The chittering was replaced by a violent screech and the worm rounded back on him. Further back down the tunnel, the roof had collapsed and two more worms were sliding along the walls towards them. Kimmy swirled her hands around, whispering her incantation and a sheet of flames roared forth, blocking the two worms behind it. The heat from the firewall was intense, but so was the light. Zack found his feet, blinking away the tears as his eyes adjusted.

Another two worms burst through the stone and into the tunnel and more of the debris fell from the ceiling. Zack could see them clearly now and noticed they had a pink-orange centre inside their translucent flesh.

Bast stabbed at one of the worms while Jackie and Tabitha fended off another.

"Forget the worms," Nell shouted over the sounds of fighting and cracking stone, "we need to get out of here before we're buried alive."

Zack followed along with the others as they ran towards Nell, but Max's barking drew his attention. A little further up the tunnel, Charlie was standing still, facing the direction of the worms. Her eyes glowed with russet light and her face was strained.

"Bast!" Zack called out. "Help me."

Bast joined him at Charlie's side and they slipped her arms around their shoulders to carry her as they ran up the tunnel. A massive slab of stone crashed down where she had been standing seconds before, close enough that Zack's feet wobbled from the impact.

The tunnel floor shook violently as more stone fell. A piece the size of his head struck Zack between his shoulder blades and pain, rather than Life, told him he'd broken something. With the last of their strength, Zack and Bast hurled their bodies forward, landing on the tunnel floor with a heavy impact as the tunnel collapsed behind them in a wall of rock. The shaking ceased and the dust settled. Charlie sat up, wincing.

"It was hard to connect with them, but I've sent the worms away. We're safe."

Zack breathed a sigh of relief, but it was cut off by Jackie's scream.

"Where's Art and Kimmy?" Her eyes were wide and frantic.

Zack pushed himself off the floor, ignoring the searing pain in his back and looked around. Jackie was right, they were missing two members of their group. Panic growing in his chest, he pushed out with his mind. He sensed the five worms burrowing away at speed and then, maybe twenty metres down the tunnel, he found two familiar Life signatures. Art and Kimmy were on the other side of the collapsed tunnel.

CHAPTER 10

"Art!" Jackie shouted and her echo bounced around the tunnel.

"He's okay," Zack said, "they both are. Their Life signals are strong."

"Are we okay?" Bast asked. "I can't see my own hands in front of my face."

"Hang on," Nell said, "it won't be as fancy as Sunshine's floating candles, but…"

A moment later, the tunnel was bathed in a lazy lime-green light. The head of Nell's pickaxe glowed like it had been smeared with some kind of phosphorescence, but it was bright enough to see in detail.

"We need to get back to them before those bugs do." Tabitha ran her fingertips along the collapsed end of the tunnel.

Charlie knelt beside Max, scratching her between her ears while inspecting her for wounds.

"The worms aren't coming back. I've made sure of that."

Is everybody okay? Art's voice entered Zack's mind and, by the expression on their faces, everybody else's as well.

Art! You're alright! Jackie's thoughts screamed out.

Ouch, Art replied. *Yeah, Kimmy and I are okay.*

What happened? Zack asked.

We were right behind you, Art answered, *then a chunk of the roof fell in front of us. We tried to squeeze past it, but then other parts started collapsing around it and forced us back. It seems stable here now, but we're completely cut off.*

"What are you all doing?" Nell said aloud.

"Art's speaking to us with his mind," Tabitha replied, "they're okay, but we've got to get them out. I don't suppose we can dig our way to them?"

Nell shook her head.

"Not a chance. Even ignoring how long that would take, it's not safe. You could trigger another cave in."

"Okay, how about a gate?" Tabitha looked at Bast.

Bast didn't look confident.

"I can try."

Bast closed his eyes and traced his patterns in the air but after a few seconds he stumbled forward and had to catch himself on the tunnel wall.

"Sorry, Cap. I can't get a handle on this place's Movement."

"What do we do then?" Jackie's voice had a panicked edge to it.

What's going on people? Art's thoughts sounded. *You didn't reply.*

Sorry, Zack replied, *we're working through some options.*

"We need to get my mother," Nell said, "her magic is strong with earth and stone. She can get them out."

"That's like a four hour return trip!" Bast replied.

"We'd better start moving then," Nell said.

"No," Charlie stood up, "I'll go. I can do it in half that."

Nell looked her up and down. "You seem fit and all, but if we stick together and push ourselves, we'll get there in good time."

Charlie smirked and knelt back down next to Max, red-brown light creeping over her body. The light faded to reveal not the wolf Zack had been expecting, but a cheetah.

Nell took a step back, her eyes wide.

"Oh, okay then. Will you… will she be able to find her way back?"

Charlie-cheetah gave an awkward nod. Zack channelled a thin stream of Life into Charlie to boost her reserves.

"Run fast."

The savannah cat raced up the tunnel, toward the surface.

Honestly, if you think I'm being impatient for an update, you should see Kimmy. Art's thoughts had a tone of frustration to them.

Charlie is going to get help, Tabitha replied, *Nell's mum is some kind of Earth mage.*

Terramancer, Art's thoughts returned. *So, what are we supposed to do in the meantime?*

Sit still, I guess. Tabitha glanced at Jackie. *Are you two really okay in there?*

A couple of scratches and bruises, but nothing to worry about. And given the company, I don't imagine getting cold will be a danger. Art's tone shifted. *You don't suppose I could get away with putting her to sleep until you saved us?*

Art! Jackie did not sound amused. *This is serious.*

Plus, Zack added, *that would leave you alone with Mr Shanks.*

Oh, go straight to hell, dude, Art replied, *I was having a nice casual entombment until you shared that little treat.*

You're welcome.

"We should move outside." Nell's voice brought Zack's attention back to the tunnel.

"No," Jackie replied, "we can't leave them."

"I'm sorry, little pea." Nell placed her hand on Jackie's shoulder. "Right here, or up on the surface, we're no good to them. But up there, we lower the risk of any more cave-ins and, when my mother arrives, I'll be able to lead her straight here."

Jackie's lips tightened and she looked to Zack and the others for support. Zack frowned in sympathy.

"She's the expert here, Jacks. We should follow her lead."

Jackie's head dropped and she fell in behind Nell and Tabitha as they moved back up the tunnel. Bast stepped in beside her and wrapped his arm around her shoulders as they walked, while Max plodded along beside her, nuzzling the top of her head against Jackie's hand. Zack took one last look at the rockslide before following them.

He noticed it was easier to find his way back through the tunnels. Apart from being all right turns, the tunnel floor sloped upwards noticeably and he found the knowledge that he could find his own way out comforting. Still, it was a deflated group that exited the shadows of the tunnels and stepped back into the light of the strange orange sun. It now hung directly overhead and the clearing felt pleasantly warm after the coolness that had clung to the stone of the tunnels.

Tabitha and Nell claimed a seat on a flat stretch of stone, facing the path back through the forest. Max lay down on her belly in the sunlight, her nose pointed at the path, while Zack followed Bast and Jackie to where they sat on the ground with their backs against the main stone outcrop. In the daylight, Zack could see the red rings under Jackie's eyes. She didn't try to hide them.

"It's my job to protect him," she said, tucking her knees up to her chest.

"And you do, li'l Sis," Bast said, gently prodding at her legs. "You protect us all. And he's going to be okay."

Jackie shook her head, her blonde curls bouncing off her face.

"You don't get it. Art looks ahead, not behind him. He's always been like that. Ever since I was little, I had to watch him get himself into trouble again and again. Now I can finally do something about it and…" she gestured to the tunnel entrance. "I should have been keeping a better eye on him."

Zack slid along the wall to sit closer to her.

"I know what you mean. Better maybe than anybody other than you. It takes a lot of work to look after our boy down there. Who knows, maybe that's why you and I have the magic we do. So, you can stop him from getting hurt and I can patch him up when he finds a way, despite that. We've got this."

Jackie sniffled and raised her eyes to his.

"Yeah, we do."

⟫⊱━━━━━━━⊰⟪

The sun had travelled across the sky before, with an excited bark, Max leapt up onto her legs and bounded down the path and into the woods.

She returned a moment later with Misha and Charlie, once again on two legs.

"A cave-in, Nell? Really?" Misha asked with a tone of exasperation.

Nell stood up to face her mother.

"When was the last time five worms struck at once? Not much I could do."

"Alright, take me down and we'll dig our guests out."

They followed Nell and Misha back down the tunnels. Even under the soft lime glow of Nell's pick, Charlie looked exhausted.

"You made great time," Bast said, "I'll have to race you some day."

Charlie gave a tired smile.

"Fine. But only I get to cheat."

Bast laughed.

"No Traveller?" Zack asked.

"Nope," Charlie answered, "he was setting up for a ritual and said he needed to be well rested for it. He seemed confident Misha could handle it."

"Can you make sure that the worms haven't come back?" Jackie asked her.

"Sure thing, Jacks." Charlie stopped and closed her eyes, placing a hand on the tunnel wall, before opening them again. "Not a trace of them."

"Thank you," Jackie said, shuffling forward to walk beside Tabitha, directly behind Nell and Misha.

Before long, they reached the front of the cave-in. Misha stretched out her arms and cracked her knuckles.

"Okay, you lot, give me some space. This is simple enough, but there's a lot of loose rock here and I'll need to pace myself."

Zack awkwardly raised his hand.

"Excuse me. Sorry, but maybe I could help with that? I'm sure we'd all be happy to share out the load a bit."

Misha looked at him with open curiosity.

"How does that work, exactly?"

Zack's nerves ratcheted up. He had assumed this was a normal, relatively simple piece of magic, but if Misha didn't know what he meant, was there something taboo or problematic about it? Was he about to offend her?

"Um, I'm a Lifer - a Life mage, I mean. I can connect us together, so we share our Life energy. When you use your magic, you can draw from us as well as yourself."

Misha blinked in thoughtful silence, the whites of her eyes reflecting the yellow-green glow. And then she smiled.

"Never had that experience before, but it does sound useful. What do I need to do?"

"Nothing," Zack replied, feeling a wave of relief. He turned to his friends. "Charlie, I might leave you to recover, but are the rest of you good?"

Tabitha and Bast nodded while Jackie looked at him with a fierce expression.

"Take whatever you need to get that tunnel open."

Rather than argue with her, he nodded and formed channels between them, linking their Life with flows of his own. A task, that had once felt impossible to Zack, had been tamed. The whirl of distracting thoughts was never gone, but with practice and confidence they no longer interfered with his simpler magic. With the Life now rolling around between them he reached out to Misha with a final channel.

"Oh, wow." Her eyes widened and she looked from Zack to Nell. "Make sure you get this one's number before he leaves. He seems smart, good height and, if it works out, this kind of magic might be a nice addition to the family."

Practice and confidence aside, Zack nearly shattered his magical plumbing and he looked around at his friends for some clue of how to react. Bast's face was frozen in delight, while Jackie looked shocked and Charlie seemed more bemused than anything. Tabitha, however, was looking away, as if she found the nearest tunnel wall fascinating.

Nell rolled her eyes.

"Mother, don't."

Misha held out her hands in innocence.

"I'm only saying, you always complain about how hard it is to connect with people when you have to keep our family a secret." She pointed at Zack. "It wouldn't be a factor here."

"Can you focus?" Nell pointed at the rubble. "People in need of rescue, remember?"

"Fine, fine." Misha turned to face the cave-in, still muttering. "I simply think it would be nice, that's all."

Nell gave no further response and Misha set to work. There were no incantations or gestures; she simply touched her fingertips to the loose rock and pushed. Waves of brown light rippled out from her hands and the stone began to move or, perhaps melt. Regardless, as Misha stepped forward, the tunnel opened up around her and returned, at least to Zack's amateur eye, to how it had been before.

With each further step, Misha's bubble of Earth magic repaired more of the tunnel and Zack felt her draw Life from the channel to fuel her progress.

"Should we follow?" Bast asked.

"Let her get a little further," Nell replied, "my mother knows what she's doing, but there's always a slight risk that firming up one bit puts pressure on another."

Hey, is the sound of stone moving around a good thing, or do we have worms again? Art's thoughts appeared in Zack's mind.

The flow of Life wavered from the surprise of the intrusion. *Talk to Tabitha. Busy.*

Misha had repaired around thirty metres of tunnel when Nell led the rest of them forward. Life had been flowing steadily out of Zack's plumbing for close to ten minutes and the combination of fatigue and strain slowed him down to short, cautious steps.

"Art and Kimmy can hear what your mum is doing," Tabitha said, "we must be close."

Nell shrugged.

"Maybe not as close as it feels to them. The vibrations can travel a decent distance. Still, tell them to get back from that wall."

Tabitha nodded and fell silent again.

"I'd better move up though," Nell continued, "if she is getting close, I can add a little support. Don't want to tunnel through to them only to bring their roof down in the process. You should keep following at this pace, I'll call you when it's secure." She walked down to be a few steps behind her mother.

Jackie gave a soft squeal at the thought of another cave-in.

"I should go too."

"I need you here," Zack said, putting his hand on her arm. "Misha's spell is heavy."

"We can trust them," Tabitha said, "Nell seems calm about this."

Jackie sighed in frustration but stayed with them as they followed behind the tunnelling's steady progress. Misha didn't slow and Zack began to monitor his friends' Life more closely. There was no immediate danger but he'd have to consider cutting the connections soon.

"Art says they can see the rubble on their side starting to shift," Tabitha said.

Jackie gave a weary smile and the group shuffled down the tunnel.

"Almost there," Misha called back to them.

A deafening crunch sounded overhead and a deep crack zigzagged out from the remainder of the cave-in and along the ceiling back toward Zack and his friends.

"Mother, stop." Nell threw her pickaxe to the ground and, with a grunt of effort, whipped her right arm in a circle toward the wall on the left. Half a dozen columns of shimmering yellow light sprang up along the tunnel wall. She mirrored the motion with her left arm towards the opposite wall, creating an equal number of yellow columns. The light dissipated, leaving behind iron scaffolding embedded firmly into the stone of the tunnel.

The crack along the ceiling ceased its growth, but the scaffolding groaned as it strained against the shifting mass of the tunnel. Misha broke away from the rubble and thrust the brown light of her Earth magic along the path of the crack. As it passed, it left solid stone and, when it faded away, the tunnel was silent again. Nell leant back heavily on the tunnel wall, catching her breath.

Misha reached out and squeezed her hand.

"Strong and fast work with that steel. Your father couldn't have done better."

Nell smiled and touched her fingers to her lips.

"Okay, back to it then." Misha straightened up and faced Zack. "Are you and your friends good to continue? We only have another five or so metres to go."

"Ready when you are," he replied.

Zack narrowed the channels between himself and his friends, restricting how much Life they were feeding into Misha's magic. It would be a stretch for him to cover the balance on his own, but he didn't want to bleed them dry when they might be needed for something important. More layers of loose rock gave way to Misha's will, reshaping into solid stone walls and Zack felt the shift from fatigue to pain. His head ached, his muscles burned and the taste of bile and metal crept into his mouth. Misha had slowed too, but as Zack was about to break off the channel, a warm orange glow appeared through a gap in the rubble, followed by another and then half a dozen more. With one last heave, Misha forced the remainder of the cave-in back into place and opened up the rest of the tunnel.

Several metres deeper, the source of the orange glow was revealed to be a compact wood-free campfire. On opposite sides of it, illuminated by the flickering light, were Art and Kimmy.

They rose to their feet and Kimmy dispelled the fire with a flick of her hand.

"Thank god, you're here. The company has been unbearable."

It was dark by the time they returned to the homestead and the orange sun had been replaced by three moons in differing shades of green. Following Misha's lead, Zack and his friends left their shoes and weapons on the veranda and trudged inside. The interior was well lit by an ample scattering of glass lanterns that had the appearance of gas lamps but, if Zack's suspicions were correct, probably weren't.

The lighting revealed the Traveller splayed across one of the couches deeper in the room. He clambered to his feet and gave a sluggish stretch, looking more weary than any of them.

"I'm sorry," Kimmy said as she collapsed into a chair, "did we keep you up, Trav?"

Zack watched for any hint of a reaction to Kimmy's use of the shortened name, but the shaggy man only shrugged and joined them at the table.

"Not at all. I was not idle this afternoon and, while it wasn't as dramatic as your adventure, it was its own kind of hard work." The Traveller looked at the sack Art had placed at his feet. "Is that it?"

Art nodded and lifted it onto the table. With a wave of her hand, Nell dispelled the sack and revealed the four nuggets of orange ore they had collected from the tunnels. In the brightness of the dining area, it wasn't as shiny as the metal it was named for and gave off a more muted reflection of the light. The Traveller thrummed his fingers on the table's edge in obvious delight.

"Excellent. That is more than enough."

"More than enough for what?" Tabitha asked, with no small amount of frustration in her voice. "We're having no more part in this until you explain."

The Traveller held up his hands in supplication.

"That's more than fair. More than fair. As I said, while you were busy, so was I. Making these."

He reached into his pocket and poured the contents onto the table. Pearls. Thirteen of them. With a gesture, he invited the others to pick them up. Nell scooped up the one closest to her and Kimmy, Art and

Bast were quick to follow. On impulse, Zack reached past the pearls closest to him and picked up one towards the centre of the table. He felt it the moment his fingers touched the pearl: Life.

The Traveller's eyes met his as he sat back down and Zack felt the weight of some silent judgement.

"Using the magic you helpfully captured in the opal, I have attuned these pearls."

"One for each School of magic?" Zack asked.

The Traveller smirked.

"Close, but not quite. One for each of the Thirteen."

"Keep going." Tabitha tapped the top of the table. "What do they do?"

"Once inside the Tower, each pearl will build up a resonance with the proclaimed 'Master' of its school. Over time, this resonance will help us identify them."

"And?" Tabitha's stare bored into him. "For what purpose? So, you can hunt them down? We won't be a part of that."

"No, please. That's not my intention at all," the Traveller replied, "I don't want to harm anybody; I'm only interested in the truth. These are the most powerful members of the most powerful organisation in human history and, not only is the organisation a secret, but they themselves are a secret within it. Nothing good can come from that much shadow and I merely want to provide some sunlight."

Tabitha opened her mouth to reply but no words emerged. She looked for support around the table, but Bast shrugged.

"It's hard to argue with that," Bast said, "you can't hold people responsible for the things they do if you don't know who they are."

"I assume your plan is for us to sneak these into the Tower," Charlie asked.

The Traveller nodded.

"Well then, I have a question." She snatched a pearl from the table and rolled it around in her palm. "In what version of reality do we not get caught? I could feel the Animal in this thing across the table. They'll get found and traced back to us."

"That is where your efforts today come in. Misha, could you please do as we discussed?"

Misha rubbed her face in her hands.

"Very well. I didn't think I'd have such a busy day when I agreed, but it's for a good cause. Would you please return the pearls to the table?" She turned to Art. "My dear, could you pass me the bronze-stone?"

Art replaced his pearl before picking up the ore and laying it in front of Misha.

"Thank you." She placed her hands around the pile, clutching it in a loose grip. "This is not the easiest of materials to work with, but I suppose that is the point."

Misha stared at the bronze-stone and her hands glowed, bathing the stone in brown light. Strain appeared on her face but, after a moment, the ore melted into a puddle and oozed across the table towards the pearls. It rippled over the pearls, leaving them cocooned in a thin orange layer. The remaining puddle, a third its original size, returned to Misha and hardened. She relaxed back in her seat.

"Marvelous," the Traveller said. He gestured to the pearls. "Try them again."

Zack hovered his hand over the pearls, trying to sense the presence of Life that helped him find it the first time, but there was nothing. The others, similarly, had no luck sensing their Schools. Zack picked up one after another until he finally felt the faintest touch of Life and he twisted it about in his fingers. The pearl was not entirely encased in the bronze-stone and he could still see it through a thin hole.

"Yes," the Traveller said, "it would defeat our purpose to cover it completely. But the peculiar properties of the bronze-stone, the ones that make this realm so hard to reach, will mask the pearls while they do their work."

Tabitha sighed.

"Okay. We'll smuggle them inside for you. Then what?"

"First, hide them separately around the Tower, near the quarters of each respective school," the Traveller replied, "I'll mark them for you, so you know which is which. In a month or so, you'll reclaim them, bring them back to me and we will see what we've uncovered."

"Agreed," Tabitha said, "now, we'd better get back."

"I'll walk you all back to the gate point," Nell said.

Tabitha smiled for the first time since they'd sat down at the table.

"Thanks, that'd be great."

CHAPTER 11

The front door to the girls' townhouse opened and Jackie entered, her backpack hanging from one shoulder. Zack looked up from his seat on the couch and closed the novel he'd been reading.

"Hey, Jackie. How was school?"

"Fine. Thanks, Dad." She rolled her eyes at him, but her smile betrayed the joke.

Bast laughed from the opposite couch before finally glancing up from his phone.

"Hey, where's big bro?"

"Not coming. The Tower called him in to go on a 'Men in Black' run." Jackie used her fingers to make the air quotes. "I really doubt the Tower actually calls it that."

"He said he was going to discuss the plan for the pearls with us," Tabitha said, entering from the kitchen with Kimmy.

"Sorry," Jackie replied, "he says he's happy to take your lead, but thought it would be both suspicious and a bad idea money-wise to turn down the offer."

"Yeah, that's fair enough," Tabitha said.

Kimmy walked past them and sat down next to Bast.

"Suits me. We got the smart Stevenson, anyway."

"I'm going to get changed, then I'll be right out." Jackie disappeared into her room.

Tabitha joined Zack on his couch.

"Charlie was also happy to go with the flow and is apparently in Thailand right now."

"Laos," Bast corrected.

"So, it's up to us to decide how we take this next step in turning against the Tower," Tabitha said.

"Come on, Tabs," Bast said, "after everything we've learnt about the Tower, this is the right move."

"And the Traveller has been pretty above board," added Zack, "he's trusted us with magic that could lead the Tower back to him and he's introduced us to other people who seem to trust him."

"They did seem like good people," Tabitha said, "and if they trust him, maybe that's enough. I mean, Nell seemed like somebody who was pretty cluey. Like she could read people well."

Bast smirked. "Well, if Nell trusts him."

"Yeah." Tabitha stared off into empty space. "I just get good vibes from her, you know?"

"You do, do you?" Kimmy's smirk was twice as wide as Bast's.

"Yeah, you don't?" Tabitha looked over at the two of them. "Why, what are you smiling about?"

"She's been like this for three days," Kimmy said to Zack and Bast, ignoring Tabitha.

Jackie walked into the room, changed into a t-shirt and jeans and looked back and forth between the others. Zack shrugged and patted the seat next to him.

"I've been like what?" Tabitha looked confused.

Bast leant forward, looking closely at Tabitha. "Like…"

"Like?" Tabitha's voice trailed for a moment before her eyes widened. "Oh. Oh! I guess… yeah. Well, that answers that, at least."

"Finally!" Kimmy threw up her hands in obvious melodrama, her smile wide.

"So, you guys knew?" Tabitha said, looking around.

Zack nodded, a smile on his own face.

"Well, obviously," Kimmy replied.

"Smitten as a kitten," Bast added.

"Well, I need to think about this a bit later." Tabitha had a look of pleasant shock on her face. "But back to the task at hand. How are we going to manage the pearls?"

"I think it's easy enough for each of us to hide our own near our School's quarters." Zack said.

Kimmy nodded along.

"But how do we get the other six in place?"

"You and I can sneak into Earth and Water," Tabitha said, "we're always going into each other's spaces anyway."

"Yeah, good idea," Kimmy said, "so that leaves four."

"Those will be harder," Zack said, "have any of us had a reason to go into the Creation, Knowledge, Plant or Body quarters?"

"What about getting Art to do it?" Bast asked. "He could mind wipe anybody that got suspicious."

Zack shook his head, eyes wide.

"Way too risky."

"I can do it," Jackie said, "everybody knows Mr Smith, my mentor, is weird. If I get caught, I'll claim it's a training exercise."

"Are you sure?" Tabitha asked.

Jackie nodded.

"I'd probably sense somebody coming, anyway."

"Okay, sounds like a plan." Tabitha handed the shielded pearls out to the others, claiming three for herself and giving five to Jackie, before leaving one each for Art and Charlie on the table. "Hide them well and then come back and we'll write a list of where they are in case somebody else needs to retrieve them. Now, if that's sorted, I need to go and send a text."

"Want some help with it?" Kimmy asked.

Tabitha wore a lost expression on her face.

"I think so, but probably not from you, Kims."

Kimmy gasped in outrage.

"Excuse me?"

"You've shown me some of your texts to guys. They're mostly times, locations and distressing collections of emojis."

Kimmy crossed her arms and barely mollified annoyance while Bast stood up and held out his hand to Tabitha.

"C'mon, let's take a crack at it together."

With a tight smile of relief, Tabitha followed him out of the room.

"Can I ask her out for a drink or is that a mixed message?"

A second helping of potato dumplings, more generous than the first, was piled onto Zack's plate. He looked up at his mother in open question.

"You seem skinny," she said as she served his father a more reasonably-sized portion, "I don't think you've been eating enough since you moved out."

Zack glanced down at his body. Not that it was visible under his baggy hoodie but, if anything, he'd been bulking up a little. His father caught the look and gave a gentle shake of his head, which Zack took to mean that he was, in fact, not getting skinny.

"Probably just half a cupboard of instant noodles and an empty fridge." His mother sat down in front of her own plate of beef goulash.

"He looks fed enough to me, mum." His sister, Ellen, pushed her food around her plate.

"Thank you," Zack replied.

Her brow creased as she stared at him.

"I'm not defending you; I just want her to stop going on about it. It's making my headache worse."

Ellen didn't look well. Beyond her bleary, red eyes and runny nose, Life had revealed the high load of virus inhabiting her respiratory system. She had a brutal case of the common cold.

"Too many late nights out are what's made your headache worse," his mother said, "you need to go to bed early and get a full night's sleep."

"What I need is antibiotics," Ellen replied.

"Antibiotics won't help, it's viral," Zack said before thinking it through. Quickly, he added, "Probably."

"Oh, I was mistaken," Ellen said through a cough, "I thought you'd taken a gap year, but instead you've crammed in eight years of medicine and become a doctor."

"Isn't that exactly what the doctor said to you when you asked for antibiotics, though?" his father asked.

"Yeah, well neither the real one or this wannabe have an assignment due Monday morning that's worth forty per cent of the subject." She pushed herself back from the table. "I'm going to have a shower and go to bed."

"Good night, honey," Zack's mother said, "I'm sure you'll feel better in the morning."

"She's been stressed about this one," his father said after Ellen had left, "She had big plans for it, done lots of prep and just needed the weekend to pull it all together."

"We can help her out." His mother speared a dumpling and rolled it around in the sauce. "She'll be fine."

"You might be able to," his father replied, "I haven't even been able to pretend to understand her subjects since the end of her first year."

"Well, it's a good thing you're pretty." She gifted him a warm, genuine smile before turning back to Zack. "But you're honestly getting enough to eat, right? Everything at the supermarket is getting so expensive."

"Yes, Mum. I'm doing fine. It's not as good as this, but we're eating healthy. Fresh fruit and veg and everything. Actually, our work has been sending us travelling a little and they always give us an allowance when they do, to cover our expenses. Rather than blow it, we try to pocket as much of it as possible."

His father nodded. "Smart."

Lies were simply built into his relationship with his parents now. He still felt guilty, but he had decided that if the message behind the message was honest, then the lie in between wasn't a big deal. In essence, he had now told them that his job occasionally took him out of Sydney, that money wasn't a problem and that he was eating healthy. And that was all true.

He still felt guilty.

"I'll pack you some leftovers, anyway." His mother was not going to admit defeat.

"I'd never say no to leftovers," Zack replied, surrendering.

A few hours and two card games later, Zack and his father were watching a movie in the lounge room. The credits began to roll and his father yawned, louder than was strictly necessary.

"Are you sure you don't need a lift home?"

"No, I'm all good," Zack replied, "Art's going to swing past in a bit and pick me up."

His father stood and tossed Zack the remote control.

"Well, lock up behind you when you leave. And for god's sake don't forget to take the goulash with you."

"I won't. Thanks, Dad."

"Good night, Zack." His father patted him on the shoulder as he shuffled out of the room.

Zack flicked over to another movie and pulled out his phone to text Art.

Finally, they're all in bed. Can you pick me up in 30 mins?

Yeah. No worries, Art replied, moments later.

Zack waited another fifteen minutes to give his father a chance to settle in before he crept upstairs. He listened to the sounds of snoring and slow breaths coming from his parents' room and the more laboured breathing from his sister's. Loitering outside her door, Zack reached out with his Life, observing the way her immune system was struggling against the virus plaguing her body.

Zack sent a thin stream of Life towards her, not to her lungs or sinuses, but to her brain. The memory of a night in a hospital, a little over a year earlier, leapt into his mind and nearly knocked the spell out of his control. It had been the first time he had successfully performed this magic and he had used it to send his grandmother into a deeper, more restful sleep. Now he was casting it with ease and doing it more to ensure Ellen didn't wake up and interrupt him.

Life found his target and Ellen's breaths steadied. Zack's next stream of Life was anything but narrow. Instead, he launched a flood of Life into his sister where it bonded with white blood cells, bolstered her body's hydration and targeted her immune system against the virus. And boosted her own depleted Life reserves while he was at it.

Zack's body ached from the effort as he plodded down the stairs and into the cool Autumn night, remembering in the last moment to pick up the three containers of goulash and dumplings his mother had set aside for him. His quiet sense of pride in being able to help his sister had a deeper and darker shadow lurking behind it; the shame he still felt at not being able to save his grandmother. He would never visit his parents or his sister, without finding a moment to monitor their Life signs. Viruses would be repelled. Fractures repaired. And the earliest appearance of cancers would be destroyed. They would live long healthy lives. Anything less would be a failure.

Art's van pulled up in the driveway and, as Zack climbed inside juggling the three containers, Art's eyes widened.

"Is that your mum's goulash?"

⁂

"How's the pain now?" Zack asked.

Misheel, a dark-haired woman and his only current patient, sighed up at him from the bed. "I suppose it's less now, but it was fine before."

Zack thought that was doubtful. His shift in the Tower's infirmary had been uneventful - three shallow cuts and a sprained ankle - until three of Misheel's companions had dragged her in. The sleeve from her leather jacket and the shirt beneath, were missing, revealing a red-raw arm covered in blisters. Zack's eyes watered when he saw it and he pointed at one of the empty beds. It had been some kind of acid, they had explained, while he poured Life into her arm to repair the cells and fight off potential infection.

Misheel had wanted to leave immediately, against the objections of Zack and the other three mages. Then a huge eagle, which Zack had not noticed was in the room, leapt onto the end of Misheel's bed and screeched at her. She shot a stern look at it but lay back down.

Her companions had since left, but the eagle, whose name was Anchin, sat in watch.

"If you promise to come back tomorrow, or earlier if you notice anything unusual, then you can leave." Zack knew that more than a few Tower members were uneasy about being treated by a Lifer as young as him, but he'd earned the respect of most of them. "I've repaired the damage but secondary issues, like infections or allergic reactions, could spring up."

"Good." Misheel rolled up off the bed and picked up the backpack the others had left behind. Anchin made soft piping sounds at Zack and Misheel sighed again.

"Okay, yes. Thank you for taking care of my arm. I promise I'll return tomorrow."

Anchin piped again, hopped off the bed and trotted along the ground behind Misheel as she left.

Zack got to work, stripping the bed sheets before moving to the linen cupboard for a fresh set. His eyes were drawn to where, a month or so ago, he had found a tiny hidden nook at the back in which to hide the gilded pearl. As casually as he could muster, he glanced around the room and, seeing that he was alone, he reached inside to check that it was still there. The cupboard was deep and he was in up to his shoulders before he felt the cool touch of the bronze-stone and the faint wisp of Life magic.

"Hey, mate."

Zack jumped in shock, slamming his head into the shelf above, before stumbling backwards out of the cupboard. Art greeted him with an overly pleased grin.

"Did you see any other Lifers around?" Zack asked him, rubbing the bump that was forming on his skull.

"Nope, just you," Art replied.

"And have you recently learned any Life magic?"

Art looked at him confused before glancing around the infirmary. "No."

"So, if I had a bloody heart attack from you sneaking up behind me, who would have been able to resuscitate me?"

Art's chuckle was sheepish.

"Yeah, sorry. Anyway, I just stopped by to ask if you've seen Jackie?"

"No, sorry. I've been on shift for five and a bit hours."

"She was supposed to meet me after school in the Training Room, but she's not there and I knocked on the door to her mentor's room and there was no answer. I was hoping she might have swung by here or something."

"Maybe she's running late from school?" Zack replied.

"That's not like her though. Me? Sure. But not Jackie." Art looked worried.

Kristian, an older German man with wispy hair that was somewhere between a transition from blonde to white, entered the room. He wasn't due to take over the infirmary shift from Zack for another twenty minutes, but he was often early and this time, Zack was extra grateful.

He approached Kristian, greeted him and gave a brief account of his shift, with particular attention on Misheel.

"Do you mind if I skip out a bit early? I need to help a friend out."

"Of course." Kristian spoke softly and seldom wasted words.

"Thank you. I hope your shift is a quiet one." Zack scooped up his backpack and led Art out. "Let's go back to the Training Room. You probably just missed her."

The two friends bounced down the stairs in silence until they reached the room. A woman trained in the corner with two short blades against a Greco-Roman statue, but otherwise the room was empty.

"See?" Art gestured with an open hand.

Zack approached the Commander, who stood in the centre of the Training Room.

"Commander, have you seen Jackie today?"

The massive stone form did not move, but the Spanish tenor rumbled in reply.

"I have seen nothing unforged for days."

"Okay," Zack said, "let's try Mr Smith again. Maybe they're both inside and didn't hear you."

Back up the steps they went and, on the way, Zack realised he was starting to worry as well. Art was right, this wasn't like Jackie at all. They knocked and then banged on Mr Smith's door, but there was no answer. Art's hammering was turning frantic when Mr Smith appeared behind them from around the corner. Zack had only seen the man a few times over the past few years. He was a short, skinny man with oily hair and the faintest pencil moustache on an otherwise shaven face.

"Can I help you, gentlemen?"

"I'm looking for my sister," Art answered, the unnecessary volume communicating his growing anxiety.

"Jackie," Zack added.

Mr Smith looked them both up and down.

"It is not my normal practice to confirm or deny the identity of any of my associates, much less my knowledge of their movements. But I will say that I have not seen any students today." He stepped towards his door, brushing past them. "Now if you'll excuse me, I have a lot on my plate right now."

He entered and closed the door firmly behind him.

Art stared at the door.

"I've never liked that guy. So, what do we do now?"

At Zack's suggestion, they left the Tower to get mobile reception, but after a few minutes outside, neither of their phones had any message and, when Art tried to call Jackie, the phone went straight to voicemail.

"Maybe we should head to the school," Zack said, "see if she's still there?"

Art nodded but then stopped.

"Actually, let me check something first." He tapped at his phone's screen.

"What are you doing?" Zack asked.

"When I set up Jackie's mobile plan with global roaming, I maybe also gave myself access to her location information."

"Dude!"

"I've never used it. It was for emergencies." Art showed Zack his phone. "But look, she was last here forty-eight minutes ago. She's in the Tower."

"So, what now?" Zack asked, "Back to Mr Smith?"

"Yeah, maybe." Art patted his jacket pocket and a look of confusion replaced the open worry on his face. He reached in and withdrew a scrunched-up piece of paper.

"What's this?"

Zack stepped closer as Art unfolded the paper, revealing a scrawled note and one of the gilded pearls. Zack's heart dropped into his stomach at the sight of the pearl and kept falling as he read the note.

Your activities on behalf of our mutual friend, Mr T, have been noticed and Ms J has been taken. The pearl will guide you to one who has her, like it was ink. Act with haste.

Mr S.

A hundred scenarios ran through Zack's mind, each of them begging a thousand questions. Art stood motionless, gripping the note and pearl in dull hands. His skin looked paler than Zack had ever seen it before.

"I don't know what to do."

"Neither do I, mate," Zack said, "but we'll work it out together. We'll find her."

CHAPTER 12

Together they had faced demons, angels, renegade mages and frostbite, but Zack had never seen his friends look as serious as they did right now. They were gathered at the girls' townhouse, the six of them and Max, and in the shared silence that followed Art and Zack's retelling, most eyes flickered once or twice to the door to Jackie's room.

"What are we going to do?" Charlie asked.

"We're going to go get her," Art replied, "now!"

"Hold on," Kimmy replied, "are we going to walk right past the fact that Jackie's mentor knows what we were doing? And that he had a pearl?"

"Kimmy's right," Tabitha said, "this could be a trap."

"I don't care if it's a trap!" Art shouted.

Zack put a calming hand on his friend's shoulder.

"Trav said he had allies in the Tower. The fact that it was one of our mentors might explain why he was willing to trust us so quickly. I can't see what the angle is for Mr Smith to set us up."

"I'm just trying to think it through," Tabitha replied, "if the Thirteen have her, then that means they know what we're up to. Maybe it'll be safer - safer for Jackie - if we go and admit what we did."

"What?" Bast looked at Tabitha in confusion.

"Why the secrecy?" Zack asked. "If we're busted, why not come for all of us and arrest us or whatever they do? I was alone in the Tower for most of the day and Art was wandering around it for a while too. No.

They came for Jackie and took her in secret. We need to go after her and get her back."

"And make anybody who touched her explain themselves," Charlie added, "slowly and clearly."

Max growled in deep and menacing agreement.

"Okay," Tabitha said, "let's do this."

"We're going up against one of the Thirteen," Zack said, "so we need to go in prepared."

Art pulled a broadsword and a rapier from his duffel bag, passing the latter to Bast. "You ladies should get your own weapons."

The three of them disappeared into their rooms and Zack passed the pearl to Bast. "The note suggested you could use this like the magical ink."

"Yeah, I'll give it a shot." Bast claimed the pearl and his eyes grew wide. "Well, that's not good."

"What's not good?" Charlie asked, entering the room with a denim jacket, her bow and a quiver.

Bast held up the gilded pearl.

"If Mr Smith is right, it's the Master of Movement that has little Sis. And that means we'll have to be fast, because they'll feel my gate opening up the moment I start. No chance we'll give them much of a surprise."

"Then that leaves total and overwhelming force as our best option." Kimmy returned patting the side of her axe, with Mr Shanks floating beside her.

"I'm on board with that," Art replied.

"That's our plan then," Tabitha said as she joined them. "We go in hard and fast. We get our girl as our first priority and answers as our second and then Bast gets us out again."

"Everybody ready?" Bast asked, moving to where the set of runes had been carved into the floorboards beneath a rug. "If you've got a game-face, better put it on, because I'm going to rip this gate open as fast as I can."

At a flick of his own hand, a ripple of orange light bathed Bast and his movements sped up. On the other side of the room, Kimmy ran her fingers over the head of her axe, which burst into flame. Charlie knelt on the floor and incanted in wide patterns. The russet light collected in her hands but then flowed across to Max, who grew in size, becoming more wolf than dog. The glow returned to Charlie and then there were two wolves in the living room.

Zack clutched his new quarterstaff, which was the only game-face he had. Beside him, Art stood with his sword low, staring at where Bast worked his magic on the pearl. A sliver of grey light appeared in the air and Bast delivered on his promise. Where it normally would have grown slowly, this time it widened rapidly and the strain was clear on Bast's face.

When it was barely a metre tall, Art charged forward, diving head-first into the void.

"Art!" Tabitha called, but it was too late.

Charlie and Max bounded after him, more easily slipping through the growing gate and then the others followed behind. Zack brought up the rear with Bast, who slammed the gate behind them.

Zack wasn't sure where he had expected the pearl to lead them to, but this was not it. The smells of sawdust, oils and stains struck him first, reminding him of his grandfather's workshop. It was dark, but there was enough light to get a sense that they were in a massive room, filled with tall benches and, further into the room, a pair of fluorescent hanging lights. He reached out to the nearest of the workbenches and his fingers brushed against some short cuts of timber and some sandpaper.

"This doesn't exactly look like wizard prison," Kimmy said.

"Where is she?" Art managed to keep his voice low but it had a frantic edge.

Charlie and Max pushed past him, their noses low to the ground. The rest followed behind them, weaving between the benches and then they saw her. Lit by a single dangling bulb, Jackie lay strapped to a bench, tape over her mouth. Art bolted past the wolves towards her but Zack didn't need access to Protection magic to know what was coming.

"Art, it's a trap!"

It was too late. Art crashed against an invisible barrier before he reached Jackie's side. A brighter light turned on with a loud clunk, catching Zack and the others in a white circle and blinding them to the rest of the room.

"How did you find us?" a harsh male voice asked from the darkness.

"I don't think it matters," another said, "the fact that they are here tells us more than we've got out of hours of asking her. They are part of a move against the Tower."

"We should inform the others," the first voice replied.

"Agreed. But not empty-handed. Let's capture them first."

"Are you right?" Kimmy stepped to the edge of the light, brandishing her axe forward like a torch. "You're not capturing shit. You let her go now and we might leave before I burn this place to the ground."

A length of plastic cabling flew in from the darkness and whipped around Kimmy, binding her arms to her sides. Her axe fell to the floor and extinguished and, as the cable continued to whirl around her, Kimmy fell beside it.

"Quiet, child." The second voice sounded annoyed rather than aggressive. "The grownups are talking. Now, the rest of you will drop your weapons. I'd recommend kneeling as well, but if you want a more painful fall to the floor, that's your choice."

None of them dropped their weapons and the only movement was Kimmy, muttering and thrashing about on the ground.

"Very well," said the voice and another length of cabling snaked in at them, this time toward Tabitha.

An inch from her shoulder it stopped, as Bast, hands alight with orange magic, sent it flying upward with an aggressive fling of his arm.

"Oh," the first voice said, "Stefan's little pupil. Adorable."

Zack had had enough. The blinding spotlight was no impediment to Life.

"One of them is three metres past that workbench on the left and the other is against the wall on the right." He pointed with his staff and free hand.

The wolves darted out to the left, while Tabitha and Art moved to the right. Bast sprinted in a third direction and Zack took the moment to reach out with Life toward Jackie. The barrier around her was no impediment to his magic sense, so Jackie's Life reading was clear. And bad. The bruises and abrasions on her arms and legs told only part of the story. They had done something else which exhausted her almost entirely and whatever it was, had likely been painful.

Zack drew together a stream of Life, mostly his own, as there was not much going spare in this musty workshop and sent it toward her. This time, the barrier rejected his efforts and the stream dissipated on contact.

Right, thought Zack, whichever one of the two mages out there that wasn't the Master of Movement was likely responsible for this barrier. He would be the first to fall.

Announced by a cascading series of clunks, the building's lights turned on. As illumination waved down the room, it first revealed Bast, who had found the control panel, before exposing the two mages.

The one to Zack's left, engaged with two wolves, looked like he was in his late forties or early fifties, with dark, silver hair slicked back and a matching goatee. He was dressed in a long-sleeve white t-shirt, jeans and work boots.

The mage on Zack's right, with Art and Tabitha now closing in on him, was a similarly aged man, with short dark hair, dressed in well-worn shirt, waistcoat and trousers.

The man on the left reached out to a workbench over a metre away and a hammer leapt into his hand. Zack clutched his staff and ran toward the other, while the wolves circled around the Master of Movement.

Kimmy clawed her way to her feet and casting off the last of the cabling, she reclaimed her axe and ran to join the wolves. The Movement mage looked at her in surprise and then realisation washed across his face at the sight of Mr Shanks hovering beside her.

"Cute," he said, "you've got an animated knife. I have similar allies."

Blowing through his fingers, he produced a long, shrill whistle and immediately there was rustling throughout the room. Life-sized wooden mannequins rose up from behind crates or underneath clutter and shambled towards Zack and his friends. Seven all up, at Zack's quick count and they were snatching up saws, chisels and other improvised weapons as they approached.

"You picked the wrong woman to threaten with wooden soldiers," Kimmy said. "Get him, Shanky."

The enchanted dagger zipped forward, but the Master of Movement scoffed and, with a flick of his finger, Mr Shanks streaked off path and embedded itself deep into a wooden crate.

"Mess with mine and I mess with yours." Kimmy traced patterns in the air with her left hand and red light bloomed around it before engulfing it with fire down to her elbow. The flames did not appear to harm her and, instead, when she pointed at the nearest mannequins, fire spurted from her hand and immersed the constructs.

Charlie and Max circled around another mannequin. Max feinted forward, drawing its attention and Charlie leapt at the opening. Her jaws found their way around its calf, but without muscle, tendons and nerves to bite, her teeth could do little but bore into the wood. The mannequin, unfazed by the attack, struck down at her, slicing into her muzzle with its short hand-saw. Charlie clenched her jaws harder against the pain and reefed her head away, pulling the construct off-balance. Max followed her lead and bit down hard on the other leg, tugging back against the strain. The mannequin slashed twice more at Charlie, scoring glancing cuts to her cheek and back, before the two wolves pulled it apart. Their victory was short-lived as three more mannequins bore down on them.

Bast raced back in with magical speed, leaping rapier first from a workbench toward the Master of Movement. The instant before the tip of the blade skewered him, the man pivoted in a blur of movement so fast it made Bast's movement seem slow and clumsy. Bast landed hard but absorbed the impact by rolling forward and the hammer strike, that would have connected with the side of his skull, sailed through empty space. At the end of his roll, he spun in a low crouch and the two locked eyes. The Master sneered and rushed toward him.

"Kimmy's brilliant decision to make these things into flaming faceless nightmares is going to burn down this place before we can get Jackie out." Art's eyes were wide.

"Focus, Art. We've got this," Tabitha said, as the two of them moved in on the other man.

This second man didn't seem to be concerned that they were approaching him, weapons drawn. His stance was relaxed and he looked at them with little more than mild interest. Zack was sure he wasn't as unprepared as he looked, but he couldn't work out what the man was up to, so he hurried to back them up instead.

Art reached him first and pointed his sword at the man.

"I should cut you in half for kidnapping my sister, but if you surrender now, we can work something out."

The man's only reply was a smirk and he half-turned away as if Art's ultimatum was nonsense.

"Fine then." Art gripped his hilt with two hands and swung hard at the man's ribs.

A foot away from contact, the blade bounced hard off a familiar shimmering steel light. While Art was off balance from the surprise deflection, the man sidestepped towards him and punched him in the throat. The sword clattered to the ground as Art stumbled backward, clutching his neck and sucking in air.

Before the man could pursue him, Tabitha moved in, her flail whirring at her side. She whipped it forward in a low arc and it crashed against another magical shield, but she was ready and, as it bounced back, she let the momentum carry it around to strike from the left. The man flicked his index finger toward it, with the briefest flash of steel light and this time, when the flail's head struck the shield, it was deflected straight back at Tabitha and slammed into her thigh. She turned at the last instant, but the force of the blow still tore at her skin and knocked her to the ground.

Zack raced forward, putting himself between the Protection mage and his friends. The man gestured with his empty hands, but Zack wasn't going to be goaded after what he just saw. The man looked at Zack in open evaluation before drawing two short, wide knives from under his waistcoat and lunging at Zack. One after the other, the man's swings were strong, but they were clumsy and left him wide open for a counterattack. Zack's brain raced with thoughts. His opponent was most likely a Protection mage and something Jackie had once said to him stuck out in his mind. That danger was a separate thing, apart from whatever object created it. It was the danger itself she could sense and the danger she could block. Resisting the hours of training and physical memory, Zack pulled back on his quarterstaff and focused on knocking the blades aside. Twice more, the man came at him and each time Zack fought back against the impulse to follow his parry with a strike to the knee, ribs or throat.

Art and Tabitha reclaimed their weapons and circled around the mage who, for his part, did not seem worried about being surrounded.

"He's a Protection mage," Zack said, "His magic is only useful if we're trying to hit him."

"I don't think we exactly have a long list of other options," Tabitha replied.

"I can think of one." Art scribbled in the air with his finger, purple light following in its path and he reached out towards the man. An instant later, Art groaned in pain and dropped to a knee, clutching his temples. The man laughed.

"You children really have no idea what you've blundered into. I am not 'a' Protection mage, you little morons., I am 'the' Protection mage."

"Any ideas, Zack?" Tabitha asked.

"I think we need to—"

The Master of Protection lunged toward him, knife first. Zack twirled his staff to deflect the blow, but the man blocked it with his other forearm. The force of Zack's swing should have broken his wrist, but instead the staff bounced off like it had struck stone and Zack stumbled a step backwards. Tabitha rushed forward and lashed out with her flail, but it crashed against a shield. The Master of Protection's knife slid in between Zack's ribs.

"No more ideas from you," the man said, yanking the blade back out.

Blinking back tears from the pain, Zack clutched at the wound and felt warm and wet blood against the skin of his hand. Life told him what had been damaged inside, but he was finding it hard to breathe and he couldn't concentrate.

Art and Tabitha were flanking the Protection mage, striking at him with coordination born of training and trust, but the attacks bounced off a continuous stream of shields and they struggled to avoid the backlash from their own weapons as often as from his knives.

Across the workshop, the others battled against the Master of Movement and his wooden soldiers, four of which were now aflame. Kimmy lashed out with more and more heat, while Bast used every inch of his speed and training to dodge hammer swings aimed for his head. Charlie and Max were being herded into a corner by more of the mannequins.

Against the wall, Jackie was still trapped behind a magical barrier, injured and alone.

And Zack was on his knees, bleeding out.

CHAPTER 13

No. They needed him.

Zack reached for Life, but between the pain and his shallow breaths, it slipped through away and the sounds of the ongoing battle clashed around him. The worries and doubts that lived in the corners of his mind flooded out. What kind of Lifer was he if he couldn't even look after himself? What would happen to his friends without him? Why was he so unprepared and weak that it took one hit to drop him? And woven through the thoughts, pain.

But he knew what to do with those thoughts. He reached for them, making these sharp rocks into the handholds he'd use to pull himself out of this pit. He reached for Life again, responding to the doubts, fears and the pain, with the only answer that ever worked: this is why I have to do it right.

His mind calmed and Life responded to his call, flowing inward and mending the damage that had been done. As his skin knitted itself closed, he gripped his staff and regained his feet. He was okay. If he held his focus, his magic would keep him going as long as the Life in his body held out.

His eyes widened at the idea: as long as the Life in his body held out.

"There's no trick to this," he said to Art and Tabitha, "we just need to wear him out. Eventually, his shields will fall or that barrier around Jackie will."

The man scoffed at him.

"You are out in the deep waters, boy. You have no idea what a master of the Tower is capable of doing."

"I probably don't," Zack replied, "but I know you're human, just like the rest of us and you use your Life to feed your shields. You're going to run out."

"Not before you run out of blood." The Master of Protection leapt at him, cutting down in a wide arc.

Rather than parry, Zack dodged to his left and lashed out with his staff at the man's legs. The blow bounced off a shield and jerked strangely in his hand. If Zack hadn't been ready, the staff might have spun in his wrist and struck him in the head, but he followed the odd energy and brought the weapon back around.

"You sure about this plan, mate?" Art asked as he squared up against the man.

"Nope," Zack replied, "but it's all I've got."

"That's good enough for me." Tabitha choked up on the length of her chain and charged the Master of Protection.

He ignored her and lunged at Art, landing a slice across his upper left arm. While Art hissed in pain, Tabitha's flail bounced off yet another shield, but shortening the chain saved her from wearing its returning arc in the face. It glanced off her shoulder, though and she winced at the impact. It was still the only plan Zack had, so he thrust forward with his staff.

Nearby in the workshop, Kimmy's flames had spread to one of the timber piles and smoke poured up towards the ceiling.

"Quit it with the fire, Kimmy." Bast desperately rolled away from a swing that would have shattered his collarbone. "They aren't going to burn up before they take this whole place with us."

"I could make the fire hotter," Kimmy replied.

"No!" Bast turned to shout at her and the Master of Movement's hammer struck him in the calf. He grunted. "Use your damn axe."

Kimmy scowled but she shook her hand and the fire surrounding it dissipated. Gripping her axe with two hands, she waited for the closest mannequin to approach before swinging at it with her full weight. The broad blade cut into its upper arm and, while it didn't chop all the way through, it left a splintering crack. She pulled the axe back with a determined cry and swung again.

Charlie and Max were running out of space to manoeuvre, with three wooden soldiers herding them into a corner. One of the mannequins, wielding a long chisel, stabbed at Charlie over and over. She had dodged it so far, but that had left her an easy target for the hammer and saw the other two held and she was slowing. The two wolves had little to show for their efforts. They had left the wooden creatures splintered and scratched, but being outnumbered and boxed in meant they couldn't repeat their successful attack against the first soldier.

The mannequin thrust the chisel towards Charlie's head and she leapt to the side to avoid it, but her landing was clumsy and her front left paw folded under her body. The mannequin with the hammer loomed over her and swung down to strike the back of her neck, but with a howl, Max launched herself at the creature. Her jaws snapped around its arm, knocking the hammer strike astray and the mannequin spun. Max's weight carried them both around and down, but as the wooden soldier fell, it punched Max in the ribs. As if sensing the opportunity, the other mannequins turned away from Charlie to where Max had become pinned under the heavy wooden figure.

Charlie howled and russet light collected around her. The mannequin with the chisel held it above Max, ready to plunge it into her thrashing chest, when it was ripped off the ground. Where a wolf had been lying on the workshop floor, a seven-foot brown bear was now rending its long claws through the wooden soldier's body. The mannequin reversed its chisel, attempting to stab behind it and the soldier with the saw slashed at Charlie's body, but she held strong to her target. Carefully, she dragged her left claw to its shoulder joint and, despite the saw cutting her twice more in her side, with a roar, she tore the mannequin apart. Its broken and motionless body clattered on the ground.

The strike Bast had taken to his leg was not too serious, but it slowed him. And he was already not fast enough.

"I know you," he said to the man, "I've seen you on gate duty. Harry?"

"Harvey," the Master of Movement replied, "and I know you. Stefan has done well with his training, but you can't win. Why even try?"

Bast fended him away with his rapier, using the extra inches it gave him to prevent the man from coming straight at him.

"You think I don't know you're faster? That only matters if I'm trying to beat you."

"You'll be dead long before any of them can help you." Harvey flashed towards him in a blur.

Bast threw himself to the side, panting as he landed, while the mage's missed swing landed the hammer on a workbench with a loud crash. Bast scrambled to his feet, his rapier at the ready again.

"We'll see."

The Master of Protection leapt toward Tabitha, slashing out with his knives. Tabitha caught one in the length of her chain, but the other nicked her along the hip. It was a shallow cut, but it wasn't the first.

Zack darted forward and snapped a well-timed strike to the man's knee. As it had every time, it thumped against a silvery shield and Zack braced to prevent it from bouncing backwards and striking him. Like Tabitha, he bore half a dozen cuts and scratches, but it was the ache in his wrist that hurt the most.

Tabitha and Art charged at their foe and Zack fell back. With the Master of Protection distracted, he gathered two threads of Life and pushed them towards his friends, closing as many of their wounds as he could before the man turned back on him.

Unlike them, the Master had not been harmed. None of their attacks had made it past his shields. But that didn't mean they had lost yet. Zack dropped the threads of Life and sent his magical sense towards the man. He may have been unharmed, but his defensive magic was draining him.

The Master of Protection turned and rushed toward him. Zack frantically knocked away the knives before launching a counterattack that, yet again, bounced off the man's shield.

"It's working," Zack said through gritted teeth, "we're draining him."

The Master sneered at him and attacked again. Zack's aching wrists spun his staff too slowly and the knife slipped past, cutting a deep slash into his shoulder. It was going to be a matter of who could outlast who.

Across the warehouse, Kimmy's axe found its mark, chopping deep into the broken part of the mannequin's shoulder. The blow cleaved its arm from its body and forced the crack deeper into its torso. Still, it marched on, its two blazing allies at its side and Kimmy was forced back as she readied her axe for another swing.

The centre mannequin lunged at her with its remaining arm and Kimmy kicked it back with the sole of her boot. The leather protected her foot, but the flames from the wooden soldier licked up her leg. Kimmy gritted her teeth through the pain and, as the mannequin stumbled back, she used her momentum and brought her axe around in a low, broad sweep. The blade crunched straight through a second mannequin's knee joint and it toppled over, flailing and burning on the floor.

However, the blow's impact caused Kimmy to stumble and she fell on her knee. Off balance and with her back to the third mannequin, she offered no defence as it leapt at her from behind and buried its chisel deep into her shoulder. Kimmy wrenched her body away with a scream, pulling the length of the chisel from her body and swung her axe in retaliation. She struck the mannequin in its hand, shattering it and sending the bloodied chisel scattering across the floor. Kimmy stumbled to her feet and shifted her axe painfully as the two remaining wooden soldiers lumbered toward her.

Nearby, Bast was now panting heavily and the Master of Movement bared his teeth in a cruel smile. He pointed past Bast at Kimmy with his hammer.

"There's one friend who isn't coming to your rescue. Even if she nearly burned down my workshop before she fell."

Bast kept his eyes locked on Harvey, whose smile was knocked from his face as half a wooden soldier slammed into the back of his head. Charlie roared from where she had hurled it, standing amidst splintered and broken mannequins, her fur matted in blood. Bast darted forward and skewered him through the thigh with his rapier. Charlie and Max bound towards him, but he pointed over his shoulder.

"Help Kimmy out. I got this."

"Only because you outnumber us." Harvey shifted his weight to his uninjured leg. "Perhaps it's time to even those odds." Orange light collected around his fingers and a sliver of grey light opened behind him.

"I don't think so." Bast strained to reply through his pain. His hands glowed with his own orange light and the gate closed before it opened. "I like this ratio fine."

Harvey snarled at him, lashing out with his hammer while still trying to force the gate open, but Bast's magic held.

Zack's vision blurred, which was one of the earlier signs that he was running out of gas. He had decided against opening a channel to connect the three of them and was instead pushing his Life out to Tabitha and Art to heal their wounds but also to slow their growing fatigue. And it was taking a toll.

The Master of Protection leapt toward him, his knives ready. Zack spun his quarterstaff to catch the blades and Tabitha dashed in with an attack from behind.

But it had been a feint.

The head of Tabitha's flail ricocheted off the man's shield and flew back toward her. The head missed her face by an inch, but the chain wound around her left arm, catching her in a tangle. In an instant, the Master bounced off his toes and spun around, slicing across her throat with one of his blades. Tabitha's eyes went distant and she stumbled backwards, a thin line of blood gushing from the cut.

Zack ran towards her, gathering Life with each step, but the older mage moved to get in his way. Zack didn't slow or even move to defend himself and the side of the man's dagger found his arm as he ran past. The Master of Protection followed, ready to strike at Zack's unprotected back, when Art slid in between them, his raised sword catching the blades.

Doing his best to ignore what was happening behind him, Zack wove threads of Life into Tabitha's wound. There were so many blood vessels, nerves and minor muscles to repair and he prioritised stopping the blood loss. Tabitha's skin was pale, even in the dim light of the workshop, but her pulse calmed as Zack continued.

Behind him, Art found his feet and pushed the mage back a few steps. He swung his broadsword at the man's shoulder and it still stopped against his magical shield. The hilt twisted in Art's hands and the blade bounced back, nicking his calf.

"You're alone now, boy," the man said with a sneer, "you can't think to beat the Master of Protection in a duel."

Art corrected his grip and thrust the point of his sword at the man's chest. The steely light caught the strike and pulled him forward and to the side. The mage cut at him with both knives as Art stumbled past, slicing into his arm and thigh. Art pulled his sword back into place and turned, ready to strike again.

"Really?" the Master of Protection said with a mixture of disdain and genuine surprise. "It's okay to surrender. You must be in so much pain. And be so tired."

Art stayed silent, his eyes fixed on the man. He feinted a low swing before twisting his wrist and stance to bring the blade high, but the attack was too slow and the mage parried it away with one of his knives. Art didn't stop. Thrust, slash, thrust, he kept up his attack, but each time, the man flicked them away with one or both of his knives.

"Enough!" the mage shouted. "I will not warn you again. If that is the best you can do, you're done."

But Art smiled and threw himself at the man, bringing his sword down in a brutal, double-handed swing. The man crossed his knives above him to catch the sword, but the strength of Art's blow snapped one off at the hilt and knocked the other away. Art's sword continued down, cleaving through the mage's shoulder and into his torso.

The Master of Protection collapsed to his knees and looked up at Art, his eyes staring wildly.

"I probably am in a lot of pain." Art yanked his blade free and the man fell forward, where he lay in a growing pool of blood. "But I switched that part of my head off a little while ago."

Zack had stopped Tabitha's bleeding and was moving on to the trachea.

"Is she okay?" Art asked, stepping behind him.

"She will be." Zack was running on fumes and could already taste metal in his mouth. "I've got this. Go get Jackie. The barrier should be down now."

Art turned and ran toward his sister while Zack mended the cartilage in Tabitha's throat. She took a long, steady breath and wrapped her arms around him.

"I thought I was a goner this time."

Zack helped her back onto her feet.

"It was close. But try not to talk. I'll need to have another go at it when we get out of here. And I think I'm going to have a few more patients on top of that."

Around the room, all his friends were in need of healing. Kimmy was covered in burns and cuts, pulling apart the last of the mannequins with Charlie and Max, themselves covered in wounds. Bast was locked in his duel with Harvey, limping as he moved and Art had likely done extra damage to himself by turning off his sense of pain.

"We'd better get over there," he said to Tabitha, "we're not finished yet."

Art moved through where the barrier had been and tore the restraints off Jackie. He pulled her up and threw his arms around her in a fierce squeeze. With much less force, she returned the hug, her weakened arms barely lifting higher than his waist.

"You're okay." Art pulled back from the hug without quite letting go. "You're okay, aren't you?"

Jackie gave a soft nod and awkwardly pulled the tape from her mouth. When she spoke, her voice was faint and dry.

"Yeah, I'm okay."

"Good." Art smiled. "And see, no matter what kind of magic you have, sometimes it's a big brother's job to protect his little sister."

Bast glanced over his shoulder at the reunion before turning back to his foe. Both of them were slowing as the wear from their physical duel and their efforts over the mage's attempted gate built up.

"It's over," Bast said, "you've lost."

"I decide when it's over," Harvey replied.

With a gesture and a flicker of orange light, three pointed lengths of wood whipped off the nearest workbench at Bast. He dropped to the ground, but they were moving so fast that one gouged into his shoulder as he fell. The other two kept flying, streaking towards where Art stood with his back turned.

Jackie's eyes widened and she threw up her hand past Art. A shield of weak light flickered into place, but while one of the two stakes bounced astray off its surface, the other broke through. She brought her hands back and pushed Art away an instant before the piece of sharpened timber would have pierced his spine.

Instead, it embedded itself in her chest, knocking her down onto her back.

Art rushed back to Jackie's side, his lips trembling. Blood oozed from around the wood, staining her school shirt. She stared up at him.

"Zack!" Art screamed.

Jackie squeezed his hand. "I. Protect. You."

"No, no, no. Zack!"

Tabitha pushed Zack free of her and braced herself against some shelving.

"Go."

Zack ran towards Jackie and Art, wobbling on unsteady legs to close a distance that now seemed so far. Jackie's grip loosened and her hand dropped away from Art's. When Zack made it to her side, her blank eyes peered up at the ceiling. He fought against the dizziness and turned his senses toward her. There was still some Life there, in the muscle, in the blood, but it was different; it no longer belonged to the whole.

Art took a step back, his confused eyes darting around the room before they locked onto the Master of Movement. Confusion melted before certainty, shock evaporated into anger and he strode toward him.

Zack wrenched flows of Life from around him, as much as his fatigued mind could gather and he poured them into Jackie. He slid the wooden stake out and threaded Life into the wound. It responded. The muscle, the bone and the heart repaired under Life's urging. But that was only tissue. Something greater was missing.

Harvey held out his hammer, ready to defend himself, but purple light gathered in Art's eyes as he strode closer. Harvey grimaced and shook his head away to the side, whispering, "No."

He forced his face back around to Art and made as if to lunge at him before he instead collapsed to his knees. His hammer clattered to the ground and he grabbed the sides of his head, screaming. Harvey's scream was more one of terror than pain and his eyes flickered around the room, hovering for moments on shadows and then twitching away again.

Art, his eyes now ablaze in purple light, was screaming too. His was one of rage and anguish and, when he reached the man, Art pushed Harvey's hands away, holding the man's head between his own.

Zack threaded more flows of Life into Jackie, closing the wound and reshaping blood vessels and nerves. He coaxed her heart to beat and guided the blood flow around her body. His thoughts grew slow and clumsy, so he dropped his precise threads and poured streams of Life into her instead. Perhaps there was a sliver of her left and, if her body was well enough, that sliver could climb its way out of the dark. His wounds reopened and blood seeped down his body, but he ignored it and persisted. Jackie's cells brimmed with Life, but her body lay still. A little more magic, a few more seconds, maybe her chest would rise. Pain pulsed across his body. And then a hand touched his shoulder.

"Stop, Zack." Charlie's voice was soft in his ear. "She's gone. We can't lose you too."

Zack took a breath and released Life. The pain lessened. He looked away from Jackie to Charlie. She was human again and covered in dozens of minor wounds that had nothing to do with the tears in her eyes. Charlie pointed past him to Art.

"He needs you now."

Zack limped over to where Art stood, still holding the older mage's head between his hands. Both had stopped screaming, although the mage's mouth was still open in terror. Zack nudged toward the man with his mind. There was nothing there.

Zack placed his hands over Art's and pulled them apart. Harvey's body slumped to the floor and Art looked across at Zack, dazed and disoriented.

"C'mon, mate." Zack squeezed his hand. "We need to get her out of here."

Kimmy's errant flames grew as they consumed more of the plentiful fuel and Bast forced himself upright to coax open a gate home. With Zack by his side, Art gathered Jackie's tiny body into his arms. They left the workshop and all that was in it, to be taken by the fire.

CHAPTER 14

Silence clung to the living room like a giant squid, threatening to drown them in their shock and sorrow. Charlie wrapped her arms around Max, her face wet with tears. Kimmy sat next to Bast, holding his hand in two of hers, both staring at the ground. Tabitha stood leaning on the kitchen counter, chewing a long strand of her light-brown hair and looking past them through the back window. And Zack sat on the edge of the couch, elbows on his knees and head between his hands. His mind was so full of thoughts it might as well have been empty, a cupboard of dark clutter he might lose himself in.

His eyes drifted to the closed door of Art's bedroom, behind which his best friend had retreated with his sister's body. The cyclone of thoughts slowed to a violent storm and the events of the workshop played over again and again in his mind. And as they did, they began to beg questions.

"If only I could have—" he muttered to himself.

Tabitha cut him off before he could continue; her voice soft but still coarse from the wound Zack hadn't finished healing.

"Don't, Zack. This isn't even close to your fault. Just don't."

"But if I—"

She interrupted him again.

"Hadn't needed to save my life? If I hadn't let my guard down, you might have been able to save her?"

That was absurd, Zack thought. Besides, he should have been strong enough to save both of them.

Tabitha continued before he could object.

"A lot of things could have changed what happened."

"I could have stopped those stakes somehow," Bast said, staring forward into space.

"I could have helped Bast out instead of Kimmy." Charlie bit her lip as she spoke.

"Art could have moved Jackie away," Kimmy added.

"Kimmy!" Charlie looked at her in horror.

A look of realisation, followed by a rare one of shame, appeared on Kimmy's face.

"No, I didn't mean it like that. Just that so many things were all happening all at once. Shit, I didn't mean it like that."

"I know, Sis." Bast pulled her towards him in a tight hug.

Art's door opened and he stepped out into the room. His eyes were clear of both tears and the rage he'd shown half an hour before.

"There are some things I need to do today before it gets too late." He spoke in a calm voice.

"Of course, Art," Tabitha said, stepping toward him, "anything you need."

"No." He shook his head. "That's not what I mean. That'll be later. We need to follow protocol for Jackie's death."

"Protocol?" Charlie looked confused. "What are you talking about?"

"Jackie's dead," Art said more plainly than he should have been able to, "and when somebody dies in Australia, there is a whole paper trail behind that. If that doesn't happen, it risks the Silence."

"Who bloody cares about the Silence?" Bast said.

"The Tower does," Zack said, catching up to Art's thoughts, "and if we can be blamed for endangering the Silence, they can come at us more openly. Or at any of our families who might know too much."

"Exactly," Art said, "so, I need to go and create that paper trail."

"Do you need any help?" Tabitha sounded lost.

"Just his." Art pointed to Zack. "I know what I need to do. The Tower taught that to me. I never thought the first time I'd do it for real would be…"

Charlie muffled her sobs behind her hands. Art shook his head.

"No, that's for later. Zack, I know you're tired, but can you patch us up enough to not look like massacre victims. Then we need to get changed and get moving."

"Of course, mate." Zack moved to follow Art.

"Are you sure you don't need us for anything?" Tabitha said.

"One thing," Art said, turning around, "I could use some help carrying her to the van."

⸻ ⸻ ⸻

He had channelled more Life that day than he ever had before and the partially healed wounds scattered across his body were threatening to reopen. But neither were the true source of Zack's fatigue. No. With the streetlights turning on behind him as he followed Art up the driveway, the thought of what came next made Zack exhausted with despair. But then, he considered his friend, who had spent the last few hours moving from hospital to ambulance station to police station with methodical discipline.

"You ready for this?" Zack asked.

Art nodded, without looking back.

"Last one. For today at least."

He unlocked the front door and Zack followed him inside.

"It's about time, young lady!" Art's mother called from another room, her voice more cheery than her words suggested. "You'd better have a good reason for ignoring my messages."

Zack bit his lip to distract from the pain in his heart, but Art's face remained stoic. They followed the voice and found both of Art's parents in the kitchen, his mother cooking dinner and his father at a nearby table with his laptop open.

"Hi honey," his mother said when Art and Zack entered the room, "Jackie didn't pass on whether you'd be staying for dinner or that you'd be bringing a guest. Hi, Zack, you're of course always welcome to stay for dinner. It would just be nice if either of my children used their phones to let me know their plans. Even a simple 'I'm not dead in a ditch' would be nice from time to time. Where is she, anyway?"

"Are you alright, mate?" Art's father looked at Zack with concern, which was reasonable given that Zack was worried he was going to faint, throw up or both.

Before Zack could respond, Art traced his fingers through the air and spoke the strange arcane syllables of an incantation. His parents furrowed their brows at him in confusion, but only for a moment, before their eyes lost focus and they ceased moving or speaking.

"Mum," Art spoke with precise enunciation. "Sit at the table next to Dad."

His mother complied, bringing the wooden spoon she held with her as she walked across the room. Zack slipped past her and turned off the stove.

Using the same clear tone, Art spoke to them again.

"Jackie died today." And he told them the lie that he had told several times already that day. The lie that had been captured across the police report, the paramedics' notes and multiple hospital records. The lie that would keep them safe.

Jackie had been walking a few blocks from the high school to meet up with Art and Zack. She saw a little boy lose his hat in the wind and chase it into the street. A car was speeding by and it wasn't slowing down. Jackie pushed the boy to safety and was hit by the car instead before it sped off. She died instantly and painlessly. Art and Zack saw it happen, but there was nothing they could do. Art called his mother, who then called his father and they all met up at the hospital, where they formally identified Jackie and completed some forms.

Zack had heard versions of this several times now, but this was by far the worst. Both Art's parents were silent and still, their eyes fixed on an invisible point in space, but with every word of Art's, their demeanour changed. Their mouths slipped open, their lips trembled, their shoulders slumped and their backs curled. Within moments, without them quite knowing, they had been withered by grief.

"And then you came home with me from the hospital and both decided to go to bed," Art finished. "Now, go up to bed and sleep until morning."

Still entranced, Art's parents rose and followed Art upstairs. A few minutes later, he returned and approached the stove.

"We need to get rid of all this. Half-cooked dinner isn't in their version of today anymore."

Zack nodded and the two spent the next fifteen minutes cleaning the kitchen and throwing the evidence in the outside bin.

"I think that's everything," Art said after he had replaced the kitchen bin liner.

He sat down on the living room couch, and Zack sat beside him. They were silent for some time before Art's gaze wandered up the stairs.

"She would have hated what I did to them tonight."

"Maybe," Zack replied, "but she would have understood why you had to do it. To keep them safe. If anybody would have appreciated that, it's her."

"Safe." Art's top lip turned in disgust. "It should have been me today, not her."

"Don't." Zack shook his head. "Look, if you want to play the 'what could I have done differently' game, I'm with you. I already played a few rounds with the others. But don't take that last moment away from her. Jackie made her choice. She wanted to save you."

"Stupid choice," Art replied, "She's worth a thousand of me."

"Still her choice."

Silence descended upon them again and Zack faced his friend.

"You've done what you need to do for tonight. You can stop whatever it is you've done to your mind."

Art replied without looking back at him, "I didn't turn the feelings off.

I just trapped them behind a wall. And I can feel them battering against it. There's a lot there." Art turned to face him. "I could make it all go away, you know. A couple of surgical strikes and it won't hurt."

Zack squeezed him on the shoulder.

"I wouldn't blame you if you did."

"I would. That pain in there, that's all I've got left of her. Okay, here we go."

There was a faint flash of purple behind Art's eyes and then tears flooded from them. "Oh god, Zack. She's gone."

Zack opened his arms and Art collapsed into them, sobbing. His chest heaved with the strength of his crying and all that was left for Zack was to hold onto him, tears streaming down his own face. No more words were spoken and about half an hour later, Art passed out. Zack laid him out on the couch and found a blanket to cover him before crawling under another blanket on the nearby recliner. Sleep was whispering to him as well, but he checked his phone first. There was a message from Tabitha.

I hope it's going ok. We're all here for you if you need us.

He tapped out a reply. *All done for the night. He's asleep now. I'm going to stay here in case he needs me in the morning. Are you all ok? I can come and heal if you need it.*

We're good. Don't forget to look after yourself while you're looking after him.

I'm fine. I didn't just lose a sister.

We all lost her, Zack. Stay safe, c u soon.

Zack thought about replying to assure Tabitha he was okay, but his eyelids were getting heavy and he was too tired to lie.

A discoloured station wagon that had seen better decades picked them up from the side of an Arkansas highway. Bast's long legs claimed him the front passenger seat, so Zack squeezed into the backseat with Tabitha and Kimmy, while Charlie crouched with Max behind them. Their driver, a gruff woman with broad shoulders and short hair, had said less than ten words since she had pulled up, but her frequent glances at them through the rear vision mirror spoke loudly of suspicion.

"We might regret not bringing a Mind mage with us," Charlie whispered over the backseat.

"He needed to be with his parents to manage the funeral prep and make sure no flags get raised," Zack replied.

"I think he needs some time with them as well, for him," Tabitha added.

The trees lining the highway were a rich green, swallowing up the late spring sunshine and entirely at odds with the vibe inside the car. Zack had spent the last day and a half healing their injuries and, while there was no scratch nor scar left behind on the surface, the sharpest wound of all remained fresh and open. Jackie was gone, but only parts of Zack's brain knew it. Other parts looked for her in the corner of his eye, waited for her voice when others stopped speaking, or even tried to find space for her in a station wagon when one arrived to pick them up. But she wasn't there. She would not speak. And there was not enough room in the vehicle to fit her absence.

At some stage, the driver left the highway, but Zack didn't notice until they turned again onto a gravel road. The car slowed and, as they rounded behind some tall trees, a trailer park came into view. The signage reading 'Free Acres' was desperate for fresh paint and the No Vacancy sign hung from rusted and cobwebbed chains.

Their driver pulled up outside an old brick building that might have been a reception office and switched off the car before turning to face them.

"Word's got out about you lot and the right people have vouched, which is why you're welcome here at all. But you're Tower, so don't expect it to be a particularly warm welcome. Keep your thoughts friendly and your hands to yourself."

"What is this place?" Tabitha asked.

"Nuh-uh," the woman replied, "I'm the driver, not the tour guide. Now, follow me."

They clambered out of the station wagon and filed in behind the woman as she led them past the brick building and deeper into the park. There were only a few rows of trailers and, if the rows ended where they seemed to, Zack estimated a total of fifty or sixty trailers. And despite the sign hanging out front, several appeared empty. Closer to the centre, space had been given over to a vegetable garden and ripe produce hung from well-ordered rows of plants.

Zack focused on these details, which allowed him to avoid the gazes of the park's residents. Dozens of eyes followed the group's movement down the path: some curious, some appraising and others openly hostile. One elderly man hurried a trio of preschool-aged children inside his trailer, while another man leant against the front of his car and spat on the ground as the group passed.

Kimmy's body tensed when she saw him, but Charlie slipped a hand into hers and gave it a gentle squeeze. Zack was glad the Traveller's message had included the instruction not to bring weapons. Not that his friends needed them to be a threat, but if this was their reception arriving unarmed, the sight of a blade or two could have lit the match. And Zack couldn't blame them. From the locals' perspectives, he and his friends were the Tower and there was good reason to be fearful of the Tower.

The Traveller was waiting for them at the side of the path, in front of a very run-down caravan. Unlike the other residents, his eyes were filled with sympathy and concern.

"Thank you, Monica. I've got it from here," he said to their chaperone before addressing Zack and his friends, "I am so very sorry. If I… Please, come inside."

The Traveller ushered them inside and any idle thought Zack had that the dilapidated facade hid some kind of illusion-masked luxury was dispelled by the sight of torn couches, foldable chairs and a lopsided picnic table.

"I love what you've done with the place," Kimmy said in a flat voice.

The Traveller returned a faint smile.

"The people who come to stay at this park typically have so little, it would be selfish to claim any of the better furniture for myself. Especially, when I rarely stay overnight. Sit anywhere you like." He claimed one of the folding chairs and sat with his back against the wall.

Zack sat on the edge of a sofa, ignoring the spring pressing against him through the thin cushion. When the others had taken their own seats, the Traveller leant forward.

"I regret coming to you all with this plan." He shook his head as he spoke. "I accepted that there were risks, but this…? How could they do something like that? We should call this off and focus on making sure the rest of you are as safe as possible."

"What would that involve?" Charlie asked.

"Are you serious?" Kimmy curled her lip. "Running?"

"I'm only asking the question," Charlie replied.

"We would hide you," the Traveller answered, "there are places like this scattered all over the world. After some time, you could get new identities and, if you kept your heads down, you would be safe."

"I don't know." Bast scratched his chin. "By the time I convinced my dad and brothers that I wasn't delusional, the Tower would probably have already caught us. I mean, they've got to be looking for us now, right?"

"Art!" Tabitha bolted upright.

"Calm down." The Traveller held out his hand in reassurance. "According to my contacts in the Tower, there's nothing unusual going on."

"According to Mr Smith, you mean," Kimmy said.

"Not anymore, I'm afraid. Losing Jackie was too much for him. He's cut and run."

"So, no alarm bells or anything?" Tabitha asked.

"Not that have been passed on to me, no." The Traveller looked at each of them. "Your message was understandably short, but if you can,

I'd like to hear more about what happened and then maybe we can piece together some new information."

Zack retold how he and Art had searched for Jackie before finding the note from Mr Smith. His heart ached with each word and he focussed on the minutest of details to distract himself from the pain. He was grateful when Tabitha, aided by Kimmy's regular interjections, took over the story and Charlie shuffled closer, slipping her arm around him, as the recounting reached its awful conclusion.

"Thank you. I just…" The Traveller wiped at his eyes and sat straighter in his chair. "Let's consider that you did indeed kill the Masters of Movement and Protection. What does that mean?"

"The Thirteen are now the Eleven?" Bast asked.

"Yes," the Traveller replied, "although, maybe not for long. If my theory is correct and if the Master of Plant was linked to the Tower back in March, then that means that Animal was linked in April and the now-deceased Master of Movement was linked only a few weeks ago. But Protection would be next. Meaning that in a little over a week, they could replace him."

"So, taking on the Thirteen is like whack-a-mole." Kimmy threw up her hands.

"Yes, perhaps. But you have provided an opportunity I've never had before. The remaining members of the Thirteen will have to recruit a replacement. I can't imagine that can be done without creating some disruption to the status quo. Maybe my contacts will notice something and if we're lucky, we'll know the identity of another one of the Thirteen."

"We can keep an ear out, too," Charlie added.

The Traveller shook his head.

"That is very brave, but I can't recommend it. It would be far too dangerous for you to go back there."

"So, we do nothing?" Tabitha asked.

"Take some time," the Traveller replied, "grieve. Support your friend. I'll let you know what I find out and we can discuss the next steps then."

"Feels like you're sidelining us," Kimmy said through narrowed eyes.

"I'm not," he replied, "you make your own choices. But I was reckless with what I encouraged you to do and I share in the blame for what followed. Please let me gather more information and I promise I will reach out to you again."

Tabitha looked around at the others before answering.

"Okay, but promise to contact us when you know something."

"Deal." The Traveller stood and walked them out of the trailer. "And it's not enough, but please tell Art I am truly sorry."

CHAPTER 15

Zack's mother blinked back tears as she smoothed an imagined wrinkle in the shoulder of Zack's suit. He had spent the night at their place so the four of them, Ellen included, could travel together to the church.

It was larger than the cemetery chapel where his family had held the service for his grandmother and, unlike the chapel, the church was full. Zack didn't recognise most of the people, although he did see some faces that could have been Art and Jackie's cousins and there were dozens of students in their high school uniforms, chaperoned by a few teary-eyed teachers.

"There's Sandra." Zack's mother used her chin to point to where Art's mother was speaking with a group of five women. "I don't know how she's holding it together so well. I can't imagine."

Zack's father pulled her closer as they shuffled towards an empty pew. When he saw Art standing alone near the front, Zack broke away from his family and approached his friend.

"Hey, mate." Zack wrapped his arms around Art in a tight hug.

Art hugged back. "Hey, thanks for coming."

"Of course I came."

"I know," Art said, stepping back from the hug, "it's just what you say at these things, apparently. I've said it like a hundred times already."

"I can imagine," Zack replied, "there are a lot more people than I expected. Not that Jackie isn't worth it or anything, it's just…"

"That she didn't really make a splash, yeah." Art nodded. "A lot of them are here for Mum and Dad. Some of the kids are only here for a day off school, but others? I think the story I made up has drawn in a few extras. They see her as a hero for saving that kid."

"Well, if they knew what a hero she really was, the line would stretch down the block."

Art nodded again, his lips tight.

"I'll be happy tomorrow when this is all over and I can start mourning her my way."

"And that is?" Zack asked.

"Tomorrow." Art's voice was firm. "Today is about my parents and maintaining the damn Silence. Speaking of which, my dad's calling me over. I'll see you after, yeah?"

"For sure," Zack replied, "and if you need anything, ask."

"Thanks, mate." Art squeezed his shoulder and walked to sit in the front pew.

On his way back to his family, Zack spotted Charlie, Bast, Kimmy and Tabitha sitting together. Charlie lifted her hand in a gentle wave and Zack returned it. There was a woman sitting next to Tabitha. With her hair hidden under a scarf and a hefty amount of foundation, it took him a moment to recognise Nell. She met his gaze and touched two fingers to her lips before reclaiming Tabitha's hand in her own.

Part of him wanted to sit with them, but Art was right. Today was about letting the normal world say goodbye to the Jackie they knew. Saying goodbye to the real one would come after. He claimed his seat beside Ellen as the minister stood at the lectern and began to speak.

"We are gathered here today to celebrate the life of Jacqueline Elizabeth Stevenson." The minister's tone was soft and, as he spoke about the pain and confusion of losing someone so young, the sounds of grief from the pews often overwhelmed his words.

Zack's mind drifted as the ceremony continued, first to the recent memories of his grandmother's funeral and then to thoughts of what his own might be. For two years now, he had been facing magical creatures and renegade spellcasters with his friends and, while he had always known it was dangerous, it had never truly felt like death was a possibility. Not even when they had been captured, tortured and lost in a snowstorm. But it certainly did now. Zack had seen the devastation Jackie's death had wrought on her parents. He could still see it now in the church and he thought of what his own death might do to his. Part of what had motivated him in the Tower had been what he could offer his family, how he could use what he learned and gained to improve their lives, but now he wondered about what he might take from them. Did he have that right? Did he still have a choice?

His attention was drawn back to the hall when Art approached the lectern.

"Thank you all for coming today. Mum and Dad have let me give the eulogy and I'm grateful for that because I would like to let you all know about my sister, Jackie." Art's voice carried through the church with calm strength. "I've known Jackie her whole life and, since I can't remember much from before she was born, she basically knew me all of mine. And nobody I've ever met can or will be as annoying as she was, because only somebody who knows you, as well as she knew me, could ever compete."

Laughter tittered through the pews, but as Art continued to speak, the sound of his voice became muffled.

Sorry about that, guys. Art's voice sounded clear in Zack's mind while he looked straight at Zack and then across to the others. *I'm giving the normies what they expect to hear, but I can't let her go without speaking the truth, even if it is in silence.*

We're with you, brother. Bast replied with his thoughts. The others nodded and Nell sat straighter in the pew, looking intently at Art.

Art's lips continued moving as he spoke his muted words and his thoughts flowed out. *Jackie was so much smaller and younger than us, so quiet and reserved, that it took me far too long to see just how strong and brave she was. I wondered, in our early days with the Tower, whether I should have found some way to keep her away from what we were doing, to keep her safe. I've been asking myself that same question again these last days. But I know those are selfish thoughts, about protecting my sister, a sister who means so much to me.*

No. She taught me that she was more than just my sister. So very much more. She was a young woman with a role to play in keeping her friends and the world safe. A Protection mage who stood like a fortress in the face of danger. She was our Viking spearmaiden, a freakin' Valkyrie who never backed down. She had our backs and our fronts and our flanks. Her last act was to save me. I'll never forgive her for that. I'll never be able to thank her for it. And I'll never be able to live up to it.

Art's thoughts stopped for a moment and Zack wiped the tears from his eyes with the back of his wrist.

Zack, she loved having you as her second brother. One that showed her that, unlike her loud, pushy brother, quiet and calm could still be strong. She idolised you a little, I think. Bast, you saw her strength and your confidence in her helped her find her own. She loved you for that. And girls, she adored you. You opened your arms to her and showed her what friendship was. The magic gave her faith in what she could do, but you three gave her faith in who she was.

She was the best of us. The strongest. The toughest. We are less without her. But whatever comes next, I will never stop loving her, missing her, or trying to live up to her example.

Goodbye Jacks.

Zack sniffled back against his tears and the sounds of the church returned to his ears. He heard a strange gulping sound and looked across to see Kimmy sobbing and crying into her hands. Charlie pulled her close, tears streaming down her face and the two clung to each other.

Art finished up his spoken eulogy with a similar sentiment and returned to sit between his parents, where they each wrapped an arm around him. The ceremony continued until, at last, it was time for the coffin to be carried outside. Art and his father stood on either side, supported by Jackie's uncle and three cousins. Zack had expected that but had not expected the surge of jealousy that roared up from his stomach. He and the others should be carrying her from here. She had trusted them to face danger with her.

But in the end, they had failed her. He had failed her. And perhaps it was right that it should be her family who looked after her from here. Zack waited as the church emptied, pew by pew, and followed behind with the others to watch on as the coffin was placed in the back of a waiting hearse and taken away.

It was Sunday when Art came back to the townhouse. Zack had not long returned from dinner at his grandfather's house when he heard Art's van pull up out front. Art entered with Tabitha behind him. She sat beside Zack on the couch while Art lugged a duffle through to his room.

"Bast is collecting the others," Tabitha said, "they should be here soon."

Zack nodded. "How was he on the drive over?"

"Hard to tell," Tabitha said, looking across at Art's bedroom door, "he seems mostly himself. A bit quieter and a bit more serious, but you'd expect that."

Art entered the room in a fresh t-shirt and dropped onto the other couch, putting his feet up on the coffee table.

"It was nice that Nell came to the funeral. I didn't get a chance to thank her on the day."

"Yeah, sorry," Tabitha replied, "she couldn't stay after, but she wanted to pay her respects. I hope you didn't mind."

"Nah, it was good of her." Art sat up straighter. "So, what's the deal there with you two?"

Tabitha waved him away.

"It's not important at the moment."

Art shook his head.

"It's super important. Good things happening is important."

Tabitha blushed.

"I don't know what it is, but it's nice. We've been catching up once or twice a week since we met. I really like her."

"That's great, Tabs." Art shot her a genuine smile.

Their phones pinged with a message on their group thread from Bast. *Incoming.*

A moment later, a gate swirled into being in the corner and Bast, Kimmy, Charlie and Max stepped through. They each found a place to sit and Zack pushed away the heart-aching thought that the room felt too empty.

"It's time to talk about next steps," Tabitha said once everybody was settled.

"I've been thinking about what the Traveller told us at Nell's place," Art said, "and about what Zack told me he said the other day. And I think we have a chance to take out the Thirteen."

There was a sharp intake of breaths.

"I get why you want revenge," Charlie replied, "but this—"

"I don't want revenge." Art stood up and paced to the front of the room to face them. "Honestly, I don't care about revenge. The guy who killed Jackie and the guy who helped him are dead. I don't want payback. I don't want to get even. I don't want an eye for an eye or any of that."

"So, why do you think we should take them out?" Tabitha asked.

Art's voice was calm when he responded.

"Because who they are means crap like this can happen. They can't be held to account, not when they are protected by power, secrecy and lies. And there's nobody to hold them accountable anyway. The only option is to remove them from power."

"You mean kill them," Zack said.

"Not necessarily," Art replied, "but probably, yeah."

"Mate, I get it." Bast leant forward. "Break the power structure. But I don't see how we stand a chance. If we manage to take them one or two at a time, which is the only way we'd have the slightest hope, they'll just replace them. Trav says they've probably already replaced the Protection one."

"No, they didn't." Charlie's eyes sparkled with fervour.

"What do you mean?" Tabitha looked across at her.

"The ritual was yesterday," Charlie replied, "but it didn't go ahead."

"Who told you that?" Bast asked.

"Oh, no." Zack guessed at what had happened. "You didn't."

Charlie nodded.

"Sure did. The place was busy as usual. People scurrying around to their assigned posts. But then something happened. Or didn't. The ritual got called off. All the liaisons were running up and down. Lots of attention in the Protection quarters."

"Are you out of your mind?" Tabitha screamed, her face red. "After everything that just happened, you went in there alone?"

Charlie rolled her eyes.

"I wasn't alone. Max came too. And there was too much going on for anybody to notice two field mice creeping around. And so, if the wise and wonderful Traveller is right, then the Thirteen is still down to eleven and at least one of them can't be replaced for a year."

Kimmy slapped her on the shoulder. "Amazing."

Before Tabitha could retort, Art continued, "Okay then. If that's true, then we have a window to defeat the remaining Masters and stop them from replacing their numbers. At the moment, that window closes in May, when they can replace the arseho… the Master of Movement."

"Just hold on a second!" Tabitha shot to her feet. "I think we're all getting a little carried away. We're talking about fighting the most powerful members of the Tower. We don't even know where they are."

"We know how to find one of them." Charlie held a gilded pearl between her fingers. "I picked it up while I was snooping."

Bast clapped. "One hundred percent deadly, Sis."

"Animal?" Zack asked.

Charlie nodded.

Zack counted through the months in his head.

"That would shrink the window to February."

Tabitha looked around at each of them, eyes wide with frustration and worry.

"The Traveller said—"

"Doesn't matter what the Traveller said," Kimmy interrupted, "we're not trading a bunch of secret leaders for a crazy homeless one. If the Traveller can help us, we'll use him, but this is on us. And the only leader we want is you."

"But—"

Kimmy interrupted her again, "No buts. The Thirteen have to be defeated and we're the only ones who have the knowledge and the ability to do it. And if you still need convincing, consider this: Art and I are on the same page."

Tabitha scanned the room, facing each of them in turn and as she did, her expression changed from worry to determination.

"Alright then. If we do this, we do it right. When possible, we give them a chance to surrender - we don't know that they are all bad. And we plan as much as we can. And train."

"For how long?" Art asked.

Tabitha thought a moment.

"A month. I reckon by the next ritual our absence is going to be noticed. So, we spend the next few weeks preparing…"

Art's smile was without humour.

"… and then we take the fight to them."

CHAPTER 16

Addison, Zack's cousin's toddler, sat on his grandfather's lap, clutching a gherkin in her hand. Zack and his grandfather smiled widely while she brought the pickled cucumber to her lips, only to scrunch up her face and thrust it away as the powerful vinegar assaulted her taste buds. She glared at the gherkin and pulled it closer again. This cycle had been repeating for a few minutes now and Zack was enjoying how his grandfather lit up, with his great-granddaughter holding onto his thick hand to steady herself, ready for another attempt.

He was also using the shared moment as an opportunity to scan his grandfather for any health issues. Apart from a little arthritis, which Zack cleaned up as best he could, his grandfather was in good shape.

Zack's phone vibrated in his pocket. It was a message from Charlie in the group chat.

We're in trouble! Girl house, now!

"Is everything okay?" his mother asked from across the table.

Zack calmed his expression, ignoring the knot of anxiety in his stomach.

"Yep. Well, no, actually." He scrambled for a lie. "Art went in to work today to set up for tomorrow and the wrong merchandise has been ordered. I need to go in and help him."

His mother frowned.

"And this can't wait until tomorrow? Family Sundays are important."

"The boy is showing responsibility," his grandfather interjected, "it's good to see. Not like this one was at his age."

Zack's father, who had been pointed at, held up his hands in defence.

"I was busy with university."

"You were busy with chasing girls." Zack's grandfather turned and patted Zack on the arm. "It's always good to see you, Zacharias."

Zack leant in, hugging his grandfather and Addison together.

"You too, Deda." He broke away and circled the table, giving goodbye hugs and kisses before bolting out the door.

He pulled out his phone. *I'm at my grandparents' house.*

I could swing by and get you, Art replied.

Faster would be better, Charlie messaged.

Get somewhere private and send me the location, Bast added.

Zack thought through his options. *Heading to the local shops, there's a disabled toilet there. 5 mins.*

I'll be ready, Bast replied.

Zack took off at a run and once he made it the four blocks to the nearby shopping complex, he headed directly for the toilets. At this time on a Sunday, the small complex was mostly deserted, but thankfully, the disabled toilet was still open. He sent Bast a screenshot of his phone's location and a photo of the room.

Stand back against the door, Bast replied.

A gate spun into being and Zack stepped through, into the girls' townhouse. The others were already there sitting in the living room, while Charlie paced back and forth in front of them.

"Okay, Zack's here," Tabitha said, "what's going on?"

Charlie stopped.

"I think we've been made."

It was still a week before the next ritual and their self-made timeline for when they would move against the Master of Animal.

"How?" Kimmy asked with obvious impatience.

"I decided to go back in, to snoop around a little." Charlie avoided eye contact as she spoke.

"Dammit, Charlie!" Tabitha leapt to her feet. "Don't tell me, you got caught?"

"No, that's just it," Charlie replied, "I couldn't get in. I stepped through the shadow of the entrance, and I just ended up outside that papered-over office, like last year."

"Could the doors be down again?" Art asked.

Bast shook his head.

"Maybe, but I doubt it."

"And then the only other conclusion is—" Kimmy added.

"What I've been saying!" Charlie's voice was filled with anxiety and frustration. "They've worked out that we're up to something and they've locked us out."

"Okay then, what's our next step?" Bast asked.

"We need to get out of here and lay low," Tabitha said, "grab your go-bags and anything else you need. We'll find somewhere to stay that'll take cash and work out where to go from there."

"I know a few places," Charlie said, pulling out her phone.

Bast opened a gate to the boys' townhouse and he, Zack and Art stepped through, heading to their rooms. Zack grabbed his hiking backpack from the bottom of his wardrobe. A few weeks before, Tabitha and Art had come up with the idea that they should each put together a go-bag. Zack's had a compact sleeping bag, spare clothes, toiletries, water, food, a wad of US dollars and Euros, and some battery packs. And every gram of it pulled down as he slipped it over his shoulders. He snatched up his 'walking stick' and rejoined the others in the girls' living room.

Charlie showed Bast a map on her phone.

"This was where I stayed in Indonesia a couple of months ago. They'll take cash and there's no Tower entrance anywhere nearby."

"Can do," Bast replied, "I'm going to need to take us to that nearby patch of trees to hide the gate. So, watch your step."

Tabitha looked around at the inside of the townhouse.

"We may not be coming back here until this is over, one way or another."

"What about our families?" Charlie asked. "What if the Tower goes after them if they can't find us?"

"They won't," Art said, "they care too much about the Silence. If they are coming, they'll be coming at us. And the further we are away from our families, the safer they'll be."

Zack looked toward the gate that Bast had opened and hoped that was true.

<hr>

The smell of burnt toast, followed by a string of Kimmy's favourite swear words, woke Zack and he looked around, attempting to remember where he was. Slovenia, the answer came to him, in a bed and breakfast tucked away in the forested hills. They'd moved twice since their stay in Indonesia and this time, Art had dumped a pile of Euros into the hands of the middle-aged couple who ran this accommodation. After a little 'inspiration', the husband and wife had decided to enjoy a few days in the city, leaving the property to Zack and his friends.

Bast and Charlie had spent the previous day surveilling three different Tower entrances and reported back that they had seen several people enter and exit. So, it was confirmed, the entrances were not down. They had been excommunicated.

Tabitha was in the kitchen with Kimmy when Zack entered. She was sipping coffee and staring out at the hillside.

"I wonder what they've told people about us to explain kicking us out. Or what they've told Junie."

Kimmy scraped her toast above the sink.

"Maybe that we killed two of the Thirteen?"

Art plodded down the hallway past Zack and looked through the refrigerator.

"I doubt it. Not good for morale to say a bunch of teenagers took out a pair of archwizards."

Zack sat down at the table.

"They might have said we killed those two people though. It's not like anybody would know they were part of the Thirteen."

Art pulled a block of cheese from the fridge and nibbled on it.

"Good point. Well, whatever story they've told about us, I think it's fair to guess it'll make us look bad. We don't have any allies in there anymore."

"We might have some." Tabitha's voice carried a hint of desperation. "Some of them are bound to know us well enough to give us the benefit of the doubt."

"Nobody we can rely on," Art said firmly.

The rest of the meal was a silent experience. Even when Charlie and Bast joined them. Zack found he had even less appetite for breakfast than usual. His stomach was already full with apprehension for what was coming next. Tabitha stood and placed her empty cup and plate into the sink.

"Okay, folks. Finish up and get ready. In one hour, we head out up the hill and Bast opens up a gate to wherever that pearl takes us. We need to be prepared for anything."

True to Tabitha's word, precisely one hour later, Zack was trudging along with the others, his backpack over his shoulders and enjoying the leverage his quarterstaff was giving him. When the trees were sufficiently dense, Bast dropped his bag and marked out the ground for his gate.

"Remember the plan, everybody," Tabitha said, "we locate the Master of Animal. Do our best to convince them to surrender. If that fails, we take them out."

"Just an idle thought," Art said as he watched the orange light of Bast's incantation, "what if Bast's gate opens up into the Thirteen's weekly book club meeting and we walk into a room with eleven angry masters of magic?"

"The last ritual was due two days ago," Tabitha replied, "let's hope they go off and do their own thing."

Zack nodded.

"Based on what Charlie told us, they were surprised when the Movement guy didn't show up for his turn. That suggests they don't keep in regular touch."

"Good point." Tabitha unhooked her flail from her side and shook out the chain. "And if we don't like our chances, for whatever reason, we jump back through the gate."

"And hope they don't have a Movement mage on hand to follow me," Bast added from the ground. He reshouldered his backpack. "One little surprise before I open this thing; I'm pretty sure the pearl is directing me to another realm."

"So, they are on a mission or something?" Kimmy asked. "That's good, maybe they'll be distracted."

"I guess we'll find out." Tabitha nodded to Bast. "Knock, knock."

With a twist of his wrist, Bast brought forth a flash of orange light that swirled into a gate.

"It's not my imagination," Art said, "you are getting really fast at opening those, right?"

Bast beamed.

"You can thank Charlie. She did so much travelling this year, it gave me a lot of practice."

Charlie gave a shallow curtsey, her bow and an arrow in her hands, before plunging through the gate with Max at her side. The others followed. Zack stepped through last and found his friends all crouching amongst some trees. He dropped down to join them and Bast closed the gate.

With no immediate threat evident, Zack took a moment to look around. If Bast hadn't warned him, he could have believed this was Earth. In fact, he may not have believed he had stepped through a gate at all. The trees around him looked enough like the ones they had left in Slovenia that he was unable to pinpoint the differences. The grass and soil felt familiar, the air smelt the same as the hill in Slovenia and the blue sky, visible through the gaps in the trees, held the merest tint of an approaching pinkish-orange sunset. Everything was normal. With the exception of the massive tree, shaped like a fortress, half a kilometre in front of them.

At its base, it was maybe three times the size of an ancient redwood, except that it did not seem to be uniformly solid, with gaps and ridges creating doors and steps. As it rose high above the trees around it, the branches twisted out at unnatural angles and at some places the limbs grew thicker, rather than thinner, away from the trunk. These unlikely features meant the tree had taken the rough shape of a multi-storey building and, with the way some of the branches snaked out over and around its base, a defensive building at that.

"Huh," Art said, staring at it.

"Anybody picking anything up?" Tabitha asked. "The Air feels pretty normal to me."

Zack reached out to Life. It was mostly normal, but there was an odd edge to it, a kind of quirkiness he couldn't quite place. He pushed outward through it, towards the strange tree. At this distance he was pushing the edge of his range, but there was a lot of Life concentrated there. The tree itself was most definitely alive, but it was not alone.

Art's brow was furrowed when he opened his eyes.

"I'm not sure about Mind here. At first, I thought it was normal, but at the very least there's something weird going on with it over there."

"I think what you're feeling are the animals inside that thing." Charlie's jaw was tight as she looked towards the tree. "There are a lot of them and I reckon our Master of Animal is there too, because something has been done to them."

Max whimpered.

"It's okay, darling," Charlie replied to her. "They aren't going to get a chance to do anything to you."

"They're not here on a mission, then," Art said.

"So what, they live here?" Kimmy asked.

Bast gritted his teeth loud enough to be heard.

"These bloody hypocrites. Pretending it's all about protecting our world from magic invasion."

Tabitha squeezed his arm before beckoning them forward.

"Keep low and quiet. We'll try to get closer before we decide how to move in."

Following Tabitha's lead, they dropped their bags and crept from trunk to trunk. But a little less than a hundred metres away from the tree-fortress, the shorter trees abruptly gave way to a clearing that would provide no cover.

"Hold up," Tabitha whispered. "One last chance. Can anybody sense anything important? Bast, they have to get out of here somehow. Can you detect a gate in there or anything?"

Bast closed his eyes and reached out and Zack did the same. The tree still held a massive volume of Life and not all of it was the tree itself. At this distance, he could pick up other minor sources of Life and not all of them were plant. There were animals there too and - he forced his sense to narrow in on one source in particular - a human Life source was amongst them.

"No gates or anything like that," Bast said. "At least that I can sense from here."

"There's a human in there, though," Zack added.

"Just one?" Tabitha asked. "Is it the Master of Animal?"

Zack shrugged.

"Sorry, I can't tell that kind of thing."

"What about you, Art?" Tabitha stared intently towards the strange tree.

"I'm not sure," Art replied. "I'm getting so much white noise from things that are almost minds, it's hard to pinpoint. But yeah, I'm pretty sure there's an actual mind in there, too.

"Charlie?" Tabitha asked.

"We need to be careful. There are a lot of animals in there and they have been warped. They'll be dangerous." She took a long, sad breath. "And we may have no choice but to kill them."

"Alright then," Tabitha said, "let's keep going, but be—"

"You're not going to ask me what I sense?" Kimmy asked.

Tabitha looked at her in surprise.

"Sorry, Kims. I just assumed that, like me, Fire wouldn't really provide any intel. What could you sense?"

"Nothing important," Kimmy replied, "but it's not fair for you to assume that."

"Oh, for—" Tabitha shook her head. "As I was saying, let's keep going, but be ready to react if we get spotted. If we can get close enough, we'll spread out and then call them out."

"I kind of feel like that gives up the element of surprise," Art said.

"We agreed to give each of them a chance to surrender," Tabitha replied. "I'm holding us to that."

Art stared at her for a moment before giving a single nod. Without the cover of the forest, they crept closer to the tree but had barely covered half the ground when a high-pitched screech sounded from the top of the tree's upper canopy. The noise repeated in short, regular bursts.

"Is that some kind of alarm?" Bast asked, wincing. The screeching was not loud enough to deafen, but it was not gentle.

"Some kind of one, yeah." Charlie pointed to where a dozen dark shapes burst from within the canopy's foliage.

They looked like crows or ravens, but even from this distance, their eyes were visibly too large and their talons too long. They continued issuing shrill calls as they soared towards Zack and his friends.

"This realm's birds do not look very friendly," Art said, gripping his sword with two hands.

"Those aren't from here." Charlie's anger coated each syllable. "Those are crows from our world. Or at least they were before this was done to them. And they aren't responding to me either."

"Then I'm sorry for this, but I don't want our eyes clawed out." Tabitha swapped her flail to her left hand and drew precise, rapid patterns in the air before flicking her wrist at the crows.

Her hand lit up with a blue flash and the air in front of the crows became a swirling vortex of violent wind. Several of the birds crashed into each other and each one was flung from the whirlwind and fell to the ground where they stilled, their screeching silenced.

"You don't suppose there's a chance they were in the shower and didn't hear all that racket?" Bast asked.

Before anybody could answer, a deep roar sounded from the tree and something like a tiger leapt from the second level, landing on the ground with a thud.

"What the hell is that?" Kimmy shouted.

It was the shape of a tiger, perhaps half again too large, but rather than fur, it was covered in thick scales and where a soft tail should have been was a long raised scorpion-like stinger.

"It's like he's tried to make his own manticore," Art said, sounding stunned.

"It's awful," Charlie said. "That poor creature is so twisted up and confused inside."

"How uninspired," a voice called out in reply. A man leapt from the tree and landed beside the beast. "Sandokan is a masterpiece. And you… well, you are simply uninvited trespassers in my home."

Tabitha moved a few steps in front of the others.

"And you would be the Animal member of the Thirteen."

"Uninspired and rude," the man replied. "This is my domain and if you are going to intrude here, you will at least address me as the Master of Animal."

In a ripple of rust-coloured light, his hands grew into claws and two rubbery tentacles emerged from his back. Zack's mind scrambled to process the scene before him, but Tabitha stayed the course.

"Okay, Master of Animal," she shouted back, "even with your pet and your extra limbs, you are outnumbered. It's clear that you and the rest of the Thirteen have been lying and abusing your power and we will not allow that to continue. If you surrender, we promise we will not harm you, but no matter what, you will not be the Master of Animal after today."

"Good speech, Sis," Bast whispered.

"How dare you," the man replied. "You trespass in my domain, my home and interrupt the important work I am doing. And then you threaten me? I'm afraid I'm not quite as outnumbered as you think. Cynthia, these intruders seek to force us from our home."

A feminine figure emerged from the base of the tree. She was covered in bark and leaves sprouted from her scalp like hair.

"That's not a dryad or anything," Art whispered. "She's human."

"Life is telling me the opposite," Zack replied. "She's vegetation all the way through."

"Only one way both of those things are true," Kimmy said. "She's the Master of Plant."

CHAPTER 17

"We've still got the numbers," Tabitha said. "There's only two of them."

Her words fell a little flat in the face of what it cost them to defeat the first two masters. And her words fell off a cliff when more than a dozen creatures burst from the tree branches and charged towards them. Each appeared to be a hybrid born of multiple animals. A boar with alligator scales and sharp claws raced down a branch, while a chimp with the head of a snapping turtle and crab-like pincers swung towards them, violence in its eyes.

Bast's eyes widened.

"Um… can we have the nightmarish wooden soldiers back instead?"

"Let me try again." Charlie stepped out in front and held her hands forward.

A flash of russet light came from her hands and each of the beasts paused. Even the manticore, named Sandokan, shuddered. And then, each of them focused their eyes on Charlie and charged towards her.

"Well, I got their attention," Charlie said, with a little fear in her voice.

The man growled.

"It is not enough that you mean to take me from my home, but you seek to take my pets from me as well? They know their master and it is not you."

Sandokan streaked ahead of the others, but Max bolted forward to intercept. Charlie shook herself out of her shock and muttered a brief incantation. A shimmer of russet light passed over Max and she emerged from it as a grey wolf.

Art's eyes flashed purple and Bast nodded. The two raced towards the Master of Animal, Bast several steps ahead.

Kimmy pointed her axe at the Master of Plant in open challenge and charged, Mr Shanks hovering over her shoulder. Zack remembered his first encounter with a Plant mage and flung his quarterstaff as far away as he could before following behind her.

Sandokan was still intent on Charlie and it was only at the last moment that he saw Max on her intercept path. Max had leapt in the air with the intent of latching onto the manticore's throat, but Sandokan pulled up short and Max's teeth raked against his face instead.

The remaining creatures funnelled towards Charlie, but Tabitha was by her side. She traced shapes in the air and a wall of wind rushed outward from her and crashed into the creatures, flinging them away. Charlie used the distraction to reach out to them again, her eyes turning reddish brown.

Kimmy had closed most of the distance on Cynthia, but when she was a metre away, the Master of Plant gestured to the ground and a trio of roots jutted up like stakes, their tips impossibly sharp. Kimmy veered to the left to avoid the first, but the second pierced her thigh clean through. Hissing in pain, Kimmy hacked it off and pulled it from her leg before staggering forward. Mr Shanks zipped forward and stabbed itself at the mage, but the thin blade bounced off the hard wooden exterior.

Zack held back and instead, reached out with Life to close Kimmy's wound. Rushed and at a distance, the repair was not perfect, but it would stem any further bleeding. She'd be able to put weight on it without too much pain.

Bast closed in on the Master of Animal, but he darted to the side at the last moment and the man's sharp tiger claws raked at the air. One his tentacles lashed out at Bast, but he leapt over it, slicing into it as he went. Art feinted forward and the man responded with his second tentacle, which battered aside Art's broadsword before he could parry with it.

A kangaroo with a wolf's head and, what may have been oversized praying mantis hooks for arms, bounced towards Charlie, only to be jetted away by a blast of wind from Tabitha.

Charlie's eyes remained shrouded in rust-coloured light.

"He has a hold on them. I'm trying to unpick it."

"Whatever you're doing, it has them all homing in on you," Tabitha said, knocking back another two hybrids. "Well, all but one of them."

Max was posing enough of a threat to keep Sandokan's attention away from Charlie. The cost of owning all the creature's attention came crashing down at Max in the form of an enormous scorpion stinger. Max bounded forward, past the stinger and latched her jaw onto Sandokan's leg. She found purchase, but her sharp teeth couldn't get through the tough hide.

Kimmy's rapid recovery from her wounded leg must have surprised Cynthia, who was unprepared for the axe swing that bit into her shoulder. No blood came from the wound and the Master of Plant did not react except to step away. Dark green light collected in her hand and she gestured again to the ground. More roots sprang up, but these were slimmer and, instead of piercing Kimmy, they wrapped around her legs. Entangled and unable to move away, Kimmy flailed her axe toward Cynthia.

She screamed in frustration.

"Mr Shanks! A little help, please."

The floating knife broke off its pointless attack and sawed away at the roots holding Kimmy in place. Zack pulled a foldable knife from his pocket and rushed to Kimmy's side. It was a demonstration of how useless he was, that this was all he could do, but whatever got Kimmy - someone who was actually useful - back into the fight faster, was worth something, at least.

Art regained a proper grip of his sword in time to fend off a flurry of tiger paws raking towards his face. Bast took the opportunity to slash at the Master of Animal with his rapier but, while the blade easily pierced his clothes, the man had an unnaturally thick hide of his own.

"No good, mate," Bast called to Art. "He's like a wombat's arse."

"What?" Art replied, fending off a slash aimed at his chest. "He does square shits?"

"Square….? No, I mean his skin's all thick."

"Then just say that!" Art moved his blade forward to ward off any more attacks, but he had lost track of the tentacles and one flew in from the side and slapped him against the temple.

He staggered backwards, but the second tentacle snaked around his ankle and yanked him forward. Art fell hard onto his back and the breath rushed out of his lungs.

The Master of Animal crouched ready to pounce claws first, onto Art's prone body, but Bast dived between them and slashed at the man's face. Whatever bestial reinforcement he'd given his skin, he'd neglected his face and Bast's blade cut a thin, but deep, cut across the man's cheek, narrowly missing his right eye. The Master of Animal growled in pain and stepped back, releasing Art from his tentacled grasp.

Art scuttled backwards but stayed on the ground.

"Thanks, mate. If our swords aren't going to work, I'll try the other way."

His eyes flashed purple and he reached his palm out at the man, moving it in slow circles. Tabitha switched from jets of air to a narrow whirlwind that moved back and forth, protecting her and Charlie from the relentless aggression of the hybrids.

"How's that connection going?" she asked, without turning around.

"It's no good," Charlie replied. "Between whatever change he's made to their brains and his hold over them, I can't get in."

Max continued to hold Sandokan back from Charlie, but her focus in avoiding the creature's deadly stinger left her open to a swipe from its claws. Longer and sharper than nature would have allowed, the claw cut deep across Max's side and she whined in pain.

Mr Shanks and Zack were only halfway through cutting the entangling roots, but Kimmy waved them off.

"Shanky, Max needs your help. Zack, you back off too, I'll do this my way."

The blade zipped through the air and Zack scrambled backwards and onto his feet.

"I know you can heal leg burns, so get ready if I screw this up." Kimmy mouthed an incantation and flames sprouted from her hands.

As she chanted, a ring of fire moved along each of her wrists, to her shoulders and down her body.

It was working, but it was distracting her and the Master of Plant was moving in. There wasn't time for anything clever. Zack charged forward past Kimmy and leapt feet first at the plant woman. In a burst of inspiration, he wove a thread of Life and bound it to himself with a loose purpose, hoping it would work as intended even after he released it. His feet connected with the Master's wooden body, pushing her backwards, but she responded by stabbing at him with her thorny hands. Her sharp fingers pierced deep into his sides and, as he fell to the ground, they were torn out of him.

Zack lay in pain, shock and no small amount of blood on the ground, but the Life magic he'd set within himself kicked into action, stemming the flow of blood and repairing the damage. He could sense it working within him but, as the Master of Plant loomed over him, his blood dripping from her splintery claws, he realised it would not be quick enough.

Bast danced back and forth in front of the Master of Animal, forcing the man's attention away from Art. His supernatural speed had helped him avoid the tentacles, but he'd taken two decent scratches from the tiger claws and blood dripped down his arm and chest. Behind him, Art grunted in frustration and the man hissed in laughter.

"Your tricks won't work on me, you pathetic novice. I've made some improvements to myself. I'm something more than human now."

Art smirked and his eyes lit up.

"Something more or something in between? Hey, Charlie!"

"Yep, I'm right there with you," Charlie answered. "Time for some Gaga."

Art laughed as he leapt to his feet.

"Change up, Tabs. Help Bast out. We got this."

"You sure?" Tabitha asked, guiding her whirlwind back towards the kangaroo-creature.

"We're sure," Charlie replied. "Just try and keep him as distracted as you can."

"What do you think I'm doing?" Bast shouted as he ducked under one tentacle and slashed at another.

Tabitha ran past Art and swung her flail into the Master of Animal's side, knocking him off balance. Bast took advantage of the distraction and snapped his rapier at one of the man's tiger paws. His blade cut clean through, slicing almost a third of it off. The Master roared in pain and retreated a few steps.

Zack's focus was just clearing as the Master of Plant brought her long, thorny talons down toward him. Light bloomed behind him and an instant before Cynthia would have impaled him, a flaming axe head caught her attack. She screamed in pain and stepped back, but Kimmy followed.

"Get away from him, bonsai-bitch. This fight is between you and me."

Cynthia screeched in reply, "You who bring an axe against me and my home? Yes, you will die first."

Green light collected around her limbs and they changed. The burnt tips fell away and the wood that replaced them was thicker and covered in heavy moss. Kimmy launched herself at the woman, bringing her axe around in a downward arc. Cynthia caught the axe with her left arm and, while the blade bit deep, the flames did not catch. Instead, the moss on her arm latched onto the axe head and grew over it, dousing the fire in a hiss of steam. Kimmy gasped and Cynthia raked at her with her other arm, cutting Kimmy across the chest. Zack scrambled back to his feet and sent a flow of Life to close the wounds.

Sandokan's relentless attacks had knocked Max onto her side. The wolf shuffled frantically and still avoided the scorpion stinger, but the hybrid leapt forward, landing on her with one of its oversized talons. As it was lining up its stinger for another attempt, Mr Shanks soared through and pierced Sandokan's left eye.

The hybrid screamed, tilting its head upward in an effort to dislodge the knife. With its weight shifted, Max freed herself and leapt up at Sandokan's exposed throat. The hide there was thick but not enough to withstand Max's bite and she clamped her jaw tightly, throwing her body weight up and around. Sandokan, frantically shaking, toppled onto her back, where Max stood firm, her jaws locked.

"Sandokan!" The Master of Animal's cry sounded more like a growl than anything else. "You will pay for this."

With renewed fervour, he lunged with his tentacles. One slammed into Bast, catching him in the ribs and knocking him through the air where he landed hard on the ground. The other wrapped around Tabitha's waist and pulled her in close to him, hanging her upside down in front of his face.

"I'm going to crush your ribs until the splinters tear into your lungs and heart." He stared at her with inhuman eyes.

Straining against painful constriction, blue light collected in Tabitha's hand and she spun her flail in a whirling blur.

"None of that." The Master of Animal snatched the weapon from her hand with his other tentacle.

Tabitha smiled.

"Thanks."

A bolt of lightning shot down from the sky and arced through the metal flail into the man's body. There was a deafening boom and Tabitha was thrown through the air, contact burns snaking around her waist and chest. The Master of Animal was covered in deep burns, but despite them he still stood.

Bast forced himself to his feet.

"What is this guy made of?"

"Yes!" Charlie and Art cried out in unison, and a pulse of magenta light rippled from them.

The Master of Animal stared in disbelief at his pack of hybrids. The creatures had been inches away from Charlie but, as one, they turned and charged at him.

"No!" he shouted, fear in his voice for the first time since the fight started. "Obey your master!"

The kangaroo made it to him first, landing its feet onto his chest and bringing him to the ground. When the other creatures caught up, they swarmed over him and he screamed once more.

"Declan!" the Master of Plant screamed.

Kimmy swung her moss-covered axe into the woman's thigh knocking her to the ground. Cynthia's screams continued and a cloud of dark green light coalesced over her whole body. Kimmy swung again, hacking into the woman and the cloud cleared, leaving the still wooden body behind.

Zack hurried to Tabitha's side and discovered she wasn't breathing. He sent a dozen threads of Life into her body. Some to keep the oxygen flowing to the brain, others to stimulate her lungs and diaphragm, but his main focus was her heart. The shock of the lightning bolt had stopped it, but before he started it up again, he needed to repair any damage and he had to do that carefully.

"What was that green cloud?" Bast asked behind him.

"Dunno," Kimmy replied, "I think I snuffed her before she could finish it. Speaking of finishing, that's pretty gruesome." She pointed at the pack of hybrids still attacking the Master of Animal's body.

Each of the creatures stopped and stuck their heads up, twitching as if trying to sense something. The next second, they bolted away into the trees.

"I guess they're keen for freedom," Bast said.

"No." Charlie's eyes were scanning around. "They were scared."

"Of us?" Kimmy asked.

"I don't think so," Art said. "I think they were scared of that."

He pointed up at the tree-fortress where the dark green cloud had reappeared amongst its branches. And those branches were starting to move.

The lowest limbs, those that had been shaped into a platform around the second storey, trembled, before whipping out. The wide arc of the branches sailed over Zack and most of the others, before it dropped and slammed into Kimmy. She shouted and fell, tumbling along the ground from the impact.

"Run!" Art shouted.

CHAPTER 18

Art and Charlie dashed back toward the treeline with Max on their tails, while Bast sprinted to Kimmy's side. Another branch, from higher up in the tree, flailed out. Its mass of foliage and wood struck the ground inches behind Bast, who scooped up Kimmy mid-stride.

Zack remained crouched over Tabitha, only partially aware of the chaos unfurling behind him. With her heart repaired, he used a thread of Life to coax it back into beating. It found its way to a gentle rhythm and, when her chest began to rise and fall with her own breaths, he smiled in relief. And then a branch slammed into his side, sending him hurtling through the air. He crashed to the ground, dazed and in pain.

Nearby, Tabitha crawled to her feet.

"Um, when did the tree come to life?"

"I think Lady Groot transferred her mind into it," Art called out.

He ran to Zack's side and pulled him backwards. Zack cried out as his broken ribs flared in pain, but Art didn't stop until they were behind a tree. Art's face was a worried blur, hovering above him.

Zack held his thumb up.

"I'm okay. Need a moment."

The thin, autonomous cycle of Life magic he'd placed inside himself earlier was still active and finding its way through his damaged body. It would have to be enough.

"Any ideas how we fight that?" Tabitha's voice asked nearby.

"Don't suppose retreating is an option?" Bast asked, joining them.

"No. We may not get another chance to take her down," Art replied.

"Where's Kimmy?" Tabitha asked. "Is she okay?"

"Better than our boy here," Bast replied, "but she can't walk. I've left her propped up behind a tree."

"I've got an idea," Charlie said. "She's done the same thing with the tree as he did with the animals. She warped it far beyond what nature intended. Look at it. It makes a cool-looking house, but it's a terrible tree. It's thin where it should be thick, thick where it should be thin. It's all out of balance."

"So?" Tabitha asked.

"We help it along," Charlie replied.

"She's right," Bast said and pointed to the base of the tree. "Some of its roots have come up already."

"What are you suggesting? We run out there and get the tree to take swings at us?" Tabitha looked concerned.

"Yep," Charlie said. "Well, that and don't get hit when she does."

"I'm on it." Bast raced out of the treeline shouting. "Over here, you overgrown treehouse."

He hadn't made it far when two long branches swung in from either side and he slid along the ground as they crashed together over him.

"He needs some help out there," Tabitha said.

"We're a lot slower than him," Art said.

"Speak for yourself," Charlie said with a wink. "Maxie darling, you stay here, okay?"

A russet shimmer flowed over Charlie's body and a gazelle stood in her place. Max whined as Charlie bounded off, then curled up to lick at her wounds.

"Come on," Tabitha said, "we'll hang back, but if Charlie is right, we need this thing flailing as much as possible."

She and Art ran back into the clearing and Zack was left with the sounds of crashing and shouting. The pain and fogginess had lessened and Zack was able to weave more deliberate flows of Life together and repair his damaged ribs enough that he could sit up and watch the others.

Bast stood still, a few metres away from the tree, goading it into attacking him. Enraged, the Master of Plant swung her heaviest branch down at him and, using his magical haste, he dashed away as the branch came down. But as it hit the ground, the oversized branch snapped off the body of the trunk and exploded in a spray of splinters. Several of them cut into Bast, but he kept moving, shouting to draw more attacks.

The gazelle that was Charlie leapt around, making loud honking noises. Two slimmer branches came at her, one after the other, but she skittered away from the first and cleared the second with a single long jump. And her plan was working. On the opposite side of the tree, roots were tearing up through the soil as the weight of the tree shifted from the attacks.

Art and Tabitha circled around to opposite sides of the tree line and alternated between running in and out. The Master of Plant lunged a branch at Art and he retreated back into safety.

A ball of fire rocketed out from the forest and struck the massive tree's centre mass. It blackened rather than ignited the wood where it hit, but it sent the tree into a further rampage. Tabitha and Art scrambled back to cover, but the Master stretched its branches further, knocking some of the closest trees in the pursuit of her attackers. Two more heavy branches shattered against the ground as Charlie bounded about. She was no longer trying to provoke the plant mage; she was trying to survive.

Three more branches lunged at Bast, but rather than dodge away, he muttered an incantation and jumped onto the thicker of the three. In a blur, he raced up the length of it toward the trunk and was halfway there before the Master of Plant seemed to notice. Another branch came crashing towards him, but he slid forward and the branches collided with each other, both snapping at the points of impact.

With his ribs repaired, Zack made his way to his feet, ready to respond if, or when, anybody was caught by the berserk tree. More and more roots tore free of the soil and the Plant mage became entirely focused on Bast, bouncing his way from limb to limb above the ground. He was bleeding from a dozen scratches and piercing splinters, but he kept moving, and the tree twisted and bent in its pursuit of him.

Tabitha raced into the clearing, bright blue light collecting in her hands. Striding over a hunk of fallen branches, she hit the ground and unleashed a torrent of air at the base of the tree. Without all its roots, the tree tipped to one side, but then the roots sprang into motion and began to burrow back into the soil. Tabitha screamed in frustration and exertion as she maintained the localised gale, fighting against the pull of the roots.

Mr Shanks flew into the base of the tree and sawed at the roots, but the blade struggled with their thickness. Art ran in, sword ready, but before he could reach Tabitha, Kimmy hobbled out of the treeline, using her axe for support. Through the pain, she hissed an incantation and a beam of hot, white fire shot from her finger, slicing through the roots. Kimmy's magical laser cut them in half faster than the burned ends could regrow and with a final wind-propelled shove by Tabitha, the tree-fortress crashed towards the ground, tearing free of all remaining roots.

An instant before impact, Bast flung himself up and away from the tree. His climb had taken him at least thirty metres high and now he was falling. Zack limped out of the treeline, readying threads of Life, but orange light bloomed on the soles of Bast's sneakers and his descent slowed to the gentle pace of a leaf.

The same could not be said of the tree, which hit the ground with such force that Zack was knocked off his feet and the impact shattered the tree itself. With a thunderous tearing and cracking sound, it erupted into a shower of debris, covering the clearing and beyond, on the side it fell.

Zack hobbled out and gathered with the others amidst the tree's remains.

"The Master of Plant. Is she…?" Tabitha looked to Art and Zack.

"I'm not getting anything like a mind from there," Art replied. "I think that killed her."

"I agree." Zack pulled back his senses. "There's still a bit of Life left amongst the tree, but hers is gone."

"Two more down!" Kimmy whooped.

"What now?" Bast asked.

"We should search through this wreckage," Tabitha said, "see if we can find anything useful."

"Before that, everybody line up. Most of you need patching up." Zack stepped closer to Kimmy. "You first. You shouldn't even be standing."

He sent a stream of Life into Kimmy, mending her broken bones and completing the patch job he had done on her earlier. He left the splinters and scratches alone for now and moved on to Bast.

By the time he was done, the others were sifting through the remains of the tree fortress. Zack joined in, following a line of debris that took him out of the clearing. Most of the wreckage was pieces of the tree itself, but every so often, he'd find a piece of furniture, like a chair leg or a shard of broken crockery. A few steps past the treeline, he found a couple of torn textbooks, heavily annotated in pen. He shook them out and placed them against the trunk of a tree.

A piece of metal caught his eye. At first, he thought it was another piece of furniture, but closer to it, he realised it was part of a cage. Sifting through more of that area, he found more pieces of cage. Zack was about to call out to the others when, a couple of metres away, a patch of debris stirred. He reached out with Life and felt a faint, wounded signal. Caught between the urge to help something injured and the fear that it might be an angry hybrid, he snatched up a metal bar from the wreckage and approached it.

He heaved aside a leafy branch and found a two-foot tall creature. He tried to determine what this was a hybrid of. It was a bit like a monkey and its shape reminded him of a marmoset, but it was more the size of a lemur and without a tail. But, unlike the hybrids that had attacked them, there was nothing about this creature that didn't match. Its eyes stared back at him with fear but also with intelligence. Zack wasn't sure this was a hybrid at all.

The creature was pinned under another heavy branch and its side had been lacerated by a thick splinter. Zack dropped the metal bar and stepped closer. The creature shuddered in fear and squealed at the pain the movement caused.

Zack crouched slowly and considered what to do. He needed to lift the heavy branch, but if he did so, the creature might flee and die later from its wounds.

"It's okay," he said softly, "I'm here to help."

He reached out and carefully slid the splinter from its side. The creature whimpered and cowered away from him, but Zack wove a thread of Life into the wound, mending it. The connection with its Life revealed how fatigued and weakened it was and not only from these recent injuries. He didn't want to risk anything specific about this creature's biology, so he poured in a general helping of Life and hoped its own would know what to do with it.

The furry creature had calmed and looked at Zack in silence; the fear in its eyes was now mixed with curiosity.

"Okay, I'm going to lift this up now." Zack placed his hands on the branch. "Please don't run away, I'll need to mend the bone."

He doubted that it understood English, but the only alternative was to bring Art over, which would likely terrify the creature all over again. Hoping his tone conveyed enough, Zack raised the branch and the creature shuffled back a few inches, allowing Zack to drop it again.

"Thank you," Zack said, and wove another stream of Life to mend the creature's bone. He was careful not to lead the Life he introduced too much and, instead, allowed it to follow the host Life's instructions.

The creature sat up and crouched, chirping a soft cooing noise at him. Zack smiled but then noticed the creature was looking over his shoulder. He turned, ready to ease off whichever of his friends was approaching and found himself with a knifepoint held against his neck.

The wielder of the blade appeared to be a young woman and, at first, Zack thought this might be the Master of Plant out of her plant form, but then he noticed the woman's pointed ears and inhumanely large eyes. Eyes that narrowed at him in open hostility.

"Threpik honar!" she said with a hiss and pressed the blade against his skin, piercing enough to draw a few drops of blood.

Zack raised his hands slowly, stammering in an attempt to find something useful to say, but behind him the creature chirped again with a series of coos. Was it talking?

It must have been, because the woman inched to the side and looked past Zack and then back to him. The pressure from the knife eased and she replied to the creature with a few coos of her own. The strange conversation carried on for a few more moments, with Zack standing as statue-like as he could, before it ended with the creature scampering out of the wreckage and into the trees.

The woman stepped back and lowered her knife, eyeing Zack up and down in open appraisal and allowing him the opportunity to look at her properly for the first time. She looked elvish, similar to those of his childhood fiction and to elves he had seen in the Fae realm he had travelled to when rescuing a toddler. But different too. Her ears were taller where they poked out from her golden-brown hair and her eyes and face were more angular. She was a little taller than him and dressed in dark green hunting clothes, with a bow and quiver strapped to her back.

"Dilar minatu?" Her voice was stern but had lost some of the heat it held before. That didn't make it any more understandable.

"I'm sorry," Zack replied, knowing it was useless, "I don't understand."

Her brow creased in thought, her nose crinkling in a way Zack was surprised to find appealing, given she had threatened to kill him moments ago. She stepped closer, gesturing past him to the wreckage of the tree-fortress.

"Dilar minatu?" she repeated, this time slower, ending by tapping Zack's chest with her finger.

Was she asking if they did this? He nodded and pointed to himself. Her eyes narrowed and she pointed towards the clearing. Abandoning words, she held up two fingers before switching to a single finger and pointing back at Zack but reaching above his head.

He nodded, hoping he understood. There were two people who lived there and one of them was a man taller than him. He held up two of his own fingers and pointed back at her and then gestured to a nearby tree with some low-hanging leaves.

The elfin woman's eyes lit up and she nodded.

"Vitu?"

Not sure of what she was asking, Zack took a guess at what might be the most relevant information. He pointed to her knife, still held in her left hand and then ran a finger across his neck.

"Dah vitu?" she asked, her voice excited.

Zack wasn't confident this conversation was going well and he looked through the trees to see if Art was in sight. Maybe he could call him over in a way that wouldn't alarm her. Art was better with women anyway. But there was no sight of him. The woman stepped past him and crouched next to where he had healed the creature.

She picked up the long splinter that had cut the creature's side and held it toward him.

"Um, no, thank you." Zack shook his hands.

The woman rolled her eyes with a sigh and sheathed her knife before reaching out, taking his hand and placing the shard of wood in it. He looked at the piece of wood confused and when she drew her knife again, he stepped back, lowering the shard. The woman shook her head and reversed the knife, offering it to him hilt first. He reached out to grab it, but she retracted it, holding out her empty hand and pointing to the splinter.

Oh, Zack thought, she wants an exchange.

He held out the piece of wood and held his hand open to receive the knife. The woman's eyes brightened and her face split into a beaming smile. Zack's heart rose into his throat; she was beautiful. She claimed the splinter and held it close, while Zack examined the knife. The blade was thin and strong but, otherwise, unremarkable. The hilt, however, was an intricate combination of leather and metal.

Zack looked up from the blade and found her close to him, her eyes staring into his.

"Th… thank you for the—" he started to say.

And then she leaned in and kissed him. His surprise quickly gave way to the soft warmth of the kiss and he returned it, leaning in closer to her. The eternal buzzing of his mind faded and all he felt was the shared moment of a mix of passion, kindness, curiosity and playfulness.

After somewhere between a second and a thousand years, the kiss ended, but they stayed close to each other, her hand on his cheek.

"Zack, where are you?" Tabitha called from the clearing. "Bast has found something in the wreckage."

The shout drew his eyes and he looked through the trees to faintly make out Tabitha approaching.

"Would you like to—" When he turned back, the woman was gone.

The only evidence that she'd been there at all was the knife in his hands and the rapid thumping of his heart. He allowed himself a long sigh before he called out, "On my way, Tabs."

Zack took one more look around and made his way into the clearing, where Tabitha was waiting. He followed her to where the others were sitting around in a circle, using pieces of the debris as makeshift benches.

"What's that?" Art pointed at the dagger in Zack's hand as he approached.

"Found it out in the trees," Zack said, showing it to the others.

Art narrowed his eyes in suspicion.

"Nice," Kimmy said. "Does it fly?"

"I don't think so," Zack replied.

She shrugged.

"Still nice though and maybe it'll let you set it on fire without being a sook about it."

Mr Shanks was hovering nearby and shook its hilt, indicating, according to Charlie, that it didn't like the idea.

"But if you let me ignite you," Kimmy said, turning to face it, "then you'd be able to do things like slice through those roots faster. And it wouldn't hurt you."

The floating knife shook with more enthusiasm.

"Fine, fine." Kimmy turned back away.

"So, um, you said Bast found something?" Zack sat down.

Bast held out a silver cube, the size of his fist.

"What is it?" Zack asked.

"It's a beacon," Bast replied. "The Tower sometimes gives them out to teams that don't include a Movement mage if they are going off-world."

"How does it work?"

Bast turned the cube in his hand.

"It sends a signal to the Tower and whoever's on duty opens up a gate to wherever this thing is. I haven't done it myself, but I've seen it done."

"It's our backdoor in," Tabitha said.

Charlie shook her head.

"This from the one who went off at me for sneaking in last time."

"For sneaking in alone," Tabitha replied. "But think about it. We need to find the nine remaining Masters. Their pearls are still in the Tower and we can't get in through the front door anymore."

Zack nodded.

"Thus, the backdoor."

Tabitha's smile was grim.

"Let's go get our bags, have a meal and rest up. After that, we're breaking into the Tower."

CHAPTER 19

Kimmy used her magic to warm their canned meals and Zack laid back on the grass, using his backpack as a pillow. With his eyes closed, he let his mind drift into Life and it flowed all around him. The forest's abundance was a background to the familiar signatures resonating nearby. The Life within his friends was recuperating, like water into a sponge.

The most familiar signature sat down beside him, and Zack turned his head towards it without opening his eyes.

"Nice dagger there, mate," Art said.

"Thanks."

"And you just found it amongst the bits of exploded tree."

"Yep."

"Well, seeing as you don't like the idea of cutting people, could I have it?"

"Nah, I think I'll keep it as a souvenir."

"Fair enough." Art laid down next to him. "Did you get her name, at least?"

Zack sat up and opened his eyes to Art's smug grin.

"Are you using your mind powers on me?"

"Nah, best mate powers did the trick. That look on your face said everything. Gonna tell me about her?"

"Maybe later." Zack laid back down.

"Awesome." Art closed his eyes and dozed off.

Half an hour later, they sat around a cozy campfire discussing the plan.

"We need to get as many of the remaining pearls as possible and that means splitting up," Tabitha said.

"Is that a good idea?" Bast asked.

"I don't know," Tabitha replied, "but we should be less likely to be noticed than if we're all together. Kimmy and I will go and get the four elemental pearls."

"I'll get the Mind one," Art said.

Zack leant forward, enjoying the warmth from the fire.

"Maybe Charlie and Max should go with you. Worst case, if you get caught, Mind magic won't work on Max. It might give you an edge."

Charlie nodded. "Good idea."

"Should I go with Zack to get the Life one?" Bast asked.

"Maybe not," Tabitha said. "Life's not exactly dangerous. What if you get the Creation one that Jackie hid."

"Yep," Bast replied, "I think I know where that is."

"So, we go in, grab as many pearls as we can and then run out through the Entrance before anybody knows what we're doing." Tabitha looked around at each of them. "Don't take unnecessary risks, though."

They all nodded in agreement and shouldered their backpacks. Bast confirmed they were ready and activated the cube. It pulsed with soft, orange light. A few moments later, a gate stretched into existence in front of them.

"Me first," Art said and plunged into the grey disc.

The others followed and Zack stepped through into the Tower's Gate Room, somewhere in the heart of the building. Art was speaking with a middle-aged woman who had been the Movement mage on duty.

There was a wisp of purple light as he spoke softly into her ear.

"You will walk through the gate and stay in the clearing until sunrise. Then you will forget everything since this morning."

The woman nodded, her face void of emotion as she moved through the gate with stiff steps.

"Sorry, Teema," Bast said as she passed before looking at the others.

"She's actually a bit of a rude cow, so if it was going to be someone, I don't hate that it's her."

"Good luck, everybody," Tabitha said. "Meet at the Entrance Chamber in fifteen minutes."

"What if the doors won't let us out?" Charlie asked.

"They will," Bast replied. "They only lock you out, not in."

Zack and Bast split off from the others and crept down a corridor before Bast headed in a different direction, leaving Zack alone. He reached the edge of the Life quarters and a strangeness crept up on Zack in a way he hadn't been expecting. Over the past two years, he had spent so much time here. It had made him feel safe and special and now he was sneaking through it like a thief. It was necessary and for the right reasons, but he hated it.

Hurrying past other rooms, he found his way to the main infirmary and listened outside the door. Silence. The infirmary was almost never unattended, but maybe he was luckier than he thought. He opened the door and Tom looked up from where he was reading a book in an armchair. An expression of confusion on the Scotsman's face fell away to realisation and he leapt to his feet.

Zack darted inside and shut the door behind him. The middle-aged man had often been a source of advice to Zack throughout the last years. Maybe he would listen.

"Tom, give me a chance to explain."

"Explain?" Tom replied. "Lad, we're past explaining. The Tower's labelled ye and ye pals, renegades."

"The Tower is what I need to explain. They aren't what they seem." Zack walked further into the room, his hands up in a gesture of peace. "They've been lying to us."

Tom approached without the corresponding gesture.

"Really? And ye and ye school mates have uncovered this great conspiracy, have ye? C'mon Zack, ye still basically bairns."

"I can prove it," Zack said, shuffling sideways towards the cupboard where the pearl was hidden. "What does Life tell you about the creatures we fight? Think about it. They're as alive as you and me."

Tom moved closer.

"Nay. That's just magic and its trickery. It's magic that's deceiving ye, nay the Tower."

He was not going to be convinced, at least not then and there. But Zack needed to get the pearl and make it to the Entrance Chamber.

"Okay, another bit of proof. What about this, then?" Zack pointed to part of the Tower's wall next to the cupboard.

"What now?" Tom said, stepping closer to look. "The Tower's made of smoke and secrets instead of stone?"

Zack lashed out with his foot, sweeping through both of Tom's and, as he fell, Zack used all his own body weight to slam Tom's head against the wall.

"No, it's definitely still stone," Zack said as Tom slumped unconscious to the floor.

Zack pulled open the linen cupboard and fumbled around in the back corner until he found the pearl. Relieved, he stuffed it into his pocket and returned to Tom's side where he used a thread of Life to check the injury. There was significant trauma to the skull, but he had time.

"I'm sorry, Tom," he said, dragging his body across the room and levering him onto a bed.

He pulled a sheet off another bed and used it to bind Tom's hands to the bed frame and then used a pillowcase to gag him. Only then did he use streams of Life to repair the damage he had done, while also coaxing Tom's brain into letting him rest to recover. He would be fine and someone would likely find him soon. Which was all the more reason for Zack to get moving.

He looked over Tom one more time to try to assuage the guilt that had gripped him before he stood and moved to the door.

Sara stood watching him.

"What precisely do you think you are doing, Zachary?"

"He's okay," Zack said, his heart lurching.

"Yes." Sara sounded as unimpressed as he expected. "He looks it."

"He wouldn't listen and left me no choice. But I know you will. The Tower, the Thirteen, they have been lying to us, about a lot. Like, the magical creatures, they are as alive as you and I."

"Oh, Zack." Sara rubbed her forehead and sighed.

"It's true." He had to make her believe him.

"Of course they are alive."

"You know?" That couldn't be true.

"What difference does it make?"

"What difference?" Zack replied. "You taught me to value Life, to heal and nurture it."

"I taught you to prioritise and to make hard choices." Sara pointed a bony finger at him. "Or at least I tried to. They invade our world and kill our people and you want to value their lives aside ours?"

Zack's surprise gave way to anger.

"Protecting our world is one thing, but the Tower sends us into their worlds, invading their homes."

"The Tower does what it must," Sara said, "as do I."

An alarm sounded throughout the corridor, with a deep tone that pulsed against his bones.

"You've been delaying me here on purpose," Zack said.

"You may not be capable of making the hard choices," Sara replied, her face stone, "but I am."

Zack ran past her, into the corridor and towards the stairs, where Bast came tearing down another hallway in his direction. Bast slowed down to let Zack keep up as they bounded down the steps.

"I don't love the alarm. Did you get your pearl?"

Zack nodded. "You?"

"Yep." Bast patted his left pocket.

Art, Charlie and Max joined them at the next landing.

"Please tell me you got pearls," Art said, following them down the steps. "Mine was gone."

"Never mind that now." Charlie was right on Zack's heels. "We need to get out of here."

They rounded the final curve of the stairwell and the Entrance Chamber came into view, along with Tabitha and Kimmy. Each was struggling to escape the restraining hold of a stone statue. Black scorches marked where Kimmy had failed to weaken the grip of the arms around her.

Bast raced forward and, as Art rushed past after him, Zack joined them in their charge, with Charlie and Max following.

"No!" Tabitha shouted, but it was too late.

As soon as Zack and the others entered the room, there was a grinding sound of stone on stone and a dozen statues stepped into view, circling them. The Commander was among them.

"Surrender, enemies of the Tower."

"Commander, please," Charlie said, pointing at the shadowed doorway, "we just want to leave. We don't mean the Tower any harm."

A sharp jab pushed into Zack's back. He turned to see the bronze samurai looming over him, herding him to the centre of the room with a prod of his spear.

"That is not possible," the Commander replied. "My duty is to the Tower and its inhabitants. Now, do the right thing and comply."

Bast scoffed, a wary eye glancing around at the nearest statues.

"By comply, you mean let the Thirteen kill us."

"If that is what is necessary to protect the Tower and its people, yes." The Commander's voice was unyielding and the ring of statues tightened around them.

Kimmy thrashed in the vice grip of the statue.

"Oh, brilliant. You protect the Tower's people by killing the Tower's people. Do you hear yourself, or do the words just bounce off that thick rock head? How is that the right thing?"

The Commander was unmoved. The hulking mass of stone stood motionless on the edge of the closing circle.

"It is right if the Tower says it is right. Sometimes a sword must be melted down or discarded when it is not fit to be wielded."

A metal hand closed down on Zack's shoulder, holding him in place and beside him, Charlie cried out as another statue grabbed her around the waist. Max barked at her captor while Art and Bast slipped forward, avoiding grasping stone hands.

Art clutched his broadsword in two hands, his eyes alight with rage.

"You and your soldiers are going to have to kill me now then, Commander. I'm not letting the Thirteen torture and kill me like they did Jackie."

"What?" It was brief, but there was a touch of confusion in the Commander's voice.

"Look around," Tabitha replied, "Jackie isn't here. Before the Tower ordered our capture, they kidnapped, tortured and killed her."

"But why?" The Commander's voice raised in volume and emotion. "She was not complete yet. Why would you destroy something before the making of it was finished? Before it could be properly tested? That is wasteful. That is wrong."

Footsteps sounded from across the Entrance Chamber and, through the gaps between the statues, a dozen people came into view and approached them. At the head of them was Erik, his battle axe in hand.

"Ah, well done, Commander," he said, "we've been looking for these troublemakers. We can help you escort them to the cells."

The Commander turned to face Erik.

"Apologies, but no. These six are under my protection and will not be surrendered to the Tower."

"Excuse me?" Erik and some of the other mages looked at each other in confusion. "You have your instructions, don't you? You must obey."

"No, I must not. Not today. Not in this." The Commander glanced towards the statues. "Release them."

The samurai released its grip on Zack while Charlie, Kimmy and Tabitha's captors opened their arms, dropping them to the ground.

"Stand aside!" Erik pointed his axe at the Commander. "You may have lost your loyalty, but we have not."

The Commander's only response was still silence.

"Last warning, golem," Erik bellowed, "I have killed dragons, giants and vampires. I've bested you one to one a dozen times. And I will go through you if I need to."

Erik's shouts echoed off the Commander's unmoving body.

"Fine." Erik waved his hand, and a ripple of deep blue light washed over his body, leaving behind icy armour in its wake before flowing across his axe to create a wickedly jagged edge. With a shout, he charged at the Commander, swinging the axe in a downward blow.

The Commander was always quicker than a chunk of mountain should be, but Zack had never seen it move so fast, so smoothly. Erik's brutal swing passed through the space where the Commander had been moments before, clanging against the Tower's stone floor. In the same fluid action, the Commander threw a left hook that landed squarely in Erik's chest. The icy armour shattered and the force knocked Erik halfway across the room.

"You did not best me," the Commander said, "you were simply assessed as adequate."

In the stunned silence that followed, Zack saw that the other mages had positioned themselves between his friends and the Tower doors.

"Back up the stairs, now," Tabitha called.

The Commander pointed to the four statues at the back.

"Go with them, take them to safety. The rest of you, hold the line. Defend the friends of the unforged!"

With the silence broken, the Tower mages launched into a magical and physical assault against the wall of statues while Zack and his friends turned and raced up the stairs.

Tears streamed down Charlie's face, and she looked across to Art as they ran.

"She still manages to protect us."

"I can't," Art replied, his lips tight, "Not now."

The sounds of statues clashing against mages faded as they raced up the stairs and down a hallway, Bast out front. A brutish figure leapt out at him from a doorway as he passed, but he ducked, sliding across the floor under the grasping arms. Off balance, the attacker stumbled into the hallway and was revealed to be an eight-foot-tall man, with thick, leathery skin. Judging by the torn shirt and pants, Zack assumed he was from the School of Body.

The brute rounded on Bast and, this time, was able to grab him by the ankle. He lifted him upside down off the ground and made as if to swing him against the wall but turning his back to the group had been a mistake. A stone statue in the shape of a Greek hoplite charged forward and, rather than using the short sword in its right hand, brought its left hand around in a savage uppercut to the Body mage's kidneys.

The man yelped in pain, dropping Bast, who tumbled forward to end up on his feet. The hoplite slammed his foe against the wall and used the weight of its stone to pin him there.

"Keep going," Tabitha yelled, leading the others past the grappling figures.

"Keep going where?" Art asked, following.

"With the entrance blocked, there's only one other way out of here," Tabitha replied.

After three more corners and another half-flight of stairs, they arrived back at the Gate Room. The shouts and footsteps of pursuers had hurried them along and while the echoes made it hard to judge the distance, they'd have company soon.

"Where to?" Bast asked, approaching the symbol-carved arch on the side of the room. "Back to Slovenia?"

"They can follow us, right?" Charlie asked.

Bast nodded.

"Assuming one of my lot gets here in the next couple of minutes, yeah."

"Maybe you make a bunch of gates," Art said, "confuse them."

"That would wipe me out," Bast replied, "and there's too many of them to make a difference."

Footsteps pounded on the stones nearby. A voice shouted out, "They're in the Gate Room. Hurry!"

"We could go back to where we just left," Charlie blurted, her eyes fixed on the doorway. "Try and lose them in the forest."

"Or lose ourselves," Tabitha replied. "We don't know what's out there."

Despite everything else happening, Tabitha's comment drew Zack's thoughts to the kiss he had shared in those woods. He did know something that was out there, elves. Elves! An idea flashed in his mind.

"We know what's about to be in here," Bast said. "I need a destination."

"Can you remember how to reach that Fae realm we rescued the baby from?" Zack asked.

"I think so," Bast said. "First gate I ever closed. But why the hell would we want to go there?"

The full idea was still forming in Zack's mind, but they were running out of time.

"We can ask the Queen for sanctuary."

"I don't know, Zack." Tabitha looked uncertain.

"I order you to stand aside, statue!"

Several mages had reached the doorway where the three remaining statue escorts had formed a barrier with their bodies.

"Do it, Bast," Tabitha said, "Get us out of here."

Bast's hands whirred into motion and he mouthed his incantations. His orange light brought forth a grey disc, but before it was more than half a metre wide, the terracotta soldier hurtled through the air, clipping Art on the shoulder, before crashing against the wall. The remaining statues, a hollow set of medieval plate armour and the bronze samurai, moved closer together to close the gap, but the doorway was too wide. A pair of mages forced their way through, with more coming behind.

"Kimmy. Firestorm," Tabitha said and her fingers wove through the air with faint wisps of blue light streaking behind them. A gust of air poured forward, strong and steady, but nothing like the jets of air Zack had seen her throw around.

Kimmy moved beside her and worked her own incantation. She poured spurts of flame into Tabitha's windstream and, by the time it reached the doorway, had unfurled into twirling waves of fire. The flames did little to their statue protectors except to heat their bodies, but the mages fell back away from the doorway, patting out where their clothes had caught alight.

"Zack," Art said, rubbing his shoulder, "how is it that you and I don't have a cool codeword like Firestorm?"

Charlie laughed before pulling an arrow from her quiver and nocking it to her bow. "You do have Gaga."

Art groaned.

"That won't hold them off for long," Tabitha said, "There's at least one Air mage out there. How are we going, Bast?"

"Almost there." Bast's voice was strained as he focused on the growing gate.

"Forward, now," a voice shouted from the corridor and the flames fell away. "Don't let them escape."

Mages charged in from the left and right of the doorway. One incanted, her hand blooming with orange light as she gestured towards Bast, but Charlie released her bowstring and sent an arrow through the woman's hand.

A gorilla appeared from the right and caught the plate armour in a crushing grapple, pinning its mace and shield to its side. Kimmy flung a fist-sized ball of fire at the beast, but a few inches away from its target, it collided with a flash of steely grey light and fizzled.

With the armour occupied, two mages, armed with a sword and warhammer respectively, forced the samurai back. And more mages poured into the room.

"It's open," Bast yelled, "let's go."

"Stop them!" one of the mages shouted.

Bast jumped through the gate, followed by Art. Charlie was backing toward it, firing arrows as fast as she could, with Max at her heels, but Tabitha and Kimmy had inched forward while they whipped wind and fire in all directions to buy Bast time. Zack lunged, moved up and half guided, half pulled them to the gate. They stepped through, each throwing one final spell. Zack nodded to Charlie to jump through and Max followed her. As Zack stepped back to do the same, his eyes latched on to a man across the room, finishing a gesture with a blur of red light. A blue-white ray of heat shot toward Zack, but before it struck him, the bronze samurai leapt into its path. The ray struck the statue in its shoulder and the heat rippled out, turning the bronze into molten drops. Its arm clanged to the floor and, off balance from the weight change, the rest of it toppled over. Zack looked at it helplessly and fell backwards through the gate.

CHAPTER 20

Bast snapped the gate shut before Zack had landed on the grassy earth, his backpack somewhat softening the fall.

"Is everybody okay?" Tabitha asked as Zack climbed to his feet.

"The samurai statue isn't," Zack answered, "I watched it get cut in half."

"Sorry to hear that, mate," Bast said, "but it is just a statue."

"Is it?" Charlie asked. "The Commander isn't. It… or they, I guess, went against the Tower to help us."

"Which will be wasted if we don't get a move on," Tabitha said.

They were in the same clearing they had visited once before, encircled by a thick mist and with a single hill in the centre. And, as before, a wooden door sat embedded in the side of the hill.

"May we enter, please?" Art asked when they reached it. "We humbly seek an audience with her majesty, the Queen."

Kimmy groaned.

"I almost forgot the stupid voice he made last time he was here."

The door swung open and, ignoring her, Art led them through. Smooth, wooden steps guided them down in a gentle spiral and, as the light from above faded into murk, light from further down softened the shadows. A few more metres and the stairs finished in soil, sunlight streaming in from an uneven gap in the wall.

Art was the first through.

"Well, this is different." He stepped away to make room for the others.

The stairs had led them into a sparse forest, with grass and wildflowers growing in the warm yellow sunlight that streamed through the loose canopy.

"Spring?" Tabitha asked. "Last time we came here we entered into Autumn and had to move through Winter before we got to Spring."

Art shrugged.

"I don't know. Maybe because I asked to see the Queen, we got a little head start? But that's good, right?"

"I guess so," Tabitha said, "but if those nymphs and things show up this time, the five of you need to keep your pants on. If you lot devolve into another disgusting orgy, I swear you'll be smelling what I summon up for a week."

Zack wasn't so sure the change in seasons was a good sign and his mind started filtering through possibilities, but the others were walking down the path, so he hurried to catch up.

"Will you be able to help us this time, anyway?" Kimmy asked. "Now that Nell has cured you and everything?"

"Whoa!" Charlie replied.

Art turned and walked backwards a few steps, shaking his head at Kimmy.

"There's nothing to cure."

Tabitha rolled her eyes.

"Thank you, you two. I'm still ace. Nell hasn't changed that. I'm romantically attracted to her, not sexually."

Kimmy seemed unfazed by the looks she was getting from the others.

"I don't see the difference."

Bast laughed.

"That's because your idea of romance, Sis, is when a guy buys his own con—"

"Over there!" Charlie pointed to a cluster of trees, where two figures were watching.

As they travelled down the path, the watchers wandered towards them. One was a satyr, standing tall on his fur-covered goat legs that ended in a bare and well-chiselled human chest. Next to him, slinking her way through the wildflowers, was a dryad. An almost transparent sheet of moss was all that obscured her oak-coloured body. Zack forgot how to swallow.

"No, thank you. We are not interested in any of that today," Tabitha called out to them before whispering to the others. "Help me out a little?"

"I seriously forgot how hot these goat dudes were," Bast said. "Look at his arms."

Zack tore his eyes away from the approaching beauty and fixed them instead on the path. He placed his hands on Bast's and Charlie's backs and nudged them to speed up.

"We can do this together. Just keep moving."

Bast and Charlie reached forward, looking down at their feet and the six of them shuffled in a loose scrum along the path. Time oozed by and Zack's nose was filled with the perfume of flowers, the cloying sweetness of berries, the dry scent of sun-warmed wood and the freshness of leaves. He shook his head to clear it and noticed through his periphery that more than a dozen forest dwellers had joined them on the path. His eyes latched on to a pair of slim, bare feet, as dark pink as a lotus flower and his neck craned against his will to follow up past the ankles and up the legs. He felt Bast slip away sideways from his grasp and focused as hard as he could on why that was a problem.

"Tabs, this isn't working," he cried out, "I think you need to go full skunk."

"No!" Art's voice was distraught.

Zack looked up to see him reaching out to a tall, muscular woman, with grey skin and moss-coloured hair. Next to him, Kimmy was trying to climb on the back of a centaur and struggling, both because he had no saddle and also because she had not stopped kissing him to do so.

Tabitha began her incantation but before she could continue, a ball of fire crashed into the grass beside them, unleashing a wave of sizzling heat. The nymph beside Zack released a shrill scream and his senses flooded back to him. The forest dwellers bolted for the trees and Kimmy was flung into Bast as the centaur galloped away. Zack turned around to see a mob of mages in the distance. He leapt to the side as an arrow landed where he had been standing and, while some mages incanted their own spells, others charged forward down the road.

"They've found us!" Zack shouted. "Run!"

They sprinted down the path and Zack focused on keeping up with the others, but Bast shot frequent looks past him, over his shoulder.

"We're doing okay," Bast said between breaths, "We're keeping our lead."

"And there's the door to Summer," Art said from in front. "The Queen's sanctuary awaits."

Up ahead, the path ended in a massive oak tree with a door at its base. Bast sprinted to reach it first and held it open for the others. Zack huddled in after Max and Bast followed, closing the door behind them.

"Um, where's the court?" Tabitha's voice held more than a hint of distress.

Zack's eyes adjusted to the light, brighter here than it had been in Spring. Unlike the last time they had visited, there were no ivy-clad stone walls, no rich carpets, no thrones and, worst of all, there was no Queen.

"What's going on?" Bast asked.

"I don't know," Art replied.

"Perfect." Kimmy glared at him. "Just perfect."

"They are right behind us. The Queen's not here, but the path is." Charlie pointed to a path of dry earth that meandered its way over and around the soft hills of Summer's landscape. "We need to move."

"Agreed," Tabitha said, "but let's keep an eye out for any sign of her court."

Tabitha set out in a jog and the others matched her pace. There were fewer trees and colourful flowers here than in Spring. And there were more hills, covered in longer, drier grass. And there was the heat.

It was not the scorching heat of an Australian summer like burning rays from the sky. Instead, it was a softer but more heavy heat that came up from the ground as much as from the sun. Zack caught himself in a yawn as he ran.

There had been no sign of the Queen's court and, thanks to the path's curves, no longer any sight of the door from Spring. A bend in the path had brought them to where a hilltop tree cast a shadow on a sloping recline of grass and clover.

Tabitha brought them to a halt.

"Let's take a break for a moment. We can have a rest and listen out to see if we can hear them following us."

Bast dropped his bag and pulled out a bottle of water. Tabitha reached out and stopped him.

"Is it safe to drink here?"

Art nodded and drew his own bottle.

"If we brought it with us, it's fine. The rule was eat and drink nothing from here."

It was almost pleasant, sitting on the hillside, bottles of water and snacks in their hands. In the still silence, in between crunching, gulping and more than a few yawns, nobody could hear any sign of their pursuers. They were still out there, but for a moment, there was at least the illusion of safety.

"Aw man, we gotta come back here sometime when we're not running for our lives," Bast said, laying back against the warmth of the hill.

"It's nice and soft, isn't it?" Kimmy said with a yawn.

Murmurs of agreement sounded between them.

They needed to get moving, but Zack figured that resting a little bit longer would help them push themselves more later. Plus, the Tower mages were probably resting themselves. They had time for a brief respite. He laid back against the grass and let the soft warmth embrace him. Soft, except for something hard and pointy pressing against his lower back. Stifling another yawn, he rolled onto his knees and parted the grass where he had been laying, looking to find and move whatever stone or stick had interrupted his rest. His hand brushed against something long and slender - a branch then. He closed his hand over it and made to throw it aside when its pale white colour became visible. A bone!

Dropping it, he rummaged through the grass and found several more and a belt buckle. Even with his adrenaline coursing, the drowsy desire to lay back down crept through his brain. He reached for a thread of Life and directed it into his adrenal glands, stimulating them into overdrive. His heartbeat dangerously fast, but with his fatigue dissipating, he would have a chance to worry about that later. Beside him, Art snored peacefully.

Not for long. Zack slapped him across the cheek.

"Wake up!"

Nothing.

He slapped him again and shouted louder into his ear, "Wake. Up."

Art's eyes snapped open in startled confusion, but they were still thick with sleepiness.

"Whuh… what?"

"Get up," Zack yelled, "We're being Rip Van Winkled!"

He held up a pair of bones to emphasise his point. Art stumbled groggily to his feet and looked around at the others sleeping on the hill.

"Oh yeah, this is bad."

His eyes glowed with purple light and when they faded, he looked more alert.

"Wow, whatever this is, it's strong. I can't hold it off for long. What's the plan?"

"I don't have one," Zack said around a yawn, "We need to wake them up at least."

Art rubbed the handprint on his jaw.

"Maybe I'll be in charge of that."

His eyes flashed purple again and the other four sat up with a chorus of startled screams.

"What's happening?" Charlie asked as she climbed to her feet.

"Summer is putting us to sleep." Zack held up the bones for his friends to see. "Permanently."

They stared at the remains with expressions of horror.

"Okay, let's get moving again then," Tabitha said.

They reshouldered their backpacks and Charlie coaxed Max awake before setting out down the path again. They had barely made it five minutes when each of them was yawning and their strides slowed and shortened.

"This is not good," Bast said, covering his mouth, "Can't either of you do something about it?"

Art shook his head.

"This is so much stronger than my Mind magic."

"And I can't keep charging up our adrenaline," Zack replied. "Getting sleepy just isn't enough of a threat for our bodies to get charged up about."

"You say we need a threat?" Kimmy asked.

"No… I didn't say that." Zack didn't love the look in Kimmy's eyes.

"Hold still," she said, "I think I've got something."

Kimmy's hands flared red and she reached out to Zack.

"What are you doing?" he asked.

"Sharing my first lesson," Kimmy replied, "Fire is hot."

A pinprick of heat seared in the back of Zack's neck and he gasped from the pain.

"What did you do to him?" Charlie asked.

"It's okay," Zack replied, "I think she's onto something. It hurts a little, more than a little actually, but there's no way I'm drifting off with this burning into my neck."

Kimmy cracked her knuckles and got to work and they were soon walking back down the path, each with a pinpoint of burning pain keeping the drowsiness at bay. Art sidled up to Zack.

"There's no way anybody else's burns as much as mine," Art said through gritted teeth, "but I'm not going to give her the satisfaction of complaining."

Zack nodded along, but he wasn't really listening. His eyes, open now to the dangers of Summer, were drawn to the hills and clumps of tall grass they passed. A pair of boots stuck out from one on his left and, shortly after, a skeletal hand, half buried in the soil on his right. The pain didn't seem too hard to bear in comparison.

The path wound around several more hills and Charlie called out from the front. "Look! Walls!"

In the distance, stone walls, like the back of a cathedral, stood clad in ivy.

"Is that the court?" Tabitha asked. "Like, have we just come in behind it this time?"

"One way to find out," Art replied, "The path leads straight to it."

When they were only a few hundred metres away, Art spoke again.

"The walls look right, pretty much how I remember them."

"Yeah," Zack replied, "but it's too quiet. The Queen had attendees, courtiers, musicians even."

"Maybe they're breaking for lunch," Art said, but he didn't sound like he was even trying to convince himself.

Zack's suspicions were confirmed when they followed the path around the wall. This was indeed the Queen's court. Rich carpets of green and gold covered the ground, wrapping around a platform, atop which sat two massive thrones. And in those thrones sat two figures. On the left, a tall, thin man with pointed elven ears and blond hair held within a golden crown. On the right was the most beautiful woman Zack had ever seen, as tall as her companion, a slightly more ornate golden crown sitting atop her rich, tangled auburn hair. The Queen and her consort. Both deep in slumber.

"What?" Kimmy asked with clear exasperation. "Why are they asleep?"

"Should we wake them?" Bast asked.

"No." Zack's voice was firm. "Remember back to our first time here. Jackie warned us about waking the two people in Winter."

"Yeah, but they were scary," Charlie said, "The Queen was nice enough. And she seemed to like you."

Despite himself, Zack blushed at the memory.

"I don't think it matters. This Queen is asleep, which means it's not her time."

Tabitha narrowed her eyes at him.

"'This' Queen?"

Zack nodded.

"We need to keep travelling through the seasons and ask the Winter Queen for sanctuary."

"That wasn't the plan," Tabitha replied, her arms crossed.

"We don't really have a choice," Art said.

"And we don't have any time, either." Bast pointed back down the road. "They've caught up."

Rounding the last of the hills, their pursuers came into sight. There seemed to be less of them than there had been in Spring, but still over a dozen— more than Zack and his friends could withstand.

Charlie and Max ran behind the throne.

"The door's back here, just like in Winter."

Zack followed the others through the door, his mind buzzing with the implications of negotiating with the Winter Queen. But first, they had to lose their pursuers and make it through Autumn.

CHAPTER 21

Music, singing and the sounds of revelry met them with an almost physical force as they stepped through the door. As in their first visit to Autumn, they seemed to be in a massive banquet hall adorned with tapestries and ribbons of yellow, orange and red. A carpeted path ran through the room between long tables piled high with a variety of food and drinks. And, still startling after years in the Tower, hundreds of fae creatures celebrating. Satyrs, elves, dwarves, centaurs and dryads.

"Let's hurry before they catch up to us," Tabitha said.

"Can you drop the magic first, Kimmy?" Art said, rubbing at his neck.

"Can't handle the heat?" Kimmy replied with a smirk, but she waved her hand and the pain disappeared.

Together, they strode down the carpet to reach the other side. They had only passed a few tables when a pair of gnomes approached them, reaching up to offer a pewter stein of frothy liquid.

"No, thank you, my good friends," Art replied, "but I hope you enjoy the festivities."

They were a few tables deeper into the room and had given several more polite declines when Zack pulled them to a stop.

"What is it?" Tabitha asked. "We need to hurry."

"I have an idea," Zack replied. "They'll be here any second now and I think a fight in here would go really badly for them and us, but I think we can make this room work in our favour."

"Okay, what do we do?" Charlie asked.

Zack pulled the oat cookies he'd been eating in Summer from his pocket.

"Quickly get out whatever food you have and follow my lead."

Sharing confused looks, the others complied while Zack approached a table next to the path.

"Excuse me, my friend," he said to an oversized badger sitting upright at the table, "Do you mind if my friends and I join you for a moment?"

"What are you doing?" Tabitha whispered in a hiss that did nothing to hide her worry.

"Not at all," the badger replied and scooted to the side.

A pair of dwarves and a satyr also shifted in their seats, making room for the others. Zack gestured for them to take their places around the table. Tabitha and Bast looked at Zack nervously as they sat down, but Art's smile suggested he was catching up with the plan.

"Those look a bit dry," the satyr said, pointing at Zack's biscuits and pushing a tray of roasted ribs toward him, "Try some of these instead."

"They smell delicious." Zack's stomach growled from the truth of the statement. "But unfortunately, my allergies won't allow it."

"What are we doing?" Tabitha spoke with more insistence.

The door opening echoed through the room and Zack glanced to see the Tower mages enter.

"Now, make a big show of eating," Zack said, "then we get up and hurry to the next door."

Tabitha still looked a little confused, but she bit a wide mouthful from her muffin and chewed away. The others did the same and Art shared a look of understanding with Zack across the table.

"Quick," Art said, his voice carrying further than their table, "finish up the meal so we pass through to the next room."

Kimmy glared at him but stuffed her last cookie into her mouth and stood up. Zack thanked their fae hosts and joined the others back on the carpet.

"Stop there!" One of the mages shouted at them, but they kept shuffling down the path, weaving past the fae revellers who continued to offer them food and drink.

Zack glanced over his shoulder and, to his relief, their pursuers had paused and were engaged in an argument with each other. One of them pointed to the food on the nearby tables and then to Zack and his friends. Another shook his head and the disagreement grew more heated. Zack held his breath in anticipation and then it happened. A female mage, on the side of the first mage, leant across to the table beside her and ripped the leg off a roast turkey. The three elves at the table cheered and a gnome stood on the bench seat and offered her a flagon. The male mage beside her snatched it and swallowed down a mouthful of its contents. Four of the other mages grabbed at food from the table and gulped them down, while the remaining mages watched on, shaking their heads.

Tabitha pulled at his shoulder.

"Zack, c'mon, we need to hurry while they're distracted."

"Something's going on with them," he replied, "watch."

The mages who had taken the food did not stop at their first mouthful. The woman with the drumstick tore the last piece of flesh from the bone and then claimed a seat at the table, reaching for a flagon of her own, while the man with the first flagon sat down beside her and scooped a helping of roast potatoes onto a waiting plate. The mages who had not partaken, shouted at them to get up and were ignored by those who had sat down to eat and drink. But when one of them put their hands on the woman and tried to pull her from the table, everything changed.

The three elves, who had been singing to each other while sliding more side dishes down the table, stood in unison and shouted at the mages. The fae creatures at the nearest tables leapt to their feet and closed in around their reluctant guests, the mood of revelry replaced by one of coiled hostility.

A burst of fire erupted out of the encircled mages. The heat forced the creatures back but drew the attention of dozens more who rose and moved toward the source of the flames. All the while, the mages at the table continued to eat and drink, seemingly unaware of what was happening behind them.

"What is going on with them?" Charlie asked.

"It's brilliant," Art whispered, "Most of them obviously don't know the rules here and, when they saw us eating, some of them probably assumed you needed to eat to get through this room. But they ate fae food and now they are stuck here. And the ones that didn't eat broke the hospitality rules by fighting. Brilliant work, Zack. I wish I thought of it."

"You're right, Tabs," Zack replied, "we should go."

Tabitha prodded them forward in the direction of the door and they hurried on, the sounds of a fight erupting behind them.

"Next stop, final station, Winter," Art said, holding the door open for the others.

Zack took a deep breath and stepped through.

An icy stillness hung in the air, biting at their exposed skin as they entered. It was night, as it had been the last time they entered Winter two years ago, but this time, they were not met with complete darkness.

It was dark. It clung to the sky and to the edges of their vision, but it was kept at bay by two dozen torches, their meagre flames struggling to cast back more than a shred of the lurking night. Inside this fragile bubble of light was a throne room, a pale echo of the one they had found in summer. The carpets were white and dark blue, the walls were half consumed by a leafless creeper and the creatures in attendance within the room gathered in only a whisper louder than silence.

In the centre of the room, sitting in a pair of thrones, were two figures. Also, a reflection of the Summer court, but not one that could be called paler. Sharper, perhaps. Zack had seen them before, but only while they slept. They were awake now and their eyes were fixed upon the group of young mortals who had entered their domain.

The man was tall, with broad shoulders that spoke of strength despite his otherwise lean build. His long beard, knotted and white in his slumber, was darker now and had been somewhat tamed. He wore armour of black metal, that gleamed in the frost, and a long, wicked spear rested against his throne. On his head sat a crown of jagged icicles.

To his left sat a tall, thin woman. Zack was shocked at how similar she was to the Summer Queen; they might have been twins. And like the Summer Queen, she was beautiful. But it was a beauty like a frozen lake; a layer of idyllic perfection that rested upon the threat of danger. Her hair shimmered white and her skin was whiter still, in stark contrast with her dress, which was of darkest blue. Her icy cyan eyes rested upon Zack for a moment before she turned away and spoke with her companion.

Accepting that it was his hurried plan that had brought them here, Zack stepped forward first, leading his friends closer to the thrones. The attendees parted, although it felt less to give them space and more to emphasise how exposed the group was before the court. There were dwarves, elves and satyrs, but each looked more gaunt and with darker hair than their counterparts in the other rooms. There was a pair of gnomes that stared at Zack with such open malice that he wondered if they owned red caps as well as the navy ones they were wearing. And there were several attendees whose features were hidden under long cloaks and deep hoods.

But all of the fae faded from focus when the Queen looked upon Zack and his friends once more.

"Welcome, once more, to my domain. You have accepted the offer to return in good faith and you have overcome the trials of the journey and thus have earned an audience. What is it that you seek?" Her voice was quiet but clear and it was as if the wind itself stopped while she spoke.

Art glanced at Zack before replying, "We thank you, your Majesty, for your most generous welcome. We come before you to request sanctuary."

"Sanctuary is well within my power to provide." The Queen sat back against her throne. "Be it a place to stay for a time or an escape from those who pursue you. It is simply a matter of determining a fair price."

"We are more than willing to discuss what that price would be," Art said, with an eagerness in his voice.

"I am sure you are," the Queen replied, "although it will be more than a dance, I'm afraid. In the depth of Winter, true value is laid bare. And it is the true value we must investigate. To seek sanctuary is a simple request, but other mortals followed you through my realm, where they met with Spring's allure, dreamt in Summer's warmth and tasted of Autumn's abundance. And at each step, my domain's touch worked in your aid. Now, if this was an unforeseen boon, that is one thing. But if my domain was wielded, however deftly, as a weapon against one's foes, without my leave, then that is a different thing, with a different price."

The Queen's eyes drifted to Zack. His tongue sat too big in a mouth that was too dry.

Art bowed low at the waist.

"I can assure you, your Majesty, that none—"

Zack forced himself past Art and interrupted.

"It was not unforeseen, your Majesty. While I had no specific plan in mind, I anticipated I would be able to use the rules of your realm against our pursuers. But my friends had neither part nor knowledge of this." His heart was crashing against his ribs.

The Queen leant forward and raised an eyebrow as she stared with intent at Zack.

"This makes things interesting indeed. Negotiating for a favour already granted makes it hard for one to reject the price asked."

"We'll just leave then," Tabitha said, "Sanctuary or not, if your price is unreasonable."

"You misunderstand, young captain." The Queen spoke that last word with a tone that made it unmistakably clear she understood who she was speaking to. "To leave with a debt unpaid would render my hospitality forfeit."

Something drew Zack's eyes across to the Queen's companion. The tall man hadn't moved; his posture and facial expression remained passive. But somehow, regardless of that, everything about him had changed. Before, he may have been likened to a fierce guard dog waiting for his mistress's call. Now, he was a crouching wolf, pulling against his leash and eager to sink his teeth into—

"One year." Zack blurted out his offer, his mind having raced through a dozen other options.

"Zack, what are you—?" Charlie stepped forward.

"Silence." The Queen's voice remained soft but held a sharp edge. "One year? Go on?"

"I offer one year of my life, of my future, of your choice, given to your service," Zack replied.

The Queen threaded the fingers of her hands together.

"And you think you, within this year, are of particular value to my court?"

"Probably not," Zack said, thinking about how much more value Art's Mind magic might be to the Queen, or Bast's ability to open gates for her, or the dozens of other things his friends could do. "But the worth of something to its owner must also be considered and my future is precious to me."

"Well said," the Queen replied, "but one is not sufficient. Six years is the price. For the favours taken and sanctuary."

"Six?" Kimmy did not so much ask as she did shout.

"Six?" Zack repeated, quieter, around an involuntary gulp.

"Six," the Queen answered, "One year for each of you. You assumed responsibility for them when you included them in your plan. Now accept that responsibility."

"No, mate," Art whispered beside him, "we can work out another way."

"Accepted." Zack held eye contact with the Queen. "On three conditions."

"List them." Her icy eyes stared back at him.

Zack counted them off on his fingers.

"One, a maximum of one year's service at a time, with a minimum of one year's break in between. Two, the first period of service cannot start until at least one year from now. And three, that time in service passes equally in this realm as it does in my home realm."

"Accepted. Sanctuary for you and companions and all debts paid in exchange for six years under those conditions." The Queen's smile was both genuine and wolfish. "Yes, I think this will be perfectly acceptable."

"Hang on," Tabitha said.

The Queen paid her no notice.

"The door behind you will return you to your home realm, safe from those who seek you."

Bast hooked his arm around Tabitha and pulled her towards the door.

"Remember, no turning back around," Art said, "no matter what she says."

But the Winter Queen did not call out to them. With her bargain made and the audience completed, she had returned her focus to her attendees, leaving Zack and his friends to withdraw from her court and step through the door.

CHAPTER 22

The hot water poured down, turning Zack's pale skin pink and washing away the last of the soap and shampoo. But he wasn't yet ready to leave the shower. In here, it was warm and relaxing. Out there was a hotel room and difficult conversations. Conversations he'd managed to avoid while Bast had hopped them through a series of gates in the hope that the Tower would be unable to follow. They had been too busy to talk as they had bounced from the Irish forest where the Queen had sent them, through six gates, to a modest hotel in the centre of Seattle. But he hadn't avoided the looks.

The water turned cold, and he rushed to turn off the tap before wrapping a towel around himself. No more avoiding.

Dried and clothed, he stepped out of the bathroom and was relieved to find only Art waiting for him.

"I used up all the hot water, sorry," Zack said.

"Six years?" Art looked equal parts angry and terrified. "A fae contract for six years. And you didn't even try to negotiate."

"Yes, I did," Zack replied, "She had me over a barrel on it, but I got the conditions I needed to stop it really screwing me over. And we got away."

"That doesn't mean it was okay for you to make these kinds of calls. We're supposed to be a team."

"And I'm trying to contribute to that team. Everybody else has powerful magic, helping us fight, hide or escape. I'm just trying to do my part."

The fear on Art's face slid away as his anger grew into full-bottle fury.

"I can't do it anymore, Zack. I can't keep trying to convince you how important you are to us, how powerful you are in your own right. I don't think you're going to be happy until one of these archmages runs a sharp piece of wood through your own heart. Then you'll have finally done enough and I'll have lost another person. Fine, I wish you a very merry ultimate sacrifice, I'm having a shower."

Art stormed past Zack, slamming the bathroom door behind him. Zack sat on the bed in silence before the connecting door to the next room opened and Tabitha poked her head in.

"We… heard a lot of that," she said, "Why don't you come in here, and we can discuss next steps."

Relieved to have something else to focus on, Zack followed her into the room where Bast, Charlie and Kimmy were sprawling across the two beds. Tabitha offered Zack an armchair while she sat on the television cabinet, facing the others.

"I'll catch you up," Tabitha said, "Using the usual channels, I reached out to the Traveller. He's given us the address of a safehouse in Estonia. A place we can lay low for a few days. He said he can't be there, but he'll let them know to expect us."

"I don't know why we're bothering," Kimmy said, "We're doing fine on our own."

Tabitha shook her head.

"We're doing the best we can, but we've been hiding from the Tower for a week. It might be safer to get help from people who have been hiding from them for years."

"Sounds good to me," Bast said, "I'll look up the address and find a good place to gate in."

"Thanks." Tabitha turned to Charlie. "When Art gets out of the shower, can you go with him to buy some more supplies to refill our stocks?"

"I need some things," Kimmy added, "I'll write you a list."

Charlie rolled her eyes.

"Sure thing, Kims."

Without a task of his own, Zack tilted his armchair to look out the window into the rainy Seattle evening.

***

Zack lugged his backpack through the gate Bast had opened, into an alley across the road from the safehouse. The buildings on either side of them appeared to be old warehouses, with grimy bricks, rusted sheet metal and faded graffiti.

"It's a little close, isn't it?" Charlie asked, her eyes scanning the nearby buildings.

"I was worried we'd stand out if we had to walk too far," Bast replied. "A little hard to push the backpacking tourist bit in the middle of an industrial zone."

"It's like you spat directly in my face, that was so insulting," Art said with exaggerated outrage.

"Yeah, it's fine if people approach us and ask us what we're doing," Bast answered, "but if they notice us from a distance and then tell people, we might have a problem."

"Just because you have a good point doesn't make it less offensive," Art said with a smirk.

"If you two are finished, I'd like to get off the street and into safety," Tabitha said, her eyebrows raised.

Art and Bast fell silent and the group followed Tabitha across the road. It was the middle of the day and the entire district looked empty. It wasn't. Zack could sense human Life in the buildings all around him, but if he had to guess, this area had ceased its participation in industry years ago and had become a slum for squatters and the homeless.

And perhaps for six teens hiding from a secret, mystical organisation.

They approached a side door, as instructed and knocked. An elderly woman, crooked with age, opened it and peered at them with unfocused eyes.

"Tere?"

Tabitha looked at her in confusion before stammering the passphrase they had been given.

"Watermelon in a hat."

The woman blinked at her, showing no sign of recognition until, after several long and awkward seconds, she spoke in accented English, "Okay then."

She ushered them inside before shutting the door. When she walked back past them, she was standing straight and Zack noted that her exaggerated stoop had hidden that she was a tall woman with broad shoulders.

"You have been vouched for, which is why you have been met with an open door and not violence. But I cannot go so far as to say you are welcome here. The Tower has caused many here harm."

"We're fighting against the Tower," Art said.

"Now, yes." The woman shrugged. "But not so much before. As I said, though, an open door. Follow me and I show you around."

Their tour of the safehouse only lasted around ten minutes. The warehouse had been crudely converted into rows of rooms set up like tight bedrooms. The ones closest to the front doors looked like the kind of stark squats Zack had seen in documentaries, but further in they were more furnished and adorned. Still, far cries from luxury, but with personal touches of warmth. And some of the doors were closed.

"These are yours," the woman said, gesturing to three rooms side-by-side. "Two to a room. I take it the dog is bound to one of you?"

"To me, yes," Charlie replied.

"Very well, it can stay with you too. The toilets, showers and laundry are down to the left, common room with kitchen to the right. Eat only what you brought." The woman turned to leave.

"Thank you," Tabitha said, "you didn't tell us your name."

"I know," the woman replied and walked away.

"Alright then," Tabitha murmured under her breath before turning to the others. "Okay, let's pair up."

"Bast and I'll take this one," Art said, stepping inside the nearest room.

Bast looked at Zack with an expression that was half confusion, half apology before following Art in.

Tabitha seemed surprised as well.

"Um, well, I'll pair up with Zack then and you three ladies can take that one."

Charlie nodded and entered her room with Max while Kimmy lingered a moment to put her hand on Zack's shoulder.

"Breakups are tough, buddy. But you'll get through it."

"Not helpful," Tabitha said, brushing her arm away.

Kimmy winked at him, which went a little way to softening the tease and entered her room.

"Come on, Zack." Tabitha squeezed his arm. "Let's drop our bags and then check out the common room."

The room was tiny, with barely enough space for two mattresses, a chest of drawers and a narrow table and chair. It was warmer than Zack expected and he discovered an old oil heater in the corner that was radiating heat, despite not being plugged in.

"That's pretty cool," Zack said.

"I just hope Kimmy doesn't blow this place up trying to see how it works," Tabitha replied.

The common room was a more expansive space, taking over the back corner of the warehouse. It had been roughly divided into a makeshift kitchen, a dining area with five mismatched tables and a lounge area with a scattering of discoloured couches and armchairs facing an old television. The room was mostly empty, except for a middle-aged couple preparing food in the kitchen and a man tinkering at the side of the television.

The latter looked up and gave them a friendly wave, screwdriver in hand. He was tall, with a sandy brown beard and clean-shaven head and dressed in jeans and a long-sleeve t-shirt. He returned his focus to a metal device, roughly the size of a shoebox, that he was attaching to the television.

"Just one moment, please," he said in careful, heavily accented English, "It is near finished."

As he worked, Tabitha tilted her head in curiosity. She stepped closer to the man and the television.

"Did you just use Air magic?"

The man tightened the last screw and tucked the tool into his pocket. Facing Tabitha, he shrugged.

"I do not know. I have heard of this Air magic from others. I cannot make the wind blow or read the weather, so maybe, no?" He held out his hand. "I am Arie."

Tabitha shook it.

"Nice to meet you. I am Tabitha, and this is Zack. We came with some others who might be out soon."

Arie shook Zack's hand as well.

"Yes, I have heard. You are, or were, from the Tower?"

"We were," Tabitha replied, "Now, they are hunting us and we're trying to fight back."

Arie nodded with sadness in his eyes.

"We were told you were coming. Some people left. The Tower scares them. Others stayed but maybe will not be friendly to you."

"You seem friendly," Zack said.

Arie shrugged again.

"I have been lucky. When I learned what I could do, I found others who taught me what it was. Now, I move around helping where I can."

Tabitha pointed to the augmented television.

"And what is it that you can do?"

Arie's face split into a wide grin.

"I talk to machines, make them more than they were. Sometimes it is fixing an oven or turning some cameras into a security network. Other times, it is free Netflix." He clicked his fingers, and the television turned on, revealing a familiar cascade of movie covers.

"That's amazing," Tabitha said, "How does that work, though? None of the thirteen Schools cover machines."

"I do not know," Arie replied, "it is just what I do."

Zack's thoughts were filled with theories and questions he wanted to ask, but he held them back for now to avoid overwhelming Arie.

"Not bad at all," Kimmy said, looking around the room beside Charlie and Max. She was holding a tin and some fresh vegetables in her hand. "Let's see what this kitchen has to offer, I'm starved."

Tabitha introduced them to Arie, who shook their hands, including Max's paw.

"Did you see the boys?" Tabitha asked.

"They went to check out the laundry," Charlie replied, "to see what kind of facilities are here."

"Two working washing machines and a dryer," Arie answered with a hint of pride.

Kimmy placed her food on the counter and rummaged through the cupboards in search of cooking utensils. The couple nearby hurriedly finished preparing their food and took their meals to a table on the side, where they ate in silence. Kimmy didn't show any sign of noticing and pulled out a chopping board, knife and saucepan. She called out to Arie.

"Hey, what's the water situation here."

"It is okay but boil it." He scrunched up his face and turned to Tabitha and Zack. "Plumbing is silent to me, no matter how nice I ask. I will leave you to get settled. I have some other things to see to."

"It was very nice to meet you," Tabitha said, "Maybe you could join us for dinner tonight?"

"That would be good," Arie replied, "see you then."

Zack walked with him back to the hallway and pulled him aside.

"I'd like to help while I'm here," he said, "I use Life magic and can heal people."

The sadness returned to Arie's face.

"I can tell people, but I think that many will say 'no'. The Tower, it is the cause of a lot of fear here."

"I understand," Zack said, "but the offer is still there."

Arie patted him on the shoulder.

"I will tell them."

Zack left him and returned to his room to find something for lunch.

With night fallen and no windows in his and Tabitha's room, Zack sat in pitch-black darkness, except for the glow of his phone screen. His finger hovered over his mother's number, keen to simply listen to her voice as she spoke about all the mundane things his life was supposed to be filled with and to let her know he was alright. But it wasn't worth the risk. He didn't want to give the Tower any excuse to think his family was a danger to the Silence. And he consoled himself, despite everything that had happened, it hadn't even been a week since he'd last seen her. That fact felt as fantastical as journeys through a fae kingdom or a secret kiss from an elven woman in an otherworldly forest.

He wanted to talk to Art about it but he was all but ignoring Zack's existence and he wasn't sure how to fix that.

The door opened and the dim light from the hallway streamed into the room. Tabitha stepped in, her towel and clothes in one hand and her phone held to her ear in the other.

"And you promise me that you're safe," she said into the phone. "Okay, then. Yes. I miss you too. It was really good to hear your voice. Yep. I'll call you again when it's safe. I will, I promise. Talk soon. Bye."

Tabitha ended the call and switched her phone's flashlight on so she could find her bags.

"Nell says hi."

Zack smiled. "That's nice."

"Ugh," Tabitha said, "it's disgustingly nice, isn't it? I'm still not used to it. I haven't really had a chance to get used to it but it's definitely nice."

She turned the light off and settled onto her bed before speaking in a whisper.

"She was also able to provide a bit more info on what's happening.

The reason why the Traveller couldn't meet us is that the Tower has stepped up raids on the non-Tower mages. Mostly, just making their presence known, giving ominous warnings about people endangering the Silence, but rumours are that a few people are going missing. They might be in hiding…"

"But the Tower might have taken them," Zack finished.

"Yeah. And on top of that, they are throwing our names around. Harbouring us is a risk to the Silence, apparently," Tabitha said, "so that's where the Traveller is. He's helping move people around to keep them safe. A lot of them look up to him."

"No wonder they're not wild about us, though," Zack said.

"That'll change. We're on the right side of this now. Speaking of which, first thing tomorrow, we're planning our next steps in tracking down the remaining nine of the Thirteen."

"Sounds like a plan." Zack couldn't keep the glumness from his voice.

"He's just worried about you," Tabitha said, guessing correctly at one of the sources of Zack's mood. "Six years is a big price to pay, and I'm not sure I even really understand what it entails, if I'm honest."

"It's not as long as the time those mages I tricked will be spending there. And it's a lot shorter than the price Jackie paid."

Tabitha was silent a few moments before she asked, "Is that why you accepted the price? You feel guilty?"

"I don't know," Zack answered, "Maybe? I'm not sure how much choice I had in the end, but yeah. My plan from the start was to lose anybody who was following us in Autumn and Spring and maybe even in Winter's darkness. And they were people who were our allies, even our friends."

"Allies and friends who didn't bat an eyelid before hurling fireballs at us," Tabitha said, "I know there must be some good people in the Tower still, but some of them have shown just how little it takes to turn them into killers. Luring them into the Fae was the right thing and the smart thing, neither of which is that surprising, coming from you, Zack."

"I still feel like crap, though," he replied.

"Good." Tabitha reached out and squeezed his hand. "I'm sorry you're feeling that way, but I'd rather you feel that than nothing."

With that, she rolled over and fell straight to sleep while Zack lay in the dark with his thoughts.

⊰───────────────⊱

The next morning, they sat around a table in the otherwise empty common room. Zack, as usual, wasn't up to eating much for breakfast, so he picked at a travel-sized bag of frosted corn flakes.

"Now that we've had a chance to catch our breaths, let's plan our next moves," Tabitha said, "What pearls do we have?"

"I've got Life," Zack said, placing the metal-coated pearl on the table.

"And I assume I've got Creation," Bast said, placing another beside it, "at least it was where Jackie said she hid it."

Art tensed the way he always did when Jackie's name was mentioned.

"The Mind pearl wasn't where I left it."

"That's not a good sign," Tabitha said, "I'm not sure about ours, there were too many people around for Kimmy and I to get close and then the alarm kicked off."

"So, we have a lead on two of them, with seven more still to find." Charlie used her fingers to count them off.

"Maybe we'll get more leads as we go," Tabitha replied, "but let's focus on the pearls we have. Who should we target first?"

"Life won't be much of a threat," Kimmy said, "let's start there."

"Will you give it a rest?" Art snapped. "It's bad enough the way he talks about himself, but the way you talk about his magic isn't helping."

Zack's cheeks started to burn.

"It's okay, Art. Really."

"No, it's not. You're like a freakin' sponge to this crap." Art turned back to Kimmy. "Think of all the fights we've been in against monsters stronger than us, against mages more powerful than us. What's the one thing we've had that they haven't had? A Lifer."

"I didn't mean it like that." Kimmy crossed her arms. "I just mean that Life can't exactly hurt us."

"Well, what you mean and what you say aren't always the same thing," Art said.

"What can we expect from Life in a fight, Zack?" Bast asked, clearly eager to move the conversation away from Kimmy and Art. "I know what you do for us, but how do we counter it?"

"I'm not sure," Zack said, "if the Master of Life is alone, then we can wear them down, maybe even make them surrender. If they're with somebody else, then we should focus on one of them at a time. That'll put the most drain on them."

"Can't you interfere?" Kimmy asked. "The way other Fire mages can syphon off my magic or the way Bast destroyed those weird gates last year?"

Zack shook his head.

"No. Life is different. It's connected to a living thing and can only be given freely. If I was to interfere, that would be taking it without permission. Corrupting it and maybe me, in the process."

"So that's off the table, then," Charlie said. "What about Creation, maybe we target them first?"

"Nell does Creation magic, not that she thinks of it quite that way," Tabitha said. "She can create pretty much any solid object she can think of."

"So, it's basically a Green Lantern," Art said.

"I'm pretty sure Creation is yellow," Kimmy said with a smug look.

"No," Art replied, "it's a… never mind."

"I think we should go for the Master of Life first," Tabitha said, "if they're alone, they might be our best chance of getting them to surrender."

"I might even recognise them," Zack said, "maybe I can convince them."

The others murmured their agreement.

"Okay," Tabitha said, "let's take a couple more days to rest and get our heads clear. And get ready."

CHAPTER 23

Zack pulled his clothes from the dryer and dumped them in a pile on one of the benches in the laundry. Charlie and Tabitha sat across the room chatting while their own clothes sloshed around in the two washing machines.

"Is it safe for Max to be outside on her own?" Tabitha asked.

"I can still feel her up here." Charlie tapped the side of her head. "She'll let me know if anything is bothering her. And she was going stir-crazy in here. She needs to run and chase things for a bit."

Zack half-folded, half-rolled up his clean clothes, knowing that any extra effort would only be wasted when he crammed them into his bag later. He had finished the last shirt when a group of six men and women walked into the laundry. Zack readied himself for trouble. It wasn't only that they had no dirty clothes with them, their entire body language shouted danger. Two of them hung back by the door, blocking the only exit from the room, while the others sauntered up to Charlie and Tabitha.

Zack's staff was in his room, so he looked around for a potential weapon. A mop rested in the corner; that might do. One of the men took a step forward from the others.

"Hey. Tower girls. You are not welcome here."

Tabitha and Charlie stayed seated. If they were intimidated, neither was showing it.

"We were invited," Tabitha said, her voice calm, "by the Traveller."

The man sniffed.

"He doesn't speak for us. And I say you aren't invited."

"Look," Charlie said, "we're going to be gone in a couple of days. Let's just stay out of each other's way until then, then you don't have to worry about seeing us ever again."

"I don't think so," the man said, "my friends have been chased from their homes because the Tower is hunting you. Petra here has been run from her business by them."

"We're sorry about that," Tabitha replied, "we are trying to take the Tower down."

"That is not what the rumours say," the man said, taking another step towards them. Zack shifted the weight on his feet, ready to leap up. The man continued, "They say you are trying to take control of the Tower, to become the ones in charge."

"What?" Charlie looked at Tabitha.

"But I don't think so," the man said, "I think this is another Tower lie. I think you still work for them and are creeping into our places like rats before skittering home to your masters."

"That's not true," Tabitha said.

"Once Tower, always Tower." Flame erupted from the man's hand. "And the Tower should burn to the gr—" He broke off his sentence, gasping for air.

Tabitha stood up, revealing her twirling right hand, glowing with pale blue light.

"You're right, in a way," she said, "once Tower trained, always Tower trained. And that means we are not easily bullied."

The man fell to his knees, the fire on his hand gone.

"Rush them," said the woman from the door, "we still outnumber them."

"Count again," Charlie said, pointing upward, "we have the numbers."

The ceiling nearest to the door was a writhing mass of black that, much to Zack's horror, was a sea of spiders. Thousands of them. They climbed upon each other, reaching out to the tallest of the men like shadowy stalactites of legs and nightmares.

The two people at the door bolted down the hallway, seconds ahead of the others, dragging their gasping companion behind them. Tabitha sat back down, like nothing had happened and the spiders scattered away, disappearing into cracks in the ceiling and walls.

"I take back everything I've said in the past," Zack said, "you two are way scarier than Kimmy."

"I told you I knew alarming statistics about local arachnids," Charlie replied with a smile.

Zack shivered. The thought of that many spiders in the walls and roof not making him too much more comfortable than seeing them all in one place.

"What about you, Tabs? What was that?"

"I turned the air around his head into pure carbon dioxide," she answered, "I would have stopped before I did any real harm. Charlie, call Max back. We'd better leave as soon as we can. Next time, they aren't going to warn us."

⁂

Two hours later they were driving south, crammed into an old SUV that Arie had coaxed into running before bidding them farewell. Tabitha scrolled through a map of the local area on her phone.

"Another twenty minutes and there should be a turn off on the right into a camping ground."

"Gotcha," Art said from the driver's seat, "I can't believe how smooth this pile of rust is to drive. I don't know how he does it. Is there a fourteenth School, tech-magic?"

"There's Movement magic at play," Bast said, "but it's weird. Like I can only hear every third note in a song."

"Fire is there too," Kimmy said.

Zack thought aloud, "Remember what Trav said, that you only see Fire because you're looking so hard at Fire? Well, maybe Arie is the same. He's looking hard at engines and machines, which is a little bit Movement, a little bit Fire, a little bit of other things, like electricity, which is Air. He's stuck in his own frame of mind, just like we are, but it's a different one."

"Different because the Tower didn't impose it on him," Charlie said, "I reckon you're right."

When they reached the camping ground, Art parked away from the three other cars in the lot and the group headed into the woods away from the recommended tent area. Despite still being summer, it wasn't that warm and Zack only worked up a mild sweat, lugging his bag through the trees. Eventually, they found a spot where the trees were dense enough to give them privacy.

"In a couple of weeks, the next ritual is due to happen," Tabitha said, "it's not Life or Creation due, right?"

"No. Life gets bound to the Tower in December and Creation is right after that in January. It's August now, so the next ritual is…" — Zack counted out on his fingers— "Fire."

"Okay, so we go after either of them and they aren't getting replaced any time soon," Charlie said.

"Well," Art replied, "it's not like December is miles away. We take Life off the table and our deadline to get the remaining eight shrinks to four months."

"Bast, let's go for Life," Tabitha said.

Zack handed him the pearl and Bast knelt on the ground, concentrating. Then he gave a short laugh.

"What's up?" Kimmy asked.

"We didn't need to choose," Bast said, "they're together."

"Damn," Tabitha said, "our only two pearls, and one's a waste."

"They're in our world too," Bast added, "Singapore. And up high… like two hundred metres off the ground high."

"You can tell where they are with the pearls?" Art asked, "With Movement magic?"

"No," Bast answered, "I can tell how far away and in what direction the gate is going to open. The rest is just maths."

"Um… I don't want to be mean," Art said, "but weren't you in the bottom maths class?"

"That's because I didn't care about maths," Bast answered, "because I was never going to use it. Now that it tells me if I'm going to open a gate on land or in the middle of the ocean, I've started to care."

Art laughed. "Fair enough."

"Back to the question at hand," Tabitha said. "That high off the ground probably means skyscraper, right?"

"Yep, a tall one," Bast answered.

"So, what do we do?" Charlie asked. "Come in on the street and scope it out?"

Art shook his head.

"We don't know what kind of security they have, especially now they have a good idea what we're doing. I say we pop in on them."

"Agreed," Tabitha said.

"It'll need to be right on them," Bast said, "so I don't miss and open the gate in mid-air."

"Right." Tabitha rubbed her chin in thought. "We leave our bags here this time. We can come back for them."

Everybody nodded and Bast knelt, beginning his incantation.

"And remember, we give them a chance to surrender," Tabitha said, pulling out her flail, "every chance to surrender."

Charlie used her magic, turning Max into a wolf, while the others readied their weapons. Kimmy pointed at Max as she spoke to Mr Shanks, "See, Max lets Charlie use her magic on her. I should be able to use mine on you."

Mr Shanks shook its blade in disagreement and Kimmy sighed in frustration.

"Ready?" Bast asked.

Tabitha nodded and Bast twirled his fingers, ripping a gate open in front of them. Kimmy charged through and the others followed,

Zack and Bast last.

Zack stepped through the grey disc and into a luxury apartment. The gate had opened in the living room beside expensive leather couches. Across from it was a long marble kitchen and nearby, stairs led up to a second floor. Behind them was a floor-to-ceiling window looking out on a Singaporean evening, high above the sea of lights from cars and shops.

The apartment was not empty. A man with long black hair watched them from the kitchen, while a woman with short, bleach-white hair looked at them with her mouth agape from the base of the stairs. Bast closed the gate, and Tabitha took a step forward.

"We don't want to fight you," she said, holding up her free hand in a gesture of peace, "surrender and you won't be harmed."

"What do you think, Amelia?" the man in the kitchen said.

"Well, Shen, they certainly outnumber us," the woman replied, "I guess we don't have a choice."

"Now," said a second male voice from deeper in the apartment.

A person shimmered into existence behind one of the couches, too close to have been the source of the voice. They kicked the centre of the couch with the flat of their foot and it flew forward. Art leapt out of the way, but it slammed into Zack and Bast with such force that it collected them and, shattering the windows behind them, knocked them out of the apartment.

The collision, both from the couch and the glass, had stunned Zack and by the time he collected his thoughts, he was falling face-first to the streets below. Fast. He could hear Bast loudly incanting to his right and thought he should do the same. Was it even possible to time a surge of Life required to heal the annihilating level of damage he was about to experience? No.

He should have called his mother.

Zack caught sight of somebody below pointing upwards and all he could do was hope he didn't hit anyone, when something grabbed him under his shoulders. The couch shattered against the road, but he was pulled upward before he could splatter beside it. Zack craned his neck to see what was holding him and found Charlie's face strained but smiling. He looked down at her arms wrapped around his chest.

"How did you…?" Then the giant eagle wings flapped behind her as they ascended. "What about Bast?"

"Look to your left," Charlie answered.

Several metres away, Bast was flying upward, streaks of orange light coming from his feet. His grin was so wide it was visible in the dark.

Zack looked back to Charlie.

"You're amazing."

"Eh," she replied, "it's about time I got to save you for once. Now, let's get back up there and help them."

Bast strafed wildly from side to side, but as he gained control over his flight, he streaked ahead of Zack and Charlie before disappearing through the broken window. The sounds of fighting became louder as they approached and when Charlie carried Zack back into the apartment, the battle was well underway.

Kimmy was chasing Amelia up the stairs, a flaming axe in her hand, while the woman cackled and said, "Finally, somebody wants to play."

Tabitha and Art were flanking the one who had kicked the couch, trying to stay out of reach of the mage's arms, which stretched in and out at them.

Max had Shen cornered in the kitchen. He looked unfazed to be fighting a wolf with a butcher's knife and a cleaver and was standing his ground.

A fourth man had appeared outside a room beside the kitchen. Possibly the source of the voice, the man was thin, bald and wearing a pair of broad glasses. Bast flew towards him, his rapier out like a lance, but at the last instant, the man pivoted to the left and Bast crashed through the door. The man followed him, out of sight.

Four mages, Zack thought, taking in the scene. Quite possibly four masters, given how much they seemed to value their privacy. Art and Tabitha appeared to be facing a Body mage but which ones were Life and Creation. And who was the fourth?

Kimmy reached the top of the stairs and faced Amelia on the mezzanine-style loft. Amelia snatched a sword from a table, but rather than attack, she whispered some words and yellow bloomed around her. There was a flash of light and then there were more than a dozen Amelias, each pointing their sword at Kimmy.

"Illusions?" Kimmy said with a mocking sneer. "How terrifying. Let's find one you can stick in, Shanky."

Mr Shanks zipped to the left, thrusting straight through an Amelia's neck, while Kimmy swung her axe through the rightmost one. The next Amelia she attacked dodged to avoid her blade.

"Ah ha," Kimmy shouted, "I have you now."

And then, an Amelia to her left slashed her across the leg. Mr Shanks spun around and soared toward Kimmy, but another Amelia stood in its way and the dagger bounced off her like it had struck stone.

"I'm afraid we aren't all illusions." The Amelias spoke in disquieting unison, shifting through each other as they moved around the room.

Kimmy screamed and a fan of flames poured from her hands. Several of the Amelias were caught in the fire but their only reaction was to laugh.

Downstairs, Art took a glancing punch to the cheek from the tall, muscular mage in the lounge area, the force of which knocked him back onto the remaining couch.

He rolled over it and onto his feet.

"This isn't working. Hold their attention, Tabs, I'm going to do it my way."

Tabitha flicked a jet of wind at the Body mage, knocking them off balance before following up with a swing of her flail. Art's eyes glowed purple, but the light faded and was replaced by a look of confusion.

"They don't seem to have a mind!"

The mage gave a smug grin.

"I'm the Master of Body and you think your sorry excuse for hypnotism is going to bother me? My animus is not some disconnected puppet master. It is one with my flesh. And that flesh is going to rip yours apart."

Their hands whipped out and grabbed Art by the shirt. He hacked at their arm, cutting into it an inch deep, but no blood was visible in the wound. Instead, their grip tightened and Art was hurled into Tabitha, knocking them both off their feet.

Max leapt up at Shen, closing her jaw over his right arm. He staggered backwards a few steps under the wolf's weight, but he seemed otherwise unworried and his face expressed no sign of pain. Instead, he chopped at Max with the cleaver, landing a shallow but wide cut above her front leg. She released his arm and crouched down.

Shen raised his arm to swing again, but an arrow appeared in his chest.

"Drop the knives, or I drop you," Charlie said, closing in on him, another arrow nocked and aimed at his head.

Shen turned his attention from Max to Charlie before using his cleaver to chop the protruding arrow in half. Assuming Shen was the Master of Life, perhaps he had used his magic to switch off his pain receptors. But Zack thought he was familiar with most of the Tower's Life mages and he didn't recognise Shen. He also hadn't recognised the man Bast was fighting in the other room. Something wasn't adding up.

A scream of pain sounded from the room behind the kitchen and the bald man stepped out, blood dripping from the scimitar in his hand.

"Will you three stop playing with them and end this nonsense?" The man flicked his sword to dislodge some of the blood. "Isn't it enough that I gave them to you on a silver platter? Or do I have to kill the rest of them for you, too?"

CHAPTER 24

Already frantic at hearing Bast's scream, the man's words pushed Kimmy into overdrive. Her fan of flames erupted into an intense burst before she turned and barrelled down the stairs, earning a cut to her forearm from one of the Amelias' swords.

"Kill him, Shanks." She pointed at the bald man.

The enchanted dagger disengaged from its fight against illusory and not-so-illusory figures and lanced through the air towards the bald man approaching Shen, Max and Charlie in the kitchen. His attention was focused away from Mr Shanks, but the moment before the knife would have pierced him through the neck, he leapt to the side and, in a fluid motion, opened the freezer door on top of the refrigerator. Mr Shanks flew right inside and the man slammed the door closed behind him.

Kimmy reached him and he turned to meet her, deflecting her axe swing with a twist of his sword.

"Art, the Creation mage is upstairs and open," Tabitha said, skirting a coffee table to dodge the Body mage's elastic arms. "Go use your Mind magic to find the real one. I've got things covered here."

"Sure thing." Art ran for the stairs.

"Excellent. I prefer to fight one on one. It's more satisfying," the Master of Body said, kicking out at Tabitha with an equally stretchable leg.

Tabitha rolled sideways out of the kick's path and launched two blasts of Air at the mage. The first pummelled into their other leg, knocking them onto their back, while the second struck them in the side of their head, spinning them as they fell.

"I'm more than enough on my own," Tabitha said, approaching the fallen mage, her flail whirling.

They gestured towards her, pink light collecting at their fingertips and Tabitha's legs twisted from under her, sending her to the floor as well.

"I am the Master of Body," they said, climbing to their feet, "and not just mine."

They clenched their fist and Tabitha's arms twisted in unnatural angles. She dropped her flail and screamed in pain while the mage watched on in dark satisfaction.

Art paused at the top of the stairs, confronted with more than a dozen sword-wielding women. He held his own sword, ready to parry, but instead of moving forward, he concentrated, his eyes glowing purple.

"There you are," he said, looking past the figures to an empty space against the wall. He muttered the beginning of an incantation, but two Amelias charged forward, swinging their blades. Art dropped the incantation and moved his sword to block theirs. The first revealed itself as an illusion and passed through his blade. He only managed to twist his wrist in time to parry the second and clanged against a solid blade. The force of the blow jarred his hand painfully.

Art ignored the illusory mage and pushed the other away, restarting his spell, but two more Amelias lunged at him.

"Fine," he said, dropping his spell for the second time, "I guess I don't get to use Mind magic today."

Art stepped to the side and kicked at the solid figure, sending it tumbling down the stairs. The impacts of the fall snapped it into pieces that lay still at the base of the staircase. The other Amelias surged forward and Art leapt into the fray to meet them, slashing wildly with his blade.

Zack passed Kimmy as he dashed to the room Bast had entered. It appeared to be a study, with floor-to-ceiling bookshelves against two of the walls and a desk against the third. Bast was lying face up in the centre of the room, blood from several deep wounds leaching into the carpet around him.

Zack dropped to his knees by Bast's side, using his eyes, hands and Life to assess the wounds. Bast was barely conscious, responding in soft groans when Zack pressed against the cuts. He didn't have long, but Zack could wipe himself out trying to get Bast back on his feet right now. He'd lost too much blood and some of these cuts were deep enough to have caused other damage, too.

The smartest thing was to get Bast stable and then get back out there and help the others, which meant stop the blood loss and patch up any organs that had been injured. He drew a thick strand of Life and channelled it into Bast. Even this would cost him and he had to be thorough.

Charlie glanced to where Art was struggling upstairs, holding his sword to block an illusory attack, only to leave himself open to the swing from a solid foe on the other side. She leapt forward, using the kitchen counter for leverage and kicked Shen in the centre of his chest. He slashed at her as he stumbled back but missed with both blades.

"Go help Art work out what's real, Maxie." Charlie kept her eyes forward, nocking another arrow.

Max whined at the idea of leaving Charlie alone but still bounded away up the stairs.

"Drop the knives and get on the ground." Charlie aimed the arrow at Shen's face. "At this range, I can't miss."

Shen's top lip curled in an expression of disgust.

"You will be the one on your knees." He lunged at her, slashing with both knives in one X-shaped motion.

Charlie skipped backwards and fired her bow. Shen turned his head at the last moment and the arrow pierced his right eye, the head puncturing out through his temple. He dropped his knives and turned back to face Charlie, who had hurriedly redrawn her bow.

Shen stared at her with his remaining eye and grasped the end of the protruding arrow before pulling it free, carefully but firmly. Something darker than blood oozed from the wound that had been his eye.

He flung the gore-stained arrow to the floor.

"When I say you will pay for that, you are about to know how literally I mean it."

Shen snapped his hand out at Charlie and despite him being well out of reach, she flinched back, releasing another arrow. It struck him in the shoulder, but he didn't react. Instead, turquoise light gathered in his hand and coalesced into a thin beam that lanced, hitting Charlie in the chest.

The light didn't burn or strike her with force, but it pulsed and Charlie wobbled on her feet. Her skin grew paler and she dropped her bow, leaning on the kitchen counter for balance. The pulsing carried a wave of sickly bright light within the beam from Charlie to Shen. As she dropped to the floor, Shen stood taller and straighter and the dark liquid marring his face retreated back into his eye socket.

A nauseating chill washed over Zack like he had been splashed by an icy bucket of sewage. The streams of Life he was channelling into Bast tremored. Something was very wrong. With a final rapid knit, he stopped the bleeding from the last of Bast's wounds and stood up. Bast was still in poor shape but out of immediate danger. At least as much as any of them were.

Zack bolted to the door, letting his senses guide him to the source of the disturbance.

Close to him, Kimmy fought the bald man with visible frustration. Every swing from her axe was blocked, every burst of flame dodged and she wore a dozen minor cuts to show she had not been able to do the same. But Zack's eyes were drawn past them to where Shen stood over Charlie.

He raced to her side. Charlie's skin was turning grey and the blue of her eyes had faded as she stared ahead, whimpering. Closer to the beam, the nature of the energy was clearer to Zack. And he recognised it. His mind flashed with images of the tiny bone creatures he had fought last year. They had been fuelled by a feverous dark-bright energy that was not Life and here it was being channelled by a mage of the Tower.

Zack looked at him closely and realised. No, not simply a mage of the Tower. This toxic aberrant energy was being cast by the Master of Life. It was wrong. It was abomination. It was a betrayal of everything Zack had learned of Life. And it was ripping the Life from Charlie.

Rational thought fled and Zack leapt at Shen with a scream bringing his staff across Shen's head. A crunch rippled along the staff, but Shen remained undeterred. Zack spun his staff and swung it down onto Shen's shoulder with so much force that the staff snapped in half, dislocating Shen's arm from the shattered bones above it. With a cry of anger and frustration, Zack switched his grip on the broken half of his staff and plunged it into Shen's chest. And nothing. The mage stood there with the makeshift stake sticking out of his chest. This near to him, Zack could sense the pulsing energy flowing to Shen's injuries, fuelled by Charlie's stolen Life to repair the damage.

"Patience," Shen said to him, his voice distant and somewhat distracted, "you'll get your turn when I'm done with her."

While Charlie whimpered, Tabitha screamed. The Master of Body wiggled their fingers in gestures reminiscent of string puppetry and Tabitha's body contorted painfully on the floor. She bit her lip to catch her breath and, between the next screams, she shouted, "Art!"

Max reached the top of the stairs and barrelled through two illusory Amelias to knock back two solid ones, giving Art some momentary space. He ran to the edge of the mezzanine.

"Hold on, Tabs, I'm coming."

"No!" she screamed back. "Stop. Pain."

Art blinked as he processed her words. "Okay…"

With some whispered syllables and a flick of his wrist in her direction, his hand flashed with purple light. And Tabitha fell silent. Her face relaxed and her eyes cleared.

The Master of Body scowled.

"It doesn't matter if you can't feel the pain. Watch as your body breaks around you." Their fingers moved faster and Tabitha's left arm jerked at such a brutal angle that it pulled the bone from its socket. Tabitha closed her eyes and incanted. The mage gestured again and Tabitha's whole body stretched out, arching her backwards against the curve of her spine.

Blue light flared around Tabitha and a violent whirlwind burst through the window behind it. Collecting the shards of broken glass as it moved through the window frame, it spun in the air above Tabitha before descending upon the Master of Body. Their scowl turned into a look of terror before they were engulfed by the whirlwind.

Tabitha's blue light faded and with it the wind. Bloodied pieces of glass scattered to the floor, dropping beside the torn and lifeless body of the mage.

"Thanks, Art," she said with a sigh, "you can stop it now."

"Okay," he shouted, swinging his sword at one of the Amelias that had chased him across the room.

Tabitha groaned in pain and clutched her dislocated arm.

"Oh crap. Maybe that was a mistake."

Art caught the sword of one of the figures on the edge of his blade and kicked her away with the flat of his foot. Max barked at him.

"Okay, Wonderdog," Art said, "our unfriendly mage is over there in the corner. You show me a path through the ones that aren't there, I'll keep the solid ones off you. Deal?"

Max barked again and leapt into the fray, scampering left and right as she moved through the illusory mages and avoided the solid ones. Art hurried to follow, knocking away any swords the created figures swung at her. When he parried the second attack, however, another copy attacked him from behind, cutting deep into his shoulder blade. He blindly kicked back at it, pushing it away, but otherwise kept his focus on Max, who wound a path through the false mages towards the corner. Art took three more cuts before they reached the corner and his steps slowed.

Max stalked towards the empty corner of the room, her teeth bared and a deep growl in her throat. In a shimmer of yellow light, Amelia appeared, crouching against the wall with her hands raised in submission.

"Okay, okay," she said, her eyes wide with fear, "I surrender. I'll do whatever you say. Just don't hurt me."

Art lunged past Max, thrusting the point of his blade into Amelia's face. There was a second shimmer of yellow light and the crouching Amelia disappeared, replaced by one standing with her sword raised, ready to strike. Art's sword was buried deep in her abdomen. She looked at him in disgust before falling to the ground. Behind Art, the copies, illusory and solid, disappeared.

He scratched Max behind the ear.

"Great job, partner."

Shen looked back at the man with the glasses.

"That's Ash and Amelia."

The man knocked Kimmy's left arm away with a lazy slap of his scimitar, disrupting her flame jet.

"I said we needed them, Shen. I never said they'd survive."

"What the hell are you talking about?" Kimmy shouted, lashing out at him with her axe.

"Who do you think you're facing?" the man asked. He shook his head. "Your impressive grades notwithstanding, you're not really the thinker of this little gang, are you? I am the Master of Knowledge."

"Big deal," Kimmy replied, "you're like the Tower's biggest nerd. The rest of us manage with Wikipedia." She feinted a blow to his ribs.

"Cute. Knowledge shows me what was, what is and what will be. And that's why you'll fail. I know what you'll do" — he stepped to the side of Kimmy's kick to his knees — "before you do." He slid his blade through her ribs.

Kimmy dropped her axe and fell to one knee.

"That doesn't look good," Shen said, turning back to Zack, "still, you've taken two of my allies out, so I mustn't be complacent."

With one hand maintaining the pulsing beam syphoning away Charlie's Life, Shen drew patterns in the air with the other and a spidery web of not-Life skittered out from his fingers. The pulsing increased and Charlie shuddered in pain.

Across the room, the Master of Body stirred and climbed to their feet.

"Oh crap," Tabitha shouted, "he's healed them."

But there was something wrong. None of their wounds had closed and their steps were rigid and unnatural as they shuffled towards Tabitha. Upstairs, Amelia rose to her feet as well, reaching out at Art with grasping hands, her eyes staring right through them.

"He didn't heal them," Zack replied, "he's turned them into—"

"Zombies!" Art yelled. He slashed at the walking corpse, cutting across her chest, but it didn't slow her down. "Stay back, Max."

Tabitha cried out as she forced herself to her knees and lashed out with a jet of Air, throwing the zombie backwards a few metres.

Zack knelt beside Charlie. She was dying from no cause but having the Life drained from her. He pulled together a thick stream of Life and channelled it into her. Straight away, her body eased and her colour improved, but it didn't last long. The stream of Life was reacting to the presence of the not-Life, creating a kind of dissonant feedback between the two energies. But even without that, Shen's syphon was stealing the Life Zack was channelling into Charlie almost as fast as Zack was supplying it.

The Master of Knowledge stood over Kimmy, a gloating look of satisfaction on his face as he surveyed the room.

"You did as well as you could, I suppose. So, maybe take some comfort that you didn't do anything wrong. You were always going to fail. You were always going to die here."

Kimmy spat at him, blood mixing with the saliva.

"I'm supposed to be impressed because you think you know my future? I was raised by a woman who told me my future every day of my life. Straight A student. No boys until I'm twenty. Law degree." Kimmy forced herself to her feet. "Partner at a firm by twenty-eight. Married. Giving her grandchildren by thirty. No. Nobody gets to write my fate but me."

"Please," the man said with a dismissive scoff, "I'm not writing your fate. I'm just reading it. And anything you do, I can see it coming from miles away."

"Not everything can be escaped," Kimmy replied.

The Master of Knowledge's smirk was replaced by a flash of fear and then Kimmy exploded into an intense ball of flame that expanded out to engulf the man. His screams were muffled by the roar of the fire. A wave of heat washed over Zack and his channelling faltered.

In every direction, there was death and pain. Tabitha's jets of Air were faltering and the Master of Body's corpse was getting closer. Art hacked at his shambling foe, but it slipped past his blade and was clawing at his shoulder, while Max tried in vain to pull it away by the calf. In the side room, Bast lay deeply wounded and, as the fire cleared, Kimmy fell, her body covered in burns, beside the Master of Knowledge's charred one. And next to him, Charlie had almost been turned into an empty husk.

"Oh well," Shen said, "it appears only I'll survive this night. When you've lived as long as I have, you get used to it."

Lived.

Half a thought flashed in Zack's mind.

"You call what you're doing living?"

"It's better than living," Shen replied, "it's eternal. Without limitation."

Zack stood up, pulling another thread of Life towards him.

"That's not true though, is it? It has one limitation. It shouldn't be. And even it knows it."

Zack thrust his collected Life out at Shen in the most forceful torrent he'd ever channelled. The mage staggered backwards and the syphon stealing Charlie's Life disappeared.

Shen glared at him with open fury.

"For that insult, I will have you screaming while I slowly drink you empty of your Life." He gestured at Zack, releasing a syphoning beam of light at him.

Whether it was instinct or whether the Life he was holding influenced him somehow, Zack split the stream of Life and wove half of it into a lattice, catching Shen's beam before it struck him. The not-Life was still eating its way through his makeshift shield, but it was buying him time for his stream of Life to burn its way into Shen.

But it wasn't going to be enough time.

The magic that had animated the corpses had not been stopped by Zack's attack and while Tabitha crawled away from her attacker now that her magic had failed, Art was screaming from upstairs. The not-Life within Shen had formed a hard outer layer that was keeping Zack's stream of Life from getting inside and doing real damage.

With his right hand outstretched to direct the stream, Zack dropped his left hand to his hip for balance. His fingertips brushed the hilt of the elvish dagger.

Inside.

Zack dropped his stream and drew the dagger, channelling every drop of Life he had gathered into the tip of the blade. He lunged forward, burying the knife deep into Shen's chest. The inky not-Life crept up the blade, but the concentrated Life reverberated against it and detonated.

In an instant, Shen disintegrated, leaving nothing but a pile of clothes, a few fragments of dried bones and an acrid smell in the air that Zack would never be able to forget. The two animated corpses collapsed to the floor and Zack did too, catching his breath and waiting for the room to stop twirling.

And a few seconds later, when the room had stopped spinning, he realised it was burning.

CHAPTER 25

Zack clambered to his feet. A few metres away, several of the kitchen cabinets were on fire and it was spreading to the walls and ceiling.

"Anybody else still up?" he called out, aware of the frantic edge in his voice.

Tabitha groaned in pain as she tried to pull herself up on the television cabinet and Art shuffled over to the edge of the mezzanine, his clothes torn and drenched in blood.

"I just fought off an actual full-on zombie. No way those things are low-level monsters." His voice was groggy.

"Focus, mate," Zack shouted, "I need your help."

"Um, yeah, okay."

Max bounded over to Art and barked.

"Great," Zack said, "Max, Charlie is in bad shape. You pull her over to Tabitha. And Art, you get Kimmy there, away from the fire, okay?

"And what are you going to do?" Art said, using his hands to support him down the stairs.

"I'm getting our one ticket out of here," Zack replied.

Before he could move, though, he heard a banging sound from behind the freezer door. He opened it and Mr Shanks soared out of it, zipping left and right around the room.

"They're all dead," Zack said to it and pointed to Kimmy, "and she's down there."

The knife fluttered before descending down to where Kimmy lay on the ground, resting its icy blade against her burnt skin.

Zack pushed away his thoughts about a soothing, animated dagger and the hysterical edge to them and ran through the side door to Bast's side. The extent of his wounds shocked him again, but he was their one chance of safety. Zack ignored the protests in his fatigued limbs and poured as much Life as he could gather, into Bast.

The wounds closed, muscles and tendons stitched themselves together and despite the dizziness setting into Zack's head, a flush of fresh blood flooded through Bast's arteries. He was breathing more easily now, but both the wounds and the healing had exhausted Bast of his Life reserves and he wouldn't regain consciousness without a full night's sleep. Or some help. Zack had run out of his reserves, but he'd also run out of options and time.

He reached into himself and found the Life woven within him, in his skin, bones, blood, muscle and organs. And he called on it. Skimming as little as he could from as much as he could, he gathered it into a stream to pour into Bast. Even gathering it, hurt. His body screamed in pain, nausea and lethargy and he almost fumbled the simple incantation. But he gathered them, too. All the distractions, the aches, the needles, the dizziness and the chorus of doubts and fears were reworked into a single purpose and with them, he channelled the Life into Bast's body.

Zack collapsed forward onto his hands and knees as Bast sat upright with a loud intake of breath. He snatched up his rapier from beside him and leapt to his feet. "Where is…? Is that smoke?"

Zack pushed himself back up onto his knees and nodded.

"Fight's over. Need a gate out."

"Can do." Bast stopped at the door and turned back. "Are you okay?"

"Yep," Zack said, his eyes refusing to focus, "right behind you."

By the time Zack's legs obeyed him long enough to reach the others, the entire kitchen was ablaze. The flames had found some cooking oil and now heat and black smoke were filling the apartment.

"We need out, now," Tabitha said through winces.

"Where to?" Bast asked.

"Anywhere," Art replied between coughs, "somewhere safe."

Bast nodded and, with a few gestures, opened a gate in the corner of the room. Tabitha stepped through, while Art and Zack carried Charlie and Bast brought Kimmy through.

The gate brought them into a dark, cool room, and while Bast closed it behind them, Zack sank to the carpeted floor, placing Charlie down as gently as he could.

Art stood up, supporting his unsteady weight on a nearby piece of furniture and looked around.

"Did you bring us back to school?"

"You said somewhere safe," Bast replied, "it's dark, empty and nobody would expect to find us here."

"Good job, dude." Tabitha made her way to the teacher's desk. "I don't suppose any healing is available?"

Zack laid on his back.

"Sorry. Need a minute."

"Well then, while we wait, does somebody want to catch me up?" Bast asked.

"What are your thoughts about zombies?" Art answered.

Zack didn't find out what those thoughts were because exhaustion carried him away into the dark.

⊷————⊷————⊷————⊷⊷⊳

Zack awoke to Art gently shaking his shoulder. It was still dark and while his head felt a little clearer, everything else still ached.

"I'm sorry, mate," Art said, "I know you need the sleep, but Kimmy's not looking good."

With Art's help, Zack stood up and moved to Kimmy's side. Under the light from Art's phone, he inspected her condition. There were heavy burns to most of her body, with much of her clothes consumed by the fire. More alarming than the burns, though, was her breathing. Her breaths were sharp and shallow, accompanied by twitches and shaking and she was whispering to herself, despite being otherwise unconscious.

He reached out to her Life and found multiple signs of organ failure.

"You're right, mate. This can't wait. I just hope I have enough in the tank to fix it."

"You can take from me," Art said.

Zack looked him up and down. While he was unconscious, Art must have found a spare sports uniform and changed his shirt, but he was still deeply injured and in desperate need of his own treatment.

"I can't risk taking from any of you; I'm the only one who didn't get hurt. It has to be me."

Zack got to work. He threaded together the faint wisps of Life he could gather and, over the next four hours, broken up by short spells of passing out, he treated his friends. He stabilised Kimmy's organs and kickstarted the healing of her burns to reduce the immediate chances of blood poisoning. He reduced the swelling in Tabitha's shoulder, which allowed him to administer a marginally less painful relocation. And he closed the worst of Art's and Max's wounds.

And then, with fatigue fighting to claim him once more, he sat beside Charlie. Max, still in wolf form, nuzzled into her while whimpering and looking at Zack with deep, sad eyes.

"I'm sorry, Max. I'm not sure how to help her yet."

Zack had scanned her Life five times now and nothing had changed. Charlie seemed to be deep in some kind of coma and, as best as he could determine, her Life was stunted. The barest amount that had survived being drained, clung to her, keeping her alive, but it wasn't rebounding the way Life normally did. Even when it was futile, when sickness or injury were so severe that death was assured, Life struggled on. It was its nature. But not Charlie's. He tried feeding in some Life, but it drifted away, which didn't make sense. It was like pouring a cup of water on dry soil and watching it evaporate.

Maybe it was simply too soon. Maybe he was too tired to think straight.

Or, maybe he wasn't up to the task and she'd die because of it. Like his grandmother. Like Jackie.

Tabitha squeezed his arm and he woke up with a disoriented start. When had he fallen asleep again? Charlie remained unchanged beside him, but something was different. He could see her more easily. Light was coming in through the windows.

"We need to get out of here," he said to Tabitha.

"Relax, Zack." Tabitha looked exhausted and she still needed more healing to repair the damage done by the Master of Body's tortuous manipulations. But she offered him a comforting smile. "We're on it. Bast and Art are finding us somewhere to move; we'll be out of here before anybody shows up for the day."

"Great." Zack's sigh of relief was long. He crawled to Kimmy's side and poured another meagre portion of Life into her. The worst of the burns had improved and her core temperature had crept down.

"You look like crap, man." Kimmy's voice was raspy, but she offered him a smirk.

Tabitha leapt across the room at the sound of her voice.

"Oh my god, Kimmy. It's so good to have you back."

"How did we…?" Kimmy looked around. "Is this our English classroom?"

"Yep," Tabitha replied, "Bast's idea of a safe place."

"Bast? He's okay?"

"Yeah, he's fine," Zack said, "In better shape than you, so lie back down and rest."

"Okay." Kimmy did as she was told and a few tears slid down the sides of her face.

A gate spun open in the corner of the room and Bast stepped out.

"Art has scored us some more suitable accommodations." Bast's grin was intense. "You're going to love it."

"Are you kidding me?" Tabitha spoke through tight lips in an attempt to keep from shouting. "What part of this is 'somewhere for us to lay low'?"

Art looked up at her from the sunken lounge in their Las Vegas penthouse apartment and swallowed a mouthful of king prawn before replying, "What's wrong with it?"

"It's like the total opposite!"

"Wrong," Art said, "there's enough space for all of us in the one apartment. It's got excellent room service, which means we barely need to leave and it's got plenty of access to people walking around with huge wads of cash, which means I've got us covered. Trust me, it's perfect."

"And the fact that it has a hot tub and a fully stocked bar didn't factor into it?" Tabitha's tone was dry.

"We deserve it," Art replied, "we've wiped out half of the Thirteen. I'm sick of slumming it."

"It's fine, for now." Tabitha collapsed across from him on the lounge.

"Nobody goes in the hot tub until I've closed your wounds and cleared you for infections," Zack added, "I'm going to check on Kimmy."

"Wait," Tabitha said, "is Kimmy in any immediate danger from her burns?"

"No," Zack answered, "I've dealt with the worst of it."

"Good," Tabitha replied, "then go get some sleep. We can all survive with what we've got so far. You need a chance to recover."

"But—"

Tabitha stared him down.

"Charlie needs you at your best."

Zack dropped his arms in defeat.

"Okay. Wake me up if you need me, though."

"Sweet dreams, buddy." Art waved before reaching for another prawn.

Zack didn't dream, sweetly or otherwise, but when he awoke several hours later, he felt like himself again. Bast was asleep in the bed next to him and Art was snoring on the chaise lounge against the wall. He scanned them both while they slept. He'd healed most of Bast's injuries already but fed in a little extra Life to help him wake up more refreshed.

Art was a different story. Zack had been forced to leave him with too many wounds for too long and a few of them were on the edges of infection. But not for long. A couple of streams of Life aimed at the right spots and Art eased in his sleep.

Zack left the room, eager to do more and entered the other bedroom, where Charlie and Kimmy were laying on the bed, Max asleep at their feet.

"How are you feeling?"

Zack jumped at Tabitha's voice; he hadn't seen her reclining in the high-backed armchair by the door.

"Much better, thanks. Have you had any sleep?"

"Not really," she replied, "drifted off a couple of times, but I'm still a bit too sore."

"Let me see what I can do about that," Zack said, stepping closer.

"They need it more." Tabitha pointed at Charlie and Kimmy with a tilt of her chin.

"I've got enough fuel in the tank now, don't worry."

Tabitha's body was a patchwork of hairline fractures, sprained muscles and torn ligaments. It was no wonder she couldn't get comfortable with all the damage the Master of Body had done to her. Zack took his time, addressing each injury with the right use of his Life threads.

Tabitha stretched in her chair when he was done.

"Thank you, Zack. I really don't know what we'd do without you."

Zack moved to Kimmy next and sent threads of Life across her body. By the time he was finished, she looked like she was simply suffering from a nasty sunburn. Then he walked around the bed and stood beside Charlie. She remained in her strange coma, her depleted Life almost hibernating within her. He tried again to feed in streams of Life to bolster her, but they fell away. This time, however, he was alert enough to catch why.

"What's wrong with her?" Tabitha stifled a yawn.

"There's a residue left over from what that bastard did to her," Zack replied, "It's stopping her Life from recovering and it's interfering with mine."

"Can you fix it?"

"I think so. I'll need to carefully counteract the residue, giving her Life a chance to recover, but not too much or the reaction between my magic and his could harm her more. It'll take some time, but I think she'll be okay."

Zack looked over to discover Tabitha sprawled across her armchair, asleep. Well, no time like the present. He drew forth a needle-thin thread of Life and probed the not-Life residue Shen had left behind.

An hour later he'd made the most modest of dents, but he was confident some progress was being made. Further, it appeared that the not-Life was not doing further overt harm to Charlie, beyond keeping her in this coma. And that meant Zack had time to fix this, but it also meant he needed a way of keeping her hydrated.

He walked back across the hall and woke up Art and Bast.

"I've got a job for the two of you."

They blinked at him as if he'd spoken in a different language.

"Job?" Bast asked.

"For Charlie," Zack replied.

"On it," Art said, standing up, "What do you need?"

"I've messaged you both the details, but basically, I need some IV drips, saline, alcohol swabs and a few meds. A hospital is probably the easiest place to get them."

"You can't just…" Bast wiggled his fingers in the air.

"No. But this stuff will buy me the time I need to heal her."

"We got you, mate." Art gave him a casual salute before he and Bast pulled out their phones to plan their supply raid.

Zack returned to Charlie and continued his painstaking efforts.

CHAPTER 26

Art sat with his feet raised on another chair and an enormous slice of pizza in his hand. He manoeuvred the slice above his open mouth like a skill-tester claw, trying to get the long strands of cheese to drop into his mouth. Zack was unenthusiastic with the proximity of the greasy food to Charlie's catheter and to the fluid bag he was changing over, but his glare went unnoticed as Art focused on capturing the falling mozzarella.

"Maybe you could be a doctor," Art said, chewing through a mouthful, "This whole thing is very bloody impressive."

"Thanks." Zack pushed a syringe of sucrose solution into the fluid bag.

"Where did you even learn this stuff?" Art asked.

"Sara taught me."

"Instead of teaching you magic, she taught you medicine?"

"She taught me both. Magic isn't always an option and even when it is, knowing how the body works helps."

"Oh man," Art laughed, "I got lucky. Bast had to study maths, you had to study biology and everything else. Timur just taught me magic."

Zack tidied up the table beside Charlie and disposed of the syringe.

"No, he didn't. He taught you a bucketload of strategies and techniques for manipulating people. I've seen you use them."

"Fair enough," Art replied, "but at least I didn't have to read any books."

Tabitha poked her head around the door.

"How's she doing?"

"Better," Zack said, "removing the residue from her Life is a slow enough process as it is, but the reaction between my Life and the not-Life is not gentle and she can't take the strain of too much."

"It's been almost a week," Tabitha said, "I thought we'd see an improvement by now. I hoped she'd be up and about."

"I'm making this up as I go," Zack replied, "I promise you there is improvement and I should be able to speed it up as I remove more and more of the taint. But I can only do what I can. I'm sorry."

"No, Zack." Tabitha hugged him tight against her. "You're doing amazingly. I'm just scared. And getting a bit stir-crazy. Speaking of which, group meeting, time to start planning again."

"Awesome." Art scooped up the rest of his pizza.

Zack took one more look at Charlie, with Max's wolf body curled up next to her and followed them into the main room, where Kimmy and Bast were lounging in the hot tub. Tabitha called them over to sit at the dining table. Kimmy stepped out of the water and narrowed her eyes at Art when she caught him looking in her direction.

"A bikini isn't an invitation, perv. This is a look but don't touch situation."

Art rolled his eyes.

"Trust me, I put you in the category of those South American frogs. Beautiful, but clearly toxic."

To Zack's surprise, Kimmy's scowl broke into a beaming smile and, as she sat opposite Art at the table, she said, "Thank you."

Tabitha slapped her hand on the table like a gavel.

"Right. I think we've all given each other enough of a chance to unwind, so let's get back to business. As it stands, we've taken out eight of the Thirteen."

Art counted them out on his fingers.

"Movement. Protection. Animal. Plant. And then the other night, Tabs beat Body, Max and I got Creation, Kimmy incinerated Knowledge and Zack destroyed Life."

Zack couldn't help the look of disgust on his face.

"That guy didn't deserve to be the Master of Life."

"So that leaves us with five more," Bast said.

"And they won't be easy," Tabitha said, "Air, Fire, Earth and Water are powerful in battle and who even knows what the Master of Mind is capable of."

"And we've only got until December to defeat them," Zack said, "after that, they'll start replacing their membership. Beginning with Life."

"Plus, we have no idea where they are." Tabitha rubbed her temples with the palms of her hands. "And we've got no way to get back into the Tower and look for more pearls."

"Wouldn't help us find the Master Psychomancer anyway," Art said. "The Mind pearl was missing."

"Where does that leave us, then?" Kimmy asked.

"Well, my dad would take my brothers and I back north to our country most years when we were kids," Bast said, "Some of the uncles up there taught us hunting and there's two ways to hunt. One way, which is what we've been doing, is to track your prey and catch it where you find it. But the other way is to lay a trap and make it come to you."

Zack shook his head.

"They won't come themselves. They'll send the rest of the Tower after us."

"No, Zack." Art nodded at Bast. "We just need the right bait. Something that makes them come themselves."

"Which is?" Tabitha asked.

"I don't know," Art replied and Kimmy scoffed at him. "What? I thought this was a group brainstorm."

"Well, what do they want badly enough that they'll come for it themselves?" Tabitha asked.

"Or, what do they not want to risk sending others to get?" Zack added.

They were quiet for a moment around the table.

"We already know the answer to this," Kimmy said, breaking the silence.

"Go on." Tabitha beckoned with her hand.

Kimmy looked at Art with raw sympathy rather than her usual hostility.

"It's what they came after us… after Jackie for the first time. To find out what we know about them."

"But since then, they've been sending everybody," Bast said.

"No," Zack replied, "the remaining eleven have been sending everybody against us, but they think we're just attacking them. The first two hadn't told the others yet."

"Okay," Tabitha said, "so how do we turn this into bait?"

"Oh, I know," Art said, "we start spreading the word around the non-Tower mages that we know who the Thirteen are and how they are connected to the Tower."

Bast nodded along.

"They aren't going to want to risk us sharing that info with anybody they send to catch us. They'll have to come themselves."

"But how do we spread the word around?" Tabitha asked. "It's not like we're popular in those circles."

"Some of us are more popular than others," Kimmy replied with a smirk.

"Yeah, alright." Tabitha blushed. "I'll call Nell and see if she can help us with that."

"Excellent," Kimmy said, "and the rest of us who don't have magical half-human girlfriends will be in the hot tub."

Tabitha didn't respond and instead took her phone to the other side of the room.

"Want to play something, mate?" Art pointed to the console he'd rented from room service. "We can toss a few ideas around while we play."

"In a bit," Zack answered, "I'm going to spend a little more time with Charlie. For any of this to work, we don't just need good bait; we need her back to full strength."

"Hold still," Zack held Art's head at the temples and probed the cut on his face with a thin thread of Life.

"Why?" Art's voice held a thick tone of sulk. "Can't you just wave your hand and fix it?"

"Absolutely," Zack replied, "and if you'd like any shards of glass still in there to work their way to your eye, I can start right away. Or you can hold still."

"Fine." Art complied.

There were indeed a few pieces of the glass bottle in the wound and Zack numbed the area with a touch of magic before extracting them more mundanely with a pair of tweezers. The wound itself was simple enough to heal after that. There was bruising and the tiniest of hairline fractures, where Kimmy had hurled the bottle at Art's face and a thin, curved cut where the broken glass had sliced into his skin above his right eye.

"She's a psycho," Art said, rubbing at the healed spot on his forehead. "She whipped that bottle at me for no reason."

"You were being a bit of a dick," Zack said, "but I agree, she had no right to hit you."

"And everybody is just going to let her get away with it, like always."

"Nobody is letting her get away with it," Zack replied, "Tabitha is out there tearing shreds off her."

"Big deal."

"Well, what do you want to happen to her?"

"Something," Art answered. "Something that'll stop her from treating everybody like crap."

"That's up to Kimmy," Zack said, "Do you want to bail? Kick her out of the group? Because then this whole fight against the Tower is over. We can't change what she does. We can only decide how we respond to it."

"Well, technically, I could change what she does," Art smirked.

"You do anything close to that and this group is definitely over." Zack looked unimpressed.

Art threw up his hands. "I'm joking!"

Art wasn't wrong; what Kimmy had done was totally out of line, but it was also the situation. They'd been trapped in a hotel suite for close to three weeks. Art was able to leave every now and then. He needed to so he could earn money for the room by scamming high rollers and then wipe all the security feeds, but the rest of them were on lockdown. Kimmy and Bast, in particular, were suffering from severe cases of cabin fever, the most recent flare-up having resulted in a loud fight and a violently flung gin bottle.

Tabitha was handling it better, but she had Nell to speak with most days as they got updates on the rumours they had been planting amongst the magic community. And Zack was fine because he had Charlie to focus on. Which was part of the problem because he hadn't pulled her from her coma yet. He had been making steady progress, but there was still so much of the non-Life taint to remove and he didn't trust himself to do it any faster for fear of hurting her.

Tabitha knocked, standing outside the open door.

"Are you okay, Art?"

"Physically, yes," he replied, "thanks to our Lifer. Can't say I exactly feel safe here, though."

"I know," Tabitha entered the room, "I've read her the riot act. But that's actually not what I came in here for. Nell sent me a message, asking to come see me… us. Bast has gone off to get her. She said she's got big news."

"Sounds good," Zack said, standing up, "Coming, Art?"

"Nah." Art lay down on the bed. "Say 'hi' to her for me, but I'm going to avoid Kimmy for a bit."

"That's fair," Tabitha said and left the room with Zack following.

Kimmy was sulking in the far corner, a pair of headphones shielding her from further engagement.

"Did she say what the big news was about?" Zack asked.

Tabitha shrugged and then pointed to the grey light opening in the centre of the room.

"We don't have to wait long to ask."

When the gate reached its normal size, Bast and Nell stepped through. Tabitha's face lit up in a mirror to Nell's and the two threw their arms around each other, sharing a brief but passionate kiss. Tabitha stepped back first, her cheeks pink with embarrassment, but her fingers stayed intertwined with Nell's. She led her over to the table.

"Come, have a seat and tell us what was so important you had to come in person."

Nell sat beside her, sliding her chair closer so their shoulders touched.

"Well, I've been angling for any excuse to see you," she said with a smile, "but I do genuinely have news."

Kimmy, Bast and Zack sat down opposite.

"Well?" Kimmy gestured for her to continue.

"Right, sorry." Nell adjusted herself so she was facing the others. "I think they've taken the bait."

"What do you mean?" Zack asked.

"Since you went on the run, they've been stepping up raids on magic folk. And it's been getting worse and worse," Nell replied, "The week you reached out to me with this latest plan was probably the worst ever. Squads of Tower folk forcing their way into communities and safehouses, including that one in Estonia. Pushing people around, claiming they have evidence that the Silence is being broken and mostly making it clear they are looking for you guys."

"So?" Kimmy asked, her impatience obvious. "What does that tell us about the bait?"

"Three days ago, the raids stopped," Nell said, unfazed by the interruption, "It took me a little while to make sure, but yeah. People are beginning to wonder if you've been caught."

Bast whooped with excitement.

"That's great news, Nell. Thank you so much."

"Now we're ready for stage two," Tabitha said, "leading them into a trap."

"Good." Kimmy cracked her knuckles. "I'm ready to work out some aggression."

"Well, we need to pick a location first," Tabitha said, "and work out a way to get caught that isn't too obvious."

Zack stood up.

"I'll leave that up to you. We can't do anything with Charlie in that coma."

He entered Charlie's room and sat at the chair beside her bed. He reached out with Life, prodding against the remains of the not-Life that still clung to her. The resonance between the two magical energies hummed with a disharmony that mapped out the taint. Her own Life was stronger now than it had been, but every patch of not-Life he removed resulted in a magical detonation that harmed her and, in her current state, it took her time to recover.

Time they no longer had.

Perhaps, if he was better at this, if he had a stronger focus and if his mind didn't drift off course… perhaps if he was somebody else, she would be awake already. Max's heavy wolf head nuzzled under his hand. It seemed she had faith in him and if Max had faith, then Charlie might have some too, given how connected they were.

Connected.

He had never tried it before. Life had to be freely given and he wasn't sure how well he could get the consent of an animal, not to mention the minor differences in her Life. But Max was smart and her bond with Charlie might make the difference.

"Max," he said, looking into her clear amber eyes, "I'm going to try bringing her back now, but to do that I need you to give me some of your Life. It's going to feel uncomfortable and it's going to hurt her a little while I do it. But if we stick to it, she could be awake by tonight."

Max stared back at him. Did she understand even half of what he was trying to say to her? But then she gave a long, slow sigh and, along with her wet breath, came the gentle push of her Life at the edges of his thoughts. Freely given.

Zack turned his attention back to Charlie and sent out a soft weave of Life to neutralise the toxic not-Life that clung to her. The two magical energies reacted with a tiny, but violent, force and beneath it, Charlie's Life strained in response. Zack reached for Max's Life, but he had barely coaxed it when it rushed through him and into Charlie.

At first, this seemed like a good thing. Max's Life energy found its way easily to the points of need and Zack was able to move on to the next piece of taint almost immediately. But after four or five cycles, Zack realised there was a problem. Max's Life was too energetic, too eager. Too wild. It was no longer waiting for Zack to neutralise the not-Life, it was hurrying him. And then it was charging into the not-Life itself. Zack flipped the roles, coming in behind Max's Life to stabilise Charlie after the traumatic reaction. It was fast, difficult and draining, but Max's Life was unrelenting. Zack clenched his teeth as the familiar depths of ache and pain told him how little he had left, but if he didn't keep it up, Charlie would die from the stress.

And it also seemed to be working. In ten minutes, Zack and Max had removed more not-Life than he had been able to all week. There was only a little left. With a last surge of Life, the final taint was neutralised and Zack flooded Charlie's body with as much Life as he could gather. But despite all they had done, Charlie remained still and locked in her coma.

Through a fatigue-addled mind, Zack tried to think through what could be done, but before he could attempt anything, Max leapt onto the bed. Straddling Charlie's chest, the wolf howled loudly, directly into her face.

Charlie's eyes snapped open and Max dropped her muzzle to give her a massive wet lick across the cheek. Charlie responded by throwing her arms around Max's neck, pulling her down into a tight embrace.

Zack fell into a slouch against the back of his chair.

"Good girl, Max."

Bast poured too much vodka into Zack's glass and raised his own in a toast.

"Here is to our awesome Lifer, who pulled the lovely Charlie back from the brink of death."

The others cheered as they clinked their glasses with Zack's and drained them. Charlie smiled at him from across the table, placing her empty glass down with a heavy thud.

"And here is to the gorgeous Max, whose howl frightened away the clutches of the dark magic that held her lady," Bast said as he refilled the glasses.

Art grumbled as he drained his.

"Any cheers for the man who had to make twenty-six people forget they had heard a wolf howling in a hotel penthouse?"

"It's Vegas, Longlegs," Nell said, her arm wrapped around Tabitha, "you could have just told them you were a troupe of magicians."

Tabitha laughed.

"It's not far from the truth, either."

"How many stage magicians do you reckon have actual magic?" Charlie asked.

"Penn and Teller, definitely," Zack said with confidence.

"Why them?" Bast asked.

"Well," Zack replied with a smirk, "Teller's obviously committed to the Silence."

The others stared at him, before letting loose a chorus of boos.

"On that hilarious note, I'd better get going, Sapphire," Nell said to Tabitha, "I've got more work to do tomorrow and you lot need to set your trap."

Tabitha walked her over to a corner of the room and kissed her goodbye while Bast spun up a gate for Nell. Once she had left, Tabitha returned alone to the table, blushing but with a contented smile on her lips.

"I still say it's unfair that only you can bring a booty call back to the room," Kimmy muttered around her drink, but even she was in too much of a good mood to worry about it.

After the best part of the month, the penthouse suite had finally stopped being a prison cell and they were able to enjoy it together, even if for only one more night before they moved against the remaining members of the Thirteen.

An hour later, Zack toddled off to find a bed to crash in; he was going to need a good night's sleep if he was going to cure six hangovers in the morning.

CHAPTER 27

Clean, bright light greeted Zack when he awoke, as did crisp white sheets. He was somewhere else. An echo of a headache, remembered more than felt, flickered past his temples.

Zack leapt out of bed and onto a soft-tiled floor, like it was made of vinyl or something similar. White walls, single bed, grey bedside table. Was he in a hospital? Glancing down, he noted he was wearing pyjamas and not ones he recognised.

What was going on? Had he been hurt? He reached out with Life to assess his body's condition. Nothing. Life didn't respond. He grasped for it again, but he could find no sense of it. Something was very wrong. And where were the others?

The door was closed, but it had a playing card-sized window that allowed him to see out. It definitely seemed to be a hospital. Two men and a woman in pyjamas wandered by, followed by two men in clinical-type uniforms, perhaps nurses. One of them turned towards him and he ducked away from the window.

His mind was racing, trying to understand what was happening. There was a knock at the door.

"Good morning, Zack." The male voice had a calm and kind tone. "Are you okay in there, mate?"

He slipped further away from the door, staying silent.

"I'm going to come in, okay?" the voice said. "I just want to check in on you."

The door opened, revealing a heavy-set, middle-aged man, one of the two he had seen in the corridor.

"You're up nice and early for once, Zack." The man noticed Zack eyeing him up. "And you look a little more alert than usual. That's great."

"Where am I?" Zack asked. "How did I get here?"

The man winced.

"You're at the hospital. You've been having a tough time lately and we've been doing our best to look after you."

Zack considered what he knew. No injuries. He didn't feel light-headed or unwell. He'd been having a 'tough time', apparently?

"What kind of hospital?" he asked.

"If you don't remember, this might come as a bit of a shock, but you're in a psychiatric ward, Zack. Look, why don't you get changed," the man said, pointing to the chest of drawers in the corner, "I'll go see if I can find Doctor Kelick. He was supposed to be coming in early to check up on you."

"Um, yeah, okay," Zack replied. Whatever got this guy out of his room.

"Great job," the man replied, giving him a thumbs up before leaving, closing the door behind him.

Zack ran to inspect the window and was disappointed, but unsurprised, to find it was not the kind that opened. It was made of thick, opaque glass, designed to let some light in but not provide much visibility. Through the blur, he could make out enough shapes to suggest he was on the second or third storey of a building within a campus of buildings. Which was consistent with a hospital.

But where? Thinking about it, the man's accent had been Australian. But how had they got back here from Las Vegas? This had to be a trap, but what kind?

Well, he needed to find some way of getting out of here and finding his friends. The chest of drawers held a few changes of clothes but no jeans. Instead, he pulled on a long-sleeve t-shirt, a pair of track pants and a pair of socks. But there were no shoes, not under his bed, by the door, or anywhere else he could see. Shoeless it was then.

Zack took a deep breath and stepped out into the corridor. No clear exit was apparent, so he picked a direction - left - and walked with a casual confidence he did not own. He rounded the corner, which opened into a communal area with couches, tables and a wide-screen television built into the wall.

"Good morning, Mr Marek."

Zack turned to see an older man in a suit and tie. He had glasses, white hair and a neat beard that screamed 'psychiatrist'.

"Micah told me you were up and about; I was just coming to see you. Why don't you walk with me to my office?"

Zack looked around and couldn't see an easy way to escape. Better to remain compliant and discover what information he could get.

"Yeah, okay."

"Excellent." The man led him down a corridor through a door embossed with the name 'Dr Samuel Kelick'.

The office was a stark contrast to the sterile environment outside its door. A luxurious three-seater couch sat on the wall beside the door, opposite a desk that took up the back centre of the room. On the left, a massive aquarium was set into the wall, while on the right, a display of insects and other creepy crawlies was displayed behind glass.

Dr Kelick took a seat behind his desk and gestured to the couch.

"Please, sit."

Zack did as he was bidden, claiming the end of the couch closest to the door. Dr Kelick watched him for a moment.

"Micah was correct. You certainly are more alert. The new medication we've moved you to has done wonders."

"You gave me something?" Zack asked.

"Of course," Kelick replied, "we've given you a fair few somethings, but this is the first one that has been successful in making you this aware."

Aware? What did he mean?

"What was it?"

"A new antipsychotic," the doctor replied, "We've been running through the spectrum, but unfortunately, most of them have done little but stifle your more extreme behaviour. This one, however… it's looking promising."

"My extreme behaviour?" Zack must have looked as confused as he felt.

"I appreciate this must be overwhelming. Your newfound alertness means you're experiencing all this for the first time but try to recognise this is actually a tremendous step in the right direction. Your mind has been trapped within delusions for a long time, but now we might be able to make the progress we've been reaching for. And with any luck, the others will be responding to the new treatment as well."

"The others?" Zack sat up straight.

"Yes, you have some friends here," Kelick replied, "We have been treating them for the same delusions as you."

Zack wanted to keep him talking while he tried to put together the pieces.

"Which are?"

Dr Kelick opened a thin cardboard folder on his desk and slid a piece of paper toward him. Looking down through his glasses, he read from it.

"A belief that you have extraordinary or magical powers, that you are part of a secret 'illuminati' organisation charged with saving the world and that monsters and other supernatural creatures are real." He placed the piece of paper back in the folder before looking up at Zack. "Does that sound familiar?"

Zack wasn't ready for it to be his turn to answer.

"And my friends have the same delusions?"

"They do, yes."

"Well, that sounds a bit unlikely, doesn't it? That six people have the exact same delusions?"

The doctor nodded slowly.

"Unlikely, yes. Exceedingly rare. In my nearly thirty years of practice, I have never seen a case like this." He clasped his hands together and leant forward over the desk, looking Zack in the eyes. "You have always struck me as a particularly smart young man, Zack, so perhaps it will help if I lay out the current diagnosis. It is called Shared Delusional Disorder. As I said, it is very rare, but it is when a group of individuals share a bond so tight that when one of them begins to experience delusions, the others are exposed to them. Due to the nature of that bond - romantic, familial or, in this case, from shared trauma - exposure to the delusions leads to them being shared."

"Shared trauma?" Zack asked.

"Yes," Kelick replied, "I can see you trying to puzzle your way through this information. I imagine you're trying to find a piece of information, a flaw in logic, something that will help prove your delusions are, instead, truth. That's okay, it's perfectly natural. I am not asking you to simply believe me. If it was as easy as that, anybody could do my job. No, instead, while you are puzzling this out, I ask you to do one thing for me."

"What's that?" Zack asked.

"I want you to leave yourself open to the possibility that you have been suffering from psychotic delusions. I know the delusions feel real to you now, more real than me, this office or even that couch underneath you, but I would like you to consider the two possible cases. On one hand, you have a reality in which you have magical powers, can travel to fantastical realms and save our world from monsters. And on the other hand, you have a reality in which something terrible happened to you and you have been unwell. Which one of those two realities, logically, is more likely?"

"What terrible thing happened?" Zack asked. "What was the shared trauma?"

"Soon," Kelick replied, standing up, "You have already made such amazing progress today. I don't want to overwhelm you."

"Can I see my friends?" Zack stood as well.

Kelick nodded.

"This afternoon, I'd like to try a group session. If the others have responded to the new regime half as well as you, I'd like to bring you together. Until then, I ask that you stay in your room."

Zack narrowed his eyes.

"So, I'm a prisoner, then."

"Hardly," Kelick replied, "you are a bright young man with his whole life ahead of him and I am simply trying to give you the best chance. Sadly, there are patients here who have been moved from ward to ward, from institution to facility, for decades. Who will likely spend their lives coming in and out of treatment facilities. Not you, Zack. I don't want you to be a lifer."

"Sorry, a 'what'?" Zack asked.

"Apologies, it's an informal term here. Lifer. A patient who returns frequently throughout their lives. But not you, Zack. Not if you and I work together."

There was all too much to process, so Zack mumbled an "okay" and headed out the door. The man he'd spoken to before, Micah, was waiting for him.

"Doctor Kelick has said we should take you back to your room for the rest of the morning," he said with a friendly tone, "but we can swing by the common room so you can grab a book and a snack if you'd like."

Zack nodded and a few minutes later, he was back in his room with a dog-eared copy of *The Hobbit* and an average-looking piece of vanilla slice. He eyed the pastry with frustration. There was no way he was eating anything in this place until he had a better idea of what was going on, but he had hoped to get some kind of cutlery with it. No luck.

He slapped the paper plate down on his bedside table and paced around the room. He was angling for a casual look or at least a normal kind of cooped-up, but his real intention was to spot any hidden cameras. His first thought was, this might be a Tower prison, like where they took mages who broke the Silence. But as far as he understood, the Tower stripped those mages of their memory and Zack still had his.

Or perhaps, this was a real facility and the Tower had fudged some memories and paperwork, so it appeared they had been there for months. But why would they do that? Surely, they were still a risk to the Silence and to the Thirteen, with their memories intact.

And neither of those theories explained why Zack couldn't touch Life.

Maybe there was a third player involved, somebody outside the Tower who wanted Zack and his friends out of the way. Or there was another explanation. He forced himself to consider what the doctor had said. That this was reality and he had been suffering from delusions. It felt ridiculous. He could remember the Tower, the creatures and the other realms. He could remember what it felt like to weave Life, guiding it with his will. But the cold, logical voice in his mind noted that if he had been having a psychotic episode, his memories couldn't be trusted.

His thoughts ran around in unpleasant circles until it was afternoon and a uniformed woman came to chaperone him to his group session. She looked at his untouched lunch on the tray beside his bed and gifted him a stern and unimpressed expression, but Zack didn't care. He was too excited to see his friends.

She led him to the corridor outside Doctor Kelick's office. Charlie was waiting there, leaning nervously against the wall and twisting a long strand of curls between her fingers. When he approached, she leapt upright and moved towards him, her eyes watering and wide. She held her arms out to hug him, but the woman with Zack cleared her throat.

"Uh uh," she said, "no physical contact. Those are the rules."

Charlie screwed up her face and leant back against the wall, gesturing for Zack to stand next to her. Zack approached.

"Are you okay?"

"Okay?" Charlie stared back at him, shaking her head sharply. "How could I be okay? What is this place? Last thing I knew, you woke me up in Las Vegas. At least, I thought it was Vegas, but now we're here? And some old guy says I'm psychotic? Maybe I never got out of that coma…" She looked at Zack with suspicion. "How do I know you're even real?"

Now, there was an unpleasant thought. Charlie didn't seem to linger on it, though.

"Whoever is behind this has done something to Animal. I can't feel it."

"I can't feel Life either," Zack said, "which is impossible because I know Life is here."

More footsteps sounded around the corner and Art entered. He looked at Charlie through narrow eyes before turning to Zack.

"How many eagles did we see at Zeus's palace at the start of this year?"

It took a moment, but Zack realised what he was doing.

"One raven at Odin's cabin."

Art nodded and turned back to Charlie.

"Which Taylor Swift so—"

"Poker face," Charlie answered.

Art smiled in relief and collapsed against the wall beside Zack.

"I can't read anybody's mind here, not even yours."

Doctor Kelick opened his door from the inside and smiled kindly at the three of them.

"Come in and find a seat," he said, "the others will be joining us shortly. There was a slight incident that has caused delays."

Zack didn't like the implications of the opaque wording, but he followed the others' lead and entered, claiming a seat on the couch beside Charlie. Moments later, Tabitha and then Bast joined them and each claimed an armchair in the cramped office, sharing little but tight tentative smiles with Zack and the others.

Kimmy entered the room shortly after and Zack was confident in guessing the 'incident' had related to her. Unlike the rest of them, Kimmy was dressed in a hospital gown and socks and was escorted by two uniformed hospital staff with tense and alert body language. However, something else was off about Kimmy, but Zack couldn't place it.

"Kimmy! Where is your tattoo?" Charlie blurted at her.

Zack gaped. Charlie was right. The orange flames tattooed onto Kimmy's neck and shoulder last year were missing.

"Please," Kelick said, "let's keep our voices and our emotions lowered for the time being."

Kimmy glared at him but otherwise sat with sullen silence on the edge of the couch. Doctor Kelick waved the two orderlies out.

"I think we can all handle behaving responsibly in this session today, yes?" He looked around at each of them and, seeming to take a lack of objections as agreement, continued, "The new treatment regime has been a marked success and I would like us to strike while the iron is hot and make what progress we can."

The doctor opened up his notebook.

"I've had a chance to catch up with each of you and even accepting one unfortunate outburst, it is clear you have each gained a level of alertness that we've been struggling to achieve since you arrived here. But that is only part of the knot that we must try to unravel together. We need to come to terms with the delusion itself. And with its source. So, let's confront that together now by going back to the beginning. Tabitha, where did this all begin?"

"What do you mean?" Tabitha replied, "I don't even know how I got here."

"We'll get to that, but what I'm asking is where did your shared experience with magic—" He emphasised the word. "—begin?"

Tabitha sat up straighter, a look of defiance in her eyes.

"The alleyway. We were attacked by a tentacled creature from another realm. That was the first time we encountered magic."

The doctor nodded and then read directly from his notes.

"The alleyway in Sydney, two years ago during the Easter school holidays. You were on your way to the cinema."

"Are we supposed to be impressed that you know that?" Art asked, "There's a hundred ways you could have found out about that."

"I know this from the police report," Kelick replied, unperturbed by the interruption, "but you were not attacked by some kind of magical octopus. Your attackers were far more mundane, if no less brutal."

Doctor Kelick put his notepad back in his lap and looked around at each of them.

"That evening in the alley, you encountered a group of men who attempted to mug you and, during this attempt, they violently assaulted you. Each of you received multiple severe injuries and ended up in hospital where you were treated and rehabilitated over the course of months."

Zack's mind pushed back against the doctor's story, but not before he had a flicker of memory. He pictured the alleyway with the grey light on the wall and the dark green tendril streaking out of it, grabbing Tabitha by the leg and dragging her.

But the image shifted to half a dozen men with knives and metal pipes. One of them pulled Tabitha to the ground, attempting to get her handbag, before the others moved it, one swinging his pipe at Zack. He shook his head to clear away the thoughts.

"After your initial rehabilitation, you returned to your families and to school and, for some time, nobody noticed anything unusual." Kelick returned his attention to his notes. "But what we now know is that you were deep within a shared psychosis or a shared delusion. It is my theory that, in response to the extreme trauma of your sudden and violent assault and the resulting prolonged shock, pain and feelings of helplessness, your minds created an alternative reality. One in which violence came from inhuman sources and, more significantly, one in which you were specially equipped to protect yourselves and the world from that violence. These delusions likely originated with only one of you, but due to the intense bonding you experienced through your shared trauma and rehabilitation, they became shared and then reinforced until it was effectively a single delusion experienced by each of you."

"This sounds a bit far-fetched," Charlie said, crossing her arms.

"It is by far the rarest presentation I have seen in my entire career," Kelick replied, "but despite its uniqueness, it is still infinitely more common than six teenagers with magical abilities."

"You smug bastard." Kimmy stood up. "You want to see something uncommon, do you?"

She traced rapid patterns in the air and mumbled an incantation. Nothing happened, but she continued and a line of sweat dripped down her neck from the intensity of her effort. Finally, she flung a pointed finger in Doctor Kelick's direction and screamed at him. He watched with patience until she collapsed back onto the couch, despair written on her face.

"I understand how difficult this must be for you, but please see this for the progress that it is. Rachel," Kelick said, using her first name, "you are clearly aware that you did not just use magic to set me on fire. This is a good sign."

Kimmy grumbled to herself but otherwise offered no rebuttal.

"Let's make a deal." Kelick leaned forward in his chair. "I'd like us to meet as a group each day and, if you can commit to working with me on this, then I'll allow you to spend time together outside of group sessions. But that means taking your medications, eating properly—" He eyed Zack. "—sleeping properly and otherwise behaving yourselves. And if there is any evidence that you are influencing each other in the wrong direction, then I'll be forced to take the privilege away. Can we all agree to that?"

Zack nodded along with the others.

"Excellent," Kelick said with a smile, "I'm truly optimistic about these next few weeks, I think we can achieve a lot for you if we work together. I'll see you again tomorrow."

CHAPTER 28

Zack toyed with his overcooked lasagne before bringing a forkful to his mouth. Eager to be allowed to spend time with his friends, he had resigned himself to eating regular meals and hadn't noticed any ill effects. No drowsiness or memory loss; in fact, as the days rolled by, he was wondering if his memory might be improving. Or at least he was somehow gaining different memories, overlaying his existing ones.

Fleeting images of the hospital and of visiting doctors and nurses with familiar faces had drifted into his mind, interlacing with his earlier memories of the Tower. Even this morning, he'd been woken up by a half-dreamt memory of a brawny, physical therapist barking instructions at him in a Spanish accent during a rehabilitation session.

Revisiting the image had distracted him from what Art had said and now his friend was looking at him for a response.

"Sorry, what did you say?"

Art sighed, "I said, we have to stay focused and look for a way out of here."

"Definitely," Zack said, chewing through a mouthful, "is it worth considering, though, that maybe this isn't a trick?"

"Are you serious?" Art replied. "Three days of this and you're willing to ignore three years of memories that tell you magic is real?"

"That's what I'm saying," Zack said in a tight whisper, "Kelick has a point. What's more likely? That we're powerful wizards at eighteen years old or that we're mentally unwell?"

"Of course Kelick has a point," Art hissed back. "It would make him a pretty rubbish captor if he didn't have something convincing to say. But to answer your question, us being powerful wizards is more likely because I have seen it with my own eyes. I have seen you patch together torn-open organs, healing until there wasn't even a scar."

"Exactly," Zack replied, his voice growing in volume, "me, doing something as impressive as that. It doesn't quite sound as realistic as me imagining something like that."

Art opened his mouth to interrupt, but Zack ploughed on.

"And speaking of imagining things, isn't it a little convenient that so many of the creatures we faced are like things from the books and games we've read, almost like our subconsciouses have brought them to life."

"We've talked about this before, dude." Art matched his volume. "And we agreed it's likely that the creatures have influenced our myths and stories."

"You boys are doing a great job staying below the radar here." Charlie sat down with her own plate of lasagne. "Just super smooth."

A couple of the orderlies were looking in their direction.

"It's fine." Art stood and picked up his tray. "I'm done with this pointless conversation, anyway."

A tightness grew in Zack's stomach as his friend stomped away. He seemed to be upsetting Art a lot lately. Unless he hadn't been and it had all just been in his head. He turned to Charlie.

"Am I weird for thinking there might be something to all this?"

Charlie patted his hand.

"No. I think I'm mostly there with you. It's not that I'm saying all this is definitely real, but I don't think we can dismiss it."

"Yeah, that's all I'm trying to say," Zack said, nodding.

"Right. And if it is real, then we'd be doing ourselves real harm, hurting our families, to not try and get better."

"Exactly." Zack took another bite of lasagne.

"Still, sometimes it's like I can still feel Max. I walked around the corner yesterday and saw one of the therapy dogs." Charlie's eyes glistened. "I dropped to my knees and threw my arms around her, calling her Max. It was a bloody staffy. Apparently, I've done that a lot in the past."

Zack squeezed her hand.

"Kelick is right about one thing. We'll work our way through this together."

※————————————————————※

"I've been thoroughly impressed by your progress these last few days." Doctor Kelick addressed them from behind his desk in their group therapy session. "The medication is doing its part, but it's important that we work to unpack what is behind the delusions. In particular, what about these false thoughts has made it possible for you to all have held on to them so tightly for so long? I believe the key to this may be the people, the characters, that star in your shared world."

"The people?" Tabitha asked. "What do you mean?"

"Through our sessions, including those prior to this recent medication, I have been able to slowly paint a picture of the secret organisation you have invented, this 'Tower.' Many of the characters in it bear strong resemblances to people who were instrumental in your physical recovery from the assault in the alley." Kelick tapped his folder. "Take this June character… Apologies, Junie. I have visited the hospital and the description you've given of her, matches the doctor responsible for coordinating your rehabilitation program. Other descriptions match nurses, physiotherapists, specialists and even some of the security guards."

"So?" Art said. "That doesn't seem to tell us much."

"Not on its own, no," Kelick replied, "but if we accept that you populated the Tower with people associated with your recovery, what then of those who stand in opposition to the Tower? Are they proxies of something that stands in equal opposition to your recovery? Do they represent an underlying source of this trauma? And if so, what can those characters tell us about the trauma?"

Zack's brow furrowed as he unpacked that theory.

"Take this Traveller person, for example," Kelick continued, "He seems to be the central figure that catalysed your rejection of the Tower. Perhaps, if we discuss him, it may be illuminating."

"What do you want to know about him?" Charlie asked. "Like, what he looks like?"

"Well, yes. But let's start with more substantial aspects." Kelick rechecked his notes. "He first appeared in your narratives around ten months ago. Initially, I assumed he was simply the next adversary you had introduced, but he quickly became something else, a centralising figure, around which you began to change the focus of your shared narrative. One in which the Tower was now the adversary. Is that a fair summary?"

"There was a little more to it than that," Art said.

"Such as?" Doctor Kelick gestured for him to continue.

"Well, we discovered the Tower had been lying to us," Art replied.

"How?" Kelick asked.

"This psycho mage, Armand, told us," Kimmy answered.

The doctor flicked through some pages.

"Yes, Armand. A previous adversary. And shortly after you defeated him, the Traveller appeared, confirming his story. And you just believed him."

"Not at first," Tabitha said, "but he could use magic from different Schools."

"And that's against the 'rules'." Kelick raised his fingers in air quotes. "Let's focus there for a moment. What kinds of magic could he do?"

"How is that relevant?" Zack asked. "If the Traveller was just somebody in our heads, why do you want to know about him?"

"I want us to understand what he represents," Kelick answered, "It's possible that your magic represents a kind of need fulfilment from your trauma. You were worried about your friends' recovery as much as your own and thus, you had healing powers, while Bast, for example, was eager to get back to his athletics and developed speed magic. The magic that has been attributed to the Traveller could tell us more about his role in your narrative. What needs are being fulfilled by his inclusion?"

"We've seen him use both Fire and Air magic," Tabitha said.

"And Movement," Bast added, "I think that's it."

"I think he has Knowledge magic, too," Zack said, "The stuff with the opal and the pearls was probably Knowledge."

Kelick scribbled in his notebook.

"So, what does that tell you?" Charlie asked.

"I don't know," he replied, "This is just a starting point. Although there could be something to the idea that he represents power, control, freedom and knowledge. All things you likely felt a lack of while being in-patients here. But let's keep going."

Over the next half an hour they discussed their experiences with the Traveller, including his appearance, mannerisms and the locations where he had been.

Doctor Kelick closed his book.

"Excellent work today. I'd like to keep unpacking this with each of you in our individual sessions, but at least in a preliminary sense, I think it is clear that the Traveller is a response to the powerlessness and confinement you have been feeling. And that's a good thing, because we push back against that by fulfilling those needs in healthier ways. We can reward your efforts and progress with increases in privileges, including individual meal choices, visits from family and friends and, in time, day trips home." The doctor leant forward, smiling. "By giving you access to feelings of personal empowerment and freedom, it will weaken the hold these delusions continue to have on you."

Zack and his friends responded with non-committal sounds.

"I know it's not easy, so as an early gesture, I'll organise to order in some takeaway for dinner for the six of you. Do you like pizza?"

"Where from?" Kimmy asked.

Zack's stomach gave a cheese-fuelled gurgle as he laid in the dark of his room. Doctor Kelick had been true to his promise of pizza, but after days - or probably months - of hospital food, Zack may have overeaten a little. Or a lot.

His thoughts were sifting through more new memories that rippled over existing ones. The images of Sara teaching him in her study were now overlaid with ones of her as a nurse, as if he could see them side by side in his head. Sara in the Tower channelling Life, next to Sara in the hospital, talking with him as she changed the dressing on his wounds. Sara in the Tower teaching him an incantation, next to Sara in the hospital discussing medications with him. Sara in the Tower, furious with him the time he nearly killed Art with untrained magic, next to Sara in the hospital lecturing him when he had been pushing himself too hard during his rehabilitation. Two lives running in parallel, like different movies playing on twin screens. Either could be real, but not both.

The life where he had magical abilities certainly felt real. Logically, though, he had to agree with Doctor Kelick; it was the less likely of the two. And while it may feel real, Zack's head could understand where it would have been drawn from. Kelick's theory, about the elements of their delusions representing what they needed, made sense. The Tower and all the power and freedom that came with it, created by the six of them in response to their shared trauma, was an escape just for them. And hanging onto those delusions would only cause him and his family more pain, no matter how much he wanted them to be true.

Did he want them to be true? They might be exciting, but they were also dangerous. A reality with the Tower was also a reality in which there were monsters attacking from other worlds, not to mention a group of powerful mages trying to kill him. Was he so desperate to escape being ordinary that he preferred a world with fantastical dangers? Or perhaps he was simply desperate to escape a world in which he suffered from psychotic delusions.

Not that this was actually a choice. One of them was true, but which one was out of his control.

His mind was a whirlpool of contradicting thoughts and, as the night carried on, it was more than grease and dairy keeping him awake. And on the edges of that mental vortex, mixed up in the overlapping memories, arguments and counterarguments, was a half-formed thought. The thought that something was missing. A piece in the puzzle that was not merely out of place but was missing from the table all together. But as sleep finally claimed him, the absent element remained out of reach.

CHAPTER 29

When the morning light woke him and he shuffled himself out of bed and into a clean set of clothes, Zack had made up his mind. There was simply no escaping the logical conclusion that magic, the Tower and everything else, was nothing but a psychotic fantasy. And from that conclusion followed that he had a mother, father and sister who were suffering by having a son stuck in a delusional world.

He would do whatever it took to get back to them.

And first, that meant breakfast. Then, a shower, followed by journalling homework that Doctor Kelick had assigned. Zack spent the morning writing as detailed an account as he could from the morning before the encounter in the alley through to today. The truthful version, in which he and his friends were attacked by men, assaulted and badly injured. He wrote about the hospital, his rehabilitation and how he and his friends had struggled with returning to school. And about how the delusions started, gently at first, turning their lingering injuries into magical powers before growing in detail and intensity. How their behaviours became more and more erratic until friends, family and teachers took notice and they were admitted into a juvenile mental health ward. And later, transferred here.

Zack read it back to himself over lunch, making minor edits as he went, emphasising the difference between the parts he could now remember and the other parts still lost behind his delusions.

On one hand, he was satisfied with the end result. It delivered on everything Doctor Kelick had asked and he hoped it would put him one step closer to seeing his family. But on the other hand, as he read through it, he was struck by the same sense that there was something missing. An oversight of some kind hidden behind every paragraph. The more he thought about it, the more it was like a scab itched inside his mind, but he hoped it would come loose and the memory would emerge like others had.

Zack pushed those thoughts away because it was time for their group session. As keen as Zack was to make progress for his own sake, he was as keen to help his friends make the progress. He wanted them released from this hospital as soon as they could be, with the best chance of resuming their lives. Zack scooped up his lunch tray and dropped it off in the collection trolley before hurrying to Doctor Kelick's office.

Kimmy and Tabitha were both waiting outside when he arrived and he noticed Kimmy was holding Tabitha's hand gently while Tabitha wiped away tears with the other.

"Hey. Are you okay, Tabs?" Zack said, acknowledging the banality of the question as it left his lips.

Tabitha shook her head in response, her lips tight.

"She had a solo session today," Kimmy said, "They covered Nell."

Zack's eyes widened as he realised what they meant.

"Oh, crap. Tabs."

"It's okay," she sniffed, "I just invented an entire person to be my girlfriend, that's all. So, alongside imagining we all had magical powers and fought monsters, I created something equally fantastical; a woman that liked me. I mean, am I even biromantic, or did I invent parts of me as well?"

"You didn't invent anything about you," Kimmy said, pulling her in for a tight hug, "You know who you are, and we do, too."

Bast and Charlie walked around the corner.

"Is everything okay?" Bast asked.

Tabitha let go of Kimmy and straightened up.

"Yeah. Or I'm getting there, at least."

Charlie swooped in for a hug, clearly unsatisfied with Tabitha's answer and Bast followed. Zack hung back, happy to see his friends banding together. Art sidled up beside him, looking at the sheets of paper in Zack's hands.

"You did the homework?"

"Yep. I want us to get out of here, mate," Zack replied, "and get our lives back."

"Me too, man." Art patted at the folded piece of paper sticking out of his pocket. "Whatever it takes."

The door opened, and Doctor Kelick welcomed them to take a seat inside before returning to sit behind his desk. Zack placed his journalling on the desk and was relieved to find all the others did the same.

"Wonderful work," Kelick said, picking them up and placing them inside a folder, "I'm going to organise with your families to see if they are available for some visits this weekend. They have been keen to visit, but I wanted us all to establish a new baseline before we added them back into the mix. I think we're there, though, as long as we can keep the progress moving."

Zack smiled and most of his friends shared his enthusiasm.

"Excellent," Kelick said, "so, to that end, let's continue building a picture of the Traveller and what psychological needs he was meeting for you. I think we're very close to breaking him down and start treating the root causes of those needs. But one thing I'm curious about is some of the places he took you. From what we've laid out previously, they seem to be substantially different kinds of places. Your stories about the Tower involved exciting locations, like hell dimensions and icy mountains, while the Traveller has seemingly led you to places of community. That is an interesting difference. I'd like us to start with the world where you met Nell. I know this will be particularly difficult for you, Tabitha, but I believe it is important. Bast, why don't you start? Describe that place for me."

Bast began his description with how difficult it was to open a gate to it and Zack wondered about the symbolism of that, combined with the implications of what Doctor Kelick had said. Were these elements of their shared delusion, suggesting they had shifted from wanting to feel powerful to wanting to feel connected? The others described their experiences in Nell's home world, but Zack's mind wandered and, with it, his eyes. He gazed into the aquarium, watching the tropical fish and other creatures swimming around the tank.

He was trying to determine whether the rock he was looking at was actually a partially submerged crab when Tabitha, stuttering over her words, drew him back into the discussion. She was describing the aftermath of the tunnel collapse.

"After Charlie raced off to get help, Nell told us we should wait on the surface because it would be safer, but… she… was so distraught about leaving Art behind."

Tabitha paused, her face tightening in confusion.

"Please continue," Doctor Kelick said.

"No, hang on," Tabitha replied, "She was distraught. Did I mean Nell? No, Nell was always so calm, plus she didn't really know us yet."

The scab inside Zack's mind started to itch.

"That's okay, Tabitha," Kelick said, "I'm more interested in your collective sense of this magical world you've created."

Tabitha wasn't listening.

"It couldn't have been Charlie. She was gone. And it couldn't have been Kimmy. Who was I talking about?"

The itching grew and a strange sensation flooded Zack's mind as if he was able to scratch at it.

"We're getting a bit off track here," Kelick said, "let's keep our focus."

"Who is 'she'?" Tabitha shouted.

The scab came loose, a short burst of familiar cool-warm energy rushing forward in Zack's mind, along with a name.

"Jackie!" he yelled.

The name echoed around the room in the silence that followed. Art's face contorted in pain, confusion, anguish and relief. Tears filled his eyes as he leapt to his feet.

"Jackie! How could I forget my sister? What is happening?"

Clarity and wonder bloomed on the others' faces.

"Yes, okay." Doctor Kelick raised his hands, gesturing for calm. "Yes Art, you have a younger sister named Jacqueline. Please, sit down."

Art complied but remained leaning forward, his weight on the balls of his feet.

"I know I have a sister named Jacqueline! Why couldn't any of us remember her?"

"I'm not sure," Kelick replied, "earlier this year, you edited her out of your shared narrative."

"What?" Kimmy asked.

"It happened when you were all transferred into this adult facility. You were originally in the adolescent treatment program, but now that you're all eighteen, you were unable to stay there. Being removed from Jacqueline was particularly triggering and it took you all some time to recover, but when you did, the narrative had been altered and she had been killed. At the hands of the now terrible 'Tower'."

"Where is she?" Charlie asked.

"She's not my patient, and I couldn't divulge too much information, even if she was," Kelick replied, "but she's alive. Another reason to focus on getting well, Art."

Art stared back at Doctor Kelick, fury filling his eyes and spilling out across his face, but he spoke in a controlled voice.

"You are telling me that my sister did not actually die? We just killed her off in our story because it was convenient and then all forgot about her?"

Kelick replied calmly, "Those are not the words I would have chosen, but—"

"Don't lie to me!" Art's control was gone and his rage entered his voice. "I felt her mind, that beautiful, brilliant, loving mind, stop."

"Art, please calm down." Doctor Kelick gestured with both hands. "Your sister is alive."

"Stop lying!" Art screamed and flung his hand out at the doctor.

For just a moment, Zack felt a flicker of 'something', like a familiarity he couldn't place and then Art collapsed back into the sofa.

"I have to say, I'm very disappointed by all this," Kelick said, "Progress does not happen without setbacks here and there, but this might just—"

"Eight," Art said, his voice weak.

"What do you mean, Art?" Tabitha said, turning to him.

"That's enough of this nonsense," Kelick said, his voice as stern as Zack had ever heard it.

"I don't know. I got through for a moment, just an instant and that's what I saw." Art turned to Zack. "Eight."

"I said, that's enough!" Doctor Kelick pointed at Art. "It appears my suspicions have finally been confirmed. Art is indeed the 'inducer', the one whose primary psychosis is putting the rest of you at risk."

Zack ignored him, looking around the room. His eyes settled on the wall clock facing the door.

"Why didn't I see it before? That clock is broken and it's stuck on eight o'clock."

"I think it's an anchor," Art said.

"That's it!" Kelick said, "If you are not going to listen to reason, you can all head back to your rooms."

"We break it then?" Tabitha looked around at the others.

"Aye, aye, Cap." Bast leapt up, grabbing his chair as he ran and swung it over his shoulder. It smashed into the clock face, shattering the glass and knocking it off the wall.

The lights in the room flickered and, for an instant, a thin, grey-haired woman sat in Doctor Kelick's place. When the lights settled, he was there as before, with a furious look on his face. The doctor pressed a button on his desk-phone.

"I'm sorry you resorted to violence, but that has escalated things."

"What now?" Charlie asked. They were all on their feet.

Art rubbed the sides of his temples, his face stretched with effort.

"Whatever it is, it's weaker for the moment. I don't think that was the only anchor."

"So? What are the other ones?" Tabitha asked.

"I don't know," Art replied, "Eight is all I've got."

The sound of footsteps thundered into the outside corridor.

"Quick, help me block the door," Tabitha said.

"But if none of this is real, what does it matter?" Kimmy asked.

"It's real enough, until we get rid of the anchors," Art said, "however many there are."

Zack eyed the desk calendar and something clicked in his mind.

"I reckon there are seven left and I think that's one of them. Unless we're all okay with the coincidence that it's the eighth of August?"

Bast spun around and slammed the chair onto the desk, smashing the wood-and- paper calendar to pieces.

"This is fun!"

The lights flickered again and fists pounded on the door.

"Doctor Kelick, are you okay in there?"

"No!" he shouted, sounding afraid, "They've become violent, help me."

Charlie and Tabitha pulled the couch in front of the door in time to block it from being forced open. As she stood back up, Charlie's eyes went wide and she pointed to the wall-mounted bug display.

"Scorpion."

"And?" Kimmy asked.

"Eight legs," Charlie replied, "The rest of them are all insects."

"Good enough for me, Animal girl," Kimmy said, "My turn."

She ran up to Doctor Kelick's desk and snatched the keyboard from in front of him.

"You are all going to be in a lot of trouble," Kelick said.

"Oh, shut your hole." Kimmy swung the keyboard like a bat into the scorpion, pulverising it against the display. "Nobody's buying it anymore."

The lights flickered again and when they came back on, the banging at the door had stopped and Doctor Kelick stood in the centre of the room.

"Fine," he said, with no trace of the patient health care professional left in his voice, "time for another reset, then."

Pain flared at the centre of Zack's brain; the same pain he remembered from when he first woke up in this hospital.

"We need to hurry. Find the other five anchors."

They scrambled around the room, looking for anything that could be an eight. Tabitha stared at the aquarium.

"There's got to be a— there! An octopus."

She stepped out of the way as Bast swung his chair again, shattering the aquarium glass. The contents poured out and Tabitha sifted through the sand before stomping on the octopus, squishing it against her slippers and the floor.

The lights flickered yet again and Zack felt a sliver of energy slip in. Life. It was faint, but he drew it close to him, squeezing it tight like a childhood blanket. The pain in his head lessened for a moment before returning with sharp heat.

Charlie was in the corner by the shelves, pulling down book after book and throwing them over her shoulder. As the pain grew, she held herself up by the centre shelf but didn't slow until she shouted, "Aha! I knew it."

Charlie held up a book titled *Diagnostic and Statistical Manual - Volume VIII* and, with a grunt of effort, ripped it half down the length of the spine, triggering another flickering of light.

This time, when the lights came back, the woman was standing there. She appeared to be in her fifties with short, messy grey hair. And she was enraged.

"You ridiculous little upstarts. It's one thing for you to think you stand a chance against us, waging your coward's war from the shadows, but now you are literally in my world. How can you think you stand a chance?"

Zack cried out as the pain grew more intense like a vice, lined with jagged glass, was crushing his brain. Even as more Life flowed into him, it was not enough to hold back the psychic assault.

Reduced to crawling, Art moved on his hands and knees to the desk and reefed the drawers out, emptying their contents all over the floor. He pawed through the debris until, pushing aside some sheets of paper, he revealed an octagonal compact mirror. Without a hard object in reach, he opened it and slammed his fist down against the glass, hitting it again and again until the mirror cracked, the jagged pieces cutting into his knuckles.

"Two left," he groaned, collapsing onto his back.

After the lights flickered, only half of them came back on, capturing the room in uneven shadows. Zack blinked away the tears in his eyes and caught a glimpse of something on a side table in the corner. An hourglass.

"There," he pointed.

Bast looked over at it from where he was holding himself up against the wall.

"What? The hourglass?"

Zack nodded and immediately regretted it when fresh waves of pain lanced through it.

"Triangular. Pyramids," he said, between steadying breaths, "Two of them. Eight sides total."

"I was happy to take your word for it, dude," Bast replied and threw the last fragments of broken chair at it, shattering the hourglass.

The room didn't flicker so much as pulse with light and dark, like two competing rings of ripples in a pond. But Zack hardly noticed any of it. The pain was so intense it was all he could see, hear and taste.

"Where's the last one?" Tabitha screamed in frustration and agony.

Art groaned and lifted his hand, pointing at the shadow figure of the woman who was Kelick.

"Her. The last eight." He collapsed flat on the floor.

The others tried to move towards her, but the pain was crippling them. The woman laughed, loud and mockingly, standing above them as they writhed on the floor.

"We'll pick this up again tomorrow," she said, "after I've wiped your memory and updated my notes and kept you in this agony for a few more hours. Not that you'll remember it, but it's more for me than for you."

Zack took a deep breath, pushing away the pain and the nausea for just an instant. Long enough to allow him to grasp as much Life as he could. The pain eased, and he wanted to cling to it and ride it away from the psychic attack. But instead, he bundled it all together and, giving into the agony, he thrust it directly into Kimmy. The woman's mouth dropped open as Kimmy stumbled to her feet.

"Seven down, one to go." Kimmy thrust her palms forward and a jet of hot, white fire shot out of her, engulfing the woman and illuminating the room in blinding white light.

The pain ceased and then there was darkness.

CHAPTER 30

Zack awoke on another white linen bed. He tried to move, but straps around his head, limbs and chest held him down and, when he tried, the stinging ache of a cannula pulled in his left arm. Not ideal.

But Life flowed around him. Not the strained Life that he had pulled through Kelick's weakening barrier, but pure, free Life. And through it, he could sense his friends, evenly spaced in a circle around him, their Life signs surprisingly strong.

"Is everybody okay?" Tabitha called out.

"Yep," Charlie answered.

"Apart from being strapped down to a bed," Art added, "How are we supposed to get out of this?"

"I got it." Bast muttered some words and the sound of velcro ripping soon followed. "Ugh," he said, in equal parts disgust and surprise.

"Is everything okay?" Tabitha asked.

"Um, yeah," Bast replied, tearing more velcro straps off himself, "While I'm freeing everybody, maybe Art can see if there are any other minds around."

"It's just us six," Art replied, "plus a fuzzy signal that feels a lot like—"

"Max!" Charlie shouted with a sob. "Please, Bast, let me up so I can go to her."

"I will, but I think I better get Zack first. I've got a needle sticking out of my arm." Bast hobbled over and appeared in Zack's field of vision.

Bast untied Zack and they both looked at the cannulas in their arms. Zack reached out with his mind and probed the sites of injection.

"I don't think there's anything weird in it," he said, pointing to the fluid bag Bast had carried over, "Seems like saline and glucose."

He drew the needle out of Bast's arm and used the lightest touch of Life to close the wound before repeating the process on his own. Bast moved over to Charlie while Zack got his bearings. They were in a dimly lit room, each on metal beds arranged in a circle and in the centre of that circle sat a leather armchair. The armchair was linked to the circle of beds with complicated chains of painted symbols on the floor and walls, but that was not what held Zack's attention. Sitting in the armchair was the woman Doctor Kelick had transformed into. Her face was twisted in pain and her eyes stared into empty space.

Bast looked over at him as he undid Kimmy's restraints.

"Is she…?"

"Gone," Zack answered.

"Good," Kimmy said, pulling at her restraints with her freed arm, "although I would have been happy to roast her in real life as well. That bitch had me thinking I was crazy for a week."

Zack hopped off his bed and moved over to Bast. His legs were a bit wobbly, but otherwise, he was fine and he joined Bast, removing the cannulas, while the others undid their restraints. They found Charlie in the next room, her arms wrapped around Max, who was licking her with extreme enthusiasm. A metal cage sat in the corner of the room. Charlie must have pried it open to let Max out.

Charlie looked past Max to Zack.

"Can you check her?"

He nodded and reached out with Life.

"She's fine. Her muscles are pretty stiff, but nothing I can't help her out with."

He sent a flow of Life into Max, enjoying working with it again.

"Does anybody have any idea of what this all means?" Tabitha asked.

"I'm putting one together," Art said, flipping through a notebook.

"Where did you get that?" Charlie detangled herself from Max and stood up, keeping a hand through her fur.

Art pointed back at the body in the chair.

"She had it. This more or less confirms she was the Master of Mind; at least she references the Thirteen as 'us'. And she was taking notes on us. Or, more accurately, on Trav."

Tabitha slapped herself on the forehead.

"Ugh, and we fell for her trap, feeding her everything we knew about Trav." She gasped, her eyes wide. "Oh, crap. We told her everything about Nell and her home, too. She's in danger!"

"She might be," Art said, "if Kimmy hadn't barbequed Kelick's psyche. But I doubt anybody else has seen this book. We're okay."

"How did we even get here?" Charlie asked.

"Let's get out of wherever here is, first." Tabitha pointed to another door in the room.

"I'll lead," Kimmy said, stepping up to the door, "Anybody who tries to stop us is going to regret it for a few seconds."

Tabitha nodded.

"Okay, but let's try and stay qui—"

Kimmy threw open the door and charged into the room. The others followed behind. Unlike the previous two rooms, this one was more comfortably furnished and better lit. A desk took up a corner of the room, filing cabinets lined one of the walls and, opposite these, a wooden staircase rose up to a solid metal door.

"Our way out?" Bast pointed to the door.

"Hopefully," Art said, "but I'm more worried about that."

He walked to the desk and put his hand on a pile of notebooks, each the same design as the one he was holding. Kimmy grabbed one from the middle and flicked through it, ignoring the scattered pile she left behind.

"This is about us too, but I don't remember these conversations. I never spoke to Kelick about my mentor, but there are pages in here about my lessons with him."

Charlie claimed another notebook and opened it in the middle.

"This one has a whole group discussion about the Commander and the statues."

Art clicked his fingers.

"She told us this. Right at the end. She said something about wiping our memory and starting again."

Tabitha pulled out the bottom notebook and opened it. She flicked through it, stopping to read a sample of the pages.

"I think this one is her first attempt. The questions she was asking us were more about us, our families, our childhoods. And it looks like it all crashed fairly quickly because of something between Charlie and Max." Tabitha read more closely. "She theorised that Max needed to be in good health and physically closer to Charlie or their connection would interfere with the mind trap."

Tabitha and the others looked to Art. He shrugged.

"This crap is well beyond my pay grade. She basically created and then puppeteered a little universe just for us. I'm getting a nosebleed simply thinking about it."

"Okay," Tabitha said, "so she's been running us through her psych ward simulation, mining us for information."

"Well, we kind of asked for that, didn't we?" Bast said, "We got Nell to spread the rumour that we knew their secrets, hoping they'd come after us. And then they did."

"And we've killed one more of them," Kimmy said, "There's got to be something down here to lead us to the last four."

"Let's turn this room over, find whatever we can." Tabitha turned to Max. "Can you keep an eye on the door up there, Max?"

Max gave a soft bark in response.

"She's got our back," Charlie said, approaching one of the filing cabinets. As she neared it, her eyes lit up excitedly and she pulled open one of the drawers. She reached in and pulled out a handful of phones.

Zack recognised his among them.

"How did you sense those?"

"I didn't," Charlie replied, passing him the devices and reaching back in, "I felt this." She pulled out a steel lockbox and handed it to Kimmy.

"Is that…?" Kimmy asked with a squeal.

"I think so," Charlie answered.

Kimmy melted the lock with a wave of her hand and pried open the box. Mr Shanks floated out, wiggling its hilt in front of her face.

"Shanky!" Kimmy said, grabbing the dagger and pulling it in tight. "Did that horrible woman lock you up? It's okay; you're back with me now." She looked at the blade more closely. "Whose blood is that on you, you naughty knife?"

The drawer Charlie had opened turned out to hold their phones, wallets and other personal items. Zack handed the phones out to their owners, but all their batteries were completely flat. Still, Zack gained a sense of security having it and his wallet in his pockets.

The next, deeper drawer in the cabinet held their weapons and Charlie excitedly took them all out and lined them up against the wall.

Bast focused on the desk and, after a moment of intense staring, pulled a drawer clean from beneath the desktop.

"You're not the only one getting a tingle, Charlie."

He discarded papers and clutter from the desk before holding up a metallic cube.

"A beacon?" Art asked.

Bast nodded.

"Great," Kimmy said with a dry tone, "we've got a one-way ticket to our suicide run."

"It's still good to have," Tabitha said.

Kimmy held up her hands.

"I wasn't voting against it."

Zack eyed the drawer Bast had removed and looked back at the desk. There was something about the size and shape of it that didn't look right. It was too shallow. He pulled out the drawer beneath it and compared them. The lower one was deeper. Driven by a flash of inspiration, he reached into the top-drawer cavity and felt around above it. His fingers found something sticking out and he pressed against it. With a soft click, what had appeared to be part of the solid desktop, slid open to reveal a slim drawer.

"Aw, hell yes," Art said over his shoulder, "you totally found a secret drawer."

"With a secret laptop." Zack held up his prize.

He opened the computer on the desk. It had been in sleep mode and, as it woke up, a chat window was open.

"Got anything?" Tabitha asked, looking over his shoulder.

"There's not much installed on here except for this private chat client. The most recent conversation is between 'Eight' and 'Twelve'." Zack counted out on his fingers. "'Eight is Kelick and Mind is the eighth school… which means she was most likely talking to the Master of Air."

"What does she say?" Tabitha said, leaning in closer.

"Not much. Kelick is pretty guarded." Zack skimmed through the chat history. "She says she's got us and that we're under control. That we've given her plenty of intel and she's building a profile on the Traveller, so they'll be able to eliminate him and start replenishing the ranks of the Thirteen soon."

"Bloody hell." Bast stared at the monitor over their shoulders.

"It's not that much of a surprise," Art said, "we knew that was likely their plan."

"Not that," Bast said, pointing at the bottom right corner of the screen. "That!"

"Oh crap," Zack said. The laptop's date read as Friday, 20 December.

"That can't be right," Tabitha said, "we were barely in that place for a week."

"That time," Art said and gestured to the notebooks, "I think a few months is possible."

Charlie looked at Max and then back at the group.

"Max says we've been here for a long time. She doesn't count days the same way we do, especially not from a cage, but it's been a lot more than a week."

Zack opened the calendar on the laptop and counted the weeks from the last ritual date he could remember. He swore again.

"The next ritual is tomorrow and they'll be replacing the Master of Life if we don't stop them before."

"Maybe," Bast said.

"I'm pretty sure I did the maths right," Zack replied.

"Yeah, but you didn't factor in the time zones." Bast stepped beside him and took over the laptop and pulled up the clock settings. "The rituals are early Saturday afternoon for us in Sydney. But according to this laptop, we're in the US. And the ritual starts in less than an hour."

Silence settled over the room as they each contemplated the significance of what Bast had said.

"We need to make a choice," Tabitha said, "either we accept the Thirteen are going to grow from four back to five members today and we take time to recuperate. Or we use that beacon, force our way through the Tower and take on the four most powerful of the Thirteen."

"Plus their Life replacement," Zack added, "who will either be another necromancer or somebody better than me at healing them while they fight us."

"I vote we go in," Kimmy said, "I'm sick of sneaking around and I want this over."

"I get wanting to end this, Kimmy," Tabitha said, "but we've got to play this smart."

"I think it is the smart choice," Art said, "they still think we're locked away in a psychic prison, so they won't be expecting us. And, for once, we know where they are going to be. Maybe we'll even get lucky and catch them while they're distracted by the ritual. It's really the best chance we're going to get in a while. We give it up and who knows how many months and how many more replacements they'll get before we get another chance."

"I don't know whether I'm reassured or terrified that Art is agreeing with Kimmy," Bast said, "but I'm in."

Charlie nodded. "Me too."

"I agree," Zack said, "but how do we find them once we're in there? We don't know where the ritual takes place."

"I got a feeling of it when I used the opal," Bast said, "there's definitely Movement magic behind the ritual and I might be able to sense its signature if we get close to it."

"So, we're just going to wander around the Tower, fighting anybody that gets in our way, until Bast can sense where the Thirteen are?" Kimmy asked.

"Hopefully most people are already assigned to their guard posts and the halls will be empty," Bast replied, "but yeah."

Tabitha looked at each of them.

"Okay, I'm on board. But if Bast can't find them, we get out, either through the Gate Room or the Entrance."

They all nodded in agreement.

"Great," Tabitha said, "How long do we have, Bast?"

Bast paused.

"Assuming we want to get in there at the last minute, when hopefully everybody else has stopped roaming the halls, we have about forty-five minutes."

Tabitha walked over to the wall and reclaimed her flail.

"Alright, everybody, do what you need to do. And then we finish this."

Zack didn't do much during that time other than worry. He fed some simple streams of Life into the others to ensure they were as healthy as they could be and practised a few basic forms with his quarterstaff. But, otherwise, he spent the time pacing back and forth, his mind afroth with thoughts and fears.

Art pulled him aside and threw an arm around his shoulders.

"We've got this, mate."

"Yeah, I know," Zack replied, in a voice unlikely to convince either of them, "I just wish my phone had charge so I could call my parents. They must be worried sick. Yours too."

"Nah," Art said, "there's Tower protocol for this. Until we're definitely dead, there's too much risk to the Silence to kill us off in the real world. And us being missing is almost as bad. Half a dozen young, middle-class teens disappear without a trace? We'd be on the news every night. My guess is, each of our parents remembers talking to us 'just a couple of days ago'. They won't be worried."

"Telling me the Tower is sending psychomancers over to my parents' house is not filling me with the serenity you might have thought it would," Zack replied.

"It's fine, mate. One more throwdown and then we can sort this all out."

"Unless we lose."

"Well, either way, they leave our families alone after that." Art's casual tone brought a smile out of Zack and he smiled back. "I wish we had enough time to explore whatever is upstairs. I'm not picking up any minds."

"No major Life signals at all," Zack said, "but it could trigger an alarm or something and we need to stay in stealth mode."

"Yeah, I know." Art spoke with an overly wistful tone as he looked up at the door. "Years of gaming tells me we're missing out on potential loot."

"It's time," Tabitha said, calling them together, "Bast, activate the beacon. When the gate opens, we go in fast. Art first, to stun whoever is guarding the room, then I'll follow with an air blast as backup. Then everybody else."

Bast placed the cube on the ground, triggered it and then stepped back. Moments later, the silvery disc of a gate expanded out of nothing. Tabitha and Art nodded to each other and leapt through.

CHAPTER 31

Zack emerged from the gate into chaos. Art and Tabitha had been unable to subdue the guards in the Gate Room. Instead, Zack, the last one through, found all his friends hovering a metre above the ground, upside down, while half a dozen Tower members incanted, orange magic swirling around them.

Zack hesitated only a moment before charging towards one of the guards, bringing his quarterstaff back for a powerful swing. But one moment was long enough and he was lifted into the air beside Bast.

"That's all of them," the mage at the centre of the group said, "Keep them spinning and I'll go trigger the alarm. And watch Bast closely in case he—"

What Bast might have done went unfinished when a torrent of wind rushed through the doorway, collecting the mages and sending them crashing into the stone walls. They fell dazed or unconscious and the teens tumbled to the ground.

"Great work, Tabs," Kimmy said, picking up her axe, "I couldn't get a lock on them the way we were spinning and I didn't want to burn any of you."

"It wasn't me." Tabitha looked past Kimmy, her face slack with astonishment.

Junie hurried into the room, glancing over her shoulder.

"Are you all okay?"

Charlie drew her bow and pointed it at Junie.

"What are you doing here?"

Junie held up her hands.

"Slow down; I'm on your side. The Traveller told you he had more people on the inside. I'm one of them."

She gestured at the scattered mages on the other side of the room.

"How did you know we'd be here?" Zack asked.

"I didn't. Nobody knew where you've been hiding." Junie looked more frantic than Zack had ever seen her. "But the Traveller said the ritual is about to happen and the last five of the Thirteen will all be in one place. I can help."

"Last four," Kimmy said with a smug grin.

"What?" Junie asked.

"Four," Tabitha replied, "That's where we've been, held prisoner by the Master of Mind. But we got free and now it's four."

"We still need to find them, though," Zack said.

"Here." Junie reached into a pocket and held out a tiny orange object. It was one of the gilded pearls. She handed it to Tabitha. "When you went missing, the Traveller sent me looking for them. This was the only one I could find. He said they could lead the way to them, but it would take Movement or Knowledge magic to use it."

"Hold up," Kimmy said, glaring at Junie with open mistrust, "we're supposed to buy that you're working with the Traveller? You're the one who sent us hunting renegade mages all last year."

"And the one who kept our hunt for those renegades as secret as possible." Junie answered with a sharp tone. "The one who sniffed Armand's fingerprints on it from the start and wanted to make sure nothing led back to the Traveller? Yes, me."

"Why send us after him at all?" Bast asked.

"Because what he was doing didn't just risk the Tower, it risked the world," Junie said, "Look, we're running out of time. If you need to leave me behind, then go, but I can help you."

Zack and his friends exchanged glances in a brief and silent conversation.

"Okay," Tabitha said, passing the pearl to Bast, "we could really use the help; please come with us."

Junie replied with a pleased nod while Bast concentrated on the pearl.

"This is tricky," he said, one eye squinting, "I can't open a gate there, because of the wards, but if I pretend that I can, I get a feel for where it's leading me. I can make it work. Follow me."

They made their way through the Tower, creeping down corridors, as Bast led them in a series of left and right turns and up and down stairs. On a few occasions, Junie pointed to rooms in which people were on guard duty and they held their breaths while they tiptoed past. Zack caught a fragment of a conversation about recent streaming shows and was relieved; the idle chatting suggested there was still time before the ritual began.

After Bast led them around three consecutive left turns, Art grabbed him by the shoulder.

"Are you sure you've got a read on where we're going? Like, at least a direction?"

Bast returned a stern look.

"A direction only works in three dimensions, which the Tower only pretends to be. So, if you don't mind, I'm building up a pretty massive headache trying to pull this off."

"Leave him alone, Art," Tabitha said and they continued down the corridor, "Junie, do you have any idea where the ritual will be taking place?"

Junie shook her head, but a few steps in front of her, Art squinted and rubbed the inside of his ear. He turned around, fixing his squinting eyes on Junie.

"We've dealt with shape-changers and illusionists before. How do we know you're really you?"

Tabitha looked at him, confused.

"Art, what are you—?"

Art held up his hand to cut her off.

"Prove you are who you say you are."

Junie looked equal parts confused and frustrated.

"I thought I'd earned some trust with the pearl and from saving you from the guards, but fine. How would you like me to prove I'm me?"

"Say your name," Art said, "that should be enough."

She rolled her eyes.

"I am Junie."

Zack wasn't sure what Art was attempting, but he'd known him long enough to be certain he was up to something. A look of realisation snapped onto Art's face.

"She's—"

A vortex of wind burst out from Junie's palms, catching Zack and the others within its violent streams and sending them crashing into each other and the walls.

"We'll have to do this the hard way, then." Junie rode the whirlwind past where Art and Bast were sprawled on the floor. "Come and finish what you started."

She was out of sight before the swirls of wind ceased and they regained their feet.

"What the hell was that?" Tabitha asked, looking at Art. "So, that wasn't Junie?"

Art rubbed his shoulder where it had struck against the wall.

"Oh, that was Junie, alright. She's also the Master of Air."

"So, what was all that about proving she wasn't somebody else?" Charlie asked.

"I wanted her to say her name," Art replied, "She's been basically rubbing our noses, everybody's noses, in it. The Tower translates other languages to sound like your own. Tabs, when you said her name, I could hear a translation happening behind it, but it was too distorted to catch. When she said it, I heard it loud and clear. Junie is Juu-Ni; it's twelve in Japanese."

"Twelve, as in, who eight was messaging in about us." Zack was hurrying to put the pieces together in his head. "That's how she knew about the Traveller and Armand."

"Then why help us now?" Tabitha didn't seem to want to believe.

"Because she didn't want other people to catch us," Art said, "I'm guessing she was leading us into an ambush."

"Well, neither of us gets the advantage of surprise," Bast said, "Let's go."

Bast led on, before stopping in the middle of a corridor and turned to look at the wall on the left.

"I think we're here."

"It's a good thing I understand the gravity of this situation." Art stared at the blank stone wall. "Otherwise, I'd be geeking out about needing to open a secret magic door."

"Game faces," Tabitha said.

Charlie waved her hand and Max transformed into her oversized wolf form, while Bast's feet glowed orange. Kimmy called out Mr Shanks before igniting a magical flame on the blade of her axe. She looked at the floating dagger.

"Are you certain you don't want some?"

Mr Shanks shook his blade from side to side and Kimmy sighed.

Watching the others prepare themselves, Zack decided to try his own preparation and wove a series of Life threads into himself, where they lay dormant, ready to respond as needed. He hoped.

The stone bricks shifted, sliding open to reveal the Ritual Chamber, the secret room hidden in the heart of the Tower. They stepped inside, ready for battle, but the figures were still, watching them. Four of them - Junie, two other women and a man - were evenly spaced around the room, standing at the tips of a thirteen-pointed star etched into the stone floor. *A tridecagram,* Zack's mind offered. But he wasn't really paying attention to that. His eyes were drawn to the fifth figure, standing in the centre of the room next to a floating stone that resembled the bricks of the Tower walls. The figure stared back at him with the familiar brown eyes that had watched and guided him for over two years.

Sara, his mentor, had been chosen to be the next Master of Life.

"You need to stop this absurdity," she said, "You all do."

"Listen to her," Junie said, "We've given Sara one chance to end this without violence."

"The Thirteen started the violence when they kidnapped, tortured and killed Jackie," Art said in a cold voice.

"Those two acted alone," the man said, "we would have held them accountable if given the chance."

"And rather than speak up or come to me," Sara said, "you sided with the Tower's enemies, hunting down the members of the Thirteen and killing them? Even killing the Master of Life?"

"I defeated the Master of Life, but I didn't kill him." Zack took a step closer to Sara. "His name was Shen and whatever he was, it was not alive."

"What do you mean?" Sara's expression changed to one of earnest concern.

"This can wait," Junie said, "will you surrender or not?"

Zack ignored her.

"Sara, you taught me about the abomination of ripping Life from something without permission and in Shen I saw it first-hand. He pulled it out of Charlie, leaving her in a coma and used what it became to animate the bodies of the other masters. He was so far gone that I had to use Life itself to destroy him."

"I think you've had your chance, Sara," one of the other women said, "It's clear they are beyond reason, a threat to the Tower and they must be destroyed."

"That's what you're joining," Zack shouted, desperate to convince Sara, "a group of people content for Life itself to be perverted if it helps them hold on to power. That's what we're fighting against."

Sara spun to face Junie, anger on her face. "Is this true?"

"Yes," Junie replied, her voice calm, "I thought you were ready to pay whatever price was necessary to protect the Tower. To protect the world."

"That is not a price," Sara replied, "that is a betrayal!"

A jet of icy slush struck Sara in the side of the head, propelling her into the floating stone with a heavy thud. She flopped to the ground. The woman who had cast it looked over the body to Junie.

"I don't think you were going to convince her."

Junie shrugged.

"There are better contenders for the role, anyway. And we'll have more time to consider them after we've dealt with these traitors."

Zack stared at Sara's still body and, in that moment, it was his grandmother lying there. His grip tightened on his quarterstaff and he charged the woman who must have been the Master of Water. No yell or battle cry escaped his lips, only the hiss of seething fury as he ran.

"I guess we're starting then," Bast said.

Behind Zack, Tabitha shouted out directions, but he wasn't paying attention. The Master of Water turned back to face him and deep blue light glowing from her hands, she conjured a slick of ice along the ground.

Focused only on her and his anger, he dropped to his knees and slid across the ice, holding his staff forward like a lance. His knees hit the ground painfully, but the ice carried him towards his target at speed. The butt of his staff slammed into her thigh and she stumbled backward.

Bast and Charlie raced past Zack to the other woman deeper in the room. Red light bloomed around her hands and a cone of white-hot flame shot out. Bast strafed to the left, but Charlie's reactions weren't magically enhanced like his and she was forced to throw herself to the right, landing on the floor in an effort to avoid getting burned. The Master of Fire stepped toward her, redirecting the flames, but Bast dashed in and whipped out with his rapier. The thin blade sliced into her forearm and she pulled back the arms and the flames. A reddish-brown glow engulfed Charlie and she emerged from it as a cheetah. She and Bast raced around the woman in opposite directions, while she responded by flinging handfuls of flames at them.

They darted in and out, avoiding the fiery projectiles and forcing the Master of Fire to spin around as she tried to keep them both in sight. While she hurled flames at them with both hands, she couldn't help but lose track of them as they circled her and, when that happened, Bast or Charlie leapt in, attacking with blade or claw.

After another two wounds, the woman incanted and the next time Charlie raked her claw across the woman's hips, flames, rather than blood, emerged from the cuts and Charlie pulled her burnt paw back with a feline squeal. The flames travelled across the mage's body, igniting her other wounds until she was almost half covered in fire.

Flames flashed on the opposite side of the room as Kimmy, with Mr Shanks hovering overhead, charged in to attack the man. Before they could close on him, he incanted. In a wave of brown light, rocky armour materialised and covered him from head to toe and the light extended out in his left hand, growing into a stone hammer. He stepped forward to meet Kimmy and his hammer clanged against her flaming Axe.

Mr Shanks zipped down, but the blade could only scrape against the rocky carapace. The Master of Earth swung his hammer in an overhead attack at Kimmy and she was forced back, barely knocking it aside with her axe. Twice more, he levelled his hammer at her and, on the second swing, her rushed parry collided at an awkward angle, wrenching her wrist painfully.

She stumbled backwards but, before the man could follow, Mr Shanks soared at the man's eyes. He raised his hand to fend it off and Kimmy used the moment to retreat a few steps further. She dropped her axe and incanted, pointing at the Master of Earth. At a spot on the man's chest and shoulder, the rocky armour glowed with heat. The man lumbered toward her, but she circled away, maintaining the spell. The air around his shoulder shimmered and the stone cracked. Mr Shanks maintained his assault on the mage's face and he slapped it away with a stone-encased hand. The cracks in the stone widened and Mr Shanks looped back. Kimmy dropped the spell and threw a ball of fire at the man. It splashed harmlessly against the stone on his chest and forearm, but it drew his attention long enough for Mr Shanks to soar down, lining up with one of the cracks and stabbing deep into the man's shoulder.

In the other back corner of the room, Tabitha and Art approached Junie. The Master of Air all but ignored Art, her eyes fixed on her former student.

"You really think you can best me?" Junie's voice was full of derision. "Everything you know, I taught you."

Tabitha replied with an incantation, spoken as precisely as her fingers moved, unleashing a jet of wind at Junie. With a flick of her hand, Junie returned a jet that met Tabitha's, colliding into a chaotic vortex of air between them. But Junie's jet was more powerful and, despite the effort clear on Tabitha's strained face, the vortex moved towards her.

When the vortex was only a metre away and Tabitha's hair and clothes were getting whipped around by the wind, the vortex stopped moving. Junie's eyes had glazed over and she twitched at the neck as if trying to snap herself back into attention. To the left of Tabitha, Art was also incanting, his arm outstretched and moving in slow circles with a purple glow. Tabitha poured more energy into her spell and the violent whirlwind between them moved back towards Junie until, when it was almost upon her, her eyes snapped back into focus.

Junie threw her other hand down and, with a resonating thud, the air between them went dead. In a smooth motion, the hand that had held the jet shot forth at Art. Sky blue light flared in Junie's palm and a windstorm the width of a barrel surged into him. The instant it slammed into Art's chest, a bolt of lightning forked through it and, amidst a thunderous boom, Art was flung across the room, crashing into a wall.

"There," Junie said, "I can't have anybody interrupting our final lesson."

Zack climbed to his feet, but the Master of Water recovered faster and pointed her palm towards him. A jet of liquid shot out, but he rolled to the side and it splashed onto the floor. Where it landed, it bubbled and fizzed, eating into the stone. Acid.

Before the mage could redirect the jet towards him, Max barrelled into her. She kept her feet, but the collision knocked her off balance. Staggering, she pointed the acid at her attacker, but Max bounded to the side and the stream only grazed her side, eating away at her fur, not her flesh.

Zack rose up and swung his quarterstaff at the mage's back, but she dodged to the side and the blow landed on her shoulder instead. She dropped the stream of acid and mouthed a brief incantation. A ripple of deep blue light flowed across her, leaving behind icy armour in its wake.

Unlike the Master of Earth's stone carapace, the ice took the form of medieval plate armour and covered her entire body. Zack swung his staff again, but it crunched against the armour and barely shifted her.

The Master of Water smirked through her icy helm, but her eyes were filled with hate.

"Did I upset you? You're the one to blame for her death. Or did you think we would just roll over as you attempt to take away everything we have worked for?"

The rage inside Zack had frozen as hard as the mage's armour and he was thinking clearly again. His weapon would do nothing against the ice and Max's teeth even less. All that was left was keeping the Master of Water occupied until his friends could defeat the others. But as he looked around, each of his friends seemed to be in a similar stalling position.

Unless somebody made a move soon, they weren't getting out of this room alive.

CHAPTER 32

As if someone had read Zack's mind, the entry to the Ritual Chamber began to close, the stone bricks sliding back into place. There really was only one way out now, but to do that, they needed to get on the offensive. Maybe they would be better off focusing on one of their opponents, but that would leave at least one of the others unoccupied and able to rain devastation down on them unhindered. All Zack could do was keep the Master of Water busy and hope she exhausted herself.

Nearby, it seemed Bast and Charlie had the same plan with the Master of Fire. Bast had braved the heat and cut her twice more, but flames had emerged from those wounds as well and now the woman resembled little more than living fire. And the wounds themselves had not slowed her down.

In fact, the opposite appeared to be true. Now that the woman was no longer worried about defending herself, she was able to focus on her attacks. Drawing from her flames, she shot fire from her palms like flamethrowers. The billowing flames were much harder to avoid and, despite Bast's and Charlie's speed, the fire licked at them both. Patches of Charlie's fur were burnt away, the rest blackened, while the exposed skin on Bast's right side, including his face, was red and blistered.

The two kept running in their rings, doing their best to avoid the flames while keeping the woman's attention. She dropped her hands and the flames ceased, but before they could hope she had exhausted herself, her hands glowed with red light and a wall of fire erupted from the ground. Around one metre deep, it reached from the Master of Fire to the nearest wall. Bast skidded to a halt before he crossed it, but Charlie couldn't and plunged right into the flames.

The speed she was moving carried her through it, but she emerged screeching in agony, her face badly burned. Charlie limped off, her screeches fading into pained mews, before she collapsed in the corner, shuddering.

Mr Shanks shifted back and forth, widening the Master of Earth's shoulder wound and the man cried out in pain. He grabbed it by the hilt and wrenched it out. Mr Shanks resisted, trying to fly away, but the man held tight, mouthing an incantation. With another shimmer of brown light, his stone armour softened and turned into mud, flowing up and down his body and stopping short of his stone mace. The mud did, however, ooze from his other hand, covering Mr Shanks. With a grunt, he flung the enchanted dagger against the nearest wall. Thick with mud, it landed with a splat and stuck to the stone bricks.

"Shanky!" Kimmy shouted.

She ran forward to reclaim her axe from the floor, but the Master of Earth turned his attention back to her and shot a stream of mud from his hand. It landed on the stone floor tiles in front of Kimmy and, in her haste to get to her weapon, she stepped into it, losing her balance. Her weight pushed down on her ankle at an awkward angle and she fell to the ground, hissing in pain. The man projected more mud from his outstretched palm, coating Kimmy's legs and chest.

The heavy mud weighed her down, but she mumbled an incantation and fire erupted from her hand. She held the fire close to the mud, where it dried and crumbled. The Master of Earth sneered at her through his mud mask and waved his hand. The mud around Kimmy's legs and waist hardened into stone and when she held her fire to it, it had no effect. With another gesture from the man, the stone crept up her body, covering her chest and holding her fast against the floor. Mr Shanks struggled against the mud, but the mud held firm. The Master of Earth stepped closer to Kimmy, winding his mace back for a killing blow.

Junie pointed past Tabitha to the others.

"And you call yourself their leader? I suppose this is a lesson for me as well. I saw so much potential in you, but all you've done is lead your friends to their deaths."

Tabitha screamed and unleashed another jet of air at Junie, which she again caught with a stream of her own.

"I should thank you," Junie said, over the roaring of the vortex between the jets, "As inconvenient as your little killing spree has been, you've done me a favour. Once you and your friends have been dealt with, I'll start recruiting replacements for the Thirteen. People who see things my way, who will be grateful for what I've given them. Unlike some."

As punctuation, she summoned a whirlwind from Tabitha's left, which picked her up and slammed her against the wall. The air jets dropped and Junie stepped closer.

"Time for your last lesson," Junie said, "Air isn't all about flashy wind and lightning magic."

She traced a symbol with her index finger and Tabitha gasped for air, clutching at her throat.

"It's a flexible school of magic. At least I'll be able to teach you that before the end."

Tabitha fell to her knees. Zack panned around at his friends, who were falling to the last of the Thirteen. They were losing.

Acid and pain splashed against his chest as the Master of Water used his distraction and despair to her advantage. The cycle of Life he had weaved inside him got to work and he forced away the pain.

He needed to do something to shake this up, but what? The Master of Water's icy armour was impervious to most of their weapons and magic, except for Kimmy's. Zack had hoped she would finish with the Master of Earth and turn her flames against the ice, but that no longer seemed possible. And if Kimmy's Fire was not an option, what did that leave him?

A spark of inspiration hit him and he dived away from another spurt of acid. Seeing it splash against the stone beside him filled in the rest of his thoughts.

"Max," he called, "try and keep her busy, okay?"

Max, covered in more blisters than fur, yelped at him in a way that sounded very much like she was saying, *What the hell do you think I've been doing?* and the Master of Water spun her head in the wolf's direction.

Zack charged at her and she turned back to meet him, throwing another burst of acid at him. He was too close for her to aim well and the acid splashed against his shoulder. Drops of it bounced onto his cheek and he screamed in pain as he felt it eat into his face, but he stayed his course. He thrust his quarterstaff between her legs, against the back of the woman's ankle, and barged his shoulder into her chest. The frozen armour slammed painfully against his acid-burned skin, but Zack put his full weight into the motion. The Master of Water tripped over his staff and fell to the ground.

Max leaped in and clamped her massive canine jaw around the woman's ankle. Her teeth couldn't get through the ice, but they found just enough purchase that she could drag the woman across the room. Zack didn't look back. He ran to Art's side and reached out with Life. It was bad. Beyond the burn from the lightning and the fractures from hitting the wall, there was internal damage, too. With no time to be precise, Zack sent thick streams of Life into Art. His friend was stirring when there was a pained whimpering from behind Zack.

The Master of Water had regained her balance and, despite still being on her back, had managed to shoot a spurt of acid. It struck Max on her side, eating away at fur and skin until her rib bones were visible. The mage wrenched her ankle out of Max's mouth and climbed to her feet. As she did, she incanted and a long, sharp icicle grew in her hand. Zack launched himself to his feet, leaving Art to recover and sprinted at the mage. The Master of Water lined up the icy spear with Max's head and thrust it down, but an instant before it pierced Max's skull, Zack threw himself at the mage. The force of his body knocked her to the side and the icicle shattered on contact with the stone floor. He rolled to his feet and, swearing, she turned a jet of acid towards him.

Tabitha gasped, her face turning red with her effort to breathe. Whatever was in her lungs was not breathable air.

"You really are a disappointment," Junie said, watching Tabitha choke, "I actually had you marked as my eventual successor, with all the potential you showed. But after the slightest moral quandary, the first dash of grey in your black and white mind, you turned away."

Tabitha, her face turning from red to purple, gestured at Junie, a blue glow on her fingertips. Junie sniffed at the air around her.

"Hydrogen? Are you trying to choke me out in return?" She inhaled deeply and dramatically. "See, this is what I'm talking about. I'm the Master of Air. Breathing this is nothing to me. That's the kind of mastery you could have risen to, but you gave it up and for what?"

Tabitha's unfocused eyes hid behind drooping lids, but she smiled as she answered, "Versatility."

A red glow shone from her palm and she clicked her fingers. A spark flashed an inch from Junie's head and she had one moment to look stunned before the hydrogen, outside and inside her lungs, ignited. Pale blue flames roared through her and what remained collapsed smouldering onto the floor. Tabitha collapsed to her knees, sucking air back into her lungs.

The Master of Earth turned to look at the localised explosion and so did Kimmy. Despite being encased in stone to her wrists and neck, she smirked.

"Tabs, you cheeky bitch. Stay in your lane." She craned her neck to see Mr Shanks, still struggling to escape the mud. "I'm sorry, Shanky, but I'm not giving you a choice this time."

Red light bloomed at her fingertips and fire rippled across the length of the enchanted dagger's blade. It swung its blade with frantic energy, to both try to escape and express its displeasure, but as it moved, it burnt away the mud and freed itself. The dagger floated into the air, strafing to the left and the right before it paused and wiggled its hilt with glee. It soared through the air doing loop-de-loops, a faint stream of smoke marking its passage.

The Master of Earth turned back to Kimmy and lumbered towards her, ready to strike with his mace.

"Um, a little help, Shanky?" she called.

Mr Shanks paused mid-loop and soared at the man, like a meteorite blazing through the atmosphere. The blade slashed past his face, burning through the mud and cutting across his face. The Master of Earth yelled in pain and fired a jet of mud at the flying dagger. Most of the mud sailed past it, but even the splatters that hit soon dried, crumbling off the blade in a shower of dust.

With the mage occupied, Kimmy refocused her efforts on the stone encasing her and incanted. Red light rippled across her body and the stone coverings glowed with heat. Kimmy hissed in pain but continued her incantation and her encasings hissed and cracked. The smell of burning skin rose from underneath the rock and Kimmy clenched her teeth until the cracks grew enough to weaken their hold on her and she tore herself free.

"Gimme an opening!" she shouted as she forced herself up.

Her clothes were singed, with holes burnt through in places to revealing blackened and blistered skin, but she snatched up her flaming axe and charged the Master of Earth. He met her advance with a swing of his stone mace, but she ducked underneath it. Mr Shanks zipped in, carving off a layer of the flowing mud and exposing the man's chest, for barely a moment. But a moment was all Kimmy needed and she buried her axe into his ribcage. He staggered, swinging his mace at her one last time, but it was weak and slow and she stepped inside it, pushing the axe head deeper into his chest.

The Master of Earth gurgled in pain and collapsed to the ground. Kimmy pried her axe free before collapsing to the floor beside him, panting.

The Life weave inside Zack was working hard to repair the damage to his body as the Master of Water hit him with yet more acid, but it was draining him and there was only so much more he could take.

Meanwhile, nearby, Bast was slowing down, the strain from fatigue and burns obvious on his face.

Zack looked past the Master of Water to where Art forced himself up into a seated position. He wasn't sure if this would work, but he was desperate, so he thought as loudly as he could in Art's direction.

Art!

Art's eyes snapped to his, but his thoughts came through groggy. *Um, yeah?*

Connect us up with Bast now. Zack replied.

Art's eyes flashed purple and another presence emerged in the back of Zack's head. Zack dodged to the left to avoid another burst of acid. *Bast, can you hear us?*

Bast stumbled half a step in surprise but rolled smoothly away from a jet of flame and kept running. *Loud and clear, mate. Kinda busy, though.*

I know, Zack replied. *The girls have done their job, but if we don't finish this soon, they're going to die before I can heal them.*

I get that. Bast's thoughts felt frustrated. *Not sure what we can do, though. I don't think the three of us have magic that can get through their defences.*

We don't. Zack replied, *but they do. We just need to get them close enough and time it right.*

Love it, but I don't think one splash either way will do it. Bast's frustration was fading into desperation.

I know, but it might be enough for a chink in their armour, Zack said. *It's the best I've got.*

Confidence radiated down the mind-link from Art. *I think I can do you one better than that. Leave it to me.*

Zack wasn't sure about that, but he didn't have any better ideas. *Okay, for this to work, we're going to have to disorient them, which means we need to run fast.*

A wordless yet unimpressed feeling came through the link from Bast.

Alright, boys, get them spinning. Art propped himself up against the wall.

Zack picked up speed as he ran around the Master of Water, trying to get her off balance while avoiding the acid jet she was shooting at him.

They're too far apart, Art said through the link. *You need to bring them each about a metre closer if they're going to hit each other.*

Zack didn't answer; he could only concentrate on running and his legs were burning with fatigue. He directed a sliver of Life into his thighs, but he was only stealing from himself, and his upper body ached even more.

That's it, Art said after they had made two more passes. *I'm going to count to three, and on three, you need to drop to the floor.*

The jet of acid caught Zack in his calf, burning deep through his skin and causing him to stumble.

You need to slow down a step, Bast! Art directed.

Bast yelled in pain as the jet of fire struck his side.

That's it. One. Two. Three. Drop!

Zack and Bast collapsed to the ground and the jets of fire and acid crossed over them, missing each other by mere inches and striking the opposite mage.

"Stay!" Art shouted.

There was a quality to the word that Zack had heard from Art before. It buzzed in his ears and Zack realised he couldn't move. On either side of him, the women screamed and there was the smell of burning flesh in the room.

After several seconds, Zack's body responded to him again and he stood up. The Masters of Fire and Water were dead; their bodies, or what remained of them, were grizzly messes that Zack chose not to linger on.

The Thirteen had been defeated.

But as he looked around the room, he was the only one standing. Bast had stayed down where he had fallen, burns covering his body and Art seemed to have passed out again. Only Tabitha appeared to be able to recover on her own and he didn't have nearly enough left in him to save the rest. There was only one thing he could do.

Hoping it wasn't a mistake that would cost them all their lives, he limped over to Sara's side. The Master of Water had been wrong: she was not dead, but she had taken a brutal head injury.

Zack ignored the pain at the edges of his brain and wove together thin threads of Life, repairing the damage done to her skull, blood vessels and surface of her brain. He could have done it more easily with a heavy stream of Life but he had almost none to spare, so it had to be precise instead.

Sara's eyes opened and came into focus. She reached up and touched her head near the point of impact.

"Zachary?"

"It's over, Sara, but my friends are dying," he replied, "Please, will you help me?"

His mentor looked around the room, taking in the four masters' bodies as well as Zack's friends.

"Yes," she replied, "I will help you."

CHAPTER 33

Zack and Sara moved around the room, weaving Life magic into his friends and, for a brief respite, it was like he was her student again. Except that he'd never seen the degree of precision Sara was now threading. She was managing to repair life-threatening injuries with the amount of magic it would take Zack to mend a shallow cut. He was in awe and that feeling reminded him she was no longer his mentor.

"I'm sorry, Zack," Sara said while weaving fine needles of Life into Bast's burns.

"Sorry?" About not being his mentor anymore?

"For not listening to you," she replied, "For not giving you a chance to explain yourself."

"It's okay," he said, "I probably wouldn't have listened to me either."

"I think you would have." She stood and they moved to Art's side. "You have always shown yourself open to other ideas. It is what worried me about you. I feared what moving away from the Tower's traditions would mean and where it might take you. I never thought for a second it would reveal how rotten the Tower's core had become."

Kimmy's burns and bruises were last and then his friends were resting against the wall, speaking quietly with each other.

"To think I was so worried about your lack of patience and maturity," Sara said, "You've done so well, even without the aid of one who should have been your guide."

Zack blushed.

"It's your teaching that got me through it."

"That is kind. And true." She smiled and tapped his chest. "Although this self-contained weave you have put inside yourself is not something I have taught. It is… interesting. Perhaps you can talk me through it one day."

"I'd like that," he said, feeling the hope behind the words, "but first, we need to get out of the Tower."

"Without being killed on sight by everybody between here and the Entrance Chamber," Tabitha said as she and the others joined them.

"Your plan is to just flee?" Sara asked, "And leave the Tower with no leaders and no understanding of what has happened?"

"We'd love to explain it," Kimmy replied, "but you see, everybody keeps trying to kill us before we get a chance."

"I will speak for you." Sara stood straight. "And enough will stand with me to make sure you are heard. Are you willing?"

Zack looked around at his friends. Their clothes were in tatters, covered in burns and tears and while the worst of the injuries had been healed, they all still wore scratches and bruises. But they had survived. They had stood against the most powerful mages of the Tower. And they had won.

Tabitha met his eyes before replying to Sara, "We're willing. Lead on."

Sara led them out of the Ritual Chamber and through the winding corridors. They were passing through an intersection when Max growled a warning. Before any of them could react, a dozen mages filed in around them from each direction and at the front of them was Erik.

The brawny man had a fierce scowl on his face and pointed his axe at Zack.

"Get away from Sara and drop your weapons."

Sara moved in between Zack and Erik's axe.

"Stop this. They are under my protection."

Erik's eyes widened in momentary confusion before his scowl returned.

"You're siding with your former student over the Thirteen? Over the Tower?"

"You know very well what I would sacrifice for the Tower, Erik." Sara stood firm against him despite being a quarter his size. "And as for the Thirteen, they are all dead."

Gasps rippled around them, but Erik's eyes went cold.

"Murderers!"

Sara slid past his axe and reached up to put a hand on his shoulder.

"I was there and these children were not given a choice. The Thirteen tried to kill me, too. They would have, if not for Zack."

Erik shook his head in silence. Sara moved her hand to his, guiding him to lower his axe.

"We need to gather everyone to the Entrance Chamber. I don't believe the Tower has ever been without the Thirteen before and we must discuss what happens next."

"Okay," Erik replied, "but we will discuss what happens to them as well. And until then, they give up their weapons."

"Fine," Tabitha said, handing over her flail and gesturing for the others to do the same, "as a gesture of good faith."

Most of the mages that had surrounded them hurried away down corridors to spread the word, while Erik and a few stayed to escort Zack and his friends. After a few minutes, they reached an area of the Tower familiar to Zack and he was able to get his bearings on their path. Sara was not taking them directly to the Entrance Chamber but, rather, had detoured through the Life quarters. And judging by Erik's displeased expression, he realised the same. A knock on the Infirmary door and a short, whispered conversation later, half a dozen Lifers had joined the procession.

Zack smiled to himself. With a simple choice of route, Sara had rebalanced the scales with mages more likely to follow her lead if trouble should break out. But then Zack caught a glimpse of Tom glaring at him with open hostility and the smile slipped from his face.

A wave of healing Life magic flowed into his body and Zack turned away from Tom to find Kristian walking beside him. The older man patted him on the shoulder before making his way back down the line, stopping by each of Zack's friends.

Tabitha caught up to Zack as they walked down the stairs to the Entrance Chamber.

"Does Sara really think we can talk our way out of this?"

"I think this is our best shot," Zack replied, "If we flee and they decide we are guilty, they'll keep sending people after us. We might have a chance if we speak up now."

Tabitha nodded.

"I suppose it's me who needs to speak for us?"

"You're the best public speaker. Unless you'd rather it be Art or Kimmy?" Zack replied with a smile before tilting his chin back at Kristian, who was walking beside Charlie, "But in case it goes south, Sara made sure we're fighting, or fleeing, fit."

"Good to have a Plan B," Tabitha said with forced calm.

They were halfway down the last set of stairs when the sound of dozens of voices reached them. When they arrived at the bottom, they were greeted by a room filled with people. Every pair of eyes turned to fixate on them as they entered the Entrance Chamber and the room fell silent, except for the hurried footsteps of those entering through the other doorways.

"Alright, listen up! This lot have just admitted to killing the Thirteen." Erik's booming voice echoed through the room, but shocked whispers still sounded between the gaps. "For what it's worth, they came willingly to speak to us, so let's hear what they have to say before we decide what to do with them."

Sara levelled a look of irritation at him and when he finished speaking, she stepped forward. Her voice was softer than Erik's, but it carried well enough to be heard.

"Thank you, Erik. Blunt and without nuance, but truthful enough. Yes, I must confirm that all members of the Thirteen are dead and at their hands."

She pointed to Zack and his friends and the gathered throng erupted into gasps and murmurs. Sara gestured with her hands for silence before talking again.

"They will speak for themselves, but before they do, I wanted to say I was there at the end when they faced the Masters of Air, Water, Fire and Earth. And where they faced me, as I had just been chosen to become the new Master of Life. They did come ready for violence, it is true, but they did not come seeking it. They tried to reason and only when the four remaining members of the Thirteen forced their hands, trying to kill me in the process, did they strike back. I ask you to please listen to what they have to say, something I wish I did months ago when some of this may have been avoided."

The room stayed quiet as Sara stepped back, allowing Tabitha to move up. She took one last look at her friends and Zack nodded to her in support.

"Everything Erik and Sara have said is true. While we took no pleasure in it, my friends and I have killed each member of the Thirteen. To help you understand why, I need to talk about something that occurred at the end of last year, when the Tower was besieged by a renegade mage named Armand and the Tower entrances were locked."

Tabitha spoke about Armand being capable of channelling two different schools of magic and then about meeting the Traveller, who confirmed that he was able to as well. She recounted how he also revealed that the magical creatures the Tower had set them against were fully alive in their own right, and how they agreed to help the Traveller uncover more about who the Thirteen were.

Harsh whispers sprung up at that point, but Tabitha pushed on, emphasising that their goal was to investigate, not attack. Zack was only half listening. Instead, his focus was on the mages in the room, trying to read their expressions. Amongst the crowd were the others' former mentors, a few of the liaisons and dozens of mages Zack had tended to in the infirmary.

When Tabitha spoke about Jackie's kidnapping, silence fell over the room, except for a tight intake of breath from Art. Even with the silence, the reactions were mixed. There were some shocked faces and even some tears, but others rolled and shook their heads in open disbelief. Too many.

"We didn't want to kill them," Tabitha said, "we just wanted to take Jackie home, but the Masters of Movement and Protection wouldn't let us. We fought and they died. And so did Jackie."

"That's awful," Sadie, Charlie's mentor, said with tears in her eyes, "but why didn't you come and say something, rather than take it into your own hands?"

Kimmy burst into a humourless laugh.

"You're kidding, right? What system of checks and balances is in place here?"

Charlie stepped forward and faced Sadie.

"She's not wrong, but we did try. Shortly after Jackie's death, we were locked out of the Tower. Nobody reached out to us before that happened and the next thing we knew, we were being hunted."

"So, we made a choice," Tabitha said, "The only way to really bring the Tower's lies and corruption into the light was to defeat the Thirteen."

"I think we've heard enough," Erik said, "Look, I'm sure there are some pieces of truth scattered through this story, but are we supposed to believe these lies about the Tower? And that the first people to uncover these so-called secrets were a bunch of teenagers?"

A piece of a puzzle that Zack hadn't even realised he was working on clicked into place.

"No," he said, "we weren't the first."

Erik waved him off with a hand, but Zack ignored him and focused on the rest of the mages. His thoughts were still connecting, but he didn't have time to work it all out, so he kept talking.

"We definitely weren't the first to work pieces of this out or even all of it," he said, "Some of you know parts of it. You just thought those lies were justified, or you didn't know who you could tell, so you kept it to yourself."

Sara met his eyes for a moment and looked down at her feet.

"But I think some people didn't keep it to themselves. I think some people questioned or prodded or poked and the Thirteen took notice. I want everybody here to think about mages they knew who suddenly disappeared. Maybe they decided to stop taking on Tower work and retired. Maybe they settled down and got a real job. Or maybe they asked the wrong question and got noticed." Zack's mind was racing now and his mouth had to keep up. "You don't snatch a fifteen-year-old girl and torture her, unless you've done it a few times before. The only difference this time was, unlike you, we all knew each other outside the Tower. For whatever reason, because of our age or because Junie never really trusted us, we were kept as a team and we trusted each other first and the Tower second. But for the rest of you, if your liaison or another mage told you that your team's Movement mage had decided to retire to Jamaica, why wouldn't you believe them?"

"Okay, okay," Erik said, "that's another nice story with a long list of maybes."

But Zack had landed on something. The crowd was whispering to each other and, here and there, he heard mages swapping names of missing or forgotten team members.

Master Cho, Kimmy's mentor, clapped his hands together and moved to the front.

"This is an important discussion that we must continue to have, but it is not the most pertinent. As of now, the Tower is without the Thirteen and, as such, is not under any mage's control. This must be remedied." He turned to face the teens. "Are you putting yourselves forward as replacements?"

Tabitha's eyes widened in surprise.

"Absolutely not."

Master Cho nodded.

"Then I think you must be asked to leave. All members of the Tower must be included in this discussion, but as was made clear, your membership was revoked. Only after the Tower has new leaders can we consider your fate, including whether you will be allowed to return."

The surprise on Tabitha's face turned to anger.

"You think we want to return?"

The crowd somehow fell more silent than before.

"The Thirteen corrupted what should have been an organisation with an unrivalled ability to do good and they did it on your watch," Tabitha said, "With the aid of secrecy, tradition and privilege, they empowered themselves and the rest of us as it suited them. When they captured us in a dream prison for three months, by the Tower's standards, they did nothing wrong. When they kidnapped and murdered Jackie, they broke no rule. The Silence and the Watch are a joke and they do more to bully and terrorise mages outside the Tower than they do to constrain anybody within it."

Tabitha glanced back at her friends, who nodded for her to continue.

"So, save yourselves the trouble of deciding whether to let us back in. Until you fix this and make sure it can't happen again, we don't want any part of it." Tabitha turned her back on the throng of mages and approached the exit.

"Hold it right there," Erik shouted, "are we really letting them just walk out of here?"

"It depends," Master Cho replied, "is your campaign against the Tower finished or must we consider you a threat?"

"Our campaign was never against the Tower," Tabitha replied, "It was against the Thirteen and it's over."

Tabitha didn't wait for a reply. Instead, she stepped past the Tower mages next to the exit and walked through. Zack followed her and the others, into the shadows and back to Sydney.

It was late on a Saturday afternoon when they stepped out onto the Sydney footpath, but the summer sun shone bright and hot in the sky.

The familiar sounds of cars and pedestrians, combined with the recognisable buildings, overwhelmed Zack and he fought to steady his breath.

Tabitha stopped in front of the neighbouring building and faced the others.

"It's over. We did it."

"I wasn't sure they were going to let us go," Charlie said.

"Me neither." Tabitha grimaced. "I hope I didn't overstep for the rest of you when I said we didn't want to be in the Tower anymore."

They shook their heads.

"Screw them," Kimmy said, "If anything, you were too nice about it. So, where do we go from here? Back to our normal lives?"

"Maybe not just yet." Bast pointed across the road. "Is that Trav?"

Zack turned to look and Bast was right. Striding towards them from the opposite side of the street was the Traveller, recognisable with his flowing trench coat and bouncing mop of hair. He waved excitedly with both hands as he crossed to their side of the road.

"You did it!" His eyes were wide with excitement and maybe something more that Zack couldn't quite place. "The Thirteen. Gone!"

"How do you know?" Charlie asked.

"I've still got a few friends in there and when one told me the big news a few moments ago, I rushed here hoping to find you." The Traveller was speaking with a rapid energy. "I've been worried sick these last months, but you pulled it out."

"Yeah, sorry to worry you," Kimmy said with a dash of acid, "We were locked away in a mind prison."

The Traveller shook his head.

"That's terrible. I want to hear all about it, but we have work to do and we must strike while the moment is right."

"Work to do?" Tabitha asked, "We've defeated the Thirteen and confronted the rest of the Tower with the truth. They're discussing a better way forward right now."

"It's not good enough, I'm afraid," the Traveller said, "They'll just replace them and the power of the Tower will remain as a corrupting and oppressive force on our world. We need to act now while the Tower is leaderless and vulnerable."

Tabitha took a step back from him.

"And do what, exactly?"

The Traveller's eyes were alight with fervour.

"We're going to rip the Tower free from our world."

CHAPTER 34

"Excuse me?" Charlie said, "What precisely do you mean by 'rip the Tower free from our world'?"

"Just that," the Traveller replied, "The Tower doesn't exist in our world. It sits on the edge of it, as a buffer between us and the other realms. Right now, for the first known time in its entire existence, the Tower is not bound to anybody. We are going to take advantage of this unique moment and pry it free from its stranglehold on our world."

"This was your plan all along!" Tabitha's hands tightened into fists. "All that rubbish about just wanting information, was a lie."

"Not a lie. Not a lie." The Traveller shook his head with frantic energy. "But surely you must agree that this is necessary. The Tower's influence does not stop at the Thirteen. The whole thing must be cast away."

"What happens to everybody in there if you do it?" Art asked.

"Nothing. The Tower is effectively a pocket realm in its own right and they can travel to and from it the same way they do to any other realm." The Traveller pointed at the office building entrance. "Those permanent gates of theirs won't work anymore, but that's it."

"That doesn't sound so bad," Kimmy said.

"The Tower is a buffer," Zack thought aloud, "so what happens when that buffer is gone? Won't that lead to a massive increase in breaches?"

The Traveller nodded with enthusiasm.

"Exactly. Magic will return to our world, giving us back the potential the Tower has robbed us of for millennia."

"And with it, creatures that will attack, injure, and kill," Zack replied.

"Only for some." The Traveller sighed in frustration. "Magic is the natural state of this world and, like any other natural phenomena, individuals and species need to adapt to survive. Just look at the six of you. Your encounter was a spark that led you to greatness."

"A spark that could just have easily killed us," Tabitha said.

"That's the point," the Traveller replied, "but it didn't. You rose to the challenge and became something even more than I had hoped."

"What do you mean you 'hoped'?" Bast asked.

"Nothing. It's not important and we're wasting time." The Traveller held up his hands and turned towards the Tower entrance.

"You opened that gate in the alley," Zack said, certain of his conclusion.

The Traveller reached the front of the office building.

"How many others did you open?" Zack shouted at him, drawing the eyes of passers-by, "How many died from the creatures that came out of them?"

The Traveller turned back to him, his face wild and his eyes unfocused.

"As many as was necessary! As many as it took until I created the perfect bait for the Tower to swallow. And they swallowed it whole. I've tried to be nice about this, but yes, you were a tool of my own making." He incanted a few arcane words, and orange light gathered between his palms. "So, either help me out or stay out of my way. Otherwise, I'll unmake you just as easily."

The orange light in his hands streaked out towards the entrance of the Tower, where it crackled and opened into the grey light of a gate. But, unlike a gate, it didn't open evenly; it looked more like a liquid poured on an uneven surface, finding the shape of its container.

"We need to stop him," Tabitha said, "He's lost it."

"If he ever had it," Kimmy said.

"Uh, we've got another problem." Charlie pointed across the road where several people had stopped to look at the grey light and the man speaking in strange syllables in front of it. "There goes the Silence."

"The Silence isn't going to be an issue if dragons and demons start pouring into the world," Art said, "We worry about it later."

"Agreed," Tabitha replied, "If we can distract him, maybe we can stop this ritual and then make him give up."

"All over it," Kimmy said, "Come on, Mr Shanks. One more psycho before we can go into retirement. Try to avoid any major organs, okay?"

The enchanted dagger rose from inside her jacket and wiggled its hilt before soaring toward the Traveller. It flew low to the ground and was on a path towards the man's thigh when, with a flick of his hand and a flash of orange light, Mr Shanks clattered to the footpath where it lay still. Kimmy screamed.

"You bastard! Zack will just have to do his best to patch up whatever's left of you."

She ran forward and unleashed a burst of fire at the Traveller. The flames rushed toward him, but again, with one hand channelling the rift energy, he flicked out with his other hand. This time, it flashed red and Kimmy's fire reversed its direction, flowing back towards her.

Tabitha summoned a torrent of air, which crashed against the flames, pushing them against the nearby building. Most of the fire sputtered against the brickwork before fading away, but the plastic signage caught alight and spread.

"Kimmy, put that out," Tabitha said, "Everybody else, attack."

Art held out his arm and his eyes flashed purple. The Traveller staggered and, for a moment, the orange light in his outstretched hand died and the rift ceased growing. He clutched his head between his hands and tittered before tightening his jaw. His own eyes flashed purple and he flung his arm away in the direction of the street. Seconds later, four people on the opposite side of the road screamed in terror and a car sped into the back of a bus. The door opened and the driver tumbled out, whimpering. The Traveller returned his attention to the rift.

In a brown-red haze of light, Charlie transformed into a wolf. She, Max and Bast charged at the Traveller. Bast streaked out ahead, his fists balled and ready, but he slammed into the invisible wall of a shield and fell back onto the footpath. Charlie and Max skidded to avoid colliding with it and circled around the Traveller, looking for a weakness. But he was covered by a shield from every angle.

"We need to coordinate," Tabitha said, "Pull back and be ready to go on my mark."

Bast leapt back to his feet, and Kimmy finished extinguishing the flames.

"Alright, now!" Tabitha shouted and released a powerful jet of wind at the Traveller.

Kimmy followed suit with a thin, white-hot beam of fire and Art redoubled his efforts, launching a second mental attack. Zack ran in to join Bast, Charlie and Max, bashing against the barriers of steely light.

The Traveller's shields held back the wind and fire as well, but after a few seconds they weakened against Zack's fists. Tabitha's wind jet burst through, striking the Traveller in the back and he stumbled forward.

He dropped the magic, widening the rift and turned to face them.

"Enough! If you refuse to accept that this is necessary, then you force my hand."

The Traveller flung his arms back and forth, the glow from his hands oscillating between red, orange, and blue. First, a wave of fire rippled out from him, roaring towards Charlie and Max and forcing them to leap away, their fur singed and blackened. Then, a motorcycle parked on the side of the road flew at Zack. He dropped to the ground to avoid it, but it still clipped his shoulder and pain crackled down his arm. Next, a spray of icy shards shot from the Traveller's palm at Art and Kimmy. They dodged to the sides, but a few of the shards still found their targets, cutting into their arms and legs.

"Fall back!" Tabitha shouted, running for cover behind a nearby bus shelter.

Charlie and Max scampered away behind the bus that had now stopped, while Zack and the others followed Tabitha to the shelter. All except Kimmy, who continued to fling fireball after fireball at the Traveller. With no other clear target, the Traveller unleashed his kaleidoscope of magic back at her. Pieces of earth and stone tore up out of the ground and flew at Kimmy, but they crumbled under the intense heat of her flames. Likewise, another wave of his shards of ice hissed and evaporated before they reached her. But when the Traveller snapped a fireball back at her, Kimmy's fireball crashed against it and they collided into an intense explosion. The force flung Kimmy back a dozen metres and she landed in a heap near the bus shelter.

Bast and Zack raced out to grab he, and even the aftershock was hot enough to suck the moisture right off their bodies. Once they were back behind cover, Zack streamed Life into the worst of her burns and fractures. Rather than pour a deluge of Life in, he used more precise weaves modelled on Sara's recent examples. He had a feeling his reserves were going to be needed.

The Traveller didn't return to his work on the rift. Instead, he strode toward them, the air around him crackling with electricity. Art closed his eyes, a strong purple glow still visible along his eyelids. The Traveller lost half a step in his approach but otherwise kept moving.

"Ugh," Art groaned, opening his eyes, "He's too strong."

"Yep," Tabitha said, "but he's not skilled, or at least, he's not using any subtle magic. He hasn't used Mind magic except to push away your attacks. He's throwing fire and ice and… well, motorbikes, but nothing else. We've been trained for more than brute force, maybe there's something there?"

"Skilled?" Bast smirked, "I think I can work with that."

He raced out from behind the shelter and weaved in and around the Traveller so fast that he was a blur. The Traveller's hands launched a bolt of lightning at him, but Bast was too quick and the lightning crackled against the footpath, then faded. Three more bolts and none got close to hitting Bast. Without losing a step, Bast incanted and pieces of rubbish and debris rose up in the air and soared at the Traveller. Discarded cans and bottles, rocks and pebbles, even glass from the crashed car. Most bounced harmlessly off the Traveller's shields, but a few splinters of glass made it through, cutting across his cheek. He roared in frustration and his hands gathered steely light as he reinforced his magical defences.

Charlie, back in her human form, stepped out from behind the car, incanting swirls of russet light around her hands. Buzzing filled the air before coalescing into a dark cloud of flying insects. The unnatural swarm flew towards the Traveller and, while many of the insects bounced or splattered against his shields, countless more made it through. Inside his defences, they stung, bit and otherwise irritated him. He screamed in pain and annoyance and his hands lit up with a red glow before a ring of flame burst out from around him, roasting the remains of the swarm.

"Fine. You see yourselves as the defenders of this world?" The Traveller pointed to where dozens of people had stopped across the street to watch what was happening, many of them with their phones held out. "Look at them! They are so coddled in their cotton wool ignorance that you want to keep them in. They deserve a chance to see the truth."

The Traveller incanted, gesturing in wild and frantic movements before unleashing a series of massive fireballs in the direction of the crowds. They arced high and the first three hit the buildings directly behind the onlookers, while the fourth hit the bus. The force of it sent the bus crashing over onto its side. The fire rippled out and with it, fear. Much of the opposite side's footpath was covered by awnings and they were ablaze. The people didn't know which way to run and so they scattered in every direction. As shouts and screams filled the street, more bystanders joined them, fleeing the alarms and flames of the buildings. It was chaos.

"See how unprepared they are!" the Traveller shouted over the screams. "This is the Tower's legacy and yours, if you continue trying to stop me."

Tabitha ignored him and spoke to the others.

"We need to help them. Kimmy, you come with me and work on the fires. Everybody else, help who you can."

Bast nodded and raced toward the flames, where he carried out those struggling to escape. Kimmy and Tabitha followed, working Air and Fire magic to bring the fire under control. Zack crossed the road behind them, moving along the edges and looking for anybody in need of healing.

Away from the buildings, the tipped bus was burning and, from the shouting inside, it was far from empty. The driver, outside the bus in response to the earlier collision, was now frantically trying to get back inside to assist his passengers and was kicking at the front windscreen to break it open. The flames in the centre of the bus were growing and there was banging coming from the back.

Art ran over to help, but the emergency release had been bent from either of the collisions.

"It's stuck!"

A deep grunt sounded behind him and he turned to discover he was face to face with a gorilla. Art blinked in surprise before smiling.

"All yours, Charlie."

Charlie reached past him and gripped the release in her strong gorilla hands before wrenching on it and the emergency panel fell open with a crash.

"I feel like I loosened it," Art mumbled.

A dozen people in the back of the bus stared in shock at the gorilla in front of them, including a young man who screamed. Art stepped in front of Charlie.

"It's okay, she's a friendly gorilla. She only eats bananas. Now, get out of there before you burn to death."

The screaming man quietened to a whimper and they all climbed through the opening to escape the bus. Art patted Charlie on the shoulder.

"Good monkey."

Zack tended to a woman who had been hit by a falling piece of awning and suffered a deep burn across her face, endangering her eye. She gazed at him through the other eye in bewildered shock as his Life magic reduced the angry red to a dark pink. Past her, the Traveller had returned to his work on the rift.

"Tabitha," he called out, "He's back at it."

The light blue glow around Tabitha's hands dimmed as the flames around her exhausted.

"Damn it," Tabitha said, running to his side, "Anybody got something special up their sleeves?"

Charlie grunted, holding up the emergency panel in her two massive hands.

"She wants a distraction," Art said, his eyes flashing purple.

"I got one." Kimmy turned from the last of the flames and incanted a brief phrase. Smoke poured from her hands and billowed across the street toward the Traveller.

Tabitha took her lead and, with a gesture, called Air magic to whip the smoke into a dense cloud centred around the rogue mage. Coughing sounded within the dark haze, followed by a muffled incantation and the smoke dispersed in a sharp burst of wind.

But the smoke had held long enough to mask Charlie's approach and, as the haze cleared, she leapt forward, slamming the panel down with both hands. The Traveller's shield held long enough to deflect the strike away from his skull and it landed with a loud crunch on his right shoulder instead.

He grunted in pain, but pink light bloomed around the damaged shoulder and rippled down the arm. The limb doubled in size, tearing through the sleeve of the Traveller's trench coat and he punched out with it. The enlarged fist landed against Charlie's jaw and she stumbled backward in a daze. He held his other hand up at her and, as it glowed red, a jet of flames flowed out, but before it could strike Charlie, the metal panel floated up and blocked it.

"Get back!" Bast shouted, his fingers glowing orange from the magic holding up the makeshift shield.

Charlie scampered away and joined the others behind the tipped bus, where she shifted back to human form. She rubbed her jaw.

"What is going on with this dude? How the hell is he so strong?"

"Armand," Zack said.

"What about him?" Kimmy asked.

"Somebody taught Armand that ritual we interrupted last year." Zack sent a thin stream of Life into Charlie while he thought aloud. "You said that Fire mage was pretty full on and that was just after half a boost.

I reckon Trav has done that ritual himself."

Art nodded.

"Maybe a few times."

"How does that help us?" Kimmy asked.

"It probably doesn't," Zack replied, "but neither does that rift opening. We need to stop it."

The sound of sirens filled the air, cutting off any further conversation and two police cars rounded the corner. They screeched to a halt in front of the Traveller and four officers climbed out, staying behind their open doors as cover.

"Oh crap," Tabitha said, "this just got a lot worse."

CHAPTER 35

"Stand with your hands where I can see them," one of the officers shouted, pointing his handgun at the Traveller.

The Traveller turned around to face the police, holding his hands up above his shoulders. A second police officer spoke into a handheld radio.

"One suspect at scene, no visible weapons. Request fire and ambulance response but hold back until the scene is secured."

"Now get down on your knees and place your hands behind your head," the first officer said.

"See how unprepared they are?" the Traveller called out. "The Tower has kept them ignorant and unready."

"We can talk all about that when you've calmed down," the officer said, "Now drop to your knees."

The Traveller looked at him directly for the first time.

"It's okay, it's not your fault. You just need somebody to show you the truth."

He snapped his left arm down, flinging a ball of fire past the officer and into the side of the police car. It exploded against the vehicle, shattering the glass and engulfing the side panel in flames. The force of the impact pushed the car and it slid half a metre away, knocking the first officer off balance and the second officer onto the ground.

The two officers in the other car opened fire, unloading several rounds at the Traveller, but the bullets deflected off the shields of steely light and ricocheted into the buildings around him, cracking bricks and shattering windows.

The officer that had been knocked to the ground crawled away, still speaking into his radio.

"Correction. Suspect is armed! Some sort of incendiary or explosive dev— He's got some kind of flame thrower up his sleeve! Request backup!"

"You need further demonstration, do you?" the Traveller shouted, "Very well."

He brought his right hand down and hurled a three-metre-tall whirlwind at the second police car. The two officers threw themselves out of the way as it slammed into the car and whipped it into the bottom of the overturned bus.

The Traveller mumbled an incantation and brought his hands together in a deafening clap. The whirlwind and the flames rushed into each other, combining into a spinning firestorm. The four police officers scrambled to their feet and fled across the street while the Traveller laughed, reflected light from the flames dancing in his eyes.

"Well, he's gone total supervillain," Art said, crouching with the others behind the bus.

More sirens sounded in the distance.

"We need to do something fast," Tabitha said, "He's just playing with these four, but if enough turn up that he sees them as a threat, then he'll kill them all to make his point."

"Too much longer and it won't matter," Bast said, "I can't say for sure, given I've never seen this kind of rip-a-hole-in-reality kind of magic, but Movement is telling me it's close to finished. I can feel a pulling away. I don't think there's much left connecting the Tower to our world."

"What's the plan then?" Charlie wiped sweat from her human forehead. "Nothing we throw at him is sticking. I'm knackered and he hasn't skipped a beat."

"How about Zack channels all our energy into me and I hit him with as much Fire as I can?" Kimmy asked.

"I don't know," Tabitha replied. "If he survives that, the rest of us will be sitting ducks. Drained sitting ducks."

"What's left, then?" Kimmy thumped the bus in frustration. "We've hit him one at a time, we've hit him all together, we've tried distracting him."

Something clicked in Zack's head.

"No, we haven't."

"Yeah, we did," Bast replied, "with the smoke and the gorilla."

"No, not distracting him. All together," Zack rambled, trying to put his thoughts into words, "We attacked him at the same time, but not all together. Or at least not as all together as we could."

Art's eyes widened.

"Are you suggesting—?"

"The full Voltron," Zack answered.

"Feel like translating?" Charlie asked.

"The Art special," Zack said, "but with all of us linked."

"How would that help?" Kimmy asked.

"We'd be able to see each other's magic as we were shaping it, communicate instantly and Zack would let us draw energy from each other."

"That sounds like it'll wipe us all out really fast," Tabitha said, "Can you two hold it together long enough to give us a shot?"

"For sure," Art answered.

Tabitha turned to Zack.

"Can you?"

Past the bus, the grey light from the rift pulsed with an eerie resonance and behind him, the approaching sirens grew louder. He had to do this; there was no other option.

"Yes, I can."

"Okay," Tabitha said, "link us up."

"Hang on." Art held up his hand and looked at Kimmy. "All of us? Because if you're not comfortable with this, I can—"

"All of us," Kimmy replied, "I trust you."

Art's mouth dropped open.

"Shit, the world is about to end, isn't it?"

"Not if we can stop it," Kimmy said, "so get singing, Lord Gaga. And no radio edit this time."

Art sighed but started singing. Zack zoned the acapella cover out and focused on his own incantation, creating the magical plumbing required to connect his friends' Life energies together. By the time he was finished, Art's spell was also complete and a purple mist surrounded them. However, it was lighter than before and Zack could still see the world outside, like looking through tinted sunglasses.

Rather than connecting each of his friends to himself, Zack threaded together a web, with each of them linked to each other. It was a dazzling lattice of turquoise light and Kimmy, in particular, had a look of astonishment on her face as she ran her hand up and down through the turquoise beam that connected her with Tabitha.

Through Art's magic, he could sense their presences, five other minds almost touching his own. No, not five others. There was a sixth on the edge that reached out to the others.

Pack! The thought came through with loud enthusiasm.

The thoughts felt familiar, but Zack couldn't place them until Bast's thoughts spoke out.

Is that… Max?

Is Max, the first thoughts confirmed. *Pack can feel Max. Very good day!*

I guess you're hearing her through me? Charlie thought. *But listen, darling. We're going up against that bad man and it's going to be super dangerous, so I need you to hold back.*

No, Max replied. *Pack fights. Max is pack. Pack strong together.*

Ugh. Charlie's thoughts felt resigned. *Fine, just be careful. Move quickly and stay out of his reach.*

I can help with that, Bast said. A line of orange light bloomed and moved like lightning toward Max, where it bounced around between her legs.

She leapt from side to side. *Oh! Max is fast, like Fast-Bast. Very good day!*

Zack's attention was drawn to the trailing line of orange light. On impulse, with Life still gathered in his mind, he reached out to it, touching it with his will. The orange light reacted with a spark and then moved through Zack and into the web of Life. He looked in shock as Movement crackled like orange lightning across the turquoise web.

What did you do? Tabitha asked.

I don't know, Zack replied, *I just kind of touched it.*

Like this? Charlie asked and russet light raced throughout the web as if it was running along a turquoise surface, chasing the orange.

Red light followed after, like it was igniting the wick of a candle and then blue light twirled along behind, wrapping around the turquoise strands. And last, wisps of the purple fog drifted in, bonding with the web.

Anybody got any idea what this means? Kimmy asked, her thoughts filled with awe.

Nope, Bast replied, *but I can kinda feel the other magic. Like…* his thoughts trailed off and then a ball of fire flared in his hand.

Now that's the full Voltron, Art said, grinning.

Well, whatever it is, we need to move fast, Zack said, *I can already feel this draining us.*

Fast, you say? Orange light bloomed around Kimmy's feet and she raced out from behind the bus with magical speed.

Bast chased after her with Max bounding at his heels and the three charged toward the Traveller and the rift.

Zack examined the multicoloured web of Life suspended within the purple mist, wondering what it meant and, more importantly, how to use it. Orange bloomed along the web near Art and Charlie and they too, raced out into the fray. How had they mastered Movement magic so quickly? Nothing had changed - he still struggled while the others seemed to pick things up as if it was as simple as willing their legs to run faster.

Orange light flared at his feet.

Oh.

Zack could sense the Movement energy inside him, willing him to race and, unlike when Bast had used the magic on him before, this time he felt in control of it.

Coming? he asked Tabitha, who was still behind the bus.

Yeah, she replied, b*ut I think I'll go a different way.*

Tabitha's back radiated orange light and she flew up into the air, beaming a wide smile.

Zack blinked in surprise and then raced out to catch up to where the others were darting back and forth in front of the Traveller. Red and light blue flashes lit up the Life web as they threw balls of fire and lightning at the mage from multiple directions. Most of the magical attacks crashed against his shields, but one of Bast's fireballs slipped through, exploding against the Traveller's side. The flames ignited the man's trench coat and he was forced to rip it off. The shift underneath had been charred by the flames and burnt flesh was visible through the holes.

Nice shot, Art thought through the link. *But he's blocking too many.*

I've got an idea, Zack replied. *Art and Charlie, you throw a couple at him. Everybody else, get ready.*

Art and Charlie, still moving back and forth, threw balls of lightning and the Traveller threw up his hands to direct the shields. Zack waited until the attacks crackled against the steely light of the shields before throwing his own Air magic at the mage. He remembered back to something he'd seen Tabitha do in the past and he destroyed several spheres of air around the Traveller's head. Not powerful enough to do any real damage, they created a rapid chain of deafening bangs next to the man's ears as air rushed in to fill the vacuums Zack had created.

The others didn't wait for more of a signal. While the Traveller reeled in distraction and disorientation, they launched more fiery attacks at him and there were no shields to stop them. The balls of flame struck his body from three directions, burning through his clothes, hair and skin.

The Traveller screamed in pain and, in a pulse of dark blue energy, a wave of acid exploded from him, splashing on Art, Bast, Charlie and Kimmy. They collapsed, gasping and groaning on the road, as the sizzling acid ate at the flesh, but turquoise light flared across the web and their bodies' Life fought to repair the damage.

Life magic sparked within the web and Zack marvelled at how he couldn't tell where it had started, whether it had been from him or any of the others. It had simply happened within their combined will.

Any more thought on the subject was pushed away as the sound of sirens became louder and three more police cars raced around the corner. They screeched to a halt alongside the upturned bus and six police leapt out, pointing their guns not only at the Traveller, but at Zack and his friends. One of them, with a look of shock on his face, had his handgun trained on Tabitha, who was hovering two metres above the ground.

"Kneel and place your hands on the ground or we will open fire," the frontmost officer shouted.

Max moved to place herself in between the police and Charlie, who was stirring as her body healed and three of the officers pointed their weapons at her.

Zack turned to face the police and felt Mind magic ripple through him as he spoke. "Leave. Now."

The two words buzzed in his ears and as they fell on the police, they all lowered their weapons. The two officers furthest away climbed back into their car and sped away, while the other four simply turned and ran.

Good work, Tabitha thought to him. *My turn.*

She flew up another few metres until she was directly above the Traveller and incanted. Light blue energy, so bright it was visible in the daylight, flared around her and the sky rumbled. A massive bolt of lightning forked down from the cloudless sky and, passing through her, struck the Traveller. The thick bolt of electricity engulfed the mage, but when it faded, he remained standing. His body was a mix of charred black and deep red burns, but he stayed, swaying on his feet and hissing with wild anger.

The others staggered to their feet, their bodies still marked with acid burns yet to heal.

How the hell is he still alive after that? Kimmy asked.

Zack reached out with Life and felt a strange connection between the Traveller and the rift. *I'm not sure he is. The rift energy is keeping him going.*

At least we've stopped him widening it, right? Charlie thought.

Um, no, Bast replied, concern heavy in his thoughts, *He might be feeding off it, but it's definitely feeding off him. We don't have long before it's done.*

Do we keep going? Tabitha asked, landing next to Zack. *If the rift is powering him, can we even kill him?*

Before Zack could answer, the Traveller gave a shout that was part scream, part cackle. His eyes, pure grey light that reflected the rift, were wide and unfocused as he threw his hands up. A spectrum of light poured out from his hands, orange, blue, brown, red and more, at the office building behind the rift. The magic struck the brickwork and the top two stories exploded, collapsing down toward them in a rain of deadly debris. Zack tensed his legs to run, knowing that even his magical speed would unlikely carry him out of the impact.

Silver bloomed throughout the Life web and the falling building crashed against a dome of steely light, shattering into rubble. When the dust cleared, they all stood unharmed by the collapse, but so did the Traveller.

Who made that shield? Charlie asked, her face a mask of shock.

Art fell to his knees. *I don't know, but I can't… I can't keep this thing up anymore.*

The purple mist dissipated, along with the Life web.

Behind them, the Traveller stirred and the rift pulsed angrily.

"I don't think we can kill him," Zack said, "He's as much a part of the rift as he is a man anymore."

"I can't shut the rift while he's feeding it," Bast said.

"There's only one thing I can think of, then," Tabitha said, and she murmured a single arcane word. A jet of wind burst from her hand and struck the Traveller in the chest, knocking him back toward the rift.

He shrieked as the wind pushed him closer and closer, scraping his charred hands along the concrete path to slow him down before drawing forth blue and orange magic to finally halt his movement, inches from the rift.

Tabitha groaned with effort.

"I can't do it. He's too strong."

"We've got you," Zack said, "Get ready, Bast."

He didn't need to ask. As Zack reached out with his magic, it was there waiting for him. Life freely given. He connected a stream from Art, Kimmy, Charlie and even Max. They were all exhausted, but their Life rushed through to him. He gathered it and poured it into Tabitha.

The jet of wind roared like a cyclone, tearing through the Traveller's remaining magical defences and hurling him through the rift. Zack dropped the channel, his body shuddering with a deep aching pain and a metallic taste filling his mouth. Around him, his friends swayed on their feet, while Bast forced the rift closed. With a last burst of orange energy, the grey light was gone and Bast staggered over to join them.

Tabitha sucked in a deep, trembling breath.

"We need to get out of here."

"Where to?" Bast wheezed.

"Anywhere," she replied.

Through gritted teeth, Bast forced open a gate, short enough that Art would have to stoop to walk through. Kimmy scooped up Mr Shanks from where he had fallen to the ground and they fled through the gate, collapsing to the ground on the other side.

CHAPTER 36

The ground beneath Zack was warm, dry grass, but it was several minutes before he had the energy to even lift his head to see where Bast had taken them. He trusted his friend had picked somewhere safe.

When his breath steadied and the pain in his head had shifted from a sharp blaze to a dull ache, he forced himself up onto his knees and looked around. He smiled. Tatters Park. Of course, this was where Bast had taken them.

The memory of the first time they gathered here rushed into Zack's mind. He pictured them discussing what to do about the monster that had attacked them in the alley. His eyes lingered over the climbing frame where Jackie had stood next to Art.

Blinking away the tears, Zack turned back to his friends who were still laying down all around him. He pushed away the fatigue and reached out to get a sense of their Life energies. Burnt, battered and bruised, but mostly drained. He laid back down. They were going to be okay, for now. He even thought about closing his eyes for a moment.

"Alright, gang," Tabitha said, "everybody up."

"Five more minutes, Mum," Art replied, but he forced himself to his feet along with the others.

"Alright, Cap," Bast said, "what do we do now?"

"Well," Charlie said, "we were discussing going back to our normal lives… and then things got a little out of hand."

"Yeah, I don't think normal is on the table anymore," Kimmy smirked.

"I doubt normal is on the table for the whole world." Art ran a hand through his dust and ash-matted hair. "I don't think the Tower has a protocol for repairing a break in the Silence on this scale."

"Then screw 'em," Tabitha said, drawing shocked gasps from the others, "I'm serious. The Traveller was off the deep end trying to pull magic into our world, but he wasn't wrong about how exposed the Silence has made us."

"So, what do we do if the Tower still wants the Silence?" Charlie asked.

"And wants to blame us for it breaking?" Art added.

"We don't let them," Zack said, "We go to the other mages and we find good people to work with. People like Nell and her mum, or like Arie, with his weird technomancy. And we help them defend themselves. The Tower doesn't get to be in charge anymore."

The others nodded in agreement.

"But first, I'll be honest," Bast said, "I just want to go home and see my dad and my brothers."

"Me too," Charlie said.

"And to have some truthful conversations." Art's eyes were serious and distant.

Kimmy burst into loud, blubbery tears.

"What's wrong?" Tabitha asked, putting a hand on her shoulder.

Kimmy pulled Mr Shanks from her pocket.

"I know you guys probably think it's silly, but I'm going to really miss him."

"It's not silly," Tabitha said, hugging her close, "In whatever way he was capable of, he clearly cared about you."

"He was terrifying and pointy," Art said, "How could you not miss him?"

Kimmy sniffled.

"Thank you, that's really sweet."

Charlie's eyes widened and her mouth hinted at a smile.

"He's still in here."

"What? How is that possible? The Traveller hit him with something and he's been…" Kimmy waggled the lifeless dagger. " … ever since."

"I don't know," Charlie said, "but I can still sense that Animal vibe."

"Maybe it's just an echo or something," Art said.

"Maybe. Give me a closer look." Bast held out his hand and Kimmy handed him the dagger. After a moment, he smiled, and orange light bloomed in his hand.

Mr Shanks leapt up into the air, hovering in front of Kimmy. She squealed in relief and delight and swept the dagger into a tight embrace. Ignoring the thin cuts it left in her forearm, Kimmy sobbed again, but this time with a smile on her face.

Tabitha smiled at Bast.

"Okay, let's catch up tomorrow and work out what we do from here. Bast, do you have enough juice left to give us lifts home?"

Bast groaned but nodded.

"Yeah, gimme a moment."

While Bast worked on a series of gates to their respective homes, Zack looked at his friends. No, he thought, 'friends' wasn't a good enough word. They were family, as much as the one he was eager to see again. Together, they had stood against an ancient, corrupted order of mages, a psychotic sorcerer, and everything else that had been thrown at them. And they had succeeded where others had failed, not because of raw power, intelligence or even luck, but because they had been able to rely on each other.

And they'd get through whatever happened next as well.

To give Bast a break, Zack used the same gate as Art, opened about halfway between their homes. The two stepped out onto a suburban street, not far from where they used to catch the bus to school together. After the gate closed behind them, they stood in silence for a few moments. Zack was looking forward to seeing his family, but the paleness of Art's face suggested far more apprehension.

"I've got to tell them about Jackie," Art said, looking down at his feet. "I've got to tell them how I lied to them for months. How I put her in danger for years until she died."

Zack nodded, unsure of what to say.

"What if they hate me for it? What if they can't forgive me?" Art's bottom lip trembled.

Zack pulled him into a tight hug.

"They won't hate you for it. It'll be rough, but they love you and you'll get through it. I can come with you if you want."

Art hugged back and then stepped back, standing a little straighter.

"No, you need to get home too. I have to do this alone."

"Okay," Zack replied, "but I'm a phone call away."

"When we charge our phones, anyway," Art said through a forced smirk.

"Then I'm a psychic shout away. I'm sure you can reach me from your place."

"Thanks, man. I love you. I couldn't have survived this without you."

Zack smiled back at him.

"I love you, too. And I wouldn't have made it without you, either. We saved the freakin' world today, mate. Again."

"Can't be that big a hero and be scared of talking to your parents," Art said, as much to himself as Zack, "Alright, see you tomorrow, mate."

Zack watched him walk down the street, wishing him as much luck as he could, before turning around and heading to his own house. While it had been half a year since Zack had seen his family and months since he'd spoken to any of them on the phone, he had to remember that they probably didn't think the same thing. During his time in the mind trap, Art was confident the Tower had been using Mind magic to make them think vaguely that they had spoken to him recently.

Zack was on his way past the next-door neighbour's house, his mind full of potential conversation paths, when his parents' car screeched past him and into their driveway. He hurried toward the car as his mother bounded out of the passenger seat and threw her arms around him.

"Oh, thank heavens you're okay. We were so worried. Why didn't you answer your phone?" She released him and stepped back, taking in his scorched and dishevelled appearance. "What happened to you?"

This wasn't quite what he expected and none of his prepared dialogue worked. Had she not been Mind-charmed after all?

"I'm okay. Why did you think I wouldn't be?" Zack looked to his father, who had approached from the driver's side. "Dad, why did she think—"

His father drew him into a closer, tighter hug. Zack hugged back.

"What's going on?"

His father released him.

"We were on our way back from the shop when we heard about this terrorist attack, or something, in the city. Huge thing, fire, explosions, everything. We couldn't remember where you worked, but it seemed to be in the area, so your mother tried calling you—"

"And you never answer, as usual. And the reports just kept getting worse and worse." His mother took a deep breath. "But you're okay. Everything is okay. Let's go inside; unpacking can wait. I need some water."

Zack followed them inside and took a deep breath of his own.

"Actually, I was there."

His parents looked at him, confused.

"You mean this morning? Before it happened?" His mother pulled three glasses from the cabinet.

"No, when it happened," Zack replied.

"Then how are you here already?" his father asked. "The news made it sound like it was only just happening."

"Are you alright?" His mother's calmness vanished.

The sound of footsteps trundled down the stairs behind him.

"I'm okay," Zack replied, "but I need to tell you something that might be difficult to believe."

Ellen walked past him from the staircase, a half-smile locked behind an expression of shock on her face.

"Yeah, I'd say you do."

"What are you talking about, Ellie?" his mother said.

Ellen didn't reply. Instead, she walked over to the coffee table, snatched up a remote and turned on the TV. A news bulletin was rolling, with a journalist at the scene, surveying the aftermath of his fight against the Traveller.

His mother gasped as the camera panned across the smouldering fires, the overturned and crushed vehicles and then rubble from the destroyed building.

"You're saying you were there?"

"Just keep watching," Ellen said, her eyes flickering between Zack and the TV screen.

"Some footage of the event, captured on smartphones by bystanders, has been going viral on social media," the journalist said and Zack's heart dropped.

The broadcast cut to a shaky video of the fight. Blurry at first and focussed more on the fire and the police vehicles, the video then panned to show Zack and his friends fighting the Traveller. Lightning shot from Art's hand while Zack moved with impossible speed across the screen.

Whatever happened next, life was going to be different. He and his friends had defeated the Thirteen and the Traveller, both of which had been in the shadows, manipulating the world for their own agendas. Killing the Traveller had protected what remained of the Tower and it would be up to the remaining members to decide what to do next now, not only because some of the rot had been excised, but because the Silence had been irrevocably shattered. Maybe they would come for him and the others, but even if they didn't, Zack still owed six years of his life to a fae Queen, had a pretty elvish girl in another realm to track down and had growing ambitions about how to bring more healing into this world. And doing any of that would be easier with the support and understanding of the three people staring at him with wide eyes and open mouths.

Zack held up his hands in a show of defence.

"Well, to start with, I don't work in promotions."

THE END